The
FATHER

MADE IN SWEDEN: PART I

ANTON SVENSSON

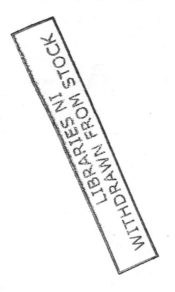

sphere

SPHERE

First published in Sweden in 2014 by Piratförlaget
First published in the English language in Great Britain in 2015 by Sphere

Based on the Swedish work *Björndansen*.
Published by agreement with Salomonsson Agency.

1 3 5 7 9 10 8 6 4 2

A CIP catalogue record for this book
is available from the British Library.

Hardback ISBN 978-0-7515-5782-4
Trade paperback ISBN 978-0-7515-5783-1

Typeset in Sabon by Palimpsest Book Production Limited,
Falkirk, Stirlingshire

Printed and bound in Great Britain by Clays Ltd, St Ives plc

Papers used by Sphere are from well-managed
forests and other responsible sources.

MIX
Paper from
responsible sources
FSC® C104740

Sphere
An imprint of
Little, Brown Book Group
Carmelite House
50 Victoria Embankment
London EC4Y 0DZ

An Hachette UK Company
www.hachette.co.uk

www.littlebrown.co.uk

The Father is a work of fiction inspired by a true story. Details of many events and characters have been changed, and others are purely fictitious. For more information on how the real case inspired this novel, please see the interview at the end of the book.

If then is now.

If now is then.

HE'S SITTING IN a yellow Volkswagen van that smells of sweat and paint and something else he can't quite put his finger on. Maybe the petrol station coffee cup on the dashboard. Maybe the remnants of loose tobacco in the passenger seat. Maybe the bag of plaster and the paintbrushes on the seat behind him, which he's just bought in a hardware store on Folkunga Street. Or the tools and the wallpaper table lying in the back that he took out of the fucking storage unit *she'd* rented – four years stacked next to his clothes and his bed, which had once been one half of their bed.

That's what that smell is.

A cellar. Storage. Time.

The sun beats down onto the car window, onto a film of dried flies and dust. The kind of mysterious heat that comes out of nowhere. He rolls down the window to cool off and lets in even more heat, the memory of a phone call buzzing through his head.

'It's me.'

'I know.'

'How's my boy? Everything OK? Everything good?'

Three hours from Stockholm. A small town surrounded by factories and a spruce forest. He's been slowly circling it since early this afternoon, on his way to a neighbourhood with a Konsum supermarket, a hot dog kiosk and a small gravel football pitch – and to an apartment building at the centre, three floors of red brick that he's never been to before.

'Everything's fine.'

'What are you up to?'

'Not much . . . we're about to eat. Mamma's cooking.'

As he left the city behind the roads got smaller and slower, cutting through a part of Sweden he hadn't seen for a long time. He'd stopped at a petrol station on the outskirts of town, rolled a cigarette, closed the door to the phone box, and dialled a number he had memorised. She'd answered the call, fallen silent at the sound of his voice, and handed the phone to their eldest son.

'And your brothers, Leo? How are they?'
'They're the same . . . as always.'
'And everyone's at home?'
'Everyone's here.'

He drove the last few kilometres slowly, past a church and an old school and the main square where sunbathers soaked up rays that would soon turn to clouds and thunder – it was that kind of heat.

'Can you give Felix the phone?'
'You know he doesn't want to talk to you.'

He was parked outside the flat, staring at the door, feeling it staring back.

'Well . . . Vincent then?'
'He's playing.'
'Lego?'
'No, he's—'
'Toy soldiers? Tell me what he's doing.'
'He's reading – Pappa, soldiers were a long time ago.'

The window at the top on the right-hand side, he thinks, that must be the flat. His eldest son has described it so many times it feels that he knows what it looks like: the kitchen directly to the left as you enter, the brown, round table with four chairs, not five; living room straight ahead, a door of milky glass you can't see through; to the right is *her* bedroom and the other half of the bed, which she's kept, then the children's rooms, just like when they all lived together.

'And you?'
'I have . . .'
'What are you up to, Pappa?'
'I'm on my way home.'

———

A four-bedroom flat is its own world of sound. When Mamma turns the tap on in the kitchen sink its dull rumbling collides with the clang of the cutlery tray and the brittle rattling of the crockery cabinet. Together they do their best to overpower the television in the living room, the high-pitched screech of the cartoons Felix is watching from the corner of the sofa, music coming from Leo's two giant speakers, and whatever's seeping out of the Walkman headphones that sit askew on Vincent's head – a deep voice narrating a story – sounds that when pushed and squeezed together intertwine and then meld.

The spaghetti is ready, and the meat sauce is hot.

Mamma lifts up the headphones and whispers, 'Dinner time,' and Vincent runs through the hallway shouting, *food*, another lap, *food food*.

The TV is turned off. The music stops.

It's almost silent as they all head towards the kitchen table, and then another sound enters, interrupts – the doorbell.

Vincent is already on his way back out to the hall.

'I'll get it.'

Felix passes the TV and hurries towards the front door.

'*I'll* get it.'

They race, and Vincent who's closest gets there first and reaches for the doorknob, but he isn't able to turn it. Felix is a step behind and lifts Vincent's hand away, leans forward, peering through the peephole. Leo sees Vincent reaching for the knob again and not being able to pull it down, while Felix recoils, turns round with fear on his face that hasn't been there for a long time.

'What is it?'

Felix nods at the door.

'There.'

'There . . . what?'

The bell rings again. A long sound, and Leo continues towards the front door. Vincent jumps up to unlock it, and Felix refuses to let go of the handle.

'Felix, Vincent – move. *I'll* get it.'

Later she won't even remember if she actually turned round, if she even had time to wonder why the boys were standing still. What she will remember, the only thing, is that his curly hair was longer and his breath had stopped smelling of red wine.

7

And that he punched her, but not like he used to.

Because if he hit her too hard, she'd fall down, and he wanted her to look him in the eye as he destroyed her, destroyed her for ignoring him, for passing the phone to his eldest son. She needed to look him in the eye when they touched for the first time in four years.

The first punch is right fist against left cheek, and his hand then continues towards her neck, grabs it and twists it so they can look at each other. The second and the third and the fourth punches are just the opposite, left knuckle on right cheek, *look at me*, quick powerful punches, and she puts her arms over her head to shield herself, spiked elbows forming a helmet, all skin and bone.

One hand on her neck and the other in her hair, he forces her to stand up even though she's getting heavier, wants to stay down, lie down, protect herself. He holds her head down while he knees her, *feel me*, knees her again, *feel me*, knees her once more, *feel me*.

———

Because Leo doesn't understand the terrible silence.

That's why it takes so long for Leo to react. Pappa's knuckles hit Mamma's face like a whip, but he takes his time and does it silently; you used to be able to hear it when Pappa threw a punch. He is both Pappa and someone else. And because Mamma doesn't scream. And Vincent is hiding behind his brother's back, and Felix is still standing by the front door.

They're not yet the same height. If they had been, Leo wouldn't have had to jump onto his back. That's what he does when Pappa starts using his knees, when Leo realises that this time Pappa won't stop until she's dead. He hangs onto his back and clenches his arms around his father's neck, until Pappa finally grabs hold and rips him off.

But at that point at least Pappa has to let go of her head.

Leo slips, falls to the floor, and his mother, confused, takes a couple of steps away, her arms protecting her heavily bleeding face, mostly from a gash on her cheekbone from Pappa's knuckles. Pappa follows her, grabs her again, the same way as before – he wants her to look at him while he's punching her.

One more punch. A fist to her nose and mouth.

But that's the only one he gets in before Leo stands up and squeezes himself between them and raises his hands.

No, Pappa.

He's standing in a void. Between a mother who is bleeding and a father who wants to hit her again, but can't because there's another face in the way.

And Leo grabs hold of him.

Not his neck, Pappa's too tall for that, nor his arms, Leo can't quite catch them. But his waist and a bit of his chest.

No, Pappa.

He tries to plant his feet on the kitchen floor. His socks slide, and he has to brace himself against the table legs, doing his best to hug his Pappa away. He can't quite do it, but at least Pappa lets go of her hair.

Mamma runs out of the kitchen and into the hallway to the front door, which is standing wide open. She slips on the polished stone floor of the stairwell and her blood pours out, and she whimpers and moans on every step.

Only the two of them are left.

Leo keeps hold of him, his arms around his father's waist, and leans into his body, as if he were still hugging him.

'It's your turn now, Leonard.'

The smell of food, spaghetti and meat sauce, and Mamma's blood. They look at each other.

'Do you understand? I won't be around any more, not here. You're responsible from now on.'

And now his pappa's eyes are different – they don't slip away, they stop, and even though his pappa doesn't say anything else, his eyes do.

Not that it matters, but this novel
is inspired by a true story.

now
part one

1

LEO HELD HIS breath. The intense, white light of a torch swept over him, and he pressed his face against damp moss and straggling sprigs of bilberry, pushing his entire body harder against the ground. Lying there – just a few steps inside the woods – it was easy to follow the inspector's routine.

First, he pointed the light at the lock on the security door, searching for signs of a break-in.

Then he walked around the cube-shaped building with his torchlight directed at the surface of the concrete walls.

Finally, he stood with his back to it and had a smoke, apparently taking a break until he was sure everything looked just as it had the night before.

Leo started breathing again. He'd been lying just like this at the same time for seven nights in a row, beside a large, square gravel yard surrounded by forest and with a small, grey concrete cube in the middle – the bunker. The night was motionless. Just the wind, and an owl hooting incessantly, and the occasional insect.

It was a peculiar feeling, lying a few metres away, watching every movement of a man convinced that he was completely alone – a man in uniform taking deep drags on a cigarette, responsible for all the military storage facilities in what was called Stockholm Defence Area 44.

Leo adjusted the microphone on his collar, raised his head above the bilberry bushes and whispered, 'Cancerman is leaving the site.'

The ditch between the forest and the gravel yard was filled with water, and the coarse soles of Leo's boots slid on the grass as he took a run up and jumped over it, a heavy bag in one hand and a square of hardboard in the other.

Jasper approached from the other direction, with moss and pine needles in his hair and an equally heavy bag in his arms.

They didn't speak to each other. They didn't need to.

Leo placed the sheet of hardboard – exactly 60 by 60 centimetres – on the ground in front of the bunker door.

He'd been pondering these walls for a long time. Blasting them would show up later in the beam of the inspector's torch and would make too much noise.

Then he'd analysed the roof. It would have been easy to remove the metal sheet that protected the building against rain, penetrate the fifteen centimetres of concrete from above, and then put the metal back on again. A blasted roof wouldn't show up in the inspector's torchlight. But that too would be heard.

One way left: the floor. With the hard ground providing counter-pressure, the force of the explosion would be redirected upwards; fewer explosives could be used and less noise would result.

Leo lifted half a kilo of heavy plastic explosive out of the bag.

He sank to his knees and kneaded it, shaped twelve balls in the light from the lamps on their heads.

'It's not enough,' said Jasper.

He placed them one at a time on the hardboard, like a clock fitted with forty grams of plastic explosive for each hour.

'It's enough.'

'But according to the table—'

'The army always uses too much. They're trying to kill people in battle. I've halved it. We want to get in – not destroy what's inside.'

Leo watched Jasper unfurl a folding shovel from his bag with a flick of the wrist and start digging. With each movement the hole in front of and below the safe-like door grew.

One piece of dough to mark each hour. A circle of time, linked by a length of brown, twine-like penthrite.

He knew it was silly, but he lived with the clock – Leo always knew what time it was, even when he wasn't carrying a watch. Time ticked inside him, and always had.

'Ready.'

Jasper was sweating, stooped over, kneeling with the shovel deep inside the hole under the door – and the floor of the bunker. Leo crept closer, their eager arms getting in each other's way as he pulled out with cupped hands whatever the shovel couldn't reach.

'Now.'

They held onto either side of the hardboard and gently pressed it inside bit by bit, making sure the twelve balls of plastic explosive didn't get stuck to anything and that the fuse ended up exposed. When they were sure that the square had gone under the door, beneath the small, one-room building, they pressed gravel into the hole and around it until it was completely sealed.

'Satisfied?'

'Satisfied.'

Hours of calculations. Days spent obtaining the materials. Weeks spent in rubber boots, tramping through one forest after another, a mushroom-picking basket under his arm, surveying Swedish military storage facilities, and when he'd found this one, in an area called Getryggen about fifteen kilometres south of Stockholm, he'd known he could stop looking.

Now there were just a few minutes left.

He taped the short fuse to a detonator, which he then attached to the plus and minus on an electrical cable, before moving as far away as he could, across the gravel and the ditch and back into the woods. Then he connected a wire on the other end of the cable to the positive terminal on a motorcycle battery.

'Felix? Vincent?' Leo said into his microphone.

'Yeah?' replied Felix.

'Have you got a clear view?'

'Clear view.'

'Ten seconds . . .'

————

Felix and Vincent lay next to each other under a tarpaulin covered with leaves and moss and grass, near a red and yellow barrier bearing a metal sign that said NO ACCESS FOR UNAUTHORISED VEHICLES.

' . . . then I'll let it rip.'

Vincent was holding tight a pair of bolt cutters nearly a metre and a half long.

Felix raised his upper body and checked his watch, rubbed his finger across the glass of the dial; the damp had turned to mist.

'Nine.'

He rubbed it until he could see the second hand and then nodded towards Vincent, whose breathing was short, intense, brittle.

'Eight.'

'Are you OK?'

'Seven.'

Vincent didn't answer. He didn't even look at his brother.

'Six.'

Even the heavy tarp across their backs shook.

'Five.'

'No one's coming, Vincent. We're all alone out here.'

'Four.'

He moved his arm from shaking shoulders to the hands clutching the bolt cutters.

'Three.'

'Vincent?'

'Two.'

'Leo's up there. He has this all planned. It'll go fine. And this is better, right?'

'One.'

'Vincent? It's better to be involved than sitting at home on the sofa not knowing.'

———————

The explosion roared, louder than Leo had expected. The bunker acted like the sound box of a guitar, a shell amplifying the sound of half a kilo of plastic explosive. And when the floor was blasted into the single room of the building, the sound box amplified the next sound, too – concrete chips being flung against a ceiling.

They'd agreed to wait for five minutes.

That didn't happen.

Leo slithered across the wet gravel with the folding shovel in his hand. He laughed out loud, not even realising at first that he was, laughing in a way he seldom did, as he crouched down on his knees and stuck his right arm under the bunker's security door and felt . . . *Nothing*. There really was a hole! He unfolded the shovel, scooped away more gravel, inserted his headlamp and turned it on.

'Jasper!'

He turned towards the woods and shouted way too loud.

'Come here! Come and see this!'

The headlamp flooded a windowless room. And there. When he stretched inside, he could see it clearly, the very first letter.

K.

Oh my God. Oh my God!

He pressed his head further into the hole – slowly the next letter appeared.

S.

Ohmyfuckinggod.

A little further. White letters on a green background.

KSP 58

'Felix? Vincent?'

'Yeah?'

'The padlock?'

'We're working on it right now.'

'Good. When you're finished drive up here.'

Jasper's shoulder was against his as they dug their way towards the hole in the floor, like an escape tunnel. They dug until he was able to squeeze his head, shoulders and arms inside, and clip with a pair of heavy pliers the rebars that formed the cement's grid-shaped skeleton. He prised it open, braced his back against the ground, and pushed his hands against the edges of the hole to heave himself up and through.

He adjusted his headlamp, which had slipped down slightly on his sweaty temples, and looked around. It was small enough for him to touch both walls and ceiling, two metres by two by two metres. Along the walls were stacks of green wooden boxes.

'How many?'

Jasper's voice came through the tunnel.

'A lot.'

'How *many*?'

Leo counted out loud.

'A platoon. Two platoons. Three platoons. Four . . .'

A total of twenty-four military-green boxes.

' . . . two whole damn companies!'

It was now Jasper's turn to squeeze his long body through the dirt tunnel, laughing the whole time. Like Leo, he couldn't help himself. They stood beside each other in the cube-shaped room, the concrete dust undulating in the light that streamed from their lamps.

'Open them now? Or later?'

'Now, of course.'

A cautious hand on top of the wooden box. A rough, almost rugged surface.

It was easy to dislodge the pins and prise back the lid.

A machine gun. Leo picked it up, handed it to Jasper, who bent his legs slightly and his upper body forward in order to brace for an imaginary recoil, going through the motions they'd learned during their military service. They looked at each other like two people at the end of a long journey trying to understand that they've finally arrived.

'How many do you think there are? If you were to guess?'

Leo was just about to open the next box. But stopped. Behind Jasper's shoulder, partially covered by white dust, the answer was hanging right there.

'I don't need to guess.'

A piece of paper in a plastic pouch hanging on a hook on the wall just to the left of the locked door, a ballpoint pen hanging on a string next to it.

'First row: 124 submachine gun m/45. Second row: 92 assault rifle AK4. Third row: 5 KSP 58.'

They opened up and checked the contents one box at a time. Metal bodies side by side. Well-greased and carefully packed.

'Damn, can you believe it, Jasper?'

Under the typed, detailed text about rules and routines, at the very bottom.

'This place was inspected . . .'

He leaned closer, headlamp on the white paper. It had been written by hand under somebody's illegible signature.

' . . . Friday, October 4th.'

'Yeah?'

'Less than two weeks ago!'

'And?'

Leo waved the paper so high it hit the ceiling.

'The guards only open the security door to check *inside* once every six months. Are you with me? That means they won't figure out what's happened here for more than . . . five months!'

'Felix to Leo!'

Felix's voice emerged with a crackle.

'I repeat! Felix to Leo! Come in!'

20

'Yeah?'

'It's about . . . the lock. We have a problem.'

Leo pressed his body through the hole in the floor of the bunker and back out onto the gravel. He hadn't counted on this. If they couldn't get the barrier open, then all this would be for nothing. He ran downhill on the rough forest road towards his two little brothers, who were sitting on either side of the barrier, which was padlocked with a steel shackle a centimetre and a half thick.

'I'm so fucking sorry.'

At some point during that warm, light-filled summer he and Vincent had become the same height. But still, a seventeen-year-old body was quite different from that of a twenty-four-year-old.

'Leo . . . it's not working. I can't do it.'

Vincent shrugged his slender shoulders and threw open his arms, which seemed too long for the rest of his body.

They looked at each other until Vincent moved aside.

'Felix – you and I'll do it.'

Leo sat down in Vincent's place and opened the bolt cutters with arms longer than a man's. He held onto one arm with both hands while Felix, on the opposite side of the barrier, held onto the other.

'Now, brother.'

They both pressed their bodies against their side of the bolt cutters. The teeth bit into the padlock, two rowers pulling their oars to their chests, pulling, pulling, pulling, until suddenly – with fingers and hands and arms and shoulders shaking, cramping, crying out – the teeth of the bolt cutters cut the thick steel in two.

———

The first net was attached to two lonely birches, and the second hung between the dense branches of a patch of young spruces. They had been practising in the garage in Skogås in the evenings, and one last time in darkness outside Drevviken, so it was easy now to pull off the camouflage nets that hid the trucks, roll them up and throw them onto the empty flatbed. Two red Mitsubishi pickups, the kind of vehicles that someone who owned a contracting firm might drive.

While Leo ran back up the hill, the other two started the pickups and drove through the moss and bilberry shrubs to the open gate.

Jasper knelt inside the bunker, passing one gun at a time into the tunnel, Leo kneeling outside to receive them; Felix stood just behind him, and Vincent was up on the truck bed. A long chain in which every transfer between sets of hands took a second and a half.

'Two hundred and twenty-one automatic weapons.'

Each object that left the concrete cube would be on the platform in six seconds.

'Eight hundred and sixty-four magazines.'

Leo looked at the red hands of his wristwatch. They'd be done in half an hour.

———

They swept away the explosive residue, filled the hole outside and under the door with gravel, packed it hard, stamped on it, packed it again. They changed into blue jumpsuits and workmen's shirts, and put on black jackets with the construction company's logo on the sleeve. They opened the gate and passed through, the two engines idling as Felix jumped out with a padlock in his hand identical to the one they had just cut – it was important that the key should slide in smoothly, even though it would be impossible to turn. The following evening, around nine o'clock, when the inspector arrived in his dirty Volvo to listen to the tawny owl, smoke his cigarette and walk around the military armoury at the top of the hill, everything would seem completely intact. The meticulously prepared inventory had confirmed it would be almost six months until the inside of the armoury was inspected again, when it wasn't going to look quite so untouched.

2

LEO HADN'T REALISED he was singing. He was taking Horns Street to the bridge at Liljeholmen on the E4 motorway, heading south away from the inner city in the rain, when he first heard his own voice enveloping him in the pickup.

He'd bought a coffee and a sandwich at a café, and then crossed the street to the Folk Opera's wigmaker. He was the first customer of the day and watched in curiosity as dancing fingers wove a few strands of brown hair at a time onto the back of a plastic head, while the young woman explained she was using real hair, purchased in bulk from Asia, bleached and then dyed. Then he'd gone to the Eye Centre on Drottning Street and picked up the contacts he'd ordered, both with STRENGTH + -0.

A glance in the rear-view mirror. Blue eyes and fair hair. Leo had always been the one who resembled their mother the most. Her fair complexion, strawberry blonde hair. And he had her nose – small, angular, cartilage as hard as granite. He'd never be mistaken for a foreigner, not even second generation. A small, sharp Swedish nose had always meant less attention – and if the wigmaker or the optician he'd visited this morning were to provide descriptions of a customer who'd paid in cash, they'd be describing somebody who looked just like everybody else.

He left the motorway at Alby, where three lanes turned into two, passed the Shell station and the beautiful twelfth-century church where the high-rises and asphalt gave way to meadows and forests.

He slowed down.

There.

The barrier on which Felix had changed the padlock just seven hours ago, and next to which just ten hours from now a man in his sixties would park his Volvo, put out a cigarette and stroll on by.

The rain that had started late last night was getting worse, wipers beating against droplets that turned to rivulets. The rain would also be falling onto their war tunnel under the concrete. He'd pass it, Cancerman, his rubber boots standing on the gravel that covered the hole. They'd packed and stamped and smoothed it over, but if this rain continued, it would slowly sink and become noticeable in the inspector's torchlight.

I need time.

You mustn't discover it now just because we've done a bad job, you have to discover it in five months when you open the door.

I need time to implement a new way of working, a way of maximising profits without increasing risk. I should get out, walk through the rain, and check to make sure the hole isn't visible.

Which was precisely what he mustn't do.

Only a fool spends months designing a plan, secures his loot, and then returns to the scene of the crime the next morning.

He stepped on the gas.

———————

Neighbours and passers-by called the site the Blue House, a large metal cube that had once been the Gamla Tumba Woodworking factory. Leo parked as he'd parked last night, far away from the wide highway and next to a locked container painted black.

They'd unloaded weapon after weapon without being disturbed, hidden from the view of the main road and any nearby houses.

He rolled down his window and listened to the familiar sounds coming from the large building site – loud music from a paint-spattered radio, short bursts from the air compressor of the nail gun. He did up the last button on his blue shirt, pulled up his blue braces, stretched, and got out.

The Blue House had long been an empty shell, and they'd spent several weeks removing all the old fittings. Then they'd reinforced two floors with beams, insulated them, laid flooring, and partitioned it with walls. Space by space, the building had been transformed into the premises of small independent businesses, a place some entrepreneur was trying to open as the Solbo Centre.

'Did you take care of everything?'

He'd never thought about what Felix looked like when he walked until now. His brother, three years younger, was walking towards him across the makeshift car park, and he looked more like their father with every step. He took up space, feet angled sharply outwards, broad shoulders, thick forearms that he swung as if he were stretching as he walked; he looked idle, like *him*.

I look like Mamma. You look like Pappa.

'Did you get it, Felix? Take care of it?'

'I think Gabbe's trying to shaft us on that last payment.'

Felix made him feel calm in a way he couldn't explain. It should have been the opposite, with those similarities; they should have made him feel worried, hunted.

'He's inside counting every damn nail.'

'Did you . . . take care of it?'

His younger brother began unhooking the plastic hood that covered the bed of the second company truck.

'Gabbe and his freaking nagging. As if he has the right to refuse to pay just 'cause we're not on schedule. As if it says that anywhere in the contract.'

'I'll take care of him. But did you take care of your part?'

'Section Eighty-three. Orthopaedics, I think,' said Felix, taking off the white plastic cover. 'I rolled it out and Vincent's legs suddenly started hurting like hell.'

A wide wooden toolbox with a shiny metal handle stood in the middle of the flatbed. And next to it, under a couple of yellow blankets bearing the logo of a hospital, was a folded-up wheelchair.

They pulled the two pickups a little closer and opened the padlock on the black container – the kind that every construction company sets up at a building site to store tools and equipment. When the vehicles' doors were thrown open, visibility was obscured on all sides, and they were able to lift the empty box and carry it in.

Broad daylight in a residential area, just a few metres from a busy road, and they stood there – in front of piles of automatic weapons.

'Where the hell have you been, Leo?'

Gabbe's high-pitched voice cut through the October day. He was in his sixties, wearing a blue tracksuit that had once fitted well but now sat tight over his expanding belly, a cup of coffee and a bag of cinnamon buns in his arms. 'How the hell are you going to finish all this today?'

He was outside, approaching the container.

'Have you even been here at all in the last week?'

Leo took a calm breath, and whispered to Felix, 'Close this up again. I'll take care of him.'

He left the container and went to meet the red-faced, snorting foreman.

'Leo! You weren't here yesterday! I called you several times! You may be working on something else, but whatever the hell it is, it's not this building!'

Leo glanced quickly over his shoulder. Felix was closing the heavy container doors. The sound of a heavy padlock snapping shut.

'But we're here now. Aren't we? And it'll be finished today. Just like we agreed.'

Gabbe was so close that he could have touched the wall of the container. Leo put his arm around Gabbe's shoulders as he pushed him back towards the Blue House, not so firmly that it was uncomfortable, but insistently enough to ensure that they moved away from what no one else should see.

'I don't give a damn if you've taken on other jobs! Do you understand that, Leo? You have a contract with me!'

Gabbe was audibly panting as they walked into the building. There, on the first floor, right inside, there'd be an Indian restaurant next to a flower shop next to a tanning parlour. On the floor below a tyre company, a print shop, a nail salon, and there, near the inner walls that would frame Robban's Pizzeria, Jasper and Vincent were screwing together a plasterboard partition.

'You see! You aren't done, damn it!'

That foreman's fucking shrill voice. Shrill and overweight and old and hotheaded.

'We will be.'

'I've got a fucking tenant moving in tomorrow morning!'

'And if I say we'll be done, we'll be done.'

'If not, I *will* be keeping the final payment.'

Leo was thinking he'd like to slug that little foreman – a single blow. Right on the nose. Instead he put his arm around him again.

'My dear Gabbe – have you ever been disappointed in me? Have I ever done a bad job? Have I ever been late?'

Gabbe wriggled his outraged body out of Leo's overly tight grip and ran towards the other corner of the metal building.

'The wall here! The hair salon! A layer of plaster is missing! Do the old ladies have to get their perms without a fire wall around them?'

He ran out into the car park and the rain that had gently started falling again.

'And . . . that damn container – you were supposed to move that. In a few weeks this is supposed to be customer parking!'

Gabbe slapped his palms several times against the container that took up so much space in the car park. The sound was muted because the storage unit was filled up to the brim.

'Calm down – we don't want you to have a heart attack, all right?' said Leo.

The foreman's face was even more flushed after running around, but now his whipped-up anger started draining out of him and flowing away in the rainwater.

'It *will* be done by midnight,' said Leo. 'I need this firm, Gabbe – I don't think you really understand how much I need it. My construction firm, our collaboration, it's absolutely necessary for me to be able to . . . expand.'

'Expand?'

'Maximise profit. Without increasing risk.'

'Now you've lost me.'

'You're breathing pretty heavily. I'm worried about you. You should go home and rest. We'll be done by midnight. You can depend on me.'

Leo stretched out his hand and held it aloft between them.

'Right?'

Gabbe's hand was small and moist and soft when it met his. Leo nodded.

'Good. The job will be done today if I say it will. And then *I'll* treat *you* to some cinnamon buns. OK?'

Leo waited between the container and the car as Gabbe left. He had stood there beating his greasy hands on a metal box filled with automatic weapons, and he'd had no idea. Next time he might want to open it.

When he was absolutely sure that the loud-mouthed foreman was far down the road, Leo set off across the street and into the residential area, towards the solution to his storage problem – a small, two-storey house, with a fenced-in yard and no lawn, right next to a major road. He'd seen the owners moving furniture out. Now it had a FOR SALE sign out the back. He walked beside a high chain-link fence towards the gate, entered the yard and, crossing the asphalt, went up to the house, peering in through the window to the left of the entrance – an empty kitchen. Through the window to the right of the entrance he saw an empty hallway. Around the corner and into the next window – an extension and an empty room. Around the corner again and into the next window – the stairs to a second floor.

Two floors, but no basement. The entire neighbourhood was built on an old lakebed. Every house was built on mud and could be extended up, but not down.

Several times in the last week he'd stopped nailing and drilling to look at the ugly little stone house that lay so close to the road. And every time he'd seen the Phantom's Skull Cave. He knew it was a childish thought. But it was also a solution.

A house you didn't really notice, for people without much money.

On the front door there was another FOR SALE sign. He looked at the picture of a smiling estate agent with a swept-back fringe and wearing a suit, searched for the pen in his inside pocket and wrote down the phone number on the back of the receipt from the wigmaker.

The big garage was a dream. He climbed up onto a pile of used tyres and wiped dirt off the window in order to see in – high ceilings and room for four, maybe even five vehicles. Perfect for the formation, the training of a group.

A door opened and closed.

He turned to the garden next door; a much larger house, with lawns covered in wet leaves and a row of apple trees like craggy skeletons. A woman with a small child stood on the gravel path; she looked at him, a curious prospective buyer, and he nodded.

The blows of hammers and the drone from across the road – the uniform an observer would see. A house with a garage to its right – headquarters and a place to train. And in the forest just a few kilometres away – the most remarkable night of his life.

And it had been so easy.

That three brothers and their childhood friend – all around the age of twenty, all snotty-nosed kids without any education – could decide to pull off the biggest arms coup of all time, equipped only with general construction knowledge, plastic explosive, and an older brother who knew the power of trust.

3

A STARRY SKY, brighter than the night before. Leo and Felix squeezed into the truck and drove to a suburb of high-rise apartments, away from the now completed Blue House and a satisfied Gabbe, away from a locked container that sleepy commuters would pass on their way to the bus stop.

The two brothers got out of the truck. Each grabbed one of the brass handles of the battered wooden toolbox on the flatbed.

'It's eleven fifty,' said Leo.

The box was the same weight as when it had held tools, despite the new contents – the new life, their other life, which was about to start.

'Eighteen hours to go.'

They carried it past some low bushes and a sparse flowerbed on their way to the block of flats and the staircase. Leo opened the door. While they waited for the lift, they could hear Jasper and Vincent laughing together in the basement storage rooms.

Fourth floor.

His door. Their door. DÛVNJAC/ERIKSSON. They put the wooden toolbox down while Leo searched for his keys, then took the stack of flyers crammed into the letterbox on the door and threw them in the garbage chute.

The lights were on inside.

Anneli was sitting in the kitchen on a simple wooden chair, the sound of the sewing machine her mother had given her colliding with the music coming from a cassette deck, the Eurythmics – she often played eighties music.

'Hi,' said Leo.

She was beautiful, he forgot that sometimes. A kiss and a gentle pat on her cheek. The black fabric twisted, captured, impaled by the sewing machine's needle. He turned to the sink and the cabinet below it. They were still there. Right where he'd hidden them, far at the back behind the bottles of washing-up liquid and bottles of floor cleaner. Three brown boxes. Not especially large, but heavy.

'Wait.'

He'd already been on his way out.

'Leo, I haven't seen you for days.'

Last night he'd come in and, without stopping at the bathroom or refrigerator, had gone straight into the bedroom and laid down in a bed smelling of her – not her perfume or newly washed hair, just her, lying close to her and holding onto her sleeping body, the force of the explosion at the armoury still reverberating in his chest. The clock radio on his bedside table had blinked 4.42, and she'd turned over, her naked body against his as she yawned and pressed herself even closer.

'And this morning when I woke up, you weren't here any more. I miss you.'

'Not now, Anneli.'

'Don't you want to see what I've made? The polo necks? You were the one who . . .'

'Later, Anneli.'

He was just about to go down the hall to the living room where the others had already started unpacking and repacking, when he saw the empty wine bottle on the draining board and the wet cork in the sink.

'Have you been drinking? You're going to be driving.'

'Just a little. But it was last night . . . Leo, you were in the woods, and I didn't know a damn thing. How it was going, if you'd come home, if someone saw you and would . . . I couldn't sleep! And now . . . what have you been doing?'

'Construction. We weren't finished. Now we are.'

He was already out of the room.

She stopped the sewing machine.

Why were her hands trembling? When she was the one who'd wanted to be involved? When she was the one who wanted to make the vests and who would put masks on Leo and Jasper and drive them to the site?

———

Leo rolled down the blinds on the window overlooking the Skogås shopping centre. The living room looked just like every other living room: sofa, easy chair, TV, bookcase. But that was about to change.

The four men worked on opening the tool chest, the Adidas bag and the paper bags that Jasper and Vincent had brought up from the basement, and the three brown boxes that had been under the sink, and then placing each item in a long row on the wooden floor, as if this were a military inspection before an attack.

A folded wheelchair found in the corridors of Huddinge hospital, the kind that could be collapsed in just two moves, and two yellow blankets with the name of the hospital on them, found in the hospital ward among sleeping patients.

A bag with two wigs of real hair from the Folk Opera and two pairs of brown contact lenses from the optician on Drottninggatan.

Two AK4s and two submachine guns taken from the black container on the building site. Shoes, pants, shirts, jackets, hats, gloves. Torches – Vincent would carry the smaller one in his pocket, and Felix would signal with the larger one. Two five-litre drums full of petrol. And four sports bags beside four indoor hockey sticks.

Leo sat down in the wheelchair and rolled across the shiny floor towards the bathroom wall, turned around, rolled back. He spun around several times, and leaned, trying to tip the chair over.

It was steady.

He stood up and went back to Anneli in the kitchen, caressed her cheek as before.

'How's it going?' he asked.

'They're ready.'

Extra fabric extended the black collar of the polo neck. Anneli pulled on it hard, and the seam held and stayed invisible. It was her design.

'Each collar has a face mask. They all work.'

She then pointed to two green vests.

'And these. Just like you wanted them. Beaver nylon fabric. Pockets for magazines.'

He tried on the vest he'd be wearing under his windcheater. It fitted perfectly. She knew his body.

He leaned forward and kissed her.

'All that stuff on the living room floor, any amateur could get hold of that. But not this. Or one of these.'

He held onto the vest and picked up one of the sweaters with the elongated collar.

'Details. That's the difference. What makes it possible for us to get close enough and transform quickly enough.'

One more kiss and back to the wheelchair again. He folded down the leg rest and put his right leg on it, tried to sit as he thought someone with an injured leg would sit. Jasper squatted in front of him, wearing thin, transparent plastic gloves, opening up the first of the three compact brown boxes – 7.62 calibre, lead and steel core – then the second – 9 calibre, metal jackets – and the third – tracer ammo with phosphorus that would make a luminous red streak several hundred metres long. He then filled each magazine with cartridges and taped them together in pairs. Four pairs for the newly sewn pockets in his own vest, three pairs for Leo's vest, and one pair each for Felix and Vincent, who would wear them in little bags on their stomachs.

'No one looks directly at people who are different. And we're going to take advantage of that. Of their prejudice, their fear.'

Leo spun around in the wheelchair.

'And if they do look, it won't be for long.'

He moved his wheelchair in the same way he remembered the disabled people that his mother worked with moving theirs. His mother, who'd worn a white nurse's uniform and let her three sons come to the nursing home sometimes, when they couldn't stay at home on their own. That's when they'd all seen it – how adults turned their eyes away in uncertainty.

'Right? Don't stare at what's different.'

Jasper handed him an AK4, and Leo tried holding it in his right hand under the yellow blanket, next to his leg on the footrest.

'You're exaggerating too much.'

'No, I'm not.'

'Yes, you are. Isn't he?'

Jasper looked at Felix and Vincent, who both nodded.

'You're overacting, Leo,' said Felix. 'It ruins it.'

'That's how they moved their wheelchairs. But you don't know that. You were too small.'

Leo got up out of the chair and looked around the room. Their very first time. None of them had carried out a major robbery before. But everyone had their roles and knew what to do. And on the floor in front of him was everything they needed.

In less than twenty-four hours, they would be transformed.

4

SIX THIRTY-FIVE P.M. Fifteen minutes remaining.

A journey in silence.

All of them were focused inward.

Anneli adjusted the van's rear-view mirror; she was tall in comparison to her few female friends, but despite that she was significantly shorter than Leo, who was sitting next to her in the middle seat, and Jasper, who was in the passenger seat. A red traffic light, the last before Farsta. It was as if she was slowly being sucked into that light – the more she stared, the more it took hold of her and carried her away.

She didn't remember the single moment in which she'd decided to be involved, the moment when someone had shoved this into her life, *my God*, because if anyone had suggested just a few years ago that she was capable of this, that she'd be on her way to rob a security van . . . Or maybe there was no single moment. Maybe there were just small moments melting together that she never noticed. Maybe one day someone says there is an arms dump in the forest, and someone else says it might be possible to open it up and empty it out, and someone else says that if you empty out a bunker full of weapons, then you might as well use them to rob someone – perhaps when you find yourself surrounded by such moments you slowly become a part of them. No one had ever really asked her a question that she'd stood up and said yes to. Abnormal becomes normal, the ideas of others become her ideas and suddenly a woman named Anneli – a mother – is driving a car towards something she could never have imagined. That was probably why she took off too fast when the light turned green, her driving uncharacteristically erratic.

She was shaking. Not very much, not enough for Leo to notice; he had long since retreated into himself. She was shaking because she'd only ever been so scared before when she gave birth to Sebastian. That had been just like this, crossing a border, knowing that your old life was over.

'There.'

Leo pointed to a pavement lined with lamp posts. She guessed there were another two hundred metres to the middle of Farsta.

'Stop right between those two – where it's darkest.'

Leo closed his eyes, feeling a calm that only existed inside him.

Only I know. No one out there knows what's going to happen. I am the only one who can feel each new step.

They sat waiting for his signal. Anneli was on his left, almost gasping, Jasper on his right, his breathing slow and steady as if he were trying to relax himself.

The van's engine was off, and it had become obvious how dark this October evening was. Leo had sat alone here for four Fridays in a row in a parking spot facing the rear of the forex office, near the bus stop and the entrance to the metro, the Tunnelbana. He'd recorded every moment of the actions taken by the two uniformed guards in an armoured security van, the route they chose, the pattern of their movements, how they communicated with each other.

'Sixty seconds.'

Her hands started trembling again. He grabbed them, looked at her, holding her hands until the trembling decreased. She did one last, very quick inspection.

First the wigs, made from real human hair. If any traces were found

33

later, they would be from a person with thick, dark hair. She reassured herself that they were on straight and covered all of their blond hair, made sure they weren't *too* perfect, tousling both Leo's and Jasper's fringes.

Then the makeup. Waterproof mascara on the eyelashes and eyebrows; she brushed them upwards, making them bushier. Their foreheads, cheeks, noses, chins, necks had been scrubbed clean of dirt and dead cells in the apartment bathroom, moisturised and covered with Sunless tanning lotion.

'Thirty seconds.'

She told them to blink so she could see if their brown contacts sat right.

She examined their jeans, jackets and boots, Leo's windcheater and Jasper's oilskin coat; they'd worked together to survey men's fashion, and this was what they'd agreed two young Arabs, recent immigrants, might wear.

Finally, the polo necks.

'Lean forward.'

Her idea, her design.

'Both of you.'

She folded them down, pulled them up, folded them down again.

'You're wearing them too high. In order for them to work, you have to be able to grab hold of them and pull them over your face without them slipping down again.'

'Fifteen seconds.'

He adjusted his vest, its extra magazines chafing slightly against his chest.

'Ten seconds.'

The thin leather gloves.

'Five seconds.'

He leaned over to kiss her, and she flinched a little as his moustache, also made from human hair, brushed against her upper lip; it was slightly awry, and she smiled as she readjusted it with two fingers until it was straight.

'Now.'

Anneli opened the door and stepped out onto the pavement, loosened the cover on the white truck bed and lifted out the wheelchair and two blankets. Right footrest up – with a new, shorter butt, the AK4 could be hidden under the blanket completely. Jasper steadied Leo as he sat him down on the plastic padded seat and nodded towards the van as Anneli drove away.

Along the dark pavement. Down the gently sloping hill, which would become much steeper in a moment – the loading bay for one of Stockholm's largest forex offices.

Leo had carefully mapped out every section of their course.

'Leo?'

Jasper had stopped the wheelchair, leaning down to unlace his shoes and then tie them up again, so he could whisper without anyone seeing.

'You're still overacting. I've seen your mother work with people who are . . . *different*. And they don't move like that. They don't drool like that.'

Jasper stood up and slowly continued to wheel the chair along a suburban shopping street where everyone was on their way somewhere else. It was at that moment that Leo saw the boy. Five, maybe six years old. Just a few metres away among a group of people waiting for the bus.

No one looks at things that are different.

The boy pointed and pulled on his mother's hand.

No one really notices what a man looks like when they're trying to decide whether to look away or not.

A boy pointing at him – the wheelchair.

But a child. A child doesn't see the world like an adult.

A boy who was now shouting out loud.

A child is fascinated, open, he hasn't had time to get so fucking scared.

The weapon under the blanket. The taped-up magazines in his vest. That wasn't what the boy was pointing at or shouting about, but that was how it felt.

One more shout and the adult standing next to him, not daring to look, might suddenly glance over, maybe even remember them later. Jasper jerked the wheelchair around and hurried away from the bus stop to a less well-lit area.

17.48.

They waited, glancing towards the entrance to the parking area. Cars, bicycles, pedestrians. On their way in, on their way out.

17.49.

Only a few minutes left.

17.50.

Maybe a couple more.

17.51.

Soon.

17.52.

'Where the hell is it?'

'It'll be here.'

'It's already—'

'*It'll be here.*'

17.53.

They started slowly rolling closer, now not even ten steps from the wall that shielded the entrance to the exchange office. The white security van would have to drive all the way down the ramp without noticing two individuals in the crowd, a disabled man and his carer.

17.54.

Jasper crouched down, unable to stand still any longer. He untied his boots and started tying them up again.

'Hey, what's your name?' shouted the boy. 'Why are you sitting in one of those? Are you hurt?'

The boy tore away from his mother's grip and ran towards the people with the wheelchair. They looked exciting.

'*You go back,*' Jasper said in heavily accented English.

'Hello! What's your name? And what happened to your legs?' the boy answered in Swedish.

Jasper put his hand through the hole in his coat pocket, clutching the submachine gun that hung around his neck.

'*Go back.*'

'Gobakk?'

'*Go back!*'

'Is that his name? Gobakk? That's a nice name.'

He turned the safety off, on, off. An annoying clicking sound. Leo prodded him in the side with a bent arm.

It had arrived – the truck they were going to rob.

'*To your mama! You go back.*'

The boy wasn't frightened, but he didn't like it when Jasper leaned close and hissed in his ear. So he stopped staring and asking questions and did as he was told, slunk back to his mother at the bus stop.

17.54:30.

Friday evening. Two hours left. Inside the security van, Samuelson glanced at Lindén, who he'd sat next to for almost seven years, but didn't really know at all. They'd never had a coffee together outside work, never got a beer. Sometimes that's just how it was – two colleagues remained just that, colleagues. They didn't even talk about their kids. He knew he and Lindén both had the same number of kids, but nowadays Lindén's only spent every other week living at his house, and talking to people about what they had lost didn't usually turn out too well.

The van's headlights followed the streetlamps as it rounded the car park. They passed the people waiting for the bus or taking the escalators down to the Tunnelbana. The security guards looked around, scanning their surroundings as always: there was the hot dog kiosk near the bike rack, three women sitting on a bench with overflowing shopping bags, a man in a wheelchair and his guardian talking to a little boy around the same age as his own son, now being jerked away by his mother, a large group of adolescents a little further away, jostling each other and trying to decide where to go – a crowd just like on any other evening.

They took the sharp bend at the bus turning area, then a small swerve, and then came the monotonous beep as the security van reversed down the sloping loading bay to the locked back door.

Lindén turned off the engine, and they looked at each other, a quick nod; they'd both read this place the same way – peaceful for rush hour in a capital city. Samuelson opened his door and took a single step towards the back door. The money was always kept two corridors away in the chief of security's office: two cloth bags on an otherwise empty desktop – banknotes and coins and a handwritten receipt in red ink: 1,324,573 kronor.

———————

Friday was the most profitable day of the week for Swedish exchange offices – and Farsta was the last collection for this particular armoured vehicle on this particular route. The point at which it contained the most money.

17.56.

Leo had chosen the target, the time, and the location of the attack. He knew the wheelchair would only get them as far as the ramp to the loading bay. Aware that there would be nowhere to hide, they would have to overpower the guard during his two steps from the building's back door to the passenger door of the van. And they would have to do it without alerting anyone.

17.57.

They waited. They squinted at the metal door down below.

Now.

The short, humming signal of a lock being opened.

Now. *Now.*

Leo and Jasper grabbed hold of their extended polo necks, pulled them up over their necks and chins and noses, and let go just below the eyes.

They exposed the AK4 under the yellow blanket and the submachine gun hanging under Jasper's long coat.

Forcefully and simultaneously, they heaved themselves onto the wall and jumped down towards the truck in the loading bay.

Samuelson was leaning against the metal door, a green security bag in his hand.

Then he heard it – two beeps from the radio. The go-ahead.

He opened the door, went out onto the loading bay and heard a click from inside the truck, just like always, as Lindén opened the rear door to the secure area.

Lindén was sitting in the driver's seat when he saw Samuelson exit with the security bag. He pressed the button engaging the internal lock and was about to turn towards his colleague when he saw something else. Nothing clear, more like a fragment, something you try to piece together without quite understanding it. First, he saw through the windscreen that the wheelchair he'd seen in the crowd earlier was lying overturned on the pavement above, empty. And then, in one of the wing mirrors, he saw a movement, as if someone was falling towards him from the wall embrasure, someone whose face was completely, almost inhumanly black. And finally, Samuelson opened the side door *Run!* and threw himself inside *For fuck's sake run!* and rolled across the floor of the van seeking cover.

'*Open door!*'

The single second he needed in order to understand.

And it gave him the time he needed to key in the first code, and the steel door to the safe slid down again, blocking the way to the money. Then the two seconds he needed to enter the second code – four digits on the dashboard in order to turn the ignition key.

'*Jalla jalla, open door!*'

It was too late. Someone had landed on the bonnet. A black mask and staring eyes and an automatic weapon aimed at him.

Lindén didn't raise his arms, didn't turn towards the door.

He did nothing.

And that big metal barrel got bigger, closer.

He'd been imagining this every day for seven years, every time he scanned a crowd, but when it happened, it wasn't at all like he imagined. It started in the chest, right in the middle, and then pushed all the way to his throat. And he couldn't get rid of it despite his screaming.

'*You open fucking door!*'

And then he understood. He wasn't able to get rid of it because he wasn't the one screaming. Someone else was. Next to him. And there was another one – outside his window. Another face with the same mask, black fabric over his chin, nose, cheeks, up to his eyes. But with another kind of voice. Desperate. Not meaner, not louder, but more desperate.

Someone was going to die. That's what he felt in his chest. Death.

The window shattered, and his only thought was how harsh it sounded to have someone stand so close by shooting at you. He was aware of two shots and threw himself backwards, his back and head pressed against the seat. The third bullet struck his chin and larynx, the fourth hit the dashboard and the fifth the passenger door, while he automatically pulled the control centre alarm.

––––––––––

'You open door!'

It takes three seconds to empty thirty bullets out of the magazine of a submachine gun. The five shots through the van window that Jasper had just fired took half a second, but it had felt so much longer.

'You open or you die!'

Leo stood on the bonnet of the van with his gun aimed at the security guard in the driver's seat, while Jasper beat the muzzle of the submachine gun against the partially broken safety glass. Until the second guard, who was lying on floor, lifted his arms over his head.

———————

Samuelson looked at Lindén, at his neck, at the blood flowing from it – he'd never thought about how red blood is when it's fresh. He'd got up, arms above his head, opened the door on the passenger side and let in the masked man from the bonnet of the van, who now stood inside the cab aiming a gun against his temple and speaking in broken English, asking him to unlock the safe. He tried to explain. But he couldn't find the words. Not in English. He wanted to explain that from now on the safe door was locked, and that it could only be opened with a code held at headquarters. He searched for words that just weren't there, while the masked man listened and waited, so quiet and restrained, not like the other one with the desperate voice, who'd fired through the window. This was the face that made the decisions, that was clear, even as the muzzle pressed a little harder against his temple.

———————

Lindén was slumped down in the driver's seat, blood running down his neck.

The hand, the hand that belonged to that self-controlled face, searched through the pockets of Samuelson's trousers, jacket and shirt, searching for and then finding his keys.

And the desperate one screamed and shoved the gun against his chest.

'*Start engine!*'

The muzzle of the gun moved from his forehead to his mouth. Into it.

'*You start! Or I shoot!*'

The gun was between his lips and against his tongue, as he leaned against the keypad, four digits, needed to start the engine.

'*I kill I kill I kill!*'

Samuelson's hand had lost all feeling, his fingers hard to manoeuvre as he punched in the code, turned the key, and started the truck again.

———————

Jasper drove slowly up the steep loading ramp and across the pavement towards the turning area and the car park exit. No one had noticed five shots muffled by the walls surrounding the loading bay and then disintegrating into the soundscape of the city.

A few metres up from the loading ramp, life went on as if nothing had happened.

If they continued to drive at normal speed. If they didn't call attention to themselves, they'd have plenty of time to empty the safe and disappear.

'Open inner door,' said Leo, holding up a key chain and handing it to one of the guards. Somewhere on the chain was the key to the security cabinet that hid seven other keys to seven boxes holding seven cash collections, with more than a million in each one.

'Please, the door is locked. With code. Special code! Can only be opened from headquarter . . . please please . . .'

'You open. Or I shoot.'

He glanced quickly through the window. Outside, a Stockholm suburb in motion. In here, one guard lying down, retreating into a world of his own, and another guard with blood on his chin and neck still talking.

'Understand? Please! Only . . . only open at headquarter.'

A few minutes left, no more.

Nynäs Road, Örby Highway, Sköndal Road. More blocks of flats, a football pitch, a school. And the crest of a steep hill – if someone were following them, they'd make it there, but no further.

Felix was breathing slowly.

In. Out.

For the last twenty-four minutes he'd been lying in long, wet grass on the top of a hill they used to run up and roll down as children, right above the outskirts of Sköndal, not far from where their grandparents had once owned a small, white house.

The gun shook, *in, out*, with every breath he lost his rhythm and had to start again, *in, out*, one hand around the grip with his index finger on the trigger, the other in the middle of the barrel, and one eye staring into the gun's sight.

Nynäs Road lay down below. He almost felt like he could touch it, though it was far away, a blurry streak of headlights melted together, cars on their way home on one of Stockholm's most congested motorways. And beyond that stood Farsta, buildings shining in neon light; it was in that direction that he anxiously aimed his gun, that was where Leo would come from.

There. The white van.

No.

That wasn't it. It was white, and large, but not a security van.

18.06. Two minutes late. Two and a half.

The gun slid, vibrated.

Three minutes. Three and a half.

There. There!

He glimpsed the roof of a white van, over the bridge and past the sharp left turn, searched through the telescopic sight and saw in the driver's seat a face covered with a black polo neck just like his, then the space behind the car's two seats, Leo squatting in front of two people lying on the floor, one with his hands over his head.

And then he saw it. Behind the security van. A passenger car, two people in the front seat.

They'll either be following us in a painted cop car or in a civilian car. Always black, always a Saab 9-5 or a Volvo V70. This one was black. He saw that when he moved the barrel of the gun. But he couldn't see the make. *Look at the right side, there should be an extra side mirror, that's how you know if they're plainclothes cops. And don't press too hard, just squeeze the trigger.*

He looked through the sight.

Felix, listen to me. I set up this weapon myself and you can't miss, and no one will be, or should be, hurt. You put a bullet in their engine and stop their car.

He wasn't sure, an extra side mirror, he just couldn't be sure it was there.

And he squeezed just a bit more, while the muzzle pointed at the bonnet of the black car.

———

Leo looked at the guards, at Jasper driving, and out of the window as they passed the hill. There was a clear shot from up there all the way down to the bridge. Especially with an AK4 with a telescopic sight he'd ordered specially because anyone could hit anything at three hundred metres using it.

If someone was following them, one shot should be enough.

Felix was shaking. The black car was still close. Too close.

Then you wait. Don't leave or let go of your gun until we've gone past and you're sure no one is following us.

The white security van turned left after the flyover at the intersection. Thirty metres behind, the same car was following them.

In, out.

He let the sight rest towards the front, on his knuckles, and squeezed the trigger. Squeezed.

The black car suddenly veered to the right, heading in the opposite direction. Increased its speed and disappeared.

Felix wasn't trembling any more, he was shivering, breathing rapidly.

Two people had been sitting in the front seat, on their way home, a single finger tap away from death because they'd been driving on the wrong road at the wrong time.

He got up from the wet grass, put the gun in his bag, and rolled the fabric covering his face into a collar again. And ran. Down the hill, through the woods and the community garden. It was dark and he fell over a low, pointed fence, dropped the bag and stood up, ran until he reached the car parked at the bottom of the hill.

They'd passed the hill. Felix hadn't fired.

They weren't being followed.

Leo looked at the locked door. Inside were seven more batches of collected cash – eight, nine, maybe ten million kronor.

They'd had a few seconds to react. They'd needed one more.

The security guard had managed to enter the code, and the steel wall had slid down to protect the safe. They were supposed to open and empty all the compartments before they got to the rendezvous. That was no longer possible. But they still had time to deviate from the plan.

'Where . . . please, please . . . do you take us?'

They could shoot open the door at the rendezvous – but that was too noisy.

'What . . . please, I beg you, please . . . will you do with us?'

They might be able to force someone at headquarters to open it from a distance – but that would take too long.

'I have . . . please please please please . . . I have children!'

The security guard lying on the floor, bleeding a little, put one hand inside his uniform, and Leo struck his shoulder hard with a gun.

'*You stay put!*'

The movement was interrupted, but the guard continued, put his hand back inside his jacket, held something up.

'My children! Look! Pictures. Please. Please!'

Two photographs came out of his wallet.

'My oldest. He is eleven. Look!'

A boy on a gravel football pitch. Thin, pale. A ball under his arm. His hair sweaty, he smiled shyly, his blue and white football socks rolled down.

'And this . . . please please look . . . this is . . . he is seven. Seven!'

A table in a dining room or living room and what looked like a birthday party; a crowd, every seat taken, everyone dressed up, sitting around a white tablecloth and a big cake. The boy leaning over, about to blow out half the candles, missing two front teeth.

'My boys, please, two sons, look, look, brothers . . .'

'*Turn around.*'

He snatched the two faded photographs and dropped them on the floor.

'Two boys, my boys . . . please!'

'*Turn around! On stomach! And stay!*'

Vincent guided a rubber boat across calm water. Drevviken. One more wide turn, his hand on the steering rod of the two-cycle engine, and to his left he saw the light beyond the forest's edge – Farsta – and the darkness straight ahead of Sköndal Beach. He turned off the engine, gliding towards the jetty and the beach. He got out, and pulled the boat into the reeds. He'd thought for the last two kilometres he was running late.

Right then he realised why Leo had chosen this place. The bay was sheltered, and beside the beach was a swimming pool that was long since closed for the winter. Their mother had once worked there with disabled children of his age, some with and some without wheelchairs.

He stood on the long wooden jetty, rocking slowly. Not far away lay a second jetty, shorter and much older, and he was reminded of the summer Leo taught him to swim. He had called it the Dock, and Vincent would

44

earn the invented swimming badge (of which only one copy existed) when he was able to swim the ten metres that separated the old wooden jetty from the new one. He'd thrashed his arms and drummed his legs, and one evening after the others had gone home he'd managed to make it the whole way without putting his feet down. Leo had applauded and given him the badge – a large piece of wood with words carved into it.

He was being rocked up, down, by a plank that sagged just a little too much – even the new jetty was getting old. The very plank he'd held onto after that last stroke, as he'd gripped Leo's hand to keep from sinking into the cold. Leo's voice was always there, telling him to concentrate on the next stroke, and only that, not on what he felt or saw, just straight ahead to the next stroke.

They should be here already. *He* should have been *there*. Anything but this – the not knowing.

He smelled bad. Vincent could feel it oozing out of his pores, a scent he'd never smelled before, strong, acrid, stifling – more fear than he could hold inside.

He leaned down on his knees towards the glassy surface of the ice-cold water and rinsed his face.

The gun pressed against his back and he readjusted it. Leo had handed it to him in the hallway before they parted, *always keep the barrel pointed down until you're ready to use it,* Leo had emphasised as he showed him, *safety off, safety on, safety off,* grabbed his shoulders tightly, *just remember, Vincent, that you decide, not the weapon.*

18.11.

They should have been here by now.

———————

Felix ran down the hill, through the woods and community gardens, towards the car. Down the narrow gravel road and then onto the slightly wider asphalt road, until he found himself at the flyover. His heart was just beginning to beat a little more regularly, his breathing starting to even out – when he heard the sirens.

When he saw the rotating blue light.

'Vincent, where are you?'

'I'm still here. At the jetty. Waiting.'

The phone he was only supposed to use for emergencies.

'They're not here yet,' said Vincent, his voice weak.

45

This was an emergency.

'Fuck . . . *Fuck.*'

'Felix?'

'Fuck!'

'Felix, what's—'

'The fucking police just drove by now! In a few minutes they'll be there, where you are!'

Vincent was holding the phone and Felix's voice in his hand. The fear poured out of him stronger than before.

It was at that moment that he saw it, heard it.

The car stopped and its headlights streamed onto the windows of the changing rooms at the beach.

And then – the voices. Talking loudly. Screaming.

Leo looked at his watch.

18.12.

No one was behind them at the checkpoint. They still had time to force open the locked door that separated them from another nine million kronor. He was just climbing out when Jasper dragged out the guard. Both pushed beyond their limits.

'*Open! Or I shoot!*'

'I . . . can't. I can't!'

Jasper stood up and shoved his automatic weapon into the guard's mouth.

'*I shoot!*'

The watchman kneeled down, weeping and trying to speak.

'Please! Please please please please!'

Jasper cocked the gun and raised his weapon. His black boot sank into the grass as he leaned forward, pressing the butt firmly against his shoulder. His finger on the trigger, his eyes unreachable.

Vincent heard shots.

Not one. Not five. Twenty, maybe thirty.

He knew he wasn't supposed to be seen. There were only supposed to

46

be two robbers. The only ones the security guards would see and report later.

But Felix had called. The cops were close. He had no choice.

Pain cut into Jasper's right shoulder: it felt good. His breath was ragged. But despite emptying his magazine into the locked door, there was not a scratch. He fished a new magazine out of his vest.

Then he heard footsteps in the darkness, getting closer.

He turned in their direction, his weapon in front of his body, ready to shoot.

Vincent had to warn them. He ran across the fine-grained sand and over the grass they used to lay their towels on, ran until he saw the outline of the van, and beside it, Leo and Jasper.

Jasper pointed his weapon in the direction of the approaching steps.

A face. He was sure of it. Out in the dark.

He fired the first shot.

Leo had heard those steps, too. He saw Jasper turn his weapon in that direction, squeeze the trigger, and then recognised something familiar: the way a person puts down their foot, moves their upper body. And he just knew.

He threw himself forward, his hand around the barrel of Jasper's gun, forcing it upwards.

'Felix called, he said . . .'

Someone who Leo recognised, who shouldn't be there, who could have died just now, was whispering, pressing his mouth to Leo's ear.

'. . . the cops are on the way – they've passed the checkpoint!'

Leo grabbed his youngest brother tightly.

You should have stayed at the jetty.

'Go back.'

I could have lost you.

'And get the boat started.'

Leo looked at Jasper and at the still intact steel door. Vincent would never have disobeyed an order if it weren't an emergency.

'*Leave. Now,*' Leo ordered.

They'd used up their nine minutes from Farsta to the shores of Drevviken lake. He'd allowed four more as well. There was no more time.

'*Now.*'

Jasper saw the bluish light above the trees, getting closer. He had an almost full magazine, thirty-five shots. Leo was going to have to wait. He wanted to make a stand, face those bastards.

'*Now!*' Leo screamed.

Jasper started running, but not towards the boat, first to the security guards, one at a time.

'We know your names, *sharmuta*.'

He tore off the IDs hanging from their jacket pockets. Names, service numbers.

'If you ever talk . . .'

––––––––––

The three-metre-long rubber boat glided through the reeds. Leo in the front, Jasper in the middle, and Vincent in the back with one hand on the engine cord.

He pulled on it. Nothing. He pulled again. Still nothing.

'Come on, for fuck's sake!'

Vincent's fingers were slippery, they slid and couldn't get a good grip – and when they did, he pulled on the cord a few more times and nothing happened.

'Damn it, Vincent, the choke!' barked Leo.

Vincent pulled the square button all the way out, then pulled hard on the engine cord.

The engine started.

Leo looked at his youngest brother. He'd always been so little, but just now he'd made his own decision, disobeyed an order and left his spot to warn them. And he watched the blue lights flashing behind him, almost beautiful against the blackness, ebbing away on the other side of the cliff as their boat reached open water and disappeared into the darkness.

5

JOHN BRONCKS LEANED his head against the inside of a large window. It was cool, almost cold against his forehead. The leaves of the wiry, newly planted trees standing in a line in the courtyard of the Kronoberg police station had recently turned from yellow to red, and were now brown, falling to the ground to be trampled on.

Ten to seven on a Friday evening.

Not much life out there. Not much life in here.

He should go home.

Maybe he'd do that.

He went to the kitchenette that stood in the middle of the office, put a saucepan on the stove, then poured boiling water into a deep porcelain cup someone else had bought and left behind, making silver tea. He usually drank it like that. Only a couple of offices still had their lights on: Karlström's four doors away, and one at the end of the hall, where a chief inspector approaching retirement was playing sixties music and sleeping on a brown corduroy couch. Broncks never wanted to end up like that, spending his nights at the station to escape the loneliness like a black hole you were falling headlong into. Broncks was here for the opposite reason. He *didn't* need to hide here. He liked going home when he felt he deserved it, when he gave himself permission.

A warm cup in hand, the water didn't taste of much, but it went down smoothly. Broncks's desk looked like everyone else's. Piles of folders, parallel investigations. Others seemed to be drowning in them, but to him it felt more like autumn on his desk, something that made it easier to breathe.

> Interrogator John Broncks (JB): She lay down?
> Ola Erixon (OE): Yes.
> JB: And then . . . you hit her?
> OE: Yes.
> JB: How?

OE: I sat on top of her, on her breasts, straddled her. Right
hand. Again.
JB: Again? As in several times?
OE: She usually pretends.
JB: Pretends?
OB: Yes, sometimes . . . usually she pretends to faint.

Every night, around the time he should be heading home, they started
pushing harder – investigations that just wouldn't allow him to leave and
let him take part in whatever lay outside.

Thomas Sörensen (TS): I took him to his room and asked him if
he saw anything different.
Interrogator John Broncks (JB): Different?
TS: The damn lamp was on. It'd been on all day. So I had to
teach him.
JB: What do you mean by that?
TS: The book. Against the back of his head. He needs to
understand it costs money! This wasn't the first time.
JB: That you hit him?
TS: That he left the lamp on.
JB: Your son is eight years old.
(Silence.)
JB: Eight.
(Silence.)
JB: You continued? Hitting him? With the book . . . a thick,
hardcover book?
TS: Mmm.
JB: And then . . . I want you to look at the pictures a bit further
down – the back, the body, neck?
TS: But you have to understand he deserved it?

Night after night he went through these investigations, most of them like
this. But he didn't do it because of the attacker. Or the person who'd
been attacked. It wasn't for their sake. He'd never met them before, didn't
know them. That wasn't why he stayed here long after the corridor was
empty. It was the attack itself. Folder by folder, document by document.

Erik Linder (EL): She didn't do what I told her to.
Interrogator John Broncks (JB): What exactly do you mean?

EL: I mean exactly that.

JB: And so . . . what did *you* do?

(Silence.)

JB: This image – according to the doctor, first you fractured the shop assistant's jaw.

(Silence.)

JB: And here – you fractured her cheekbone.

(Silence.)

JB: This is an image of her chest, which you kicked repeatedly.

(Silence.)

JB: And you have nothing to say about that?

EL: Hey!

JB: Yes?

EL: If I'd wanted to kill her . . . I would have.

And yet. Even though he didn't care about these strangers. Each time he investigated incidents where excessive force had been used, it was as if he became more alert, more interested – something that pulled him in and wouldn't let go. Until the perpetrator was sitting in a jail cell four floors above.

'John?'

There was a knock. Someone was standing in his doorway. Someone was stepping inside.

'You're still here, John.'

Karlström. The chief superintendent. His boss. Wearing a winter coat and carrying a couple of overflowing paper bags.

'Did you know I end up with an average of fifty cases a year of serious violence on my desk, Karlström?'

'You're still here, just like you always are, every night.'

Two pages of photographs of a woman's body. Broncks held them up.

'Listen to this: *If I'd wanted to kill her I would have.*'

'And this weekend, John? Will you still be here?'

More photographs from another folder. He held them up as well.

'Or this, Karlström: *But you have to understand he deserved it?*'

'Because if you are going to be here, I want you to put that aside.'

More pictures, not especially sharp, probably taken by the same forensic scientist in the same hospital lighting.

'Wait, this, this is the best: *She usually pretends to faint.*'

51

Karlström took the documents and piled them on the desk without looking at them.

'John, did you hear what I said?'

He pointed to the clock on the wall behind Broncks.

'One hour and seven minutes ago a security van in Farsta was hit. More than a million taken. Automatic weapons, shots fired. The van was hijacked and driven to a beach in Sköndal. More gunfire took place there when the two masked robbers tried to break into the safe.'

Karlström lifted the pile of pictures and waved them.

'Now forget these. These investigations are over. I want you to go there and take over. Now.'

He smiled.

'Friday evening, John. All of Saturday. Maybe Sunday, too – if you're lucky.'

Karlström was just about to grab the two bags and leave when he changed his mind, lifting out a live black-spotted lobster with rubber bands around its claws.

'My evening, John. Homemade ravioli. A basil leaf on each circle of pasta. You cover it with fresh lobster, grated truffle, salt and olive oil. Fold the circle into a crescent, press the edges together firmly to seal it. The kids love it.'

John smiled at his boss, who every Friday afternoon rushed to Östermalm Market to sample the raw entrecôte, and then sat in a café mourning the fact that free-range corn-fed chicken had been banned by the EU.

One man with lobsters wearing rubber bands. Another one with a security van robbery to investigate.

You got the weekend you wanted. And I got the one I wanted.

Felix wasn't freezing, even though he was naked. And it was for the same reason that he hadn't shot that black car before it turned.

A calm that was his alone.

If Leo, three years his senior and who took the brunt of it, had been lying on that hill he would have taken the shot just to be sure. If Vincent, who was four years his junior – protected, allowed to be a kid – had been there, he would have fired in panic. And if Jasper, who so eagerly wanted to be the fourth brother, had been up there he would have fired just because he could.

Felix looked around the dark forest, towards the dark water.

Barefoot against the damp rock, he pulled on the tight wetsuit, thin, with short sleeves and legs in order to reduce buoyancy; soon he would need to dive.

Holding the unlit torch in his hand, he searched the water ahead, but saw only long waves with foam crests rippling in the breeze.

Silent. Too silent.

Was the wind covering up the sound of a rubber boat with a Mercury motor?

He flashed his torch three times with the green light.

The signal.

First came the gently arced bay, then the jutting cape, power lines connecting two beaches like thick clothes lines above their heads, then steep cliffs and then, there in front . . .

There.

It was still far off and the trees on the beach were in the way, but Leo could just make it out: the green light, three blinks.

'Vincent?'

'Yeah?'

'Change places.'

Leo had practised navigating in this kind of darkness. For the last stretch, they'd be close to land, manoeuvring around sharp stones you couldn't see. Tiller in hand, he slowed down, turned, turned again.

'Fucking hell, we did it!' said Jasper, putting an arm around Vincent's neck. 'No one has ever hijacked a security van so fucking perfectly! What the hell's the matter with you, Vincent? You feeling OK?'

'What's the matter with *me*? You nearly shot me.'

'You had orders to remain on the boat. How could I know you would run up there?'

'If I hadn't warned you, if I hadn't—'

'Quiet now. Both of you,' said Leo. 'And Jasper, take off your wig, put it in the bag and wash your face.'

Leo slowed down a bit. The propeller was sluggish in the black water as he made a wide arc around a rock, then a small hill. Three flashes. The green light was getting brighter. He steered towards it. Their target was a low bluff with two scrawny pines. And Felix was standing on it, barefoot in a wetsuit.

They had arrived.

They jumped ashore carrying three automatic rifles and the security deposit bag, while Felix picked up from the tall grass four identical Adidas bags, which contained the jeans, shirts, jackets and indoor hockey sticks. He put on his flippers and mask, and they started filling the rubber boat with the boulders he'd rolled forward, then tied a long rope around each one and attached them to the engine.

Leo, Vincent and Jasper pushed the boat out into the cold water towards Felix, who swam beside it. When he got to the middle of the sound, he hoisted himself up onto the side and started slashing holes into the rubber with a large knife. The air hissed out and it began to sink.

It drifted slowly below the surface.

Felix couldn't see far, just a meagre arm's length ahead of him, but he knew that according to the nautical chart the lake was ten metres deep at this point, and he followed the boat down for three, maybe four metres before resurfacing. They'd gone swimming here so many times as children, swimming and diving and looking for non-existent treasure, without ever getting close to the lakebed of blue clay – so perfect for a rubber boat to get stuck in.

John Broncks had taken the report about the security van robbery and hurried towards his car in the Kronoberg police station garage. He'd driven over the Västerbron Bridge and stopped for a hot dog at 7-Eleven – four hundred calories that took the same amount of time to eat as it took to read a recipe for lobster ravioli. As he drove south past Skanstull, people were on their way out on a Friday night, making the transition from one life to another, our collective reward system.

An hour and seven minutes had passed by the time he received the report. Twenty-two minutes in the car. He knew the two masked robbers who'd hijacked the security van and its guards were already somewhere else.

He increased his speed, but his thoughts remained with the case files on his desk. The husband who'd killed his wife and then sat there waiting for the police to arrive, who couldn't handle his fear of loneliness, who'd just felt lonelier as he beat her. The father who'd taken his son to the doctor and forced him to lie, explain how the injuries made by a hardback book had been caused by a skateboard that didn't slide down the handrail as he'd hoped. And the man who'd remained silent in the face of pictures of a battered shop assistant, convinced that he'd been in control and could have stopped whenever he wanted to. Broncks had interrogated all of them this week. And they'd confessed.

He exited the motorway, on which the Friday rush hour traffic had gradually reduced to weekend levels, hurried down a smaller road into the Stockholm suburb of Sköndal, passed first apartment blocks then houses, then arrived at an empty beach on a bay. Or it *should* have been an empty beach. But instead there were three police cars, an ambulance and a security van with its doors open.

You got the weekend you wanted. And I got the one I wanted.

A helicopter buzzed overhead, dogs barked in the distance. He'd meet up with them later. First, the white van. He walked over to it, seeing five bullet holes in a side window, the congealed blood which streaked a security guard from chin to neck as he lay down, a paramedic at his side – the real damage, which wouldn't heal, was on the inside.

'Not yet.'

A young woman wearing a green uniform with a red name tag on her chest nodded first at Broncks and then towards the security guard on the ground. The guard looked around without seeing, his brain turned off so it wouldn't break.

'OK. When?'

'He's in shock.'

'*When?*'

'You can't question him yet. Understood?'

Broncks continued towards the other guard, who was making a wide circle around the security van again and again.

'Hi, I'm John Broncks and I'd like—'

'It was me. I was the one who let them in.'

A little faster, a little wider, around the front of the van.

'They would have killed us otherwise. Do you understand? They'd already fired through the window. But then, the steel door, Lindén had already locked it, and they wanted to get in, they wanted . . . they fired again.'

'The steel door?'

'Where the safe was. The rest of the money.'

Broncks looked into the van. Blood and glass and bullet casings were scattered on the seats and on the floor. On the dashboard, a receipt reading *Forex Central Station 3001* under a thin layer of glass splinters.

'They knew there was more. And he started shooting. The desperate one, he was screaming at us . . . he wanted to get in.'

The guard was standing behind him, about to start walking in circles again.

'One of the Arabs.'

'Arabs?'

'Yeah. *Jalla jalla. Sharmuta.* Like that. And the rest in English. With an accent.'

A plastic duffel bag lay between the driver's seat and the passenger's. John had seen that kind of bag before, in other robberies.

'How much?'

The security guard was already walking away.

'Excuse me . . . but how much is left in there?'

A ragged voice, but clear, and with his back to Broncks.

'Eight pickups at eight exchange offices. About a million at each one. They got one.'

The security guard, whose name was Samuelson, continued walking in circles around the van. Broncks was following him with his eyes – this man who didn't know where he was going – when the paramedic shouted for him.

'It's fine now. Five minutes.'

John Broncks returned to the other guard, who was lying on a stretcher, and they shook hands. The guard's was cold, damp, passive.

'John Broncks, City Police.'

'Jan Lindén.'

Lindén tried to stand up, but stumbled and lost his balance. Broncks grabbed him and helped him lie down again.

'How are you? Should I . . .'

'The robber . . . he was . . . leaning forward.'

'Leaning forward?'

'The one who shoved that fucking . . . that shoved it into my mouth.'

'Leaning forward – how?'

'He . . . had a low centre of gravity, you know what I mean? When he aimed. At me.'

The guard stretched out his legs, bending them at the knees, to demonstrate.

'Like this . . . as if he was holding the gun *above* himself. With his legs bent. With one boot sinking down.'

'Boot?'

He stood up from the stretcher again. It went better this time.

'You said "one boot sinking down".'

And he started walking, too.

'I have to go home now.'

The paramedic and Broncks followed him, and each took hold of one of his arms.

'They took my ID. They know where I live.'

He tried to break free, but lacked the strength.

'My kids, don't you understand, I have to get home to them!'

And he wept. The paramedic gently guided him to the stretcher.

Broncks was left alone. The questions would have to continue the next day.

The truck in front of him was lit up like an outdoor stage and a forensic scientist crawled in and out of it. Lights streamed weakly from the beach behind him as other scientists went from one jetty to the next.

He'd seen fear. He knew what it looked like, how it sounded. And this kind, he'd learned never to avoid it again.

Excessive force.

Who terrorises people in that conscious way? Who uses fear like that?

Someone who'd felt it before.

Someone who knew how it worked – that it did work.

Broncks walked towards the water and the wandering lights. They'd had a well-developed plan – location, time. They'd been heavily armed. They'd used extreme violence. They'd stayed cool during a kidnapping. They'd chosen a remote destination. These were no first-time robbers, no debutants – this was a group that had carried out similar robberies before.

He approached a long jetty surrounded by thick reeds.

And there – another forensic scientist with a torch.

Sometimes you just know.

It was dark except for that torch, but only one person in the whole world moved like that. He went a little closer. She became clearer.

'Petrol.'

She still looked young. He knew that he didn't.

'And here, on the first few planks, grass and dirt.'

She hunched down, with her torch pointed at the water's surface and at the droplets gleaming and melting together.

'They went this way.'

That was all. She said no more, turned around, and left him. Back to the security van in order to search it on her knees with infrared light.

She'd looked at him as if they didn't know each other.

Those first few years he'd thought about her every day, several times a day. About meeting again. He'd worried and hoped and dreamed. Then not every day, but almost. And now . . . this. Not even a hello or a smile.

A peculiar feeling. To not exist.

John Broncks climbed onto the jetty, slippery with dew. Farsta was just across the water behind the trees. And in the other direction a line of southern suburbs. Thousands of landing sites for a small boat.

She'd been right.

They'd fled this way. A group of criminals who used assault as an instrument, professionals who'd done this before.

And would do it again.

6

ANNELI WAS FREEZING, but she didn't want to leave the balcony. The dimly lit underpass could be seen from here – and it was from there that Leo would emerge. Besides, the cigarettes – Mindens, from green packs, cigarettes that tasted of menthol and comfort – were warming her up a little as she chain-smoked.

She'd parked the car, run up the stairs and opened the door to the flat. Without even taking off her coat, she continued through the hallway and the living room and out onto the balcony where she heard sirens.

She had no idea what was happening. The police could be there right now, could be shooting at them right now, Leo could be hit and dying without her right now.

She'd been hearing them talk for months about how you blow up a an arms dump, how you empty an armoured security van. Heard, but hadn't taken part, and the few times she'd said something, they didn't listen. Leo hadn't listened. The four of them were a closely knit group she could never be part of. Leo seemed absent when he was with her, and present when he was with his two brothers and his third wannabe brother. They didn't even eat together any more. She'd lost four kilos, which was too much if you were already a little skinny. He hadn't even noticed.

One more cigarette. She inhaled, deeply, filling the empty space inside.

The sirens were multiplying. Getting louder. They buzzed around in her head even when she covered her ears. She went in, closed the balcony door, shutting them out, drank the other half of a bottle of wine, put on the television. Seven thirty: the news. She'd never liked the news. It wasn't relevant to her, not here, not in a flat in Skogås. And the intro music, the stories that were supposed to sound so important, just sounded like the sirens outside. Pictures of people lying on cracked and parched earth with their stomachs distended, people in suits standing in front of stock prices, people jumping in front of cameras in the middle of a war and shooting at other people.

A smiling newsreader. A woman she recognised.

Two heavily armed men made off with over a million kronor in a raid on a security van in southern Stockholm only an hour and a half ago.

A mouth. The only thing she saw. Lips moving slowly.

The security guards were abducted at gunpoint and one of them was shot.

Shot.

Who?

Anneli went closer to the TV and the woman with the moving lips. *I didn't hear, don't you get that! Who? Again! Say it again! Who was shot?* She grabbed the remote control from the coffee table.

A large area has been cordoned off, but the police still have no leads on the two robbers and any possible accomplices.

Then she heard. *More than a million.* For the first time in her life, the news was actually about her. *Still no leads.* The only thing they showed was an abandoned van. Behind blue and white plastic crime scene tape that shook in the wind. And next to it there were people in uniform who were hard to make out, talking, searching.

And then it was over.

Images from the Swedish parliament turned into pictures from the UN headquarters in New York.

She had no idea how long it had lasted. Thirty, maybe forty-five seconds. But it had been *that* van, it had been about them, about her.

She went back out onto the balcony for a cigarette and leaned over the railing to get a better view of the viaduct and the underpass, her feet almost leaving the cold floor.

The sirens were gone. Now there was only wind, and music coming from an open window one floor down.

She felt so light and leaned even further out. What if she fell? It would be so painful.

She was the one who'd told Leo where to find the wigmaker, who'd said she could transform them into two immigrants. She'd brushed them and painted them, and the first few times they shook with laughter. And she was the one who'd designed and sewn the polo-neck collar that could be pulled up to cover their faces, and Leo had said they were so good they should sell them to other robbers.

And there they were.

She stood on the balcony, looking down on them as they exited the viaduct, lit by the short streetlights. They carried a bag each over their shoulders from which their hockey sticks projected, hiding their machine guns and more than one million kronor.

And there they were.

She was flooded with the kind of warmth she only felt when they made love, or like when she'd seen Sebastian for the first time, sticky and newborn on her stomach.

She wanted to run to the door, but didn't – Leo mustn't see how worried she'd been. He wouldn't like it.

Jasper entered first. And it was as if he was about to explode, as if he desperately needed to tell her something, over and over again in different words. He marched into the living room, put the bag on the floor, turned on the TV, *hurry up, Leo, for fuck's sake, come and see*, and then he laughed, or sang, still traces *We!* of adrenalin left *Made!* from pushing a gun into another *The!* human being's mouth, he tore off his *Front!* jacket and shirt and T-shirt and it smelled strongly of sweat *Page!* and unlaced his boots and pulled off his pants and his erection showed through his underwear.

Then Felix and Vincent came in. Arms above their heads in triumph, wide smiles and muffled shouts of joy as they took turns embracing her, like Jasper smelling strongly of sweat, then threw themselves down in an armchair as relieved as they were proud. Finally, she heard his step. Leo.

She kissed him and whispered, 'They don't have any leads on us, I just heard it now, on the news.'

'They had time to lock the security door.'

He passed her on the way to the kitchen with a plastic bag full of mobile phones, opening them one by one.

'The door?'

He plucked out the SIM cards and cut them apart with pliers.

'To the money.'

Filled a small pot up halfway with acetone and then put the bits of SIM card in to dissolve.

'But they just said on the TV . . . they said you got a million.'

'And missed nine.'

'Missed?'

'Nine million fucking kronor behind a locked steel door. And it was my fault. I was the one who . . . it won't happen again.'

He put the mobile phones, minus SIM cards, into a fabric bag.

'But all the rest?'

'What "all the rest"?'

Tied a string tightly around the bag until it was completely closed.

'The collars I sewed?'

'They were perfect.'

'And the makeup, how . . .?'

'It worked.'

He took a hammer from the drawer under the kitchen sink and put the cloth bag on a chopping board and struck it, repeatedly, until the four phones became impossible to piece together again.

'You did a good job. Sweetie – it's like you were with us the whole time. Right?'

His hand against her cheek. And she saw it on him. That he'd thought it would feel different. He should feel pride, joy. But he was empty, he had already left her and she knew it. Even though he'd just got home, he was already on his way to the next job.

He had the same look on his face as he pretended to be happy, beside her on the sofa with Jasper on his other side, Felix and Vincent in the armchairs; the same look as when Felix overturned an imaginary wheelchair and jumped over a wall, and everyone laughed, when Vincent picked up a large empty fish bowl and filled it to the brim with money, or when Jasper hugged him and wanted his attention, *Leo, did you see, when you were on the bonnet, how he looked at you first and then at me, did you see his eyes*, then he raised his voice and pretended to be an Arab again, *we know your names*, pretended to pull off their IDs, *sharmuta I will come for you.*

It was at that point she realised what this reminded her of: it was as if they were talking about a movie. As if they'd gone the other way, into the city, seen some new movie together, and now sat drinking a beer at a bar, comparing their favourite scenes, trying to outdo each other in recreating them. She hadn't seen that movie. That's why she sat in silence and squeezed Leo's hand until he noticed that she felt left out, and stood up and walked over to the goldfish bowl and waited for everyone to fall silent. And when they were quiet, he started taking out handfuls of notes, 20s and 100s and 500s, counting them out, and then handed them ten thousand kronor each.

'Are you kidding me?'

Felix wasn't sitting in a pub and recounting scenes from a movie any more. He got up from his chair in a shabby flat in a shabby concrete suburb and started taking more bills out of the goldfish bowl.

'Hey! Felix, what the hell are you doing?' snapped Leo. 'Ten thousand each.'

'And I'm saying – are you kidding me?'

'Ten thousand.'

'Shit, there's more than a million in there. And I'm going out tonight. I wanna go through five thousand, 'cause I'm worth it. And tomorrow I have to pay the rent. And—'

'We'll talk about that then. Tomorrow.'

'Damn it, ten thousand kronor, that's what an eighteen-year-old makes at McDonald's!'

'*Tomorrow.*'

Felix held the stack of money in his hand, looked around, trying to delay making a decision, and then dramatically started to put the notes back into the goldfish bowl one at a time.

'Are you done?' asked Leo.

One at a time.

'Are you?'

Until they were lying there again, every one.

Leo got a piece of paper from the kitchen and wrote on it while the others sat and watched.

'Yes, there's a million there. But we were counting on ten. It's clear as fuck you should party and celebrate. But we have to live until next time, too. That's my responsibility. And we have to be able to *accomplish* the next one. That's also my responsibility.'

The paper was in the middle of the coffee table, next to the goldfish bowl, and he pointed with a pen to columns of figures.

'Out there in the car park are two cars that belong to the construction company. We need to look like we're going to work every day. Cars, clothing, tools. There are ongoing expenses that have to be met so that we can do this instead: clothes that will all be burned, leasing a container for weapons, a boat that will have to be sunk. And that was just this time. Next time will cost even more. You know how a business works? In order to make money, we need to invest money until we have so much damn money that we don't need any more.'

Felix and Leo looked at one another. And they were kids again – one who challenged the other and one who accepted that challenge and would beat it every time, as you must to be in charge.

But they'd never done it standing around a bowl full of banknotes.

'Are we agreed?'

No answer.

'Are we?'

Felix pursed his lips.

'Mmm.'

Leo pulled him closer to himself, hugged him.

'You wily bastard.'

Anneli sat so close to them and yet so far away. She'd never really understood it when siblings belonged together like this. She had an older sister and a younger brother and it had never felt like this – now they rarely even talked. These were siblings who trusted each other. Needed each other. And she didn't like it; when people got that close, it was difficult for other people to get inside, to belong.

7

LEO SAT ON the edge of the bed, sweat on his face and running down his back. 03.05. Persistent rain was drumming against the windowsill.

He'd been freezing when he went to bed, and now he was suffocating from the heat.

Anneli was sound asleep on the other side of the bed, snoring, whimpering a little. She'd been so tense when he came home. Then, as he reached for her, her body had collapsed, as if she wanted to avoid explaining to him what she truly felt.

She didn't need to explain.

He knew the time he'd been spending on the firm's new project was creating a rift between them. But he was going to make up for it. When you love someone, you give back what you've taken.

Leo kissed her lightly on the tip of the nose. Held his face close to hers. Her calm breath was warm, and now, with her anxiety gone and finally asleep, he could see what he'd been unable to understand last night or the night before.

Even though I love you, Leo, I can leave you.

And it didn't get any better when he tried reversing the words.

Even though I love you, Anneli, I can be left by you.

It sounded so simple. And it terrified him.

Another kiss on the cheek, but not so fleeting, as if he wanted to wake her, whisper to her.

When you rob a bank together, you can never leave each other.

He sat up quickly on the side of the bed. *What the hell am I doing?* Adversity should never cause doubt, should never be directed at the family.

Nine million kronor locked behind a steel door – that was why he wasn't able to sleep. It had nothing to do with Anneli, they belonged together and would never betray each other. He, if anyone, knew the consequences of driving away someone you love.

He went over to the window and stood there for a moment looking out over the suburb he'd grown up in.

Same tower blocks. Same asphalt.

But he'd chosen a different life now. Bank robber. And he was going to do it better than anyone else. Because he *had* to do it better than anyone else. He couldn't fail, getting caught was not an option – his brothers were part of this, and they were all going to become financially independent together.

It was my fault.

That's why he couldn't sleep – he should have done better tonight.

It won't happen again.

He took a folder out of the desk between the sofa and the corner cupboard, laid it down on the table and opened it.

A sketch of a bank.

Four escape routes that led to four roundabouts, each with four new exits, and a search area that included a total of sixty-four possible escape routes.

The doorbell rang.

He threw a blanket over the goldfish bowl and a lid over the toolbox and the four guns it contained.

The doorbell rang again.

He stood up and looked out over the car park and the road from the centre of Skogås. Empty. The driveway to the gate, empty. He walked carefully across the floor, shut the door to the bedroom and her heavy breathing, proceeded to the front door and bent down to look through the peephole.

Felix. Leo didn't realise how tense he'd been – how prepared.

'Weren't you going to go into town? And "go through five thousand 'cause I'm worth it"?'

'We never made it to fucking Crazy Horse. Jasper went to some underground club and then Vincent went off with a girl. Can I crash here?'

Leo opened the door and nodded towards the bedroom door with a finger to his lips. He took the blanket off the goldfish bowl and threw it onto a fully clothed Felix, who sank into the sofa.

'What the hell is that?' Felix asked, grabbing the drawing from the table.

'The next one.'

'Where?'

'Handels Bank. Svedmyra. Let's sleep now.'

'Sleep? Cheers, brother! Here's to financial independence!'

'It's not about the money.'

'And that fucking goldfish bowl, then? It's filled to the brim!'

'It's about making sure no bastard can *ever* tell us what to do again. After this you and I and Vincent won't have to depend on anyone ever again.'

Felix looked at his big brother who, trying to avoid more questions, went over to the window, lifted the blinds a little and peered outside.

'Leo?'

'Yeah?'

'I don't get how you can fucking live here.'

Leo could hear in his voice that he was drunk. But he meant it.

'Sometimes you know every bush, every staircase.'

'That's what I'm saying!'

'We grew up here.'

'We grew up here – and you moved back voluntarily!'

A car reversed and turned round in the car park. A cyclist rode through the underpass. Otherwise, it was peaceful in a way that only existed between the hours of the final news bulletin and the arrival of the morning paper.

'We'll be moving soon.'

'What I don't understand is why you moved back in the first place.'

'Sometimes you have to.'

'But here!'

'And then we can move. Again. For real. Anneli wants a house. And I . . . I've already chosen one.'

'A house?'

'Yeah.'

'A lawn? Cutting the grass? You?'

'There is no lawn. And no basement. That's the whole point.'

It had been a virgin robbery by four beginners: a code to a steel door that he hadn't anticipated; ten million that ended up being only a million.

But next time, everything would be perfect.

Leo lingered in front of the living room window, which was covered with stray raindrops – outside was Skogås, a suburb south of Stockholm whose tower blocks were almost identical to all the others built in Sweden in the sixties and seventies.

The asphalt that had been his whole world.

then

part one

8

LATE EVENING WINTER darkness, and big patches of white, brown and grey snow lie on the asphalt, the steam pouring from his mouth as he counts his own big breaths.

He has no coat on. Despite that, he's not cold. They've been doing this for a while, up and down, up and down, and the skin on his forehead and cheeks is covered with shiny layers of sweat. He wipes his hands across his face, and they end up wet, so he dries them on his trousers.

A three-storey building that looks just like all the others. 15 Loft Street. Five steps to the door. He turns his head to look at the next door along, 17 Loft Street, and his opponent, who stands there looking back.

Felix. His seven-year-old little brother, already in junior school.

Leo raises his arm slightly, angles it away from the shining streetlamp. A light brown leather strap, the watch face with red hands that are short and ugly. The day he has enough money, he'll buy a new one, the kind that other people look at.

He waits. The second hand passes the nine. Ten. Eleven. He holds his hand high up in the air.

'Now!'

At twelve exactly he runs. Opens the door to number fifteen, while Felix opens seventeen.

Taking two steps at a time to each new door, a wad of paper in his hand, Leo delivers seven different leaflets from seven different companies, which they've bundled together at home on their living room floor.

He opens the first letterbox and glances at the red hand of his watch. It took twenty-four seconds to run up the stairs and deliver the first bundle of ads. On each floor there are four letterboxes that he has to press open with the palm of his hand in order to make the opening large enough. One at a time, and as quickly as he can. They slam shut when he's done and his black lace-up boots thud against the floor as he runs to the next slot.

He's lived here his whole life. Ten years. An area south of Stockholm called Skogås, thousands of identical high-rise blocks all standing in a row.

Every door is almost the same, but not quite. The names, smells, sounds are different. Often someone's at home watching TV. Sometimes someone's listening to music, bass and treble coming through the open slot. Now and then someone is drilling holes in the walls, and quite often people are shouting at each other. The dogs are the worst part. In this stairwell there's one waiting on the second floor. One jumping at the letterbox as he thrusts in the flyers, which aren't supposed to be visible from the outside in case the people paying him make a random inspection.

The dog starts barking as soon as he approaches, its heavy body against the inside of the door. He opens the slot, just a small gap, sees a long tongue and sharp teeth, and loses six seconds because those slavering jaws force him to stick his papers in one at a time.

And then there's that letterbox at the very bottom, the one that always takes twelve extra seconds – number seventeen has no such apartment.

He wonders how far Felix has got.

He takes the stairs three at a time, but knows that because of that damn dog and then this door, it's taken almost a minute and a half to do the entire stairwell. Felix will be out there smiling, a little bit cocky, fifteen seconds before him.

And he is. His little brother has won – but he's not smiling.

Felix has company. An ugly, blue puffa jacket. Hasse. He's in year seven, the kind of guy who stays in the smoking area of the playground even after the bell rings. There's usually someone else with him too, a shorter guy who wears a denim jacket even in the winter: Kekkonen, the Finn who's never cold.

But now he is alone. And he's holding his arms outstretched. Above and around Felix, preventing him from moving.

'What the hell are you doing?' Leo screams.

That's his little brother!

'Let him go!'

Hasse smiles in victory, a smile that should belong to Felix.

'And here comes another little faggot.'

'Let him go, damn it!'

'The little fucking faggot's screaming! The little fucking faggot doesn't understand! I told you last time. Right? I said "one more time". If I saw you and your little fucking faggot brother here again, I said I'm gonna *kill you*.'

70

Leo is breathing heavily, but not because he took the stairs three at a time. He's scared. He's angry. And both sensations beat against his chest from the inside.

'We're not the ones who decide where these fucking flyers get delivered!'

The anger and fear push him to walk quickly towards Hasse, still trapping Felix with his arms, and the closer Leo gets the bigger the smile on that bastard's face gets. He continues walking, a little more slowly. It doesn't make sense. Hasse shouldn't be smiling, he's tall but not strong, and he should be scared and angry, like Leo. He should be preparing.

But he's smiling, and looking at something that seems to be . . . behind Leo.

It's too late.

Leo gets a whiff of a musty, forgotten smell. From a dirty denim jacket that's only ever been taken off when a teacher has demanded it. He recognises the smell but doesn't see the fist coming at his neck and cheek. Surely he's going to fall. The snow-patched asphalt is getting closer to his other cheek and his forehead. He's on the ground, his vision blurry. Someone is standing near his face, shorter than Hasse and squarer. Kekkonen, the Finn who's never cold, has been hiding behind a tall bush and he's attacked Leo from behind, while Hasse just stands there smiling.

The ground is cold. He has time to notice that. But not to get up.

The first kick hits his cheek. The second hits him lower down, on his chin. The last thing he remembers is how strange it looks when the evening darkness disappears into a streetlight, how it's sucked up, turning white before it turns black.

9

THE PAIN IS most intense on his left side, near the ribs. When he pulls up his thin sweater and probes the skin with his fingers, the swelling is still there.

Leo lies in his narrow bed, which is too short for him, his feet reaching all the way to the end. It's not exactly light outside his window, but it's lighter than when he went to bed.

The pain throbs from a large spot in the middle of his head, as he grabs hold of the blanket and mattress and heaves himself upright. A mirror hangs above his desk. The tight half of his face is less red now, more blue and yellow and swollen like his ribs. He touches it. It hurts worse.

He tiptoes barefoot across the room. Felix doesn't move at all, lying on his stomach in bed with both his hands under his pillow, muttering something in his sleep. Leo walks out into the hall, unlike yesterday, when he crept in. And when his father had finally stuck his head into the room, Leo had made sure he was lying with his face turned to the wall, pretending to sleep.

Leo closes the door to Vincent's room, where inside is the little bed he once slept in and his three-year-old brother lying upside down with his feet on his pillow. He continues past to Mamma and Pappa's bedroom, also closing their door. And he stands there, as he usually does for a moment, in the middle of those smells. Red wine from his father's breath, menthol from his mother's, and mostly, the smell from his father's huge work trousers that hang on an iron hook in the hall, a Mora knife and a folding ruler in one of the oblong pockets. It's a smell that has always been there, like drying paint, or the smell of sunshine on skin – now it reminds him of Kekkonen's denim jacket. He extends his hand gently towards them. The carpenter's trousers have been hanging there for almost two weeks, untouched. That's how it usually is in the winter, longer stretches between jobs.

He hears a sound.

Through the closed door.

Leo waits quietly, closes his eyes, hopes it will go away. One ear against the painted surface. Quiet again. It was surely his mother. She usually makes some sounds when she's just come home and managed to sleep for a little while, when she's been working several nights in a row at the nursing home. He's learned the morning sounds. It's good when his father's breathing is deep and audible – watch out if you don't hear it any more. Leo waits a little longer, then goes into the kitchen and takes out a new kind of white bread that tastes like syrup, cheese with large holes in it, and orange marmalade. He doesn't take out the toaster, it rattles too much. He mixes orange juice in three glasses, a finger of yellow and the rest cold water from the tap. He makes sure whenever he's close to the sink not to bump against the pan of congealed wine, a dark and hard layer that's difficult to wash away. There are piles of Keno tickets on the counter covered with crosses forming different patterns, part of the system his father has been using for so long. He counts the butts in the ashtray. His father sat up late into the night and won't be getting up for a while yet. Leo goes back to the bedrooms, shakes Felix's arm and then Vincent's, with a finger to his lips – and they nod as they usually do.

They don't say anything while they eat. Syrup loaf, orange marmalade on top of the cheese, a full glass of juice. He moves his chair slightly, making sure to keep his ear towards the hallway and the bedroom. He can't hear the heavy breathing any more. Maybe Pappa's just turned over? Or what if their chewing was too loud and he's woken up? Leo shakes the last slice of bread from the plastic bag, butters it, and hands it to Vincent, who has marmalade on his fingers and cheeks and in his hair.

The door. He's sure of it. That fucking damn shitty door.

And it's his pappa's footsteps, treading slowly from the bedroom to the toilet – he can hear him peeing even though the door is shut.

Only half a sandwich to go. Two sips of orange juice.

There he stands. His long pale upper body, his thick forearms, his jeans unbuttoned at the waist, sockless feet that never seem to end. He stands on the threshold looking in and fills up the whole doorway.

He combs his hand through his hair, pulling it back; Pappa has always looked like that.

'Good morning.'

Leo is chewing. When you're chewing you can't answer. Since you're chewing and can't answer, you've got time to turn your face towards Felix, leaving only your right cheek exposed to that voice.

'I said *good morning*, boys.'

'Good morning.'

Leo hears them answer in a quick chorus, as if they want this to be over as soon as possible. Pappa passes behind his back, opens a cupboard, takes out a glass, and fills it with water. It sounds like he's drinking half of it, and then he turns towards the table.

'Has something happened?'

Leo doesn't look at him, just glances with his good eye.

'Leo. You're not looking at me.'

Now he turns his head a little more, as much as possible without revealing *too* much.

'Show me your face.'

He's not quick enough. Felix gets there before him. The sound of his sandwich plate on the table and a loud voice.

'It was two against one, Pappa. They were . . .'

Pappa isn't standing at the sink any more. There's bare skin near Leo's shoulder.

'What is that?'

Leo turns even more to the side, further away.

'Nothing.'

Pappa grabs his face. Not hard, but hard enough, and turns it upward. The stupid swollen cheek that is blue and yellow and puffed up around the eye.

'What the hell is that?'

'Leo . . . fought back. He did. Pappa! He . . .'

Felix answers again before Leo is even able to form a single word. He normally has so many, they fill his mouth. Now they aren't there. When they come, he swallows them.

'Did you?'

His father stands there, looking at him, then at Felix, then back to Leo, trying to meet his eyes, staring, staring.

'Leo?'

'Pappa, he did, I saw it, loads of times, he—'

'I'm asking Leo.'

Eyes that stare and stare. And a mouth that asks and asks.

'No. I didn't hit back.'

'There were two of them, Pappa . . . and they were big, thirteen or fourteen years old, and—'

'OK. That's enough.'

Those large hands lift up Leo's battered face a little bit more, carefully fingering it.

'Now I know. Go to school, Leo. And when you get home . . . we'll take care of this.'

10

THEY DON'T LOOK much from this far above. There's the taller one with fair hair and a backpack and the shorter one with dark hair and a gym bag over his shoulder.

He's probably never watched them walking to school together. He walked Leo to school the first week, walked beside him, explained things to him, warned him, directed him – *it's a fucking savannah, hunt or be hunted, and it will only give you what you're entitled to if you take it, you're a Dûvnjac and no bastard is going to sit where you want to sit* – until the second week when Leo asked him to walk a few metres behind, then the week after asked him not to walk him to school at all. With Felix, he'd never even considered it. He had Leo, and that was good enough.

But it *wasn't* good enough.

His oldest son can't even protect himself.

Ivan moves the two potted plants to one side and leans on the window-sill with both hands. There isn't really much to the kitchen. A narrow corridor, a dining area, and a seventh-floor window from which both Skogås and the two heads below appear small. But it's his. A four-bedroom flat with two entrances in a Stockholm suburb that didn't even exist until a few years ago, when men in suits drew a few lines on a piece of paper, trying to solve an acute housing crisis by building a million identical flats.

He cracks the first egg, the second egg, the third egg, the fourth egg, always fried to a crisp, always thoroughly salted. He stands at the stove, stirring the eggs in the frying pan with a fork, but what he sees is a face. Swollen. Blue. Yellow. A face that won't go away.

He tries to focus on the high chair, where Vincent sits and waves while his pappa cooks. He pours himself a large glass of water and drinks it. He boils water in a snorting kettle and mixes the instant coffee, heaping in several spoonfuls.

It's not enough. It doesn't block out what's in front of him.

One swollen cheek, one eye swollen shut, a battered face.

'Owww!'

His plate is on the table, coffee cup in his hand, when Vincent leans over and grabs the ballpoint pen and a stack of Keno tickets and starts drawing on one that's already been filled in.

'Not those, those . . . those belong to Pappa. No scribbling there.'

'You have so many.'

'No more. Stop it!'

He looks at his son, who refuses to let go. His little hands are a lot stronger than you might imagine. A three-year-old, but the face is that of his ten-year-old brother, and it won't leave him alone. He turns away and closes his eyes, then turns back, but the swelling continues to grow. Leo getting beaten, falling to the ground and crawling, taking it and not hitting back.

A fifth egg, another cup of black instant coffee. Ivan still sits there, even though he finished long ago, looking through the kitchen window, following the pavement towards the white brick school where two of his sons spend their days. The one-storey building that holds the junior and secondary school and where a swollen face sits at a desk, answering questions and anxiously glancing out of the window, looking for whoever beat him up. And who might be waiting outside to beat him up again.

He's suddenly in a hurry.

He puts Vincent down on the floor and tells him to go to his room and wait there and not to wake up Mamma. He throws on the closest pair of shoes, brown leather, once nice but now scuffed and missing their laces, and takes the lift seven floors down to the basement, through a corridor that's missing its lights and past the storage spaces.

The mattress is blue quilted on the outside and spun and carded horsehair on the inside, the hard kind that's almost impossible to get hold of any more now that everyone wants to sleep on air and down. The mattress they slept on together the first few years they lived in the city.

It's heavy and fills up the entire lift. He knocks down decorations in the hallway and clothing off the coatrack on his way into the kitchen. The twenty-year-old horsehair mattress covers the entire floor between the refrigerator and the dining table. He presses it down with his left knee and rolls it up, packing it tightly, and ties a rope at each end, moves it from the kitchen to his workroom and leans it against the wall while shoving a chair out to the middle. He takes down the large rice-paper lamp and presses the mattress up against the ceiling hook until it catches hold.

'What's that?' comes Vincent's small voice.

He hadn't noticed his audience. Ivan smiles, sighs, lifts up his youngest son.

'A new lamp.'

The curious eyes look at him for a long time.

'No, it's not, Pappa.'

'No. It's not.'

'What is it, Pappa?'

'A secret.'

'Secret?'

'Mine and Leo's secret.'

Ivan walks towards the kitchen, Vincent following. He removes the scraps of rope from the kitchen table, puts the little boy in the high chair at the short end of the table, and takes a new bottle of red out of the wine rack under the sink, which has empty spaces for nine more – Vranac, with the label that he likes so much, the black stallion that can't be broken, rearing up on its hind legs. Pours half of the bottle into a pan, a few tablespoons of sugar, then heats it up, stirring it until the sugar melts, and decants it into a beer glass.

'Thunder-honey, Vincent.'

He raises his glass to Vincent, who smiles and touches a finger to it, leaving a small, clear fingerprint behind.

'Thunder-honey, Pappa.'

Ivan raises the glass to his mouth, closes his eyes. As he swallows he sees a face, swollen, blue, yellow.

11

THE DAY WAS not long enough. Leo had waited on one of the low benches in the junior school playground for his little brother, who was in school for longer than him today. Then they'd sat there together, talking, waiting, talking a little more. About nothing. They both knew they were waiting for time to go by. That if they sat there long enough Pappa might have passed out from the wine by the time they got home.

One step at a time, up all seven floors.

Slowly taking the last step.

Slowly.

Their door looks just like all the others. A letterbox that slides open, almost swishes up after a light poke of the fingertips. A black doorbell that makes a prolonged, muted ring. And a metal plate above it that reads NO CANVASSERS, which Pappa always points to in irritation whenever anyone they don't know rings the doorbell.

Leo and Felix exchange a glance.

He doesn't want to go in, but leans in closer, trying to hear Pappa's footsteps without really daring to put his ear against the door.

They look at the nameplate on the door. DÛVNJAC. Three deep breaths. Then they open the door and go inside.

'Leo!'

A single step and the voice has already arrived. His legs don't want to continue down the narrow hallway, so they just stop there.

'Leo, come here!'

Pappa is sitting in the kitchen. Still wearing jeans and no shirt. An empty glass stands next to a pile of Keno tickets, the pan on the stove is empty. It's easier to look down at the floor, concentrate on the yellow linoleum floor far away from the staring eyes.

'Come here.'

Leo steps forward. Felix stands beside him until Leo stops him, *go to Vincent*, pushes him when he doesn't move fast enough, *go to Vincent's room and close the door*, one more step. His gaze never leaves the floor.

'Yes?'

'Your face.'

He looks less at the floor and more at his father's legs.

'I want to see your *whole* face.'

His father's legs turn into a stomach, chest, eyes. It's hard to see what he's thinking.

'Does it hurt?'

'No.'

A hand pokes at the tight and aching skin.

'Don't lie.'

'A bit.'

'A bit?'

'A bit more.'

'And they go to the same school as you?'

'Yes.'

'And you know their names?'

'Yes.'

'And you didn't hit them back?'

'I—'

'You go to the *same* school? You *know* their names? But you're not going to do . . . *anything* about it?'

Pappa towers over him.

'You're afraid. My son is . . . afraid? A Dûvnjac? Well, everybody's afraid! Even me. But not everyone runs. You stand your ground. Control your fear. And you grow.'

His big body is shaking. And then he points out into the hallway, towards the workroom.

'We're going in there.'

'There?'

'Now.'

It happens again. Just like in the hallway, his legs refuse to budge.

'*Now.*'

Leo starts moving, though slowly, when the door to the bedroom opens. Mamma. Her hair is dishevelled, and she's wearing a yellow nightgown that doesn't fit properly any more.

'What's all the screaming out here . . .'

Pappa whispers, but his voice is still loud.

'Go back to bed.'

'What's going on? Ivan? What are you up to?'

'Don't get involved in this.'

'What are you . . . *oh my God*, Leo, your face, what—'

'This is between me and Leo. This is my responsibility.'

He puts his arm around Leo's shoulder and pulls him a little closer, not hard, but clearly towards the room.

'Now let's go in.'

12

FELIX STANDS BEHIND the closed door, listening. He pushes on it and hears Mamma ask Pappa what he's up to, and Pappa telling her it's none of her business.

He doesn't hear Leo's voice at all, no matter how closely he listens, and he doesn't like that. He knows that's not good. It feels like when that bastard Hasse stretched his arms out on either side of him to keep him from moving forward or back. Or worse, like it did yesterday when he didn't have time to warn Leo that Kekkonen's fist was coming at him.

He opens the door and goes out into the hallway. He has to. He can't stand it any more.

And walks right into Mamma.

She hears him, but doesn't see him. Her eyes are boring into the closed door of the workroom. He stands next to her, listening with her.

A . . . it sounds almost like a thud. And another. Or maybe a . . . punch. As if someone is throwing punches. Again. Again. Again. Again.

Just like yesterday. When he couldn't do anything. When he cried and screamed inside Hasse's arms.

He opens the door before Mamma is able to stop him. It looks weird.

Pappa is on his knees, on the floor, and he's never seen him like that. His upper body leans against a large, blue, tied-up mattress. Pappa is holding it as if he's hugging it. And he never hugs anybody. Leo is also shirtless. Bare chest and jeans.

He looks like Pappa.

'Put your weight into it, like this,' says Pappa. 'Your whole weight.'

And it's then that Felix realises that the blue mattress is hanging from the ceiling where the rice-paper lamp used to hang.

'You punch with your body, not your hands, you need to put your *full* weight behind it.'

And it's *Leo* who's doing the hitting, at the mattress that Pappa is hugging. Again. Again. Again. Again.

'When someone wants to hurt you, you aim for the nose. A single punch. Go for the bigger one first. If you hit his nose, it'll make his eyes water.'

Now Pappa stands up, jumping lightly on the spot, low, quick jumps, and he punches the hanging mattress hard, very hard.

He stops hitting and nods to Leo who's rubbing the knuckles of his right hand, which are already skinned and red.

'When you hit the nose, he'll lean forward. The idiots always lean forward when their tear ducts start to squirt. That's what happens if you hit the nose just right, they open up, and then he'll stand just like this, look at me, Leo, with his forehead near yours.'

Pappa leans forward, very close to Leo's chest, like a ram about to slam his horns into another ram. And that's when he sees them. He looks at Mamma, who wants answers but won't get them, so chooses to look at Felix instead.

'Go and get some water. A big glass. Your brother's getting thirsty.'

Now he pokes, nudges his head gently against Leo's chest.

'Now punch again. But *never* straight ahead. If you do that you'll hit

80

the forehead, the skull, it's the hardest bone in the body, and you have to protect your hands. Aim your next punch here.'

Pappa points to his chin, and gestures at his cheek.

'The jawbone. You crook your arm, as if you're hitting diagonally from the side and also from below.'

He makes a fist and hits his own jaw and cheekbone.

'You aim for this, the cheekbone is fragile. With your whole body behind you. A short right hook slanted underneath.'

Leo punches. Punches and punches. Tries to crook his arm, come around with it, punch just as Pappa wants him to.

'Water? You were supposed to go and get some water, Felix. Didn't I say so? Run!'

Felix does it, runs to the kitchen, to the tap from which the water is always warm and takes so long to run cold, fills a big glass and walks slowly back, holding it in both hands.

'Good. From now on this is your assignment. You bring us some water every half-hour and hand it to your brother. Now . . . close the door.'

Pappa turns his bare back to them. And lays his arms on Leo.

'You've hit him on the nose. He's leaned forward. Now you keep on hitting. Until he's on the ground. And if there's more than one of them, they'll give up. One or two or three. It doesn't matter. It's like . . . dancing with a bear, Leo. You start with the biggest bear and hit him on the nose – then the others will run. Dance and hit, dance and hit! You wear him out, and when he's confused and scared you hit him again. You can defeat a bear, as long as you know how to dance and hit!'

Felix is waiting for Mamma to close the door, but instead she steps into the warm, musty room.

'Ivan – what do you think you're up to?'

'I told you to leave.'

'I see his face. I do. But this . . .'

'He needs to learn how to fight.'

Mamma has a different kind of voice than Pappa, thinks Felix. When she screams it cuts through you.

'You can't do it like this! Leo isn't you. You of all people should know best where this will lead!'

'Damn it! He needs to learn how to protect himself!'

'Let's go into the bedroom. You and me. Now, Ivan! And talk about this!'

Pappa is silent for a moment. Even though it looks like he's going to scream back.

He goes over to Mamma and shoves her out of the room.

'And what are we going to talk about, Britt-Marie? How he should lie down the next time he takes a beating? Which side of his body he should turn up so they can hit him even harder? He has to be able to protect himself! Or should he be a fucking . . . Axelsson?'

Mamma doesn't answer.

And when Pappa closes the door, Felix squeezes her hand.

13

FELIX'S FOOT TREMBLES a little as he stretches up towards the cabinet and Mamma's green medical box on top of it. He sits down on the lid of the toilet seat and opens the box up, taking out bandages and surgical tape. With these items in hand, Felix runs across the brown carpet of the hallway, into the living room and across its wooden floor that's always cold and creaks when Pappa walks on it.

That damn Finn in his stupid denim jacket.

He'd heard what Hasse and Kekkonen did to their prisoners, how they scraped sharp stones against their armpits until they bled and then poured salt into the wound. And what they did to Buddha who lives on the third floor, who was scared to death of spiders and was taken prisoner during the estate war. They bound him and then gathered daddy longlegs from all over the cellar and put them all in a cardboard box. Then they opened the bottom of the box, and Hasse pushed it over Buddha's head, and Kekkonen taped the open flaps around Buddha's neck. The daddy longlegs crawled over his face and into his hair and got caught in his ears and nose and mouth. Felix had seen Buddha afterwards, how he'd walked slowly back to his own street, a prisoner of war who didn't know where he was or who he was.

He and Leo had been lucky.

Felix steps out onto the balcony, cold air in his face. He passes the elastic bandages and surgical tape to Pappa, leans over the edge of the railing, looking at the asphalt of Skogås. Leo sits in one of the striped camping chairs, his cheeks a little red.

'Your knuckles will toughen up, but for now we'll have to do this instead, protect them. You have to be able to practise more often and for longer.'

Pappa takes Leo's hands, stretches them out, and winds the bandage around his knuckles.

'When your knuckles make contact, follow through, continue the movement with your *whole* body – and it's *then*, at that moment, you go through him.'

The gauze is wound over his knuckles and down between his thumbs and index finger and then diagonally over the wrist, round and round.

'Make a fist.'

Leo clenches his bandaged right hand and then waits until his pappa hits it with the palm of his hand.

'How does it feel?'

'Good.'

The same thing with the left hand, then Leo punches the air several times in front of Felix, hopping and running through the living room and the hall, punching at nothing again and again. Pappa follows him back into the room and gets down on his knees again, and boxes the mattress so that it thuds and shifts.

'What are their names?'

'Hasse.'

'And?'

'Kekkonen.'

Pappa punches at the swaying mattress, then punches at his own shoulder.

'This is how fucking Hasse and Kekkonen do it. Their punches stay right . . . here. At the shoulder! All of their movements stop here.'

He raises his right arm to the mattress, turns the right side of his upper body into it and continues the move, following through.

'And this is how *you* should punch. *You* punch through them. *You* go through, straight through.'

Pappa moves one small step at a time until he's standing right behind Leo. Felix can't see much more than two backs, but doesn't dare go any further into the room. He stretches himself, stands on tiptoe in the middle of the threshold. It seems like Pappa has hold of Leo's arm.

'You aim for the nose and it explodes like a huge fucking water balloon! And their brains are in there, floating in liquid like a goldfish in a goldfish bowl! And when you hit the nose first and then the chin . . . the brain bounces. Hasse's and Kekkonen's fucking little brains sloshing against the walls of the goldfish bowl.'

Leo hits again.

'Nose! Chin!'

One more time.

'Nose! Chin!'

One more time.

'*Nose!* Get your body behind it! *Chin!* Follow straight through! *Nose!* Their fucking brains! *Chin!* They should bounce and splash!'

After a while Felix's toes start to hurt, so he lies down and watches as Leo's arm hits the mattress from underneath, and it almost looks funny, as if it's not happening for real.

He's still lying there when Pappa steps over him and goes to the kitchen and the stove and the pan for one more glass of Thunder-honey before he has to put on the work clothes that have been hanging a little too long in the hallway – there's a job that Pappa has to tender for so that in a few days it might be his. Felix watches the feet on their way out through the front door and hears the two quick bangs as the lift opens and closes, then feels the calm that falls over the whole flat whenever Pappa leaves, as if there's suddenly more room inside.

14

LEO PUNCHES AND punches the blue mattress. He's wrapped his hands himself, just like Pappa wrapped them before leaving to paint some kitchen all day in a house in the suburbs. Leo knows he can hit harder and more frequently without that annoying pain. He begins each morning with a session before breakfast and school, runs home at lunchtime and punches without eating, then all afternoon and evening, and again if he wakes up in the night and can't sleep.

He hears the vacuum for the second time this afternoon.

And he stops punching.

Mamma is up. She's gone past by so many times, peeking in, and he recognises the look on her face – she doesn't like him practising.

He punches again. Nose and chin. Hasse and that Finnish bastard.

They could be waiting for him at any time or anywhere, so he's been avoiding them, maybe even hiding from them, until he's ready. Nose and chin, Hasse and the Finnish fucker. It happens almost automatically now. His whole body behind it. Shoulders that rotate, shoot forward, follow through and punch through them.

'It's time to take this down.'

Mamma has turned off the vacuum cleaner.

'That's a lamp hook. A lamp should be hanging there.'

She fetches a three-legged stool and steps up on it, stretching towards the ceiling and the hook while her son continues punching without looking at her.

'Can you stop that now?'

Hard punches, much harder than she'd imagined, that force the mattress upwards.

'Did you hear what I said? Stop hitting it.'

Even harder.

'Leo?'

'Nose and chin, Mamma.'

He turns and speaks at the same time, a punch for every syllable, and she grabs the mattress, holds it.

'Listen to me, Leo! Who did this to your face? What are their names?'

She hugs the mattress, stands in his way so he has to stop punching.

'Hasse and Kekkonen.'

'I want their full names.'

'Why?'

'Because I'm going to call their parents.'

'You can't do that! If you call them . . . don't you know what would happen?'

He sits down on the stool, right next to his mother's slippers, which have a little ball of fluff in the middle.

'Leo – I'll take care of this.'

'That will only make it worse! Don't you get that?'

She's not hugging the mattress any more, she's hugging him.

'Their *full* names.'

He shakes his head and his forehead scrapes against her chest.

'Well then.'

She steps up on the stool again, lifts the mattress and throws it on the floor.

'I can take care of this better by myself! Stay out of it!'

'You can start by taking off those ridiculous bandages.'

'I have to practise!'

'Now, Leo.'

'Pappa said so. I have to practise!'

'And I'm saying you have to stop.'

He doesn't say anything else. Not one word. He stays silent as she finishes vacuuming and when Felix comes home and when they eat their snack at the kitchen table, and when she asks them to put on their coats, because they're going to go and pick up Pappa like they usually do, and then go to the supermarket as usual.

He's still silent in the car.

He's sitting in the passenger seat, Felix and Vincent in the long middle seat, and Pappa's paint stuff is in the back. Mamma is driving, dropping off, picking up – it's something she does often. They're going somewhere, and usually he loves this, being together in the car, it's probably the best thing of all.

It only takes a few minutes to drive from their neighbourhood of high-rise blocks to a neighbourhood of single-family homes. They stop in front of one of the homes and load what Pappa has left outside the gate – the brushes, scrubbed clean and smelling strongly of paint thinner, rollers lying in plastic bags, cans of paint and wallpaper paste – while Pappa finishes talking to an older lady and gets an envelope from her.

Leo is also silent when he moves to the back seat, when Pappa sits down next to Mamma, kisses her on the cheek. Pappa is so happy, laughing in the same way he and his client were laughing a moment ago, when she said that in May there'd be more work, that they'd need the whole house repainted. Pappa looked at Leo when she said that, and Leo had known why: he'd need more arms and legs for such a big job.

'Your hands, son? How are they?'

Leo feels his unwrapped knuckles with the palm of his hand.

'Leo? I asked you a question.'

'They—'

Mamma interrupts him.

'I took it down today.'

Pappa turns towards her, his face unchanged.

'What?'

'I took it down. That old mattress we used to sleep on when we first met.'

Now. Now it changes. His cheeks tighten, his lips become narrower. Mostly, it's the eyes. They're on the hunt.

'What did you say you did?'

'I don't think we should discuss this in the car, Ivan.'

'What exactly are we *not* going to discuss in the car? That our son's face is black and blue and he needs to be able to protect himself?'

'Please, Ivan, can't we talk about this later? Can't we just go shopping, go home, have a normal Friday night? Let's talk about it in the morning.'

Pappa's silence makes them huddle closer together in the back seat. And he already smells like the black wine he started drinking during the last hour of the job.

'I'd practised enough. Pappa, you know—'

'Show me your hand.'

Leo holds out his right hand.

'Soft.'

Pappa pulls on it, pushes it.

'Way too soft.'

Leo doesn't look at Pappa, he looks at Mamma in the mirror, her eyes trained ahead on the cars exiting the car park they're about to enter, outside Skogås shopping centre.

'But I'm ready now. Pappa? Nose and chin, and then my whole body and—'

'You'll be ready when I *say* you're ready.'

Everyone climbs out. And it doesn't feel good. Leo hears loud voices outside the entrance to the shopping centre, glances at Pappa. He knows Pappa hates those voices. So he lingers a little longer.

They're sitting exactly where they were last time. The loudest ones are on the benches, the ones who are a little quieter on a set of low iron railings. They sit in a row, green beer cans in their hands; they're adults, but not as old as Mamma and Pappa. Often Pappa will stop right in front of them, ask them why they're there, why they don't get a job like everybody else, and then after a while he usually calls them parasites and stares at them, mostly at one guy who has blond curly hair and a black quilted jacket with a hood and another guy next to him with long brown hair and shiny moon boots. But Pappa doesn't say anything at all this time. And it feels so good. In his gut. The guy with the curly hair screams something at them as Pappa turns left towards the off-licence and Leo and Felix and Vincent follow Mamma into the supermarket. Mamma ends up with seven bags of shopping paid for in part by the money in Pappa's envelope, and they help her carry them to the car. Even Vincent holds a large plastic bag of toilet paper in his arms.

They load the shopping next to and on top of Pappa's painting equipment. Pappa is already sitting there, holding a bottle with the black horse on its label, half-empty, looking out the side window at the seven guys on the benches and the fence, the parasites.

Mamma is just about to start backing out of their parking spot when Pappa grabs the ignition key and switches off the engine.

'Leo. Jump out of the car. You're coming with me.'

Mamma turns the key again.

'We're going home.'

'Don't argue with me!'

Pappa turns the key in the other direction.

'*You* drive home. And take Felix and Vincent with you.'

He opens the door and climbs out, stands there waiting until Leo gets out, then leans in through the side window, his elbows on the metal frame.

'Just do what I say. Drive home. And take the boys with you.'

Pappa starts walking, they both do. Back to the shops. Leo shoots a last glance at Mamma, but she doesn't look at him. She starts the car and backs out of their narrow parking spot.

'Him, up ahead in the middle. Do you see him? That's the leader. The leader of the parasites.'

Pappa points at the man with blond curly hair and black quilted jacket, who's the loudest of them all and obviously doesn't have to sit on the hard railings.

'I think I'll . . . have a little talk with him. What do you say about that, Leo?'

They stop right in front of him. In front of all of them.

'Fellas. I want you to listen now.'

If they could just keep walking towards the shops. Or if those crowded benches would just suddenly give way. Or if an atom bomb fell. Then he wouldn't have to stand here. Leo hunches up, closes his eyes. No nuclear bomb drops.

'See that pizzeria over there? I'm going to go in there and have a bite

88

to eat. With my son. It might take . . . forty-five minutes. And when we come back out, you'll have disappeared.'

'Are you joking?'

'I don't want to hear your fucking voices any more. And I don't want to see you.'

The curly-haired blond waves the beer can in his hand.

'Are you kidding me? Do you hear that? That wop must be joking. And what do we do when someone is being funny? We laugh at him.'

The blond gestures widely as he talks, waves his arms, a conductor producing loud laughter from the whole ensemble.

'Do you really believe that? That I'm *joking*? A little fucking parasite who doesn't work, is that who's in charge here? I don't think so. Tell you what, son. If you and your fucking parasite pals haven't packed up your beer cans by the time I come out here again, I'll grab you by your long-haired necks and throw you into the bushes.'

Leo moves a little to stand beside Pappa, his whole body facing the pizzeria; if he stands here, he can't be seen at all. There are seven of them. In quilted coats and denim jackets. They could be Hasse and Kekkonen's big brothers, and they're screaming now, especially the one with the curly hair, *fucking Turkish bastard*, and the guy sitting next to him in the moon boots who's giving them the finger with both hands and spitting, *so you wanna get a beating, do you, Greek bastard, in front of your own son*, and grabs a clod of dirt from the flowerbed and throws it at them.

'Pappa isn't Turkish.'

Leo takes a step forward, not completely visible but more so than before. It feels important to say something.

'Or Greek. He's half Serbian and half Croatian. And Mamma is Swedish. So I . . . I'm a third Swedish.'

The one who spat and threw dirt puts down his beer can on the bench and starts laughing, for real this time.

'Fucking Greek bastard, a *third*? Take your retarded kid and get lost!'

It's not a very big restaurant. Nine tables. There are small, dark, round lamps that look like snow lanterns hanging above the red and white checked tablecloths draped over every table. At three of the tables men sit alone, drinking a glass of beer, and at two of them young couples are eating pizzas larger than their plates. Pappa goes up to the bar and to the bartender Mahmoud, orders a beer, a sixth of Finnish vodka and a large orange-flavoured Fanta, then sits down at the table by the window.

They've been here several times before. He usually likes coming here, a Fanta in the dark with Pappa. But not now. His whole throat is dry, and he can't get the drink down, as if there's a blockage somewhere between his chest and stomach.

'You're not drinking anything? Aren't you thirsty? Take a sip.'

Leo shakes his head.

'Don't you like it?'

A sip. And it gets stuck where the others got stuck. Near his heart.

'Do you know how much there is in here, Leo?'

Pappa's envelope and the thick wad of cash inside it.

'Eight thousand kronor. I have to work. Mamma has to work. Everybody needs money. And when I work, Leo . . . I can't protect you, you have to be able to protect yourself. You have to be able to protect your brothers.'

Pappa has drunk half the beer and all of the vodka.

'Your Mamma doesn't understand that – that you *have to* protect yourself. Those parasites out there don't understand – that you *have to* work.'

His father points towards the window; the men outside seem upset, one of them is standing up, the long-haired one who called Pappa a Greek bastard.

'They huddle together on a fucking fence yelling because they don't have anything else in their lives. They think they're mates because they drink from the same beer cans. Brothers, Leo! Family. That's much more! So much bigger! It means . . . belonging together. Protecting each other. Whatever happens, you stick together. People like that? Damn it! If you hit just one of them on the nose, the rest will fall into the same fucking heap.'

On the other side of the window, the guy with the long hair has stopped screaming, and walks towards the restaurant door with determined steps. And *they* are there too, Leo notices, running between the buildings across the street: Jasper and the Turks and the boys from Kullstigen. Every single time. Somehow Jasper always knows when there is going to be a fight and he always runs so he can be the first one there to watch. It's as if he can't get enough. Then again, he doesn't have a father who hung a mattress from the ceiling.

But Pappa doesn't see the other kids. He only sees the guy with the long hair. He juts his chin forward, and his bottom lip, lowers his forehead and stares through his eyebrows, like he always does when he's made up his mind – and that's when anything can happen.

'Look at me, Leo. Pappa's going to handle this. We're a family. We protect each other.'

The door opens.

The guy in the moon boots. And he's much bigger now – when *he* was the one sitting down, it was hard to see that he was taller than Pappa, stronger.

His long hair moves as he walks towards them. Flutters back and forth between his shoulders. Until he stops and looks at Pappa, who has put down his beer.

'Got a light?'

He stands beside the table. A cigarette in his mouth. Pappa sits there, completely still.

'Hey, wop, got a light?'

His long hair reaches all the way down to Pappa's beer glass, and when he leans over he dips it into the beer, moves his head, stirs his hair in the beer. Then everything happens quickly. Afterwards, when Leo thinks about it, he's not even sure it happened at all.

The hair in the glass.

Pappa unsheathing his red-handled Mora knife from his work trousers, grabbing hold of the hair tightly, while at the same time cutting it off.

'*You damn . . .*'

The long-haired man staggers backwards, one hand on the place where his hair used to be.

'*You fucking . . .*'

That damn door again. Three more come in, the curly blond and the two who had been sitting next to him. Pappa drops the hair onto the floor, like petals falling from a rose, they land near the legs of the chair. Then he stands up and does what Leo has seen Pappa do to others he's talked to like that – but what he'd never understood before. He understands it now. Right fist hits the nose and left hits the chin, shoulders rotate and the upper body punches through the knuckles. The nasal bone cracks, and it occurs to him again how loud the noise is when a grown-up falls down headlong.

It happens just as fast the second time. The one who'd been sitting on the fence – a single blow to his nose, and he falls onto the table near the toilets, which is usually empty.

The third man, the curly blond, still stands. It's as if he's waiting. And when Pappa takes the next step, he turns his face away and holds up his arms.

'No!'

He just stands there.

'We won't . . . we'll never sit there again, we—'

'Sit down. *Here*.'

Pappa pulls out the chair that he's just been sitting in. And the men who were standing outside, on their way inside, are leaving now, running away.

'Right here. But on the floor. Next to my son. And on your knees.'

The blond hesitates.

'Sit!'

Then he sinks down onto his knees. And right behind him – the bartender, Mahmoud – seems to be in a hurry.

'Ivan?'

'I'm almost done.'

Mahmoud puts a hand on Pappa's shoulder.

'Ivan, for God's sake, you can't—'

'I'll pay for the damage. Just calm down. I can pay. OK?'

Pappa shows him the envelope, they look at each other for a moment until Mahmoud nods, lets go of Pappa's shoulder, and Pappa turns to the man on his knees.

'You're no leader.'

The Mora knife. Pappa is holding it in his hand in front of the leader's face.

'A *real* leader doesn't send his favourite loser to dip his hair into my beer.'

Moves it closer.

'A *real* leader doesn't send his lackeys. He goes first. He leads.'

The knife touches his mouth and nose, and the blond man starts to cry. Not much, but clearly enough.

'Did you hear that, Leo?'

Pappa is holding the knife against the blond man's face, but he's looking at his son.

'What?'

'Listen!'

'What, Pappa?'

'A real leader *leads*.'

The blond man moves his head a little away from the knife, which still has flecks of white paint on its blade.

'Stay on your knees! Next to my son!'

Pappa's hand clutches the curly hair, baring a sweaty neck.

'Leo?'

'Yes?'

'You see that? Always the first blow right in the nose. Always your whole body behind it.'

'I saw.'

Pappa pulls on the curly hair until his knuckles whiten.

'A good leader hits hard. Is fair. Never lets his brothers get hit. He takes responsibility and leads them. This loser parasite sent someone else! He doesn't understand that a leader always goes first.'

The beer glass is still standing there, half full. Pappa nods towards the other glass, which is orange and about as full.

'Drink up. We're leaving now.'

Leo shakes his head. The place between his chest and stomach is like a messy knot, as if someone had pulled his throat apart and then tried to fix it.

'You stay there!'

When they stood up from the table, the blond had also tried to rise.

'You stay where I told you! The whole damn time! Until my son and I go through that door and you can't see us any longer!'

It's warmer outside. Or at least it feels like that.

The entrance to the Skogås shopping centre is still there. But the benches and railings are empty and the green beer cans are rolling around on the ground in the breeze, several cigarettes still burning.

Leo breathes in, breathes out, it's easier now.

15

THEY'RE WALKING ALONG the asphalt path that cuts through the high-rises, past a closed school and a deserted car park. There's just one last hill left until home, when Pappa stops, turns around.

'Do you hear that, Leo?'

The wind. Only the wind.

'What?'

'Don't you hear it?'

'No.'

'Silence.'

Pappa nods towards the shopping centre.

'The benches, Leo. The railings. Only half an hour ago the parasites were sitting there gaping. Now they're gone. Because I decided they should be.'

They're standing at a place similar to the one where Leo lay a few days earlier. The bushes, the lamp posts, the asphalt path towards the stairwell. He wonders if Pappa knows that, or if it just happened that way.

'Willpower, Leo, you understand that? That's what matters. If you have enough willpower you can change anything you want. You're the one who decides. Nobody else! You decide, then you follow through.'

He runs up seven flights of stairs while Pappa takes the lift, racing him. If he takes two steps at a time, he'll open their brown front door just before Pappa opens the lift. He passes the kitchen where his mother is standing with her back towards him at the aluminium worktop, her hands deep in a stainless steel bowl: meatballs, or steak. He passes Vincent's room, where his younger brothers sit on the carpet in a city of cloth, with exactly seventy-seven soldiers, painstakingly placing the British commandos opposite the US marines, and Leo whispers that it's all wrong, that they didn't fight each other, and Felix whispers back that he knows that, but that's how Vincent wants it.

Then he senses his father walking up behind him, quickly, straight into the workroom where the mattress is leaning against a wall. He jumps up on the stool with the mattress in one hand, and lifts it up, while taking down the lamp with his other hand.

'Ivan?'

Mamma stands in the doorway.

'I've already explained. I don't want a mattress hanging there.'

'It's not a fucking mattress – it's a punchbag. And it's hanging there now. And it will continue to hang there until our son is ready.'

She wipes a hand across her forehead, doesn't notice the streak of hamburger.

'Hans Åkerberg. Jari Kekkonen. Those are their names. They're in year

94

seven, at Skogås secondary school. We'll talk to their parents. Talk, Ivan. Solve this.'

'Talk? We're not *talking* to their damn parents.'

'Why shouldn't we?'

'Because that won't stop this bullshit! Those kind don't stop until you make them stop by yourself. That's how it works. But you don't understand that, Britt-Marie.'

Mamma rubs her hand against her forehead again. Even more stripes. She's aware of it, Leo can see that she is, but she doesn't care right now.

'You have no idea what I know about how a child confronts another child. You've never been interested, Ivan. You never wanted to listen to anyone who is associated with me. My mother and father. Erik and Anita. My friends. You're only interested in creating conflict! You want to isolate us. As a family. Just this bloody family!'

'They attacked my son.'

'Just us. Against the whole world.'

'They knocked him down from behind, kicked him, and you want me to *talk* to his father! Should we invite him over for dinner, too?'

Pappa punches the mattress, which starts dancing between them.

'It's better that they stop this by themselves. Without us getting involved.'

Leo is waiting to go inside. He glances towards Vincent's room instead, at the seventy-seven soldiers, who are actually on the same side, shooting at each other and falling down, until they all fall down, and can all be set up again.

Pappa is still standing there. Mamma is in the kitchen.

Leo walks towards the punchbag, takes off his shirt and stands in position with his weight on his left leg, strikes the first blow.

'Right hand protects the right cheek.'

He doesn't hold his right hand high enough, and Pappa takes a panther-like step forward and strikes his face gently with the palm of his hand.

'Right hand protects the right cheek, Leo.'

Leo watches Pappa, clenches his right hand and hits with his left, and Pappa puts out his palm again. This time his chin stings a little – he's still keeping his right hand too low.

He gets into position again.

16

LEO SITS ON the edge of his bed in his thin underwear, yawning, his bare feet on the cold floor. Behind him is his shelf of precious things: Felix's red VW Beetle, still in its original packaging, a silver trophy from the school championship, and his noisy New York Rangers alarm clock, with hands that look like hockey sticks and that read quarter to five. The morning is still dark behind the flimsy blinds.

Every day this week he's been practising several times by himself, then once with Pappa in the evening, then having got up early in the morning.

This is the very last time.

He goes to the workroom, hits at nose and chin. *Today.* He feels it from his arm to his chest and stomach, all the way to his groin.

He rests on the balcony for a while afterwards, looking out over the roof of the school in the distance, washes up standing over the sink, and puts out food for breakfast. Felix gets up, rouses Vincent.

'Leo – what is it?'

'Nothing.'

'It *is* something.'

'It's nothing.'

'You seem weird. You're not like usual. You don't even talk like you usually do.'

Felix digs his spoon into the yogurt.

'It's as if . . . you're sitting here, but not with me. You're sitting here with you.'

'I'm gonna take them today.'

'Take them?'

'Hasse. And Kekkonen.'

Felix stirs and stirs his damn yogurt, he doesn't care about it, doesn't want it.

'Leo?'

He follows Leo out into the hall, where he's standing in front of the mirror, putting his weight on his left leg and punching with his right hand.

'Leo?'

Then Leo turns to the hat rack and carefully grabs hold of Pappa's work clothes. The ones that Pappa usually wears – they've hardly ever seen him in anything else except when they've visited him in prison after he's hit someone too hard.

'Leo?'

They both know where the knife is. In an elongated pocket on one of the trouser legs. And that's what Leo is unbuttoning.

'What are you doing?'

Leo has crept inside himself to a place that is unreachable.

'I told you. *Today.* I'm gonna take them.'

They walk next to each other down the same path one of them has been taking for almost four years and the other for almost a year. It's not even a few hundred metres if they cut across the car park, go through the bushes, then cross the street to the school playground.

They don't speak to each other at all. They just stand there in the playground and wait. Even after the bell has rung. Eventually, Felix can't stand it any more.

'Leo. The knife. You—'

'The bell's ringing.'

'—don't—'

'And in exactly forty minutes it will ring again. Then you should run home. Get Pappa and stand on the balcony with him.'

'I don't understand.'

'Home. Pappa. Balcony. When it rings again. OK?'

Leo looks at his little brother who doesn't want to leave.

'OK?'

And who nods, reluctantly.

'When it rings like it is now. But for leaving.'

A long, ugly, annoying ring. Leo looks around. The junior school and secondary school playground, so lively a minute ago, is now dead. The children who ran and jumped and screamed and shoved and laughed and ran even more are no longer there. Six entrances to six classrooms have sucked them inside, like a vacuum cleaner, just to spit them back out in forty minutes.

He positions himself next to a brick wall and watches the secondary school playground, at the bottom of the hill. It's not empty, not yet. Down there they take more time getting to their classrooms. The two slowest are on their way to year seven, one in a denim jacket and one in a blue puffa jacket: Hasse and Kekkonen. Leo starts to tremble so much that the brick wall scrapes against his back – in fear, in expectation. Hasse and Kekkonen are standing in the middle of the playground inside the painted white lines near the flagpole, they smoke and yell at the others who are on their way inside, punch the ones who go past in the back. They're big, even from a distance. But this time Leo knows exactly what to do. This time he's the one waiting for them.

He stays close to the secondary school building, pressed against the wall until they make their way inside. He calculates the time. They should be in their classroom by now. He doesn't need a watch, he knows when five minutes have gone by. And then he hurries down the hill, across the playground, and into the secondary school building, where he's been a few times before.

He walks along a row of student lockers, his hand around the knife in the inner pocket of his jacket. It fits perfectly in the palm of his hand and the wooden shaft is smooth, as if it's been polished by Pappa's hand, day in and day out.

He walks down the first corridor, past the closed doors and hanging jackets, past someone who is playing an instrument in the first classroom; someone else wolf whistles in the second. The next corridor, and more doors. He's walking down the fifth corridor when he sees what he's looking for. The door to the physics room. The coats on the hooks next to the door. He stops in front of the puffa jacket, which has an oil stain on the chest and a cigarette burn on one sleeve, and a denim jacket with a patch on it of a tongue sticking out of a mouth.

He's not trembling any more. He's completely calm.

The knife is so smooth in his hand as he slashes it through the backs of the two coats, several times, in almost straight lines.

He then moves away twenty paces. That's enough. He sits down and waits.

A class lasts forty minutes. And he guesses there are about twenty-five minutes left. He starts counting. One second at a time. To sixty. And then starts again. He has managed to get to sixty nearly twenty-five times when the long, ugly, irritating ring drenches the entire corridor. He stands up, feet wide apart on the floor, facing the shredded jackets.

Soon. Soon.

The door opens.

The first students leave. His knees quake. One by one they walk by. His upper body is bent slightly forward.

They come out last. At the same time, through the narrow door. Hasse. Kekkonen.

And they see their jackets.

And they see the slashed backs.

And they see him.

Leo raises his hand, waves. They start running. He starts running. Corridor, student lockers, entrance, playground.

He looks behind him. They're getting closer.

Up the hill. Secondary school playground. Junior school playground. Across the road and the stones, through the bushes and the car park.

He can hear them shouting behind him.

———

Felix's legs move faster than he ever knew they could. Up the stairs and all the way to the seventh floor instead of taking the lift that never comes.

When it rings again.

Into the flat, down the hall to the kitchen, and there's Pappa sitting at the table.

In exactly forty minutes.

Pappa looks tired, a pot of coffee in his hand as he fills up one of the china cups.

Then you have to run home. Get Pappa. And stand on the balcony with him.

'What . . . are you doing here, boy? Now?'

Felix doesn't answer. He doesn't hear the question. He runs to the balcony door, which won't open, turn, turn, the damn . . . then it slides open and he stands on tiptoe to see over the railing.

———

They're screaming behind him.

But the sound of running drowns it out.

Leo's breathing starts from his stomach and fills his lungs and expands. He never knew this was what it was like to fly. Across the car park and the asphalt path towards the entrance to the building.

He stops and glances up.

There, he's sure of it, Felix's head sticking up over the balcony railing.

He turns around and waits for his pursuers. His knees sway, sink slightly.

He brings his arms up, right hand protecting the right cheek.

———————

Felix sees Leo approaching. Sees him stop outside the entrance. Sees him turn around.

And then.

He sees the two boys chasing him. Who aren't wearing their jackets this time. But he knows. He *knows* who they are.

'Pappa!'

Felix rushes back into the kitchen, to Pappa at the table with a china cup in his hand.

'Come here! Come on, Pappa! Here! The balcony!'

A big gulp of warm coffee.

'Now, Pappa!'

But Pappa continues to sit there with the cup in his hand, and Hasse and Kekkonen are down there with Leo.

'Pappa!'

He grabs Pappa's arm fiercely, he pulls, and pulls, and pulls on his arm.

'Pappa! Pappa!'

And Pappa finally gets up, goes outside with bare feet, leaning over the railing as he always leans.

And he sees. What Felix sees.

'Pappa! Leo's down there!'

'Yep. Leo's down there.'

'And they are, too! *Them*, Pappa! We have to—'

'We don't have to do anything.'

'No, Pappa! Hasse! And—'

'Leo has to take care of this. And he will, all by himself.'

———————

Leo has chosen a place that can be seen clearly from the balcony, near the bushes and the lamp posts. Hasse gets there first, panting as heavily as Leo. They stare at each other. Hasse without his jacket, Hasse who is tall and has to look down to meet Leo's eyes.

Legs apart. Hands up.

One last look at the balcony on the seventh floor. Felix is jumping and grabbing and pulling until half his body is hanging over the railing. And next to him, Pappa.

A single blow. Right hand. Right on the nose.

Hasse doesn't know what's hit him. He just sinks down to his knees, tears spurting from his tear ducts, blood flowing down his mouth and chin and neck. Just where Leo lay earlier.

Kekkonen arrives next, and he's panting loudly, quickly.

He's a lot shorter than Hasse, but stronger, and more powerful. He strikes the first blow right past Leo's cheek, but Leo's knees are so soft and his feet so fast that when Kekkonen throws a second and a third punch they're not even close.

Leo's first punch makes contact. Not quite on the nose, more the cheek. The stocky boy is still standing.

And hits back.

His legs and feet slide like before, soft, fast, and Leo hits the temple, then the shoulder, then the other cheek until Kekkonen reels and his eyes change – the Finnish bastard's eyes turn from present and angry to absent and scared.

Leo is about to turn towards the balcony, towards Pappa and Felix, when everything changes again. He doesn't see how, or why, but Pappa suddenly starts shouting and pointing, as if trying to warn him.

Someone grabs him from behind. Leo squirms. Pulls. He needs to get free! And he's almost out of his grasp . . .

When it falls out of his jacket pocket.

Pappa's Mora knife.

He's not quick enough. He bends to the ground to pick it up, and it's not there. Kekkonen is faster and waves it in front of him.

When a knife flashes in front of your face, it's mostly the blade that's visible.

Especially when it strikes.

'Cut him, for fuck's sake!' shouts Hasse to Kekkonen, lying on the filthy asphalt with both hands on his nose as if trying to hold it in place.

The first thrust sinks deep into Leo's left shoulder. Or, actually, into the left shoulder of his thick quilted jacket. The Mora knife rips open a big hole and the white, fluffy lining tumbles out.

When the second thrust comes, he angles his upper body a little, turning it to the side, and the knife cuts through the air beside him. The third comes faster and straighter, hits the jacket again, the sleeve, but the tear is smaller.

Hasse shouts, *Cut him! Cut him!* and Kekkonen stares at Leo with those demonic eyes that sneer every time he thrusts the blade forward. He's aiming for Leo's face, and manages two more slashes before the front door opens behind them.

Leo doesn't turn round, the blade is too close. If he did, he wouldn't escape the next thrust.

Then he hears them. So he knows.

Footsteps on the asphalt, barefoot footsteps.

Pappa's footsteps.

And Pappa's breath.

And Pappa's voice.

'Drop the knife, you little bastard!'

Kekkonen does. The knife falls to the ground, bounces. And they run. Hasse with his hands on his nose and Kekkonen with his square body hunched forward, they run across the car park and through the bushes, and the bell is ringing for the next period by the time they reach the other side of the road.

17

THEY STAND CLOSE to each other, staring at a mirror covered with graffiti.

One is six foot five with dark hair combed back, the other is five foot with light, ruffled hair.

'A knife.'

Pappa holds out his hand, palm up, and in it lies the paint-spattered Mora knife.

'A knife, Leonard!'

The lift goes past the second floor, the third floor, and Leo tries to read the mirror image of his father. It's shaking. Pappa usually does this before he starts drinking wine and melted sugar, or when he's annoyed by tramps and parasites. But only on the outside. Not like this. Inside.

'I've been teaching you how to fight. With your hands! And you . . . you take *my* knife!'

'Not to fight with it.'

'You don't need a fucking knife!'

'To *make* them fight. To get them here. So you could watch.'

Pappa squeezes the knife. He's so angry he's scared, so scared he's angry.

'Don't you get that, damn it, that you . . . you . . .'

'But you used it. You cut off—'

'I learned how to fight with my hands first!'

Sixth floor. Seventh. They've arrived. But remain together in the cramped lift. As long as they don't open the door, as long as they don't stop looking at each other in the scribbled-on mirror – as long as they remain in this small world . . .

'My damn boy.'

Pappa's voice, it's shaking too, and Leo looks at him in the gap near the top of the mirror, where the spray paint is a little thinner.

'But I hit him, Pappa. On the nose. Right?'

And Pappa smiles. He laughs when he gets envelopes full of money and sometimes when he's drinking black wine, but he rarely smiles. Now he does.

now
part two

18

AND IT HAD been raining every day for several weeks. Drops would be hollowing out a refilled hole in front of a grey concrete cube. Leo had decided not to think about it, but still the anxiety was always there.

He waited outside the Skogås shopping centre in the front seat of the car as the windscreen turned into a wet membrane, making it difficult to see out. The once open-air shopping centre had been transformed into an enclosed mall. The same shops in the same places. The supermarket stood next to the off-licence, and Mahmoud's Pizzeria next to the entrance on the left-hand side – the red and white tablecloths probably had bigger stains and there were more kinds of beer on the shelf behind the bar than Leo remembered, but the owner was the same and always nodded in recognition. The bare sky had become a glazed ceiling, rough stone slabs had been replaced by plaster floor tiles, and the losers' benches and railing were now doors that opened automatically when someone approached them, as Anneli was doing now.

She stopped after just a few steps and pulled the plastic from a pack of cigarettes, lit one under cover of the entrance, and inhaled deeply as she always did when she was excited. She was so beautiful. She was older than him, yet of the two of them, she was the one who always ended up digging around in her purse for ID to show bouncers. She didn't walk, she strolled. They looked good when they strolled together, he often thought.

'Are we going south?' she asked him, climbing in.

'You'll see – there are houses for sale all over the place.'

He drove first towards Farsta, northwards, and Anneli looked out the side window hopefully, then towards Huddinge, in the west, and she pointed at some of the big houses, then towards Tumba, south, and she was just as expectant, her hand on top of his on the gear stick. The car moved slowly through a very familiar area of small houses, high-rises and factories, and then there were bigger houses again. Craftsmen city. The working-class and small business owners. The world on the fringes of Stockholm.

He belonged here, with the people who didn't fit into what Anneli imagined as she boated along the coast of Drevviken looking out at rooftops visible among the trees along the shore – the kind of house she so clearly hoped they were heading for now.

Leo slowed, and she scrutinised a beautiful turn-of-the-century house with a large lawn and apple and pear trees, and clutched his hand more tightly. But he didn't stop. He continued on to the property next door: a driveway with high iron gates, a garage big enough for five vehicles, and a little tiny house with a tired, grey stone facade.

'Here?'

Her eyes roamed, trying to avoid the puddles on the uneven, paved yard wedged between two roads busy with traffic.

They'd traded an apartment on the second floor of a block of flats for an air-raid shelter on the bottom floor.

'There's no fence,' she whispered in disappointment.

'There's a fence.'

Leo opened the car door and set off across the asphalt yard. She followed him as he zigzagged between the deep pools of water towards a three-metre-high security fence topped by barbed wire.

'There used to be a car showroom here. Nobody could get in here.'

'Are you saying that . . . this, this . . . is where we're moving to? To build a life together?'

'Anneli—'

'A huge fucking garage? An awful asphalt yard? A fucking barbed wire fence? I don't want to live like this! I want a white picket fence, I want real trees and flowerbeds and grass and rhubarb leaves and . . . Leo? Like that house! A wooden house with gravel paths and beautiful flagstones.'

She pointed to the fine, big house next door as the door to the small house opened behind them and a man in a grey striped suit, white shirt and spotted tie emerged.

'You've made an appointment with an estate agent?'

'Come on.'

She stood perfectly still, her hair dripping, her coat and trousers and shoes soaked through.

'For several weeks you've been letting me imagine moving in to a real house? And then you drag me . . . here?'

He took her hand.

'Since we're already here.'

'I don't want to live like this. Do you not understand that?'

And her other hand.

'Anneli, this will be good for us. Right now.'

'I don't want to live like this. I want—'

'Was it you I spoke to on the phone?' said the estate agent.

A suit, a tie and a practised smile. The kind who squeezes too hard when he shakes hands and thinks that's the same as building trust. Leo smiled and Anneli looked at him, *did you decide to meet an estate agent without talking to me*, and he looked at her, *now that we're here, let's take a look*, and Leo took the glossy full-colour brochure from the estate agent, who seemed to perceive where the resistance lay and turned towards Anneli.

'Maybe it's no summer house in the country. Or turn-of-the-century villa.'

The estate agent pointed at their car and then at the building company logo on Leo's jacket.

'But this house is ideal if you want to have your business close to home – and at the right price.'

Leo nodded at the large blue building on the other side of the road.

'We were the ones that renovated the Solbo Centre – the Blue House.'

The tyre company in the corner, the Indian restaurant, the flower shop, the tanning salon, Robban's Pizzeria. And next to it, a locked box containing enough military equipment to supply two infantry companies. The estate agent could see it. Everyone who drove past could see it.

Without knowing.

'So, my friends, you're welcome here.'

The rain-soaked estate agent swept his arm across the asphalt yard.

'At this eleven-hundred-square-metre property, with secondary areas totalling three hundred square metres, and a living area of ninety square metres.'

They left the puddles and the barbed wire fence and went into a kitchen on the ground floor, heard the estate agent talking about almost-new appliances and opportunities and potential and a great floor plan and cost-effective heating. They heard him, but they weren't listening. Anneli didn't want to listen, because she didn't want to be there. Leo wasn't listening, because he'd already made up his mind.

From the empty kitchen into the empty hallway – where stairs led to an empty upper floor and where there stood an empty room on the left with a closed door.

The estate agent opened it fully.

'An extension. An extra room.'

And showed them the shabby walls and floor, maybe ten square metres.

'It was used as an office.'

Leo knocked at several points on the plaster walls and stamped at several places on the plastic mat that covered the floor, but heard only Anneli's heels on their way out. He excused himself and hurried after her. She stood in what was now a light drizzle, a cigarette in her hand, taking short, fierce drags, which was how she smoked when she was disappointed.

'Anneli?'

She didn't look at him.

'Listen, Anneli, I was thinking about something. Your son . . . I mean . . . Sebastian doesn't have to sleep on the sofa when he visits here, like in the apartment.'

'But there's no room.'

'Yes, there is. I'll show you. And out there, on the asphalt, it's a perfect football pitch. And I'll put up a basketball hoop on the garage door. When I was five, I would have loved it.'

'Six. Sebastian's six.'

'You wanted him to visit more often – now he can.'

He held her.

'In a year you can have any house you want, Anneli. Anywhere. At any price.'

His hand on her cheek.

'But right now we need this. Do you understand? In order to get there, to that other house. This is perfect for the construction company. An office and a place to rehearse and a warehouse. In a residential area built on the bed of an old lake, houses with no basements. My Skull Cave.'

Her fringe, forehead and cheeks were wet, and he dried them carefully with his shirt sleeve.

One more cigarette.

'A fucking leisure centre.'

Drags that were a little longer and slower.

'Even more like a leisure centre than our current flat. Your brothers will be here all the time.'

He held her shoulders, they could both see into the house's few rooms. And turned her around gently. Towards him.

'I understand it wasn't quite what you expected. Give me one year, Anneli.'

'One year?'

'One year.'

'Anywhere? Anywhere at all?'

'At any price.'

He took her hand and they walked back through the hall towards the room in the extension.

'This room will be Sebastian's when he's here.'

'So he can stay with us more often?'

'Sebastian's room up above. And my room underneath.'

The estate agent stood waiting on the stairs to the upper floor. They passed him on their way to what would be the bedroom and walked over to the window that looked out over the neighbouring house.

'A year?'

He looked at her, held her.

'A year, I promise. Then we're done.'

19

LEO DROPPED ANNELI off at Tumba station, then drove south for half an hour on minor roads through forests and farmland. He didn't usually lie. Not to her, not to anyone. He'd had no choice but to lie so many times in his childhood because telling the truth would have been so much worse. But he'd lied to her this time. He had stood outside the home they'd just agreed to purchase, held her and said he couldn't go to town because he had to go and see Gabbe. He'd lied because he didn't understand the truth himself – that he was on his way to pay off a debt to someone he didn't owe a thing to.

Four and a half years ago, when father and son still worked in the same construction company, he'd thrown down his tool belt and walked away. *Leo, you fucking got thirty-five thousand in advance. You have to earn that out – before you leave.* It hadn't all been about money. *You owe me, Leo, you can't go!* Not for him. Not for either of them. It was about getting out, away, breaking free.

He drove slowly through a tired landscape. The sheet of water on his left was Lake Malmsjön and a thin veil of fog hung over its still surface, meadows with black and white cows then four horses chasing each other; then a second lake, Lake Axaren, equally still.

You'll come crawling back when you need money! You're nothing without me, Leo, you'll never make it!

There were only a few kilometres left when he stopped the car at an abandoned petrol station with a rust-coloured Caltex sign swinging in the wind and, in the middle of the yard, a pump with mechanical numbers that used to spin, but were stuck at 76.40 kronor.

He rolled down the window, breathed in damp air.

He'd left before but always returned. Even though he'd come to despise the feeling of being a tool, a prop in his old man's picture of a family. That day he left for real. The following year, Felix had starting working with him. The following year Vincent dropped out of high school, and the three brothers started working together.

Family. Together. *You tried. I succeeded.*

The last stretch, more fields, more water, narrow roads. A few barns, houses, a school, a few shops. Ösmo Square. Only half an hour from the heart of Stockholm, but another world all the same.

Leo rolled slowly closer.

A large brick house, a well-kept garden, with yesterday's leaves in regular piles. He parked in front of the postbox and saw the windows were lit on the ground floor; his dad was usually at home at this time.

––––––––––

The last slice of onion in one hand, the last piece of smoked pork in the other, he swallowed, washing it down. The coffee table covered with piles of filled-in Keno tickets. A draw every day, at 18.55.

Ivan leaned forward, lifted the remote control, turned up the volume on the TV.

The first yellow ball was 30. The second, 40. Third, 39. A cluster. It was looking good. Fourth, 61, in the bottom left corner. Fifth, 51, in the box just above. Wrong side. Wrong cluster.

He lowered the volume, leaned back in his chair. He didn't wait for the rest of those yellow balls. The match was already over – 61 never entered into his system, it was the figure that according to his calculations occurred least often.

The vast majority of people didn't understand that this was precisely what it was about, seeing patterns. There were no coincidences. Patterns always recurred. Everything was part of a cycle and belonged together.

Ivan was holding forty Keno tickets that had just become worthless. His map towards the future. And the eleven crosses that were his directions for getting there. He crumpled them up, dropped them on the floor.

The next draw was tomorrow at 18.55.

He muted the TV and was about to get up when he heard a different sound. Outside the window. A car stopping and a car door being opened. He drew back the curtain.

A large pickup truck with a construction company logo on its side had stopped just outside. A young man was approaching. Fairly tall.

It wasn't until those powerful strides had made it halfway to his stairs and front door that he saw who it was. Shorter hair. Angular jaw. Wide shoulders that he'd grown into. Someone who had left boyhood behind.

Leo.

Ivan looked around the kitchen, which overflowed into the hall. First he moved the empty wine bottle from the table to the bin bag under the sink, then threw the crumpled Keno tickets into the rubbish.

The doorbell rang.

He hurriedly put a pair of brown shoes on his bare feet, a grey jacket over his painting shirt. He wasn't going to have time to clean up after a lifestyle that hadn't changed.

He opened the door and they stood there, Ivan looking down, Leo looking up, seven steps and four and a half years between them.

'New truck?'

'Yeah.'

'It's damn shiny – you having a hard time finding jobs, Leo?'

'Unlike you, I take care of my things.'

'A builder's truck should be dusty, Leo. Lots of work means lots of dust. Not much of a vehicle, really . . . no space if you need to bring in extra manpower. Two people working together. That must be why you've come here? Or maybe you're hiring dwarves. Are you, Leo?'

'I have two more identical vehicles. Or – we have two more. That belong to our firm.'

It wasn't much. A blink, a slight twitch in his cheek, the lower lip shooting forward slightly. But Leo saw it.

'So, son . . . you've got some . . . employees?'

'Three.'

'Three? Well . . . be wary of the union. The builders' union. They'll butt into everything you do. Like the Gestapo. And you know, Leo, employees, they only make trouble.'

'I don't think they will. You know, Pappa, I've just completed a major construction project in Tumba. Solbo Centre. Seven hundred square metres. Commercial property, good money. We've just finished it.'

'We?'

'And I didn't come here to hire . . . how'd you put it? Extra manpower. I came here to give you this.'

Leo took an envelope from his breast pocket, one he'd checked so many times. He held it out.

'Forty-three thousand.'

Ivan took the envelope, white and a little wrinkled, opened it. Five-hundred-kronor bills. Used. The kind stored in security bags in armoured vans.

'That thirty-five grand you thought I owed you. And five thousand in interest.'

Fingers smelling of onion, Ivan took them out one at a time, counting them.

'And three thousand more,' continued Leo.

'For what?'

'One for each rib.'

Four years ago, Leo had thrown down the tool belt and started walking away while the old man stood there screaming. Leo didn't remember the rest, or what they'd shouted at each other when Pappa grabbed hold of him, but he knew he'd turned round, punched as he'd been taught to punch, but not to the nose – to the body.

'I can afford it, Pappa.'

He'd looked his father in the eyes and followed through with all his weight, through the shoulder, the arm, the fist.

'So just take it. You need it.'

And could feel as soon as he connected that something had broken inside.

They had stood in silence afterwards. Pappa crouched forward with his right arm raised, not realising that it was his son who'd struck first.

'I have enough damn work. You might have broken three of my ribs, but you didn't break me.'

Ivan held the envelope in one hand, the other braced against the closed door, balancing his frozen body – thin jacket over short-sleeved summer shirt in thirty-five degrees Fahrenheit.

'But if I understand you correctly . . . You think it was OK for you to just pull out like that, just leave? This money, Leo, my money, was an advance that you never earned out.'

'I worked for you for four years and got shit pay every week.'

'You got what you deserved. No more, no less.'

'I didn't come here to argue with you. I came here to give you your fucking money. We're even now.'

Leo stepped towards the car.

'And how . . . are your brothers?'

Leo turned round.

'They're good.'

Here they come. The questions.

'So you . . . see them?'

'Yes.'

'And they still live there, with her, in that . . . Falun?'

'They live here. In Stockholm.'

'Here?'

'Yes.'

'How . . . what . . . they're studying?'

'Working.'

'With what?'

'They work with me.'

'Work with you?'

'With me.'

'Vincent . . . too?'

This man, fifty-one years old with no socks on inside his shoes, suddenly seemed so much older. The chin and lower lip even further out, the face pale, he really was freezing.

'Yep. Vincent, too.'

He held on tight to the steps' wet iron railing, as if his bones couldn't support him.

'But he's only sixteen, seventeen years old, isn't he?'

'Like I was when I started working for you.'

'I thought he lived there, with . . . *her*.'

The envelope lay awkwardly in his hand, and he stuffed it into his breast pocket.

'Is he tall?'

'About your height. And mine.'

'Good genes.'

'And in a few years, he'll be even taller.'

'Very good genes.'

The frozen body froze no more, and Ivan found the strength to walk towards Leo.

'And Felix?'

'Better than ever.'

'It's been such a long time.'

And Leo knew what was coming.

'Leo? Son? Damn it, why don't you talk to them!'

'I don't think Felix—'

'So we can meet! Together. All four of us!'

'—wants to see you. At all. Ever.'

He was close now, a few steps away, and Leo caught a whiff of the remnants of yesterday's Vranac.

'But you surely—'

'And you know how he is. When Felix has decided something, he's decided.'

'What the hell, that was fourteen years ago!'

'And you still haven't said sorry?'

'How can he be so damn unforgiving! Can't he just let it go?'

'It's like spit in your face. Right, Dad?'

'You could surely talk to him. So we could meet. Couldn't you?'

Those eyes. The conviction.

'Anyhow, I'm in the middle of a job, too. A big one. Hotel, fifty-five rooms that need wallpapering, woodwork that needs to be painted. And all the windows, you know, at least thirteen thousand per room, really fucking big. And I've been thinking a lot about you. That we should do it together. Me and you. And now – your brothers.'

Those fucking black eyes that intimidated him, that he'd grown up with, and fled from.

'Listen . . . Pappa?'

'Yeah?'

'I don't run errands for you any longer.'

This time those eyes couldn't get to him.

'You only give a damn about yourself! You know that, Leo?'

Leo looked at a man who seemed to have shrunk with age. Eyebrows that stuck out wildly like antennae, clothing that wasn't clean – and from this close he could smell new sweat bringing old sweat back to life.

'This is what you've always done. Put yourself first.'

Leo didn't answer.

'Just like a snitch.'

'What the hell did you say?'

'You come here. So fucking cocky, eh. Not a word for years. I wasn't supposed to get shit from you. So why the hell come here now with forty-three thousand? Forty-three thousand! Did you conjure it out of thin air? Is that what you want me to believe? Nah, nah. How the hell did you earn that kind of money? Without me? What the hell kind of job pays this much?'

Ivan pulled a hand-rolled cigarette out of his breast pocket and lit it.

'You come here to tell me about your brothers who don't want to meet their father. To stuff them down my throat like I'm a fucking goose? To stand there acting like you're better than me? Just like a snitch would! A *potkazivanje*!'

'I didn't say a damn word back then, and you know it!'

'You ratted on me.'

Every time. And it didn't matter if he kept shouting or broke three more of those ribs. It would keep going, remain the same. Leo breathed slowly, reached out and tapped his fingertips against the breast pocket of his father's cheap shirt.

'We're even.'

He sped through a residential area. *Snitch*. Sped past the school, the public pool, the library. *Snitch*. Then he slowed down, abruptly. Pappa's voice, *snitch*, it didn't go away like it used to.

Empty parking spaces outside the red, low-rise buildings of Ösmo Square. He stopped there for a moment with the engine off, staring at the shops, the banks, a café, a shoemaker, a dry cleaner, a florist.

I didn't say anything. I was ten years old, sitting in front of those fat fucking cops.

If he stared just a little further into the distance, past the corner with the small kiosk, he could see the brick chimney of the house where Pappa sat now, where they'd lived and worked together, back when it was still

117

possible. Where, ten years after that little boy had kept his mouth shut like he was told to, Leo had thrown down his tool belt, met a single mother who was five years his senior, and decided to move in with her in a one-bedroom flat in Hagsätra.

No snitch would have been able to rob a security van.

Three months later, he and Anneli had signed a joint lease on a three-bedroom flat in Skogås. It had been his whole world. Until now.

Did you ever do that, old man, rob a security van?

Leo opened the car door and started walking towards the little corner store. He put a pack of Camels on the counter and tried to avoid making eye contact with Jönsson, who was still hanging on to a grey tonsure, the remnants of hair he didn't have back then either.

'Anything else?'

'Nope, that's all.'

'Anything for your dad? A bag of rolling and some Rizla papers, right?'

'Not today.'

He dug some money out of the side pocket of his work trousers, a few used 50-kronor notes from the robbery, plaster dust on his hands as he handed them to Jönsson who put them in the cash register, which was always slightly open – the click of the spring mechanism as the drawer slid out, which was the same as no receipt.

'It's been a while since we saw you, son.'

He'd reached the newspapers by the door.

'Yep. It's been a while.'

'Listen,' said Jönsson, smiling. 'Say hello to your dad from me.'

They always had leads on you. And do the police have any leads on me?

Leo didn't answer. A packet of cigarettes and some change in his hands, he just nodded and left.

No. They don't. Not a trace.

————

Leo smoked quickly, pacing back and forth across the square. *Snitch*. The bastard still got to him.

Suddenly he stopped.

He'd been here before, but now it was as if he were seeing it for the first time.

Two banks. Next to each other. Like a loving couple.

They stood wall to wall between a supermarket and a flower shop, and it was possible to drive all the way up to them and still have a full view of the square.

Two targets. Same place. Same time. Same level of risk.

And he no longer smoked so quickly – he felt that sense of calm that sometimes washed over him, the calm that not even his father could disturb.

20

JOHN BRONCKS HAD tried counting raindrops. It had worked at first. Until they all flowed together and the world outside became blurry. His colleagues running across the courtyard of the police station looked thick and clumsy. Behind him on his desk lay eighteen parallel investigations in various colour-coded folders. And he couldn't remember a single day it hadn't rained since the case lying on top had taken over, obscuring everything else – like raindrops on the window.

> Max Vakkila (MV): He talked like the man in that little store.
> Interrogator John Broncks (JB): What do you mean?
> MV: Like Ali. It wasn't him. But he sounded like Ali.

The only statement from anyone – apart from the two security officers – who'd got close. A boy, six years old.

> JB: And what did the man sitting down look like?
> MV: He was dribbling.
> JB: You mean . . .
> MV: The one called Gobakk, his whole chin was wet.
> JB: Gobakk?
> MV: That was his name.

A child had seen what the adults hadn't.

> JB: And the rest of his face?
> MV: Sunburnt.
> JB: He was a bit . . . red?

MV: Brown. Like it was summer.

JB: Good. You're doing great. Do you remember anything else?

MV: His leg.

JB: Yes?

MV: It was off. Or . . . straight out. Under the blanket.

JB: You saw it?

MV: Uh-huh. And a shoe down at the bottom.

A child sometimes sees what's not real, a fairy tale.

JB: And the one who was standing up?

MV: I didn't see much of him.

JB: But you did see a bit?

MV: He was angry.

JB: Angry?

MV: Talking fast.

JB: And what else?

MV: His eyes. They looked dangerous.

JB: In what way?

MV: Dark. Very dark. Like Jafar in *Aladdin*.

Two heavily armed robbers who looked like Arabs, spoke English like Arabs. Because they were? Or because that's what you were supposed to see and hear? Their heavy accents. Their choice of Arabic interjections – *jalla jalla*, *sharmuta*, *Allahu Akbar* – words he himself would have used to sound like an Arab.

He sat in front of his piles of documents, yawned, got up and walked towards the coffee machine in the corridor for a cup of silver tea. And then on to the vending machine, where he always took number 17: a light, round bread roll with margarine, a slice of cheese, and a tomato in the middle that soaked the bread until it became spongy, a slice of tomato that he started to peel away.

You use violence to force someone to submit to you.

You threaten to kill.

This calculated excessive force was a means to an end and he, if anyone, was well able to recognise it – like the hand of a grown man repeatedly hitting a body that refuses to comply. Violence that worked, that gave you what you wanted.

John Broncks left the vending machine, left the bread roll, threw both it and the slice of tomato into the bin, walked four doors down to the chief superintendent's office and knocked on the doorframe as usual.

'Do you have a minute?'

Karlström closed his book, or at least it looked like a book, and pushed it aside. John went in, sat down in the empty chair and tried to read the title, but could only make out the spine. Some French writer, Bocuse.

'Yes?'

'The security van robbery.'

Broncks lay the technical investigation down on Karlström's desk.

'I want to prioritise it.'

'Prioritise it . . . how?'

'I want at least a few weeks to devote myself to it.'

Karlström grabbed a binder off a shelf, flipped through it, turned it towards Broncks.

'You have eighteen parallel investigations. Other investigations. Other suspects.'

'Yes.'

'AGGRAVATED ASSAULT and COERCION in the toilets at Café Opera. AGGRAVATED ROBBERY at a jewellery store on Odengatan. ARSON at Ming Garden on Medborgar Square.'

'Yes?'

'ATTEMPTED RAPE in Vitabergs Park. DRUG TRAFFICKING, Regerings Street. AGGRAVATED PIMPING, Karla Square. CONSPIRACY TO COMMIT MURDER, Lilla Ny Street. AGGRAVATED . . .'

Karlström closed the binder.

'. . . do you want me to continue? Who do you think I should order to take over your other investigations?'

'The perpetrators are experienced. They've done this before.'

'Which one of your colleagues, John, all of whom also have eighteen parallel investigations on their plates?'

'And they'll do it again.'

'I—'

'They'll do it again, and they'll be more violent than they were in Farsta. And then again, even more violently.'

The institution didn't reign in this room, as it did in John's: here sat a man who had a life he was proud of, that gave him security. On the wall behind Karlström hung a kind of map of his professional history – a law school diploma, certification from the police shooting club, and a framed notification of his appointment as chief of the City Police's detective department. On his desk there was a second map, of his personal history: the back of three photographs that John knew were of his two daughters, siblings adopted from Colombia, five or maybe six years old; and his wife, who John had never heard his boss say anything negative about. Next to the photo frames lay an ergonomic plastic dolphin whose shoulders his boss rubbed every twenty minutes, a letter opener from the police union, and the book by Paul Bocuse, which John now saw was titled *French Cooking*.

'The robbers were carrying an AK4 and a submachine gun. Military-grade weapons. I've looked into every case involving theft from the Home Guard, shooting ranges, military installations. I've looked into anyone with a similar record, either free or on probation. I've been able to exclude the possibility of an inside job, as far as I can.'

He wasn't sure if his boss was really listening. Karlström had only ever seen violence in the line of duty, but John had grown up with it, lived with it, and then decided to become a police officer in order to face it again.

'We have two robbers who act single-mindedly and without deviating from a plan. The security van was hijacked, driven at normal speed from Farsta to Drevviken beach, and since the rest of the money was behind a locked door, they shot at it without hesitation, an entire magazine. They were disciplined, extremely focused, and didn't once break character during a raid that took twenty minutes.'

'Character?'

'They haven't convinced me. I'm not as sure as the guards that these robbers were Arabs. Just like one of them wasn't really handicapped and in a wheelchair. They could have been men who were born here, putting on a good show under extreme pressure – who handled their guns like tools, as if violence was their craft, as if they were schooled in excessive force.'

The photos of his wife and children stood lined up between them, it felt as if John knew them. Karlström was the type who talked about his family. John never talked about his family. To anyone.

'And I also don't think that there were only two people involved. There must have been more. And in that case we're talking about a gang that will continue to evolve. There was nine million left behind that steel door. They'll regard that as a failure. They didn't get what they came for. This time.'

'You said . . . schooled in violence.'

'No, that's not what I said. Schooled in excessive force.'

'What do you mean by that?'

'That they've grown up with it.'

John Broncks had to hurry down the corridor. The case had just become a priority. He could now devote himself to a single folder for a month. He took the stairs three floors down, and headed towards the forensics lab, peering first into the dark room, then into the fibre room for offenders' clothing, then into the fibre room for victims' clothing. Sanna wasn't there.

Sanna, who'd walked away at the scene as if she didn't even recognise him. Sanna who had returned to the City Police just as suddenly as she'd once left. Sanna, who he'd avoided a few years ago when they passed each other on King Street – he'd seen her from afar, and he'd waited too long to cross the street, so he was forced to keep walking, pretending to look away just as their paths crossed.

Her black case lay on one of the counters in the large lab, next to a roll of gelatine film, a box of cotton swabs, some plastic containers, test tubes, tweezers and a microscope. She stood in front of a metal cabinet filled with CNA fumes, developing fingerprints.

'Hi,' he said.

She turned around, looked at him, her face revealing nothing.

'Hi.'

'I read your report, Sanna. Several times.'

This was what he'd wanted to avoid: standing here before her indifferent expression.

'I'm getting nowhere. But I've just spoken to Karlström. And he gave me more time.'

She continued to write, then put the notebook in her coat pocket and opened the door to the CNA cabinet, releasing whatever fumes were left.

'John – as you know, there's nothing more to add.'

'I want to go through it once more. With you.'

They walked down the stairs to the garage that lay below the entire block of police buildings.

He wondered if she'd seen him on King Street, and whether she'd seen him look away. She could have recognised him without seeing his face – they'd both worked in witness protection and knew the first thing you had to change in order to form a new identity was your individual way of moving. It's what the person you're hiding from recognises first in a crowd – it's movement that connects everything.

In one corner of the garage there was a small square building the size of four parking spaces, a garage within a garage where the forensic department's confiscated vehicles were kept. She opened it up and there it stood in the middle of the floor. A white van. Broncks walked over to it and climbed inside. The seats were wrapped in plastic. The shards of glass, documents and security bags were gone. He'd researched and eliminated every report of every stolen car and stolen boat near Farsta and Sköndal during the period before the robbery – and he'd come to believe that the two robbers had probably been delivered to the first crime scene by somebody using their own car and retrieved from the second scene by someone with their own boat.

He crawled into the rear compartment with the open safe. The technical report had shown level four traces of blood, fibres, fingerprints – from the two security guards who'd been overpowered and from other security guards who used the vehicle. Nothing else. No traces from the suspects.

Sanna opened the black case she always carried with her and lined up five cartridges on the bench in front of them.

'Angle of impact ninety degrees.'

She showed him the holes through the window on the driver's side and the trajectories towards the door on the passenger side.

'And here, beside them, five disfigured bullets – fully jacketed, 9 mm; they came to a stop in the truck door. They were fired from the same weapon. A Swedish m/45 submachine gun.'

Mechanical. That was the word John had been searching for. That was how she talked about her work, and he wondered if that was how her briefings usually sounded or if she was just making an effort to seem indifferent to him.

The wheelchair stood behind the car. One of the suspects had been sitting in it with a blanket over his legs. Stolen from Huddinge Hospital and, according to the forensic scientist, bearing the fingerprints of seven individuals that had been compared with the 120,000 fingerprints the police kept on file. No match.

The security guards' uniform shirt was green. That hadn't been clear in the pictures. She poked a plastic-glove-covered finger gently through a hole on the right lapel.

'He was lucky. If he'd leaned forward just a bit more the bullet would have gone straight through the cheekbone.'

'They didn't get what they were after,' said Broncks.

'They?'

'Jafar from Aladdin. And someone named Gobakk.'

'Jafar? Go . . . bakk?'

'Our best witness. Six years old. We're looking for someone who doesn't exist. Someone who a little boy and a few others saw because it was what the perps wanted them to see. I don't buy it. I don't buy Jafar and Gobakk.'

He knew how she walked, which scent he would always search a room for without even being aware of it, and how it felt when she smiled, even when she was standing as far away as she was now.

'John – I work with fibres, bloodstains, fingerprints. With facts. With what exists and can be proven. And, like you say, Jafar and Gobakk don't exist. Not really. Just like you and I don't exist any more. Do you understand?'

John Broncks stayed behind after she'd left the garage, which was cold and whose air tasted of oil and dust. He walked around the empty security van again and again, but he was still questioning two security guards, who told of one robber who listened and waited, calm and self-possessed, his face in a mask, who was precise when he pressed a muzzle hard against their heads.

Weapons like tools. Violence like a craft.

Jafar didn't exist. Gobakk didn't exist.

Schooled in excessive force.

But you do.

21

LEO LAY ON his back for a while, as he often did when he awoke, close to Anneli's heavy breathing. She was the kind who slept with her arms wide open. He, on the other hand, slept lightly and woke up easily, as he had always done.

He still got up before anyone else to make breakfast.

Snitch.

A word that penetrated his defences as a word can sometimes do, sharp, pointed. But it didn't sink in so deeply any more.

Moving boxes were beside the bed. He counted seven and there were just as many in the living room and hallway, on their way to an ugly little house next to a giant garage – the Phantom's Skull Cave, the solution to their storage problems. To no longer getting stuck renting someone else's ground floor, filled with crumpled Keno tickets.

It had rained all through the night and into the early morning. Hour after hour, into the hole they'd refilled in front of a high-specification security door – wet gravel that might start to sink, and that could be spotted by the smoking inspector.

Anneli straightened and mumbled something that he couldn't make out, turned onto her back and started snoring again. He had to talk to her. Tell her. She had to go there, she was the only one who could do it.

Leo was in the hall when he heard voices outside the door to the flat – and then a brief pause before the doorbell rang. His younger brother never acted before thinking.

'What the fuck are you wearing?' asked Leo as he opened the door.

Felix was dressed in a red check flannel shirt, worn jeans that were a bit too loose, beige Timberland boots; Jasper was behind him in a 5000-kronor leather jacket, new jeans and black Reebok trainers.

'You're supposed to come here every weekday morning in blue work trousers, a blue shirt and old work boots!'

Leo closed the bedroom door, while Felix and Jasper went into the kitchen for freshly brewed coffee.

'Our cover, damn it! What other people are supposed to see. Jasper, you look like a fucking secret agent on bodyguard duty! And you, Felix, you can travel later, I promise – buy a used Mustang in Sydney, windsurf, drink cold beers.'

As days had turned into weeks, gradually they had started doing the one thing they shouldn't – feeling safe.

He took out bread, butter, cheese, juice, yogurt, dessert plates, coffee cups.

'We're construction workers. That's what we should look like. No bastards should ever think *how are they earning the cash, they're not doing any building*. From now on we don't need to hammer in a single nail, but we'll do it anyway! Renovate a kitchen here, a new roof there. We need the firm as cover.'

The doorbell rang again. A short, careful signal. Then the door opened.

'It's me,' called Vincent.

'We're in the kitchen. There's breakfast.'

He stopped in the doorway. Blue work trousers, a blue shirt and battered construction boots. They all stared quietly at him.

'What is it?'

'Somebody gets it,' said Leo.

'Gets what?'

Leo lifted out the coffee filter and filled four cups with black coffee, then turned to Jasper and Felix.

'After we've finished eating, you two are going to take a pickup and go home. And change into *exactly* the same clothes that the youngest person here is already wearing. And when you've done that, drive to Kenta's timber yard and pick up 150 square metres of eight-millimetre oak flooring and deliver it to Grönlandsgången 32 in Kista. It's some computer office that Gabbe is fixing up. And then wait until Vincent and I get there.'

Jasper put down the cup he'd just picked up.

'Are you serious, we're going to . . . build?'

'From now on, we'll be taking a few of those kinds of jobs. OK? One hundred and fifty metres of wood flooring – we can do this in two days. And always—'

'But damn it, we—'

'—always for a fixed price. So we can make it last for at least a week. Extensive but simple jobs that four carpenters can finish quickly, but keep working on for days and charge at a fixed price. We'll come and go and make sure to be seen there sometimes.'

———

Leo and Vincent drove across Skogås, past the school and their childhood home, the big but claustrophobic flat.

Leo parked the car, and they walked down the slope through high grass between a football pitch and the school gym they'd passed after the robbery carrying identical duffel bags with their indoor hockey sticks clearly visible.

Into the woods along a track past a steep hill, the same path he'd walked several times in recent weeks to make sure the sunken rubber boat hadn't found its way to the surface. They walked out onto a peninsula that had been much larger when Leo was young, that he'd swim to from the opposite shore. Past a couple of large rocks, a row of low and thorny bushes, a few withered and crouching ferns, and there, just behind those pines – a few metres of fine sandy beach, the place where they had landed. They searched, peering out over the water.

'Yep. It's still there, right on the bottom.'

Leo put his hand on Vincent's shoulder.

'You were supposed to stand there and wait.'

Vincent wriggled his upper body, shook off his brother's hand.

'Damn it, I . . . the cops were on their way, I had to warn you, I—'

Leo smiled.

'You did damn well, little brother. You were by yourself, in the dark, and you made a decision. For us. I chose to trust you – and you showed me I was right. But next time won't be quite the same. Target two is no security van – it's a bank, and it'll be surrounded by people.'

'I know.'

'And . . . I have to be absolutely sure you understand, really understand, that if you don't want to do this, you can pull out. Now. I won't say a thing about it. Felix and Jasper won't either. It's your fucking right. And it's my fucking duty to explain that to you.'

Vincent gave him a crooked smile.

'I *want* to do this.'

'I'm your big brother. I'm responsible for you. I'm leading this, and there'll be no way back later. But there is now.'

'*I know*. And I don't want out.'

Light gusts of wind, white geese ride the small waves, as if they were in a hurry.

Leo hugged his younger brother. They were on their way. Together.

'Well then.'

And they set off side by side back along the winding forest path, in the same direction they'd travelled in the darkness.

'You'll be wearing a bulletproof vest. Kevlar. Better than what the cops run around in. And a loaded submachine gun. Black boots, blue jumpsuits, mask in front of your face – you'll look bigger, and those skinny teen legs will disappear. But not the way you walk.'

Leo stopped and waited until Vincent did the same.

'You walk like a seventeen-year-old. Do you know that? And when you ran towards the security guards and the van, when you came up behind us in the dark, and Jasper turned around and raised his rifle at you . . . I stopped him. I recognised your movements.'

Leo set off again down the forest path, slowly, taking noticeably longer strides.

'If this is going to work – you have to seem like a grown man. The cashiers need to be absolutely certain it was three adult males who opened the doors. And the uniforms have to see three adult males when they examine those few lousy seconds of tape they'll end up with. A movement can be recognised and remembered. They should see a gang, professionals who rob banks like they've never done anything else. They should think *where the hell did they come from, who are they, what are they capable of*, and be . . . very worried. And they won't if you keep walking around like a teenager.'

The path wasn't wide enough for two any more.

'Follow me.'

Leo stepped out into the grass, straight across the meadow.

'Take firm steps. Put down your *entire* foot. Feet pointed straight ahead, no flapping around taking up the whole pavement.'

Leo turned around and saw his brother trying to walk like a man.

'Good. Good, Vincent! And imagine that you weigh more, you're heavy, and that you know where you're going. Teenagers don't have a fucking clue.'

He stopped, and his younger brother stopped too. Mid-stride, legs wide.

'There's a difference between knowing where you're going and trying to take up room on your way there.'

'I get it.'

'And a lower centre of gravity. Like this.'

Leo sank down a bit, softening both knees. Vincent watched, imitated. Until Leo put his arm around him and pushed down a little.

'Not up here. No vulture neck. You should lower your dick, *here*, a little bit closer to the earth. Your cock is your centre of gravity from now on, Vincent. Lower your torso. Do you feel that?'

They stood next to each other in the open field and bounced slightly up and down, up and down.

'I feel it.'

'Are you sure?'

'Yes.'

Leo pushed his hand hard into Vincent's chest. And his little brother barely faltered.

'You feel that? You were stable. Right?'

'Yes.'

'Good. One more thing. Your voice.'

'My voice?'

'You can't sound like you're going through puberty. You need to lower your voice. "The keys." Say it.'

'What the hell . . . are you talking about?'

'Just say it, Vincent. "The keys."'

'The keys.'

'Not like that. *Deepen* your voice. Speak from your chest, all the way down to your stomach. As if you're . . . giving me an order. Say it one more time. "Give me the keys."'

'Give me the keys.'

'Again! Deeper voice. And louder.'

'Give me the keys.'

'Again!'

'Give me the keys! *Give me the keys! Give me . . .*'

'You should sound damn determined. You have a good vocal range – from now on, use it! OK?'

They walked towards the car, across the meadow, up the slope, and Vincent swayed slightly with soft knees, repeating *give me the keys* every time he put down his right heel.

————

A computer office in Kista. Leo parked next to an identical truck with an identical logo on both sides, CONSTRUCTION LTD, opened the door and climbed out. Vincent had sat quietly in the passenger seat for the entire journey, and stayed seated now.

'Come on,' said Leo.

'That's what we'll be doing from now on?'

'Doing?'

'Robbing banks.'

Leo held the car door open and looked at Vincent, who wasn't ready to get out yet. So he climbed back in again.

'Vincent?'

'Yes?'

'The target next to the roundabout – it's just *one* bank. It's just an exercise. Next time . . . we'll take two. At the same time.'

'Two? That's impossible, we'll get caught!'

'You have to dance with the bear if you want to win, Vincent. You can never get too close. Or you won't survive it. He's much bigger than you are. He can rip you apart. But you can dance around him. And wait. You get one punch in; if you hit him right, you can keep dancing and get ready to take the next one. And it's just like—'

The door to the office building opened. Felix and Jasper. In the right clothes. And they walked towards the truck, took the cover off the truck bed and gestured impatiently.

'Time to get out now!'

They unloaded the first packs of oak parquet from the truck onto the asphalt and when Leo and Vincent didn't get out of their truck, Jasper knocked on one of the side windows.

'Come on out – you were the one who thought it was so fucking important to do this job!'

'Soon.'

'That's not how it sounded this morning.'

'*Soon.*'

Leo looked at his little brother who was staring straight ahead; he'd listened and now held inside himself what he needed to understand.

'So, it's like this, Vincent . . . it's just like robbing banks. A small group, just a few bank robbers, can defeat the whole police force. And you sting the bear every time, which irritates him, confuses him. Never give the bear time to recover, sting after sting until he goes crazy. The Bear Dance, Vincent. Punch, confuse, disappear. And then do it again, bank after bank.'

Leo put his hand under the seat, took out a stuffed, tatty plastic bag, and handed it to him.

'Here. Required reading.'

Vincent took the bag and dug into it, taking out one title at a time.

Boobytraps – Department of the Army Field Manual. He'd never read any of them before. *Explosives A – Kitchen Improvised Blasting Caps.* Not even heard of them. *The Anarchist Cookbook.* Mostly thin books. *Homemade C-4 – 'A Recipe for Survival'.* Sometimes slightly thicker booklets. *How to Build Silencers – An Illustrated Manual.* All in English. *Explosives B – Kitchen Improvised Fertiliser Explosives.*

He flipped aimlessly – text full of terms he didn't understand, illustrations showing how to construct small bombs – while Leo opened the car door.

'That's your homework this week.'

Vincent watched Leo walk over to the mound of parquet flooring and stand as if he was about to slash into one of the packages – but instead he gripped Jasper's neck tightly, pretending to wrestle with him as he sometimes did when he was trying to make things work. So Felix dropped the flooring, pounced on both of them. It was hard to make out whether or not he was pretending to fight with Leo or with Jasper, he might not even know himself.

Two older brothers and their childhood friend.

Vincent put the books back into the bag with one handle. And he smiled.

He didn't want out. He wanted in. Together.

22

JOHN BRONCKS STOOD on the last plank of the jetty – one more step and he'd be in the lake. He thought about another jetty in long-ago summers on a small island in Lake Mälaren – he could almost hear the sound of feet on wood and his mother shouting for them to come back. Sam half a step in front of him, running through the pouring rain from the summer house to the lake, then lying on his back in brackish water watching the drops landing on his face.

He squatted down and split the dark November surface of the lake with his hand, so much colder than his memories, probably just above freezing. In a month or two it would be brittle ice.

'John? You there?' called Sanna.

He heard steps behind him on the wooden jetty, causing it to sway back and forth.

'Yes.'

'And we're supposed to . . . what exactly?'

She nodded towards the simple aluminium, eight-horsepower boat moored at the jetty.

'We're going to figure out where they went. Where they landed. Which table they're sitting around now, planning their next robbery. That sort of thing.'

That neutral expression again. And her voice was just as mechanical.

'And we have to sit in an unsteady boat in the rain on Drevviken Lake to figure that out? Even though you've already made this trip several times?'

'I need your help to understand how they think.'

He put one foot on the jetty and one in the middle of the boat as she climbed in, two waterproof ponchos in her arms. She handed him one of them.

'You'll need this – it's supposed to get worse.'

He jerked twice on the engine cord to get the propeller spinning. A nudge away from the jetty, through the tired reeds that knew it wasn't summer any more and bent without protesting, out towards open water.

With the plastic-coated map unfolded across his thighs, they slowly passed small islands with names like Kaninholmen and Myrholmen, according to the almost illegible signs. He held onto the tiller lightly, passing shores covered with fir and pine, sometimes broken by the upper floors of grey high-rises and the occasional tiled roof of a villa that had been built near the beach when that was still allowed. Then the lake narrowed, and Drevviken turned into a bay with lush and uninhabited land on the port side – the tranquil Flaten nature reserve, full of coniferous and deciduous forests and small community gardens – and dense housing on the starboard side – a restless spillikins of roads, houses and concrete complexes. It was sufficiently narrow for a fleeing boat hidden by darkness to be able to land on either shore with only very small changes in course.

'Which side would you have chosen?'

Sanna examined the map first, then the reality, and pointed towards the shore with the buildings on it.

'That one.'

'Me, too.'

John steered closer to that side – a criminal on the run would want to change direction as many times as possible and would have chosen a place to disappear around here.

'I've checked – there have been no reports of a stolen boat in this area.'

'And if it belonged to them?'

Sanna looked at the map. 'There are . . . five, eight, eleven . . . fifteen marinas. At least. If they own a boat they would have been able to go anywhere.'

'These guys wouldn't have landed a boat and left it there – they're not that type, they're the kind that clean up after themselves.'

The gulls approach, curious, break the moment with their shrill wailing.

'Robbers of this kind always get rid of their getaway vehicle. And if it's a boat they'd sink it. Coves, bays, jetties, swimming areas: every metre of the shore is a landing place. Someone was waiting for them – with another getaway car.'

'Or not.'

John smiled. They still thought alike. At least as cops.

'Or not. If they didn't need to keep running. If this was their last stop. If here is where they call home.'

He nodded towards a small strip of beach behind a gnarled tree that spread out, dipping its sprawling branches into the water.

'It was seven o'clock, maybe eight. The shore would have melted together to form a black backdrop – wherever they went in, someone must have been guiding them with a light signal.'

Two hares ran over the bank, frantic, terrified by the approaching boat.

'So . . . what do you believe happened?' he asked her.

'Believe?'

'Yeah.'

'You *know*, John, that I never believe things – I'm so damn boring I just write down what I can safely confirm in the technical investigation.'

'But what do you see? What are you thinking? If you were to . . . guess?'

'*You* can guess. Or, you have to guess, that's your job. I don't interpret. I establish the evidence and the facts, that's my job.'

'And if I want to know what Sanna believes, not what the forensic scientist has established?'

'I don't like this. Speculating,' she said after a moment, shaking her head.

'We're in the middle of a lake, I'm the only one who'll hear you.'

'Sanna believes the two men – so far we only know of two perpetrators – who attacked and robbed the security van had done something like that before and been punished for it. Absolutely everything about their actions suggests that: the shots, the brutality, the purposefulness, the willingness to take risks.'

They drifted towards the shore, rocks surrounded the boat, and he steered them back out again.

'And . . . Sanna knows there's always talk about that kind of thing. *Inside.*'

She looked at him properly for the first time. She knew he knew what she was referring to.

'People locked up with not much else to do. Right, John?'

She was one of only a few he'd ever been close enough to tell.

'It's not me you should be talking to. You know that. You should go there, talk to him.'

'No.'

'Why not?'

'That won't give me anything.'

'Well you have to—'

'*No.*'

They passed a forest path that followed the Skogås shore with its high-rises, and the contrast was so obvious – stillness, beauty and fragility so close to something restless, ugly and harsh.

'You haven't changed, John.'

'Neither have you.'

Every day she'd lived inside his head and chest and hung on no matter how much he'd tried to escape her. He couldn't think her away. For ten years. They'd only been together for two, lived together for one, but back then, they'd been young and a year lasted longer.

'It made me happy. When I left that shocked security guard and walked down to the jetty and saw you.'

He'd tried building other relationships, especially for those first few years afterwards, but she'd been in the way, and the women he'd been with noticed. They were competing with someone who wasn't there, with a goddamn shadow.

'You *really* haven't changed, John. Damn it . . . is this why you've dragged me out in the rain in a fucking boat?'

'I think about you – every day.'

'I never think about you.'

He was the one who'd done the leaving. And she was the one who'd mourned. And when she'd stopped mourning – she'd let go of him.

'Was that all, John?'

He sat silent, a little boy with no clue how people talked to each other, a long way from the detective skilled in communication and analysis.

'Can we behave like police again? Maybe even pretend this boat trip was something you suggested to try to get somewhere with a criminal investigation?'

He nodded, weakly.

'In that case . . .'

She lifted up the map again.

'. . . we know that not a single witness saw them disembark. We also know that despite the dogs and helicopters and roadblocks and forensic scientists, you've found no trace of them. They *must* have known this place – being familiar with it was the only advantage they were certain to have.'

The channel had become wider, and they were on open water again. Forty-five minutes to the jetty. He looked past her to where they'd come from, for the first time during this entire trip.

'You have to go back there, John – and keep looking.'

23

ANNELI PARKED THE rental car right in front of the barrier with the heavy padlock, just a short distance from the road. A rental Volvo 240. Red. Sweden's most common car.

She'd packed up everything from the kitchen cupboards and walked from room to room between the stacked cardboard boxes. They were moving, but not in the way she'd hoped. But he'd promised. Just one year. And she had gone, without him knowing, to the exclusive Saltsjöbaden area a couple of times and walked alone around the giant houses with huge gardens and as many rooms as they had cardboard boxes, and she knew that the day they started living somewhere like that, Sebastian would choose to live with her. She took out her phone and dialled.

'Hello darling, what have you been up to today?'

'Riding my bike.'

'In the rain?'

'It's not raining that much. Not here.'

She called Sebastian sometimes when she felt like this, and it always made her feel calmer.

'It's raining a little bit here.'

'Unnhuh.'

'I'm in the woods . . . picking mushrooms. And I'm thinking about my darling. And you know what? Next time you come to our house you're going to have your own room.'

'OK.'

'And Leo's going to put up a basketball net for you in the yard.'

'OK. Now I've got to go.'

'But—'

'Dad already has his shoes on. Bye-bye.'

'Hugs and kisses, I'll see you—'

He hung up. Electronic silence. That was the worst.

'— soon.'

She was just as alone and the woods were just as gloomy, an endless coffin that stank of rotten fruit and dirt.

She folded the raincoat, stuffed her trousers into her rubber boots and set off over moss and wet leaves with the mushroom basket in her right hand. She'd never been out picking mushrooms before. She spotted a brown one, a Karl-Johan, she thought as she picked it. What a name. One more, a yellow one, a chanterelle – that one she recognised.

Suddenly she heard barking.

A dog. Maybe more than one. And close by. She wasn't alone.

She picked a few more, some white, some that were almost black – the bottom of the basket should be full if she was going to look like a mushroom picker, Leo had explained several times. He had instructed her the same way he usually instructed his brothers, and she'd liked it a lot, listening attentively, keen to do exactly what he wanted.

More barking. Closer this time. A big dog, maybe a German Shepherd, and more than one. They were warning someone.

Without fully realising, she had come close to the huge, open gravel yard. Thinner forest, more air and light. The armoury. But something was moving out there. She caught a glimpse of people dressed in green between the trees and tall bushes, heard voices on the wind.

They'd discovered it.

The fear that had kept Leo up at night, sweating, awake while he thought she was asleep. It had happened.

Anneli took a few quick steps back in the direction she'd just come from. She had to tell him, he had to know. Then she stopped just as suddenly – she didn't know anything. She knew someone was there, that there were several people with dogs, but that was all she knew. She still had a mission; she was involved.

She turned around and slowly started walking towards it again.

Sharp-toothed dogs were barking and drooling. She remembered the bite on her left cheek from a boxer who'd jumped up on her as a five-year-old girl, whose owner said he was just playing around. She crossed to the other side of the street nowadays when she saw a large dog approaching. They knew how scared she was of them.

And she saw them now.

Through the forest, trees sparser with every step . . . two dogs, maybe three. And five . . . six . . . seven people wearing green. If she kept going, stepped onto the gravel, the dogs would be able to smell her fear. But she had no choice. If they'd discovered the hole, the tunnel, the empty armoury, Leo had to know.

She walked amidst the branches of a bushy tree at the edge of the gravel, and from there she could clearly see the concrete bunker.

She was convinced the door was closed.

It was still closed!

She was just about to leave, as carefully as she had approached, when she found herself slipping. Slowly. Along the muddy edge into the ditch which separated moss from gravel, the forest from the military building. A high-pitched sound cut through the air as the soles of her rubber boots scraped against fragments of stone.

The dogs were eager. They pulled on their leashes.

They'd heard her.

Anneli was almost out of the ditch, almost to the top, when she slid down again.

'Do you need help?'

There weren't seven men – there were eight, all in green uniforms. The dogs were German Shepherds, she'd guessed right, and they followed her every movement.

'Have you . . . got them on a tight leash?'

'This is a military area.'

'I'm a little afraid of dogs, I . . .'

The tall soldier with a twisted, grizzled moustache, who seemed to be in charge, turned towards the dog at the front, whose small sharp eyes were on her.

'*Here*, Calibre. *Sit.*'

He had his gun on a brown leather strap slung over his shoulder, and he looked friendly.

'I thought you could . . . say hello to him.'

Anneli – you have to get to the bunker.

'Hold out your hand to his nose. Just let him sniff you.'

I have to know if the hole's started to sink.

'You see, he's nice if you're nice.'

He smiled now, for the first time. Anneli glanced at his helmet. MP. Military police. Then she looked at the dog next to his black boots, and wondered if it could distinguish between different kinds of fear; the unconscious instinctive fear and her conscious anticipatory fear.

'I . . . is it OK if I cut through? To the other side of the gravel yard?'

'Not really. Like I said, this is a military area.'

'Ahh. OK.'

'We're military police. We're on a training exercise here. I'll have to ask you to leave.'

'I didn't know . . .'

'There's a "Don't Enter" sign over there.'

'I . . . didn't see it. I walked through the woods, parked the car at . . .'

'So what are you doing here?'

'I . . .'

He saw the hesitation. All eight saw it.

She'd put the basket down. Now she lifted it up before him.

'Mushrooms.'

'You don't have many.'

'No, I . . .'

'But that one . . . that's a black trumpet. That's rare. Where did you find it?'

She laughed, nervously, artificially, hoping it sounded at least a little more relaxed.

'You should never reveal your source. Right? But there aren't that many, you know, because of all this rain.'

'You can't stay here.'

She smiled and cocked her head slightly to one side.

'Can I just cross over? Sir? I could get out of here faster?'

He looked at her. She continued smiling, precisely as much as she thought might work.

'Of course. Cut across.'

They observed her, kept her under guard, even when she stopped at the bunker and turned around.

'What's this? This little building? Is that the kennels?'

She moved closer, as if she wanted to see it.

'No.'

'No? It could be . . .'

'It's a storage facility.'

A few metres from the door. Right here. She thought so anyway. She was standing on a spot that not too long ago had been a hole. She could almost touch the grey walls, the ones that were empty inside; 'a shell', that's what Leo had called it, a hollow concrete shell.

'A storage facility?'

She pressed her right foot harder onto the gravel.

'In the event of a war. If we need to equip a unit.'

It wasn't porous, or soft. The hole they'd dug and refilled could be neither seen nor felt.

Anneli started to walk again. They were watching her. Sharp, prickly eyes on her back.

She'd done it. Despite the dogs' salivating jaws, despite the ache in her chest and the sweat running down her back beneath her raincoat.

'Excuse me.'

She'd been so close. Now his voice chased her, louder than before.

'Excuse me!'

She hesitated. Stopped. Closed her eyes.

'Yes?'

'You're picking mushrooms, you say?'

'Yep . . . searching for them, at least.'

Head tilted towards a serious-looking face.

He knows.

'And . . . you're sure that one's not poisonous?'

They know.

'Poisonous?'

They've known all along.

'The yellow-brown, skinny one in the middle there. You should look that one up.'

'I . . . or, you mean . . .'

'The Yellowfoot. It could be a Deadly Webcap. A lot of people get them confused.'

He smiled.

'You have to be careful.'

He smiled, and it was for real. He hadn't asked her to come back. He hadn't asked any questions about the hole or the looted armoury.

She nodded after a moment and waved. She wanted to turn around the whole time she was crossing the gravel yard to see them getting further away, but she didn't.

She ran through the woods, jumping over roots and rocks, drove her rented car faster than she'd imagined towards Tumba.

24

ANNELI LAUGHED ALOUD to herself. It felt so good. She'd been consumed by the fear of not knowing what was going to happen to the man she loved, the kind of fear that can only be neutralised by being there. Now she was involved. She'd had a mission no one else could have carried out, and she'd done it better than any of them could have imagined.

A truck stood in front of the entrance to their new home, open at the back and completely empty. All the moving boxes had been carried inside. She'd hoped that Felix and Vincent and Jasper would still be there as usual so they'd hear her telling Leo the story.

She was pressing down on the handle of the unlocked front door when she saw him come out of the huge garage, and she almost ran to him.

'Leo, I'm back!'

They should have been listening. Felix, Vincent, Jasper. To her.

'And from now on I'm your robber queen!'

She held him, kissed him on the cheek and on the lips.

'There were people there,' she whispered.

'People?'

'Military police. Eight of them. With dogs. But it was only an exercise. And I did exactly as you said.'

His face changed.

'You did . . . what?'

'I checked the gravel in front of the door. Felt it with my foot. They didn't suspect a thing!'

Leo's manner changed inwardly in that way it did when he retreated into himself, thinking thoughts she couldn't make out.

'So you stood there – a metre from the caisson – and scraped your foot while eight military police with trained dogs watched you?'

'Yes, and they . . .'

Leo looked towards the house next door, towards the road, where a car was stationary in one of the lanes with traffic backed up behind it.

'Let's go inside.'

He grabbed her, not hard, but harder than usual, hard enough for her to have to follow him, shutting the front door behind them. There wasn't much light in the hallway. Just a long cord with a naked bulb hanging down, which swayed back and forth after Leo bumped against it.

'Military police. Who are trained to notice things you don't notice. And you stand in front of them and . . . scrape your foot like a cat hiding her piss!'

A bright and uncomfortable light.

'Leo, I only did what—'

'Did they get your name? Did you tell them your name?'

'No, I—'

'Did they see the car?'

'I—'

'If they saw it they can trace it!'

He was usually so careful not to get angry, never losing his temper, always in control. She'd only seen this before when he interacted with other men – when someone challenged him. She'd even liked it, it made her feel safe. But she'd never seen it directed at her, or against his brothers, or anyone that was close.

'No, they didn't suspect anything.'

'Nothing?'

'I promise, Leo.'

'If they find out that the bunker is completely empty and track you down, they'll interrogate you. You know that, right? And in an interrogation, some fat bastard cop will be sitting across from you, turning everything you say against you, he'll make demands until he gets what he wants. Can you handle that? Can you . . . *my robber queen?*'

'What's wrong with you? Stop it!'

'Because if you can't handle me right now – you'll never be able to handle an interrogation.'

'I would never turn you in,' she said, taking his hand. 'Leo, look at me . . . you know that, right? I would *never* betray you.'

'Well, you won't end up being interrogated if you play your role right.'

Leo moved two boxes and a coffee machine and made a narrow path to the kitchen and the fridge-freezer. He opened the top freezer drawer and took out the ice tray.

'You're living two lives now, Anneli. One outward, one inward. Six weeks ago I owned a construction company. Felix and Vincent and Jasper were my employees. And you, the woman I love, were my fiancée, my girlfriend.'

Out of a box on top of the stove came an ice bucket and from the box beneath it, a towel.

'Then we stole some weapons.'

He smashed the container of ice cubes and emptied them into the ice bucket.

'Then a security van.'

He opened the refrigerator door and took out the only thing inside, a bottle on the upper shelf.

'We're being hunted. Anneli, do you understand that? The police are looking for us.'

He wrapped a white terry-cloth towel around the beautiful bottle and lowered it into the ice bucket.

'You can *never*, ever leave a trace. Never risk being seen. They know nothing and have nothing. The only tracks are and should be the ones I *choose* to leave. We're five criminals working together with no criminal record – it's something they've never seen before. Hardened criminals who commit serious crimes, but can't be found anywhere in the police records. We're their worst nightmare – we don't exist!'

He grabbed her again, but not like before, softer, and he pulled her closer.

'Two lives, Anneli. One that our neighbours see and the real one – bank robbers that the newspapers write about.'

143

In one of the otherwise empty kitchen cupboards stood two glasses, champagne glasses, brand new, never used. Leo put them next to each other on the sink and pulled out the cork. It sounded like it did in the movies and foamed over a little as he filled the fragile glasses.

'Cheers, Anneli, to our new home.'

He's sent his brothers home because he knows I don't want them here.

He's put an expensive bottle of Dom Pérignon in the fridge, because he thinks I think it's romantic.

'Cheers,' he said.

She raised her glass, looked at him, drank. She'd realised what she'd really been carrying around – the fear of not belonging. Belonging was what she'd brought away with her from the forest, and what he'd just taken away from her. And it wouldn't come back now, no matter how much she smiled.

25

SANNA HAD LIKED to walk naked across the polished wood floors. She was the one who'd taught him to sleep naked, brush his teeth naked, taught him that his bony, pale body had permission to be exposed. Broncks had been at the kitchen table and she'd been sitting opposite him on that first morning when shyness turned to silence. They'd talked about nothing to avoid looking at each other, and her feet suddenly touched his. That was all it had taken for the previous night's closeness and trust to return. Even though he'd thought for a very long time that there was no one he could be naked in front of.

You know I don't want to talk about it. That I've . . . moved on. John? You know that.

He got dressed and exited his one-bedroom apartment into the courtyard, on the western side of Södermalm in Stockholm. It was November, but the morning was so warm that it seemed as if autumn and winter had slept in, and late summer had crept back to play for a while. He crossed the court-yard towards the turn-of-the-century house on Högalid Street and the huge church with its double towers keeping watch over the door. A church bell let out a muffled stroke four times every hour; he'd found the sound irritating for the first few years he'd lived here, but now he couldn't even be sure it still rang. Past a window that was always open, Stockholm Radio and local traffic reports blaring, and then into a café with two small tables, the aroma of bread and a baker who served Italian loaves while singing Italian arias, and who knew what kind John liked: coarse and with no tomato.

One day, two years after she'd moved in, he'd packed up her things from the bathroom, her unscented body wash and toothpaste, *The Second Sex* and *Purple Rain* – the kind of things that people bring with them as they move, piece by piece, inside someone else. He'd put a big yellow Ikea bag on the hall carpet and asked her to leave, and she did her best to understand. When she left, he'd been sitting right here, in the café a block away, killing time drinking enough herbal tea to be absolutely sure she was gone.

Broncks grabbed a glass of orange juice and one of the small, somewhat drier cookies still lying on a large baking sheet.

I think about you every day.

He'd asked her to move out. He'd decided she'd got too close, and at that moment he'd had all the power. But he didn't understand that it could be taken back ten years later in an aluminium boat – and she carried it with her, while he felt only emptiness.

I never think about you.

The three drawings lay in a heap on top of the next pile of moving boxes. Leo lifted the one on top and examined it. *Conveyor belt. Drainage pump. Cement pipe.* He'd designed and drawn every step for the creation of his Skull Cave himself.

He carried the drawing into the only room that contained no boxes, the one to the left of the entrance, the extension that one of the previous owners had used as an office.

As a boy he would spend break time sketching the new parking meters he passed on his way to school, learning how to remove the tops of two rivets on the back of the machine with a chisel and a hammer, prise off the loose cover plate and take out all the small coins. Or pretend to sharpen his pencil during the last class of the day while he gently propped open the window, and then hurry home to set his alarm clock – coming back in the middle of the night with a sleepy Felix, who would stand outside with a black bin bag while Leo jumped in through the open window and threw out all the building models his teacher had ordered – real Airfix aircraft from World War II and Revell cars like the ones in *American Graffiti*.

He hadn't realised it until later – if he did what other people didn't expect, if he made his own rules, then he could control his world.

He'd made up his mind never to do what his father did, make a noise and be seen and get caught. Like his father, he'd make his own rules, but he'd keep them inside where no one else could see them.

——————

John Broncks had had the same office since the day he left uniformed life for civilian clothes. No longer the kind of cop who was first on the scene with his gun ready, he was a detective who arrived later, piecing together what had happened from the fragments left behind – the echo of threatening voices, the heat of a body about to run – slowly mapping the geography of violence.

He opened the folder and flipped past the interviews with witnesses, search reports, expert opinions, to enlarged photographs of shattered glass on the car seat, bullet holes in the car door. Broncks twisted and turned the pictures, moved them from the computer keyboard and opened a register called the Rational Notification Routine, or RNR. He was going back, just as Sanna had suggested, to the place Jafar and Gobakk were last seen, searching for anyone with connections to the abandoned swimming area in Sköndal, someone who'd taken care to hide all physical traces, and yet still left a clear behavioural trace: the use of excessive force.

A large map lay in the second drawer. He unfolded it and began to follow a line with a red felt marker along the shore of Drevikken Lake. He turned his marker down the black line of a street, and then again, until finally it led back to the beach where it had begun, where the trail stopped. An area encompassing seven square kilometres.

One finger inside the square, he stopped at every new street, entered every address into the computer for the first search – people who lived inside the square who had been sentenced to prison for violent crimes.

'Hi.'

He made a second search – for people who didn't live there but had been sentenced for violent crimes committed inside the area.

'John? Hello?'

He looked up from the screen. He hadn't even heard her come in.

'Did I wake you?'

Sanna leaned lightly against the doorframe, a stack of papers in her hand.

'All the cartridges are labelled on the back with the numbers 80 700, which confirms what we already knew – Swedish manufacture, for military use.'

She looked curiously around the room and handed him the stack. An institutional room. Cardboard boxes along the walls and floor. As if he'd never really moved in.

'How long have you had this office?'

'Since I got here.'

'That's almost ten years. And there's no sign of you. Not a single personal item. Not a photo, not . . . anything.'

'Nope.'

'John . . . it doesn't even smell like you.'

'That's how I want it.'

He leafed through the stack of papers without looking up.

'Are we done here, Sanna?'

He didn't see when she turned around and walked away.

'Yes, we're done, John.'

But heard her steps, which he knew so well, fading down the hallway.

He looked at his computer screen, the RNR system and the results of his first two searches.

He'd received a total of seventeen hits.

————

The first drawing was still in his hand, the one of the Skull Cave and the solution to their storage problems, when Leo looked out through the room's only window, towards the entrance, and saw them arriving in the truck, all three sitting in the front seat.

They parked at the front door, next to the low stairs and makeshift porch. They were on time. They were properly dressed. Felix took off the cover of the truck bed and Jasper and Vincent lifted down the thirty-kilo jackhammer, four spades, four shovels, a wooden tool chest, a bag of surgical masks and gloves, and a case of Coca-Cola.

They filled the room with tools while Leo spoke.

'We're the ones who moved the boundaries, changed the rules. Those rules only apply until the day they open that armoury.'

He handed the longer crowbar in the toolbox to Felix, keeping the shorter one for himself. First, they attacked the floor's thin baseboard, then the yellow plastic underlay, then finally the layer of hardboard and particleboard. Jasper and Vincent carried the pieces out and heaped them up next to the truck.

'Now we're going to move the boundaries a little further. Remake the rules again. So that by the time they discover the theft, we'll have our own armoury.'

He got down on his knees and, using a folding rule and a rough pencil, measured a rectangle in the middle of the floor, two metres long and 1.6 metres wide.

'We have a head start. And we're going to use it – we're going to strike fast. We'll hit the bank by the roundabout in thirteen days.'

Then came the heavy jackhammer, as Leo looked up at them.

'And if some cop is sitting in a patrol car nearby, they need to understand we won't hesitate to use more violence than necessary.'

26

JOHN BRONCKS WASN'T sure he'd ever been here before. A church, a commuter train station, an indoor swimming pool, a library. The kind of suburb most people drove through without stopping. He rolled down the car's side windows; it had warmed up and the rain had turned to mist, making it difficult to see out.

Low buildings were surrounded by car parks, Ösmo Square, and right behind them, a two-storey brick house. That was his destination.

Seventeen hits on the computer screen for seventeen violent crimes recorded in the archives held in the Kronoberg basement, all cases long since closed and prosecuted. John had carried the files up, sorted them out, put them in piles on the floor of his office.

Two of the offenders had died. Three lived outside Stockholm – in Gothenburg, Berlin and on the Spanish Costa del Sol – and had alibis that were confirmed by local police. Four were in prison, behind bars when the robbery was committed. Five had been convicted of rape, aggravated rape and aggravated sexual abuse of children – acts that didn't really match the profile of this violence.

He slowed down next to a mailbox that the owner had clearly painted himself and parked in front of it. There was someone at the window watching him.

Three preliminary investigations had remained. They were the ones that required dealing with face to face, and he'd taken the files along with him in the car on his way to meeting any ex-cons from the Sköndal area who might have been capable of such deeds.

The first meeting was just two blocks from the police station, on St Erik Street. Convicted for serious drug offences, he was a forty-year-old man with the body of an octogenarian, stooped, with thin hair, sunken cheeks, eyes covered by a hazy film – Broncks had taken one look at the man and ruled him out as a suspect for a robbery that had taken nearly twenty minutes. He promptly left the inner city apartment overlooking the Karlberg canal, and only afterwards realised that they were around the same age and that, if they'd chosen each other's paths, they might have swapped places. Time wasn't only measured in hours and seconds.

A brick house with a large garden. He guessed from the veranda and the windows that it must have been built in the 1920s. And he was sure of it now – a man was sitting behind one of those windows.

He'd driven from St Erik Street and continued towards Jakobsberg and the second hit within the search area. Broncks ruled that one out, too. A 47-year-old convicted of manslaughter – at a time when he'd had functioning legs. The offender was an obese man who had retired early, with no hair, who talked quietly, almost whispering, and drank coffee in a terraced house. He'd had prosthetic legs attached at both knees after a methodical attack, reported as retaliation; the investigation had been abandoned after all the witnesses withdrew their testimony.

One left. The one sitting behind a set of ragged curtains.

Broncks opened a folder that had sat in the police station's archives for fifteen years. It described a 51-year-old man who had emigrated from Yugoslavia in the 1960s and had been to prison several times, the last time for aggravated assault, for which he served eighteen months in the Norrtälje Institution. There were photographs of a woman standing in front of a blue background as if for a school photo, her blonde hair held up in a ponytail so that her injuries were visible. There was severe swelling around her eye, and she had a pronounced fracture on the anterior frontal bone of her skull, the forehead, which a forensic technician had washed clean of blood so the deep gash there could be seen. The rest of her face was even worse – skin turned into one big hematoma, broken capillaries that shone blue and yellow. The last photos were taken further down and on the right side, showing pale skin around a white bra that intersected with a large blood blister covering the entire area between her armpit and hip. He had been methodical.

Broncks turned over the pile of photographs. But too late. Suddenly, as so often happened, he was flooded by images of his own mother, and he wondered if this was how she would have stood in front of the forensic scientist's searching lens – hair darker in its ponytail, different swellings and bruises – if she'd ever chosen to report it.

The rain was back, not much more than drizzle, but enough to blur the house in front of him. He considered putting on the wipers, but refrained – if he couldn't see out, neither could the man on the ground floor of the house.

More investigations, more convictions. Always for assault, or aggravated assault. Served time at the Österåker detention centre, at the Asptuna and Gävle correctional facilities. Assault on the construction manager of a renovation project in Huddinge, aggravated assault on a ticket inspector on the ferry between Slussen and Djurgården, aggravated assault on two men at a club on Regering Street, which led to attacks on two police officers who arrived at the scene to arrest him. Despite the hellish images of a woman's shattered body, this was not just a wife beater – this was a man who attacked other people, indiscriminately.

One document remained in the folder. The investigation the computer had signalled a match for.

HANDEN'S DISTRICT COURT CASE NO 301-1

DEFENDANT Dûvnjac, Ivan
FELONY CHARGES Aggravated arson
LAW 8 Ch. 6 § Brb
SENTENCE Prison four (4) years

Broncks flipped through densely written pages describing a completely different type of crime. Aggravated arson. Of a small house in Sköndal, just a few hundred metres from the swimming area and the jetty and the end of the trail, with a sentence served at Österåker detention centre.

A convict who usually used assault as his method, and could be linked to the search area, might be Jafar or Gobakk.

Broncks got out of the car and opened the gate.

The man he'd glimpsed behind the curtains was still there.

———————

They'd reinforced and moulded a new tiled floor around the mouth of the well. They'd stacked breezeblocks against the mud walls, from floor to ceiling, and plastered them with cement. They'd installed a sump pump at the bottom of the well and connected it to a float switch programmed to signal if the water level rose too high.

The first drawing, showing the construction of the Skull Cave's floors and walls, was done.

Leo folded it up, put it in his toolbox, took out the next. *Hinges. Black velvet velour. The hadak.* His design for an entrance through a completely ordinary floor safe, which no one else would ever be able to find. He left the room, in the middle of which was an excavation over two metres deep, and walked out across the yard towards the garage.

He heard the whine of a metallic blade, and when he opened the door, he was met by the spray of sparks. Felix was bent over a heavy safe on a long workbench, a black mask of heat-resistant polyamide over his sweaty face.

'Felix – I've set a date, a time and a place.'

The last sparks, and the back plate of the safe came off completely.

'A bank in Svedmyra, on December the eleventh, a Wednesday.'

Leo turned the combination lock and opened the safe – and looked right through its now absent back at Felix.

'And then two banks, simultaneously – on January the second, a Thursday.'

Leo unfurled a sheet of black velvet across the other half of the workbench, measured, and marked it with white chalk on the back. Newly sharpened scissors in hand, he cut the cloth into pieces.

'I've found the place. Two banks that share a wall. A small town with a small square in the middle, you can literally drive the car up to the entrance doors.'

'Escape routes?'

'You choose. The main road – Highway 73. Or a myriad of minor roads – all of which lead back here.'

The top of the tube had dried out, so Leo scraped away the hardened gunk. Then, using a small roller, he spread milky fabric glue over the interior walls of the safe.

'Where?'

'Ösmo.'

'Ösmo?'

'Yeah.'

'In that case . . . I say we take the myriad. Through Väggarö and Sunnerby. Or Sorunda. The minor roads to Tumba.'

Velvet squares were laid onto the glue-smeared interior walls.

'Ösmo, Leo? And . . . what the hell were you doing there?'

They were sitting on either side of a large safe with no back, so it was difficult to avoid each other's eyes.

'A recce.'

'You were *there*.'

Felix searched the eyes he knew so well.

'Leo?'

Eyes that couldn't quite meet his.

'You were at his place. With that old bastard!'

'Yeah. I was there.'

'Why?'

'Money. I owed him. You know that, right? I paid him back. So I don't have to hear it ever again.'

'We don't owe him shit, Leo, when will you ever get that! And you could have paid that money back any damn time you wanted to!'

One piece of velvet left. Leo glued it onto the back of the safe.

'It just happened.'

'Like hell *it just happened*! You wanted to tell him!'

'And why would I do that?'

'Why? *Why?* I know you, Leo. I know how you two work. He sets off a load of crap inside your head, and it just keeps going.'

'Damn, you're getting so worked up. Forget it, Felix.'

'Fine. I'll forget the whole fucking thing. Forget fucking Svedmyra, bro. Forget fucking Ösmo. I'm out. *Now*.'

Felix was halfway to the garage door when Leo grabbed hold of his shoulder.

'Damn it, Felix, calm down.'

'Leo, don't you understand why I feel this way? Don't you know that . . . it would never have happened if I hadn't opened that door.'

'What fucking door?'

'I opened it. Then. When our fucking old man tried to kill our mother. I opened it. I let him in.'

'You didn't open it.'

'I opened the door and—'

'*I* opened the door.'

'Leo, I'm not fucking joking.'

'And *I'm* not joking either. Why the hell would *you* have opened the door for . . . *him?*'

'Maybe I didn't know it was him.'

'You would never have opened the door. You were always so damn worried about what might happen. You remember wrong. *I* was the one who opened the door.'

'You? *You* climbed onto his back like a fucking monkey. You stepped between them. But I . . . I opened the door and let him in! And I decided right then, Leo! Never again! You hear that? So promise me . . .'

'Promise what?'

'Promise me you won't see him as long as I'm driving the getaway car!'

'I—'

'Promise me. Promise me!'

They stood there mid-stride, staring at each other for a long time. Leo put a second hand on Felix's other shoulder.

'OK. I promise. Satisfied? I promise never to have any contact with the old man again.'

Leo pulled gently on two shoulders that were slightly wider than his own, a faint smile on his lips.

'OK, Felix? Satisfied? *Never again.*'

'If we let him back in, Leo, he'll destroy all of this – everything we've built.'

———

Broncks rang a funny little doorbell that looked like a flower. He would do as he'd done with the fat man in Jakobsberg and the junkie on St Erik Street: ask questions that didn't have much to do with his purpose, but that would give him the answers he was looking for: *What sort of person are you now? What are you capable of doing? Where were you between 17.54 and 18.14 on October the nineteenth?*

Heavy steps. A shadow over the ribbed glass of the door's windowpanes. And a lock being turned.

'Hello, I—'

'Steve isn't home.'

The man was much larger than John had expected. Not taller, not stronger, just bigger in the way some people are when you're close to them. Dark hair combed back, unwashed, bushy sideburns, like a long-haired Elvis Presley.

'He owns the place. I just rent a floor, so come back later.'

The man's rough hand grasped the brass doorknob ready to close the door, two of the knuckles clearly sunken, something common among those who've thrown a lot of punches.

'I'm not looking for Steve. I'm here to speak to Ivan Dûvnjac.'

Broncks flashed his leather police badge, and the burly man glanced fleetingly at it.

'John Broncks, City Police.'

He looked at the man and then nodded at the neighbouring houses on the left and right, which also had large gardens.

'We've received several complaints about break-ins in this area in the last few weeks. Have you noticed anything unusual?'

'So the cops are out knocking on doors?'

The same tone of voice as the Junkie and the Fat Man. People who were used to opening their doors to the police, dealing with the judicial system in courtrooms, going to prison. Always suspicious, always the feeling of being accused, even before they were. Broncks hadn't expected any other reaction.

'Yes, you could say that.'

'So what the hell do you want with me?'

'I showed you my ID. Now I'd like to see yours.'

'I don't have any fucking ID.'

'Not even a passport? Nothing?'

'Why would I need any? Is that the law? Do I have to stand here and show my papers every time some cop bastard knocks on my door?'

They stood close to each other on the narrow porch. Around this time, in his meetings with the Junkie and the Fat Man, they'd started answering his questions, found some ID. Even though they too had felt accused, they wanted to be written off.

'Maybe in order to be part of society?'

'I may rent a floor here. But I'm not part of any fucking society.'

'And that car over there?'

Broncks gestured towards the driveway and a rusty old Saab, a paint roller and a folded ladder sticking out of the back seat.

'Is that yours? In that case, you must have a licence.'

The man ran his hand through the Elvis hair.

'You think I'm a fucking burglar? Really?'

'I'd like to know where you were between the hours of five thirty and six thirty on the evening of October the nineteenth.'

A short laugh landed between them.

'And what kind of burglar does a break-in between five and seven?'

The burly man, who took up so much space, now took half a step forward.

'I've done what I've done. I've lost control. But a fucking thief . . . what the hell, is that what you think, that I sneak into other people's homes and take their stuff? I don't sneak. I fight. You can see that in your fucking papers too.'

John Broncks didn't move. Not before he'd seen some identification.

You have abused your wife. Carried out violence in order to exert control. I don't need any *fucking papers*, I know all about it.

'OK. What the hell. But only if you go back to your bloody cop car afterwards.'

The man left the door open and disappeared down the hall into what seemed to be the kitchen, a pile of Keno tickets spread out on the kitchen table alongside two bottles of wine. A grey jacket lay over one of the kitchen chairs, and inside the pocket was a worn wallet.

'Thank you.'

Broncks took the plastic card. A driving licence. IVAN ZORAN DÛVNJAC. Issued seven years earlier, valid for another three. He handed it back.

'You could have shown that to me right away.'

'And why should I do that? You come here, to my house, with your prejudices. Even though you know I haven't done a damn thing in a decade. And that I never sneaked around in other people's homes like a fucking rat.'

'Is there anyone who can confirm that?'

They stood close to each other. But not close enough. Ivan Dûvnjac moved a step closer, tossed his head, thrust out his chin, stared. It had been a long time since Broncks had engaged in this sort of power game in the line of duty.

'You come here trying to throw me off balance. Maybe you will. If you carry on.'

'Are you threatening me?'

'You can think whatever you want.'

'Can anyone confirm your whereabouts on the afternoon and evening of October the nineteenth?'

'Steve can.'

'Steve?'

'My landlord. He lives upstairs. He can confirm it. Call him. He's working at . . . call the fucking Gotland ferry.'

Down the stairs and the flagstone path to the gate and his car. Broncks didn't need to turn round. He felt the eyes on his back peering through the curtains.

He'd had seventeen hits, convicted and released, criminals and ex-criminals. He had checked them out and written them off one by one. This had been the last one. And he believed him. Ivan Dûvnjac hit people, but he wasn't a thief.

Jafar and Gobakk were elsewhere.

———————

The stairs always creaked when he walked up, but never for some reason when he went down. The newspapers lay on a stool next to the stove, a couple of days old, and Ivan picked them up, and the stack in the cabinet under the sink, and headed to the recycling.

The bastard had stood outside his door. Jeans and a black leather jacket. Some idiot cop talking about petty criminals sneaking into other people's homes like rats.

He went downstairs again and put the Keno tickets and bottles to one side as he flipped through two weeks' worth of national and local news-papers. Not so much as a note about any break-ins in the area.

He would have punched that little cop cunt in the jaw if he hadn't decided never to do that again. He'd discovered something else: there were other ways to terrify people without ending up in prison. If he raised his voice and stared into their eyes, people in this fucking country backed down. It was like punching someone in the face while just standing there. They lowered their guard and their eyes, and gave up.

Not a single punch in ten years.

Still he was treated like that by some damn cop, accused as if no time had passed, as if a man couldn't change.

The hill down to Ösmo Square was muddy and slippery, and his worn-out loafers got no grip. He walked past shops, banks and cafés. The bell above the door to Jönsson's tobacco shop gave an aggravating ring – how the hell could he stand it, that sharp clang every time a customer needed a smoke?

Ivan looked around, the tobacco shelves next to the sweet shelves next to the newspaper stand. No one behind the counter. Then came the sound of flushing from the back of the shop, a small toilet that had leaked last summer and that he'd helped the owner change in exchange for a lot of tobacco.

'Ivan.'

The curtain was pulled to the side, and Jönsson ran his hands through his thin hair, as if using it like a towel.

'The evening papers. Both of them.'

'There's no gambling section today, Ivan. You know that's only on Tuesdays.'

'The evening papers.'

He took a folded and crumpled envelope out of the breast pocket of his shirt. He flipped through the 500-kronor notes and put one down on the counter.

'I don't have anything smaller.'

The shopkeeper wiped off the glasses he rarely wore, and then picked up the note, held it up towards the ceiling lamp.

'Well, I'll be damned.'

'Lotsa work right now.'

'You made all that on painting and woodwork? I'm in the wrong business. You've got a whole envelope, and I barely have enough to give you change for one note. Who can afford to pay that much?'

'I sometimes wonder the same thing. But then you just have to figure it out.'

Jönsson put the change down on the worn countertop, 100s, 50s, 20-kronor notes. Ivan counted them and then, over near the lotto counter, leafed through the papers.

'Not one fucking word.'

'About what?'

'Burglaries.'

'Burglaries?'

'In the area. Several of them. Houses.'

'I haven't heard anything. And everyone comes in here to talk. I'd know about it.'

Ivan rolled up the newspapers and pushed one down into each jacket pocket.

That bastard hadn't been to the neighbours before ringing the bell, and he'd come alone. If he'd really been knocking on doors in the neighbourhood, he would have left his car at the square and walked around, not parked outside his window. And there would have been at least two cops wanting to talk to an ex-con with a record of beating up policemen – they always went in pairs, like hyenas. He was there accusing him for some other reason.

'Have you finished reading?'

'There was nothing to read.'

'Put them back then. You don't have to pay. Take a pack of tobacco instead.'

He refolded the two tabloids, smoothing them out as best he could, and took the packet of tobacco from the bottom shelf. He turned to leave.

'Your son was here.'

Ivan stopped.

'He's big. He looks like you, Ivan, except for the blond hair. Are you working together again?'

Jönsson wanted an answer. He wasn't going to get one. Because Ivan's oldest son had his own business now, together with his brothers.

He almost smiled.

He'd at least taught his sons one thing: to stick together against everyone – even him.

Anneli lay on her stomach across the double bed, asleep with her clothes on. She'd been sleeping a lot lately. Leo caressed her cheek lightly with the back of his hand to wake her up.

'What . . . time is it?'

Her eyes were small and she averted her gaze from the light.

'Six thirty.'

'That early? Then I want to go back to sleep.'

'In the evening.'

He took her hand and pulled gently on it.

'Come on.'

She looked at him, but didn't move.

'Now. We're going to meet the Phantom.'

Anneli stood up, her arms still too soft and legs unresponsive, and followed him without understanding, down the stairs towards the room opposite the kitchen where they'd been spending so much time.

'Just imagine, Anneli, that someone's on the run and is hiding here, in this house, and the cops come looking.'

An ordinary room. Floor, walls, ceiling. The tang of fresh paint hit the back of Anneli's throat. They were all there, together, Leo and Felix and Vincent and Jasper, watching her, looking pleased with themselves.

'I don't understand. What are you talking about?'

The floor's uppermost layer was made up of black and white vinyl squares that lay under the thick rug they were standing on. The squares looked shiny, new. Leo let go of her hand and crouched down.

'This is your room, Anneli, and Sebastian's.'

She allowed herself the shadow of a smile. He glanced at her, still as pleased with himself, as he rolled up the carpet and pointed to four of the squares, and then uncovered two iron pull rings.

'The cops are here searching. And for some damn reason, they find a couple of floor tiles that are a little loose. And then these, iron rings, that you can grab onto and lift up.'

He took hold of the circular loops and jerked upward. A block of cement came up with it.

'They've figured it out too, discovered this loose piece. Then they see this. A safe. Solidly cast into the floor. Oh what a fucking joy for the cops. Now they've got us!'

He gently gripped the combination lock on the safe.

'And then, with a hell of a lot of luck, they figure out the combination. Let's imagine that, they work out the combination.'

He twisted and turned the knob, and opened the steel door. Inside was a safe with black velvet edges and no seams, sealed tight. It contained a small plastic bag filled with 500-kronor notes. A camera. Some loose cartridges. A heap of papers that looked like certificates and contracts. Leo picked it up and laid it on the floor next to the opening.

'And then they see – this. Nothing at all. The end of the line. And so they move on to another room, glad that they found a hidden stash of cash and documents that seem important and some rifle cartridges to do useless tests on.'

Leo went to the room's only window and to the junction box attached to the wall above it. He unscrewed the cover and lifted it off. Two electrical cables, one red and one blue. He looked at her and smiled like before, touched the two cable ends together and closed the circuit.

'Go over to the safe. And look down.'

A droning sound. And then . . . the back of the safe slowly disappeared while they were looking . . . *down*.

'The cops have left. And they missed it all. Everything was underneath the safe.'

A quick kiss on her cheek as he walked over to the hole and crouched, put his feet on the aluminium ladder, climbed down and turned on the light. Suddenly, there was a room where there had been no room before. Two rows of wooden shelves along the walls. Guns standing up: submachine guns on the top shelf, AK4s on the lower.

'The Phantom and his Skull Cave.'

And five machine guns right on the floor, behind the ladder.

'Don't you see? The Phantom's safe. Where he leaves messages for the Jungle Patrol.'

Her bare feet climbed down the narrow rungs of the ladder. She wobbled, regained her balance and stepped down onto the cold floor.

'You know, the safe in the police station, the Phantom had a secret tunnel into it, he was able to open the bottom of the safe and put in his messages for the headquarters of the Jungle Patrol. And every time the Phantom or the Chief went there a new message was waiting from one of them, that's how they communicated.'

A room containing automatic weapons, almost as big as the bunker they had come from. Anneli looked at the ladder she'd just climbed down.

'Feel this.'

Leo took her hand, held it against the concrete wall.

'It's dry, right? No moisture, no water.'

He got down on his knees and lifted a hatch on the floor: a large cement pipe, a sump with a pump installed inside.

'The house is built on a lake bed. So you can't build a basement. But with this, we'll be able to control the water level. When the water reaches here, the maximum limit, the pump will start running.'

Leo and Anneli stood and held each other, in a secret underground chamber with cold floors and an opening in the ceiling. And two hundred and twenty-one automatic weapons in two rows. Everything they needed for the next robbery, and the next robbery, and the next, and the next.

27

WHEN HE TRIED to see through the black ski mask, it was like looking through a pair of binoculars in an old movie – the dark edges that surrounded his vision concentrated reality; the colours were brighter.

'Sixty seconds to go,' he said.

The first thing he saw were blue jumpsuit sleeves and hands holding a long, greyish, heavy submachine gun.

'Fifty seconds to go.'

Like the others, Blue One was squatting on the floor of a used Dodge van they'd taken apart and that now lacked seats. They were all carrying automatic weapons, all had empty backpacks, all were dressed in blue jumpsuits and boots with masks over their faces. He could almost see the silence.

'Forty seconds to go.'

Blue Two was the driver – he was totally calm and knew what to do no matter what the situation.

'Thirty seconds.'

Blue Three, sitting opposite him, was to shoot down the rear surveillance camera – he hadn't been able to sleep for several days from eagerness and impatience.

'Twenty seconds.'

Blue Four, sitting next to him, was to jump on the counter, squeeze through the cashier's window and grab the keys – he was trying to hide his trembling, not sure if he'd be able to walk like a man.

'Ten seconds.'

He looked at them through the round holes in the fabric; all were hugging guns, just like him, wondering if someone inside that bank was going to die – if someone forced them to shoot, it would be just a matter of consequences. They would decide their own fate.

'Five seconds. Four, three, two, one . . . *Now.*'

The side door opened. Eight steps to the bank. Into the entrance;

diagonally above him sat the front surveillance camera, and he swivelled his body and fired. There was no sound. So he shouted, *bam! bam! bam!*

Blue Three continued in and raised his weapon, his body weight behind the butt of the gun as he leant forward and took aim at the second camera. His shots were inaudible as well, and his voice was intense as he started screaming, *BANG! BANG! BANG!*

And Blue Four, who was right behind him, stepped over two women lying on the floor and ran towards the counter, just as they had planned.

'*The cashier's locked the window.*'

Blue Four stopped suddenly. Blue One continued shouting into his mic.

'*Blue Four, act now! React! The window is closed!*'

Blue Four looked towards the cashier's window, hesitated.

'*If the window is locked, shoot it open!*'

Blue Four was sweating profusely as he finally aimed his weapon at the lowered window and the cashier sitting behind it, calling out *bam, bam, bam* more quietly than the others, and without much feeling.

'*OK. Then we'll take a break. A few minutes.*'

Blue One – Leo – rolled the black mask up onto his forehead. They'd been running in and out of a fictional bank building in his garage for four hours and were making fewer and fewer mistakes. He put down his machine gun and leather gloves on the workbench, took the microphone off his collar and tucked it in his pocket.

'Vincent – what did I say you were supposed to do if they close the window?'

Blue Four pulled off his mask.

'Shoot it open.'

'And then?'

'Jump in.'

'We should never stop moving, OK? We lose time. And everything will go to hell. We have to be in control of the time – not them.'

Giant rectangles were outlined with duct tape on the dirty floor, a 1:1 copy of the Handels Bank branch in Svedmyra – the tape outlined the outer walls and a wooden plank indicated the front door. The cash registers had been built with studs and plywood boards. Five mannequins – customers – sometimes stood up, and sometimes lay down on the other side of the cash desk, and three mannequins – the cashiers – sat in their chairs on the other side.

Cowboys and Indians on the floor of a boy's room. Or mannequins on the floor of a garage that were props for a bank robbery.

When then became now, when the game became serious.

It was a model of a room none of them had ever entered. Though Leo had traipsed across the small square and into the mini-market, and had sat a couple of times eating in the pizzeria next door, he'd never opened the front door to the bank. It was out of the question that any of them go inside. Their height, weight, and way of moving mustn't be caught on any surveillance footage. Anneli was the only one who had been on the other side of the bank's display windows, in front of the real cameras and cashiers, surrounded by real customers. During each brief visit, she'd sketched a new part of the premises on the back of an unused deposit slip, and he'd pieced it all together on the kitchen table, transforming the fragments into a floor plan.

Felix left the driver's seat of a car parked outside the bank built from tape and scraps of timber.

'Vincent, you stopped moving before, what happened?'

'I've already told you!' said Jasper, still wearing his mask. 'He can't do it! He was supposed to shoot down the Plexiglas!'

Felix moved one of the customers who was lying down and put it next to the unpainted pieces of plywood that represented the cashier's counter.

'The window might be open, right?'

'Leo told him the cashier had closed the window!' shouted Jasper.

Felix just smiled. He didn't like to yell, so he knocked on a piece of wood instead, which read Cashier 3.

'But what's this? Sure enough – the window is open.'

'We're conducting a damn exercise!'

'And you're a fucking jarhead who sees things that don't exist. So stop picking on Vincent.'

'It's not about *picking* on someone! He has to react with his gut. Never any hesitation! You hesitate if you don't trust your weapon. Right, Leo?'

Jasper almost ran over to the two pieces of hardboard that hung from ropes on the ceiling with handwritten text on them – Surveillance Camera 1 and Surveillance Camera 2 – and prodded them with the gun.

'There – and there – are cameras that have been shot down. Do you know why?'

'All I see are two bits of hardboard that you scribbled something on.'

Jasper smacked the muzzle of his gun against the two boards, which vibrated, while he shook his head.

'When you fire a shot outdoors, people might be scared, a machine gun makes quite a bang. But inside it sounds different. Shrill. Like knives hitting the walls bouncing around until your eardrums break. And the ringing in their ears makes people disoriented. Indoors, they become more than just fucking scared. They throw themselves onto the floor, not just to protect themselves – orientation is fucking crucial to survival.'

Jasper looked at Felix and Vincent, who were silent. Leo nodded slightly.

'And this is the most important part,' continued Jasper. 'The fucking cops need to know that it's dangerous to get close to where we're working. And if they still decide to approach us, they're the ones who've decided what's going to happen.'

'Jasper's right,' said Leo. 'If they aim at us, we aim back. If they shoot to kill, we shoot to kill. If it's a matter of their lives or . . . do you understand?'

He looked into their eyes and knew that they trusted him. Now he had to decide if he trusted them. A seventeen-year-old who hadn't even done his military service, a 21-year-old who'd enrolled but got out with an exemption, and a 22-year-old who acted like he trained marines. It was his job to make them work together as a group.

'Into the car. Everybody. Once more. Come on! I'll count down, three minutes from . . . now.'

In forty-six hours they'd be doing this for real.

28

THEY WERE SITTING in the same Dodge van, restored to its normal configuration. It was rolling north along the E4 motorway, in the dawn light. They had practised the attack on the imaginary bank twenty-eight times, moving from the van to the cash desks to the vault and back again. A pattern had been carved into their consciousness. But there was more preparation to come.

The asphalt road narrowed, turned into a dirt road, not far now.

A ringing sound. The mobile phone in the outer pocket of Leo's jacket.

'Hello?'

'Leo . . . the envelope.'

That voice.

'I don't have time for this right now.'

'Your fucking debt, Leo. The money in the envelope. You said you didn't owe me anything, right?'

'I can't talk right now.'

'So if you're coming around here after this many years with cash like that, and you don't even think you owe me . . . then you must have a lot more where that came from. You'd never give me your last penny. So where the hell did it come from?'

Leo hung up.

'Who was that?' asked Felix.

'It's not important.'

'It sounded important.'

'Concentrate on the road.'

Felix was in the driver's seat, as always; he knew this car now, how it accelerated, the braking distance, the steering. A Dodge van. It was the kind of vehicle they'd be using in the bank robbery, and the kind they'd switch to when they fled the scene. Felix had practised driving it but he'd also learned exactly how it was put together. He had been given the job of stealing two vehicles the night before the robbery, and he'd spent hours practising jemmying the lock until he was sure he'd be able to open the door of a Dodge in less than twenty seconds.

The old shooting range lay at the end of the gravel road. They parked and heard shots being fired in the distance.

'There's someone else here,' said Vincent.

With their bag of ammunition, four camping roll mats, and automatic weapons, they started walking down a gravel path that turned into a track. Two men were lying on a mound three hundred metres from the targets on a sandy embankment.

Leo paused, listening.

'MP5s. They must be in the SWAT team.'

'Leo, let's go, they're looking for us, damn it!' said Vincent, pulling on his eldest brother's arm. 'We have to get out of here.'

'No. You have to learn this.'

'Leo, damn it, we—'

'Listen, the cops are looking for two Arabs.'

Vincent walked more slowly, near the back. He'd seen Leo like this before, when you couldn't talk to him, when he felt the need to challenge you, to win even though it wasn't necessary, just to show that he could. And it was at that exact moment that the two men in dark uniforms stood up, packed their things and set off.

Towards them.

They looked bigger as they approached from the other end of the narrow path. Broad shoulders, wide necks, they looked like adults. Not even Leo looked like that when he moved.

'You here to do some shooting, fellas?'

The gravel rustled as they moved over to examine the weapons.

'Let me have a guess . . . Home Guard?'

Suddenly Jasper ran out into the grass, past Leo, in order to proudly show off their weapons.

'That's correct. Järva's Home Guard battalion.'

He held his AK4 like a marble statue, confident smile carved between his pointy nose and sharp chin, revealing the gap between his front teeth. Vincent took another step back, hunched over. If Leo wanted a pissing contest, wanted to win, Jasper wanted to belong.

'MP5?' asked one.

Now they'd stopped to look at the gun, just as they were about to move on.

'You're in the SWAT team, right?' replied Jasper.

Vincent closed his eyes. It wasn't enough. Showing off their stolen weapons, risking everything. Jasper also had to go and grab hold of theirs too. He stood there, exchanging admiring glances, and loving it. Brotherhood.

'Yeah. We're in the SWAT team. Good luck out there, there's no wind, a good day for target practice.'

They nodded as people do when they're preparing to leave. Vincent looked down at his feet, breathed as carefully as he could while they passed.

'You there.'

The one who'd talked the most and showed off his weapon stopped in front of Vincent.

'Aren't you a bit young for this?'

'I . . .'

Vincent tried to look up from his feet, but couldn't.

166

'HGY.'

Leo had answered.

'Home Guard Youth.'

The policeman was still looking at Vincent.

'When I was your age, I spent my time chasing women, not doing combat training.'

Vincent tried an uncomfortable smile, still not breathing. He didn't stop until they'd taken their MP5s and gone on their way. Jasper had already unrolled the mats on the gravel, and Leo had taken a pile of targets out of the barracks, and even though Felix had opened the ammunition boxes and distributed cartridges, he couldn't relax until the two police officers had started their car and were driving away.

'They didn't even check the fucking serial numbers,' said Leo.

His smile was the real thing: happy, proud. He had confronted them sure he could win, and he had won. Now he filled the magazine, threaded the strap around his forearm in a standing position, switched the gun to automatic fire, got one of those cardboard figures in his sights and squeezed the trigger. The staring paper face was torn to pieces.

'In order to learn how to use an AK4, you also need to learn how to stand,' he said.

Leo reloaded and handed the weapon to Vincent – but didn't let go.

'If you don't brace yourself for the recoil with your body weight, if you don't push on your weapon with both your shoulder and your left hand, it'll bolt upwards and your third shot will end up half a metre above the target.'

He handed it to Vincent again and let go completely this time.

It was difficult to breathe normally, to keep the sweat off his hands. Vincent pressed against the butt of the gun as Leo had shown him, put the weight on his left leg like Leo, held his hand on top of the barrel like Leo. And fired. The butt rebounded into his shoulder. And the barrel bolted upwards as if an invisible rope were pulling on it.

Twenty shots fired into the sandy ditch. And the cardboard figure stared at him with indifferent eyes.

Jasper almost ran forward, as he'd done when they met the guys from the SWAT team, and gently kicked Vincent's left foot.

'Vincent! Concentrate! Legs apart. And then push with your left hand just like Leo said. Press on it, damn it!'

'You shut up.' Felix had left his place just as fast, placed himself between Vincent and Jasper. 'When you talk to my brother there will be no shouting or kicking. Do you understand?'

'Move. Both of you,' said Leo.

He waited until they were finished staring at each other.

'Your breathing, Vincent.'

He turned his little brother's face gently until they were looking at each other.

'Breathe in, breathe out. Breathe in, breathe out. And then . . . fire.'

The butt firmly against his shoulder. Left hand like a lock on the barrel.

And Vincent took another shot. And . . . hit! The cardboard figure's head, neck, chest.

A new magazine. More shots. Until enemy after enemy gave up and fell to the ground in pieces. And sometimes, just like yesterday in the garage, Leo lingered further away, observing the little brother he'd lifted up out of his crib, built red and blue Lego cities with, made jam sandwiches for. *You're not old enough to vote. Not old enough to buy alcohol.* And smiled with pride. *But you can fire an automatic weapon and in thirty-three hours you're going to rob a bank.*

29

IT WAS LATE evening when they drove into the yard. Leo took some shopping bags inside to Anneli, while Felix, Vincent and Jasper carried the equipment and weapons into the garage. Vincent put the bag of magazines and the remaining ammunition on the floor and felt his right shoulder jerk involuntarily, a muscle memory from the recoil.

'Gun cleaning,' said Jasper.

Vincent knew what this was really about. It had always been like this. It didn't matter who or where, as long as he belonged.

'Felix, Vincent, come on, damn it!'

Jasper put his weapon on the workbench. He quickly disassembled it, piece by piece.

'Now you do it. Disassemble and clean your own weapons. And I'll watch.'

Felix put down the AK4 he'd been firing at cardboard men, leaned over and whispered to Jasper instead.

'Jasper?'

'Yeah?'

'Why do you act like you've got a machine gun shoved up your arse?'

'Excuse me?'

'You run around here like you're some kind of fucking commando. Me and Vincent don't really . . . like that.'

'This is an exercise dammit!'

'And?'

'Every combat exercise needs a combat leader. But you don't get that! Because you didn't do your military service.'

'I'll only say this once. Stop it.'

'Stop what?'

'Just stop it.'

'If we end up in a tight corner you'll thank me.'

'Tight corner?'

'If you hesitate in battle, you die. It's that fucking simple.'

'Listen . . . if we end up in the middle of a battle, it will be your fault.'

Jasper got closer, staring him down. Vincent had seen that look before – like the time Jasper had bought a nightstick and walked around waiting for someone to look at him funny. Until he decided Big Steffe had and whacked him twice on the wrist. He'd had that same look when the bone broke, *so easy, did you see that, just like a dry twig.* He'd regretted it later that evening, worried as hell, not about Steffe but about getting in trouble, that he wouldn't be able to do his military service. And now he stood there staring at Felix with those same eyes. That was when Leo opened the door and walked in with a large cardboard box in his arms.

'What's going on here?'

Neither Felix nor Jasper said anything as they both took a step back.

'Nothing,' said Vincent.

'I can see something's going on.'

Jasper dropped his weapon on the workbench for a second time.

'They're questioning my expertise, and I'm fucking tired of it!'

'Not your expertise – your attitude!' said Felix.

'Attitude? I've never questioned your expertise on a building site, when you told me I was holding my hammer too high on the handle or put it back in the wrong damn box – I've listened to you and respected you! So you need to fucking listen to me when I'm teaching you something I'm good at!'

Leo stood right between them, pushing them both gently in opposite directions.

'Jasper? Shut up.'

'You said I should teach them everything I know.'

'Keep your mouth shut and clean your gun. And you, Felix? Listen to Jasper when it comes to stuff like this – he knows what he's talking about. He knows how you should protect yourself. Just like he protected you! When those fucking idiots from the round house beat you up, and he stayed there even though he'd taken a baseball bat to the head, he stayed there and kept beating them until I could get there. Don't you remember that?'

They were tired, he knew it. And tense.

'OK?'

He waited for one of them to continue bitching, as they usually did. But this time there was only silence, the silence he'd first stepped into.

'Good. Let's do this one last time. *With* vests. Fully equipped.'

Leo opened the box and handed everyone a bulletproof vest. Never order equipment from a Swedish company. If the cops were to start investigating security companies, requesting that they disclose information, that was precisely the type of lead they might find. This, American Body Armor, a supplier to the US Army, was a safer bet.

'If everyone looks the same.'

The second box had been under their worktable for a while now. Four new jumpsuits, blue like before, all identical.

'If no one stands out it'll be a hell of a lot harder to give good descriptions.'

One last time.

Dress rehearsal. Fully equipped. Target takeover.

From a Dodge to a makeshift bank and back again.

Exactly 180 seconds.

Then the cashiers' desks would return to being wooden planks and plywood, while the bank walls and windows and vault would become a sticky ball of rolled-up tape.

'Take the petrol can and bin bag and follow me out,' said Leo, nodding to Jasper.

He led him to the back of the garage, where a wall stood between them and their neighbour's house and hedge towards the main road. A rusty oil drum was standing just a few metres away, and Leo emptied out a bin bag full of stuff that Jasper doused with petrol.

'Five fifty p.m. Ten minutes till closing time. Everybody's trying to get their errands done in time.'

Two matches. Sketches, drawings, maps all started to burn.

'And Jasper – you have to stay in control.'

'I know what the hell I'm doing.'

The flames ate up their plans and escape routes.

'Like when you put the barrel of the gun into that security guard's mouth?'

The key was not to lose control. To never, ever become part of the violence, but to direct it. He'd seen it in his father's eyes long ago, and now it was in Jasper's eyes – eyes that were being controlled rather than in control.

'Or when you shot up the security van even though we could see the lights of the cop cars in the distance?'

The difference between crushing a nose with a punch and burning down a house.

'Look at me, Jasper. I have to be able to depend on you. Can I do that?'

Nineteen hours and twelve minutes left.

'Yes. You can depend on me.'

30

LEO WATCHED AS his little brother unbuttoned his bulletproof vest to the waist and pulled the strap one notch tighter. They were crouching in the back of one of the two vans Felix had stolen late last night. They couldn't see outside, but Leo nevertheless knew exactly where they were, exactly how far they had to go.

'What if I get stuck?' asked Vincent.

'Stuck?' replied Leo.

'What if I get stuck in the window?'

'Which window?'

'The cashier's window. When I'm on the way through?'

He was going to rob his first bank in four minutes and twelve seconds.

'You won't get stuck.'

'But if I do?'

'Vincent, look at me. You won't get stuck.'

They'd been looking for a van with a handyman's insignia on its sides, and they'd found the perfect one. A huge logo saying HEATING SOLUTIONS, a vehicle that could be driven up close to a bank without setting off any immediate alarms – and everyone who saw it would be able to give a clear description later.

Leo grabbed the rear door handle for balance as the van leaned – the last roundabout. Twenty metres left – a noticeable bump as they left Handelsvägen, crossed the pavement and rolled onto the Svedmyra Square. The last stretch, tyres braking on wet asphalt, a sucking sound gliding along the floor.

Leo straightened his ear protectors and verified that the microphone was firmly connected to the collar of his jumpsuit, waiting while Vincent, Jasper, and Felix adjusted their own ear protectors. Now they pulled down the cloth over their faces – from this distance, it looked as if someone had cut three pieces out of a magazine and pasted them directly onto the fabric, paper eyes, paper mouths.

'Mickey Mouse!' Jasper smiled as he held his hands against his ear protectors, which stuck out like big round balls under the black fabric.

'Mickey Mouse, damn it!'

'Jasper, that's enough,' snapped Leo.

'Mickey Mouse, Mickey Mouse, Mickey . . .'

'Enough.'

Leo had only just calmed Vincent down; Jasper's nervousness was harder to watch, a man preparing for adult violence by acting like a child. Their first real bank robbery. They all had their own way of coping.

'Testing.'

The transmitter was in the right-hand pocket of his jumpsuit, index finger on the small angular button, and he spoke softly.

'One two. One two.'

His voice in their heads. The voice that would soon be leading them.

'Felix, the police scanner?'

Felix had parked the van in such a way that he was able to see the entire bank in the side mirror, and in the rear-view mirror he could see the three bank robbers preparing to jump out.

'Set to the right frequency. Encrypted. We'll know exactly where the cops are.'

'Good. Vincent?'

'Yes?'

'We're gonna go straight through them.'

'Straight through.'

The sound of four automatic weapons being loaded simultaneously ran around the walls and floor.

'In five . . .'

The time was five fifty p.m.

'Four . . .'

Leo put his hand gently on the rear door handles.

'Three, two . . .'

'Wait!'

Felix turned the rear-view mirror.

'There's an old man with a walking frame on his way out. And there's an old lady behind him.'

Leo lowered his weapon. He'd counted down. Vincent had been calm, Jasper focused. It had been the time.

'Felix, damn it . . .'

'We have time. We'll just let them walk out.'

'There's no fucking old man with a walking frame! No fucking old lady! From now on . . . they simply do not exist. We go straight through them. The only thing that's in there is our money!'

'Are you finished?'

'Felix, we . . .'

'An old man with a walking frame. And an old lady.'

Felix turned the rear-view mirror a little.

'They're out now.'

31

EIGHT STEPS TO the glass door of Handels Bank. Leo first. Vincent one step behind, Jasper two steps behind him.

It was raining a little, the smell of late autumn leaves through the fabric of the mask, wet and slippery and brown, glued to the cobblestones of the square. And everywhere, eyes. People sitting in a row, drinking beer in the window of the pizzeria, and the florist and his wife in warm clothes inside their flower tent, and the two customers at one of the bank's ATMs who had just turned round.

Real leaves and real eyes. Real rain. Real people. Real sky and real wind. A real bank door.

No more practising. There was no turning back.

Vincent focused only on Leo's neck. If he just looked into it and stayed there, and kept walking at the same pace, he'd make it to the bank and follow him inside.

If this is going to work, they have to see a grown man. Do you understand, little brother?

Six steps left. Five steps. Four steps.

Inside, the bank cashiers will be sitting behind their windows, and they need to be convinced that there are three adult males coming through those doors.

The bulletproof vest took up so much space, pushing against his jumpsuit, making it difficult to move normally.

You have to stand up straight when you walk. Put down your entire foot.

And the submachine gun hanging diagonally over his shoulder still chafed like before.

Imagine you weigh more, you're heavy, and you know where you're going.

And no matter how much he looked into Leo's neck, it felt as if he wasn't getting any closer to the bank by being so careful to put down his entire foot.

He wasn't getting . . .

He wasn't . . .

'Vincent?'

Leo had stopped with only a single step left to the door. He turned round, put his hand on Vincent's shoulder and spoke into the microphone they could all hear through their earphones.

'You go straight through them.'

A big brother's voice inside his little brother's head, one that had always been there. And now Leo moved his hand to his collar and the microphone in order to cover it, then leaned forward and with the other hand lifted Vincent's ear protector.

'Vincent?'

And whispered.

'You know I love you.'

And then turned round, to the bank.

Leo opened the glass doors, and Vincent followed him inside. *I love you.* Only Mamma ever said that. They walked through the narrow entrance, hot air blowing from above, and he wondered what Leo had really meant. Was he trying to make his little brother relax and walk like a man? Or maybe they were really going to die, and Leo knew it, but didn't know how to say it.

There was no longer any sound.

It was silent as Leo fired eighteen shots at the surveillance camera, which turned inside out like a flower, long wobbly petals around a lens – silent as Jasper fired fifteen shots at the second camera, which fell apart, piece by piece, onto the floor.

'Blue Four!'

Leo shouted at him, lips moving behind the black fabric, but he didn't even hear it.

'Blue Four!'

Vincent glanced towards the bodies crouched at his feet, their arms draped over their heads.

'Blue Four – the cashier's window!'

And he started moving again.

Towards the cashiers. He saw the woman in the yellow quilted jacket too late – stepped on her arm while the cashier slammed and locked the door, and threw herself down behind the counter.

If the window was closed . . .

If he couldn't jump up on the counter and crawl through it . . .

If he got stuck . . .

'Sixty seconds!'

Leo ran up beside him, shouting something, then that movement as he raised his rifle again, bouncing gently on his knee, his left hand against the wooden handle. Ten, twenty, thirty, forty shots.

'Blue Four – now!'

Suddenly Vincent was able to hear again. Everything was crystal clear.

The glass hung in the air for a moment longer, as if the thousands of pieces had not yet understood that they should fall, and he rushed towards the cashier's now missing window, wearing a vest that no longer felt tight, a belt that no longer chafed. He could hear the sole of his left boot crushing glass into the stone tiles as he took a run at it, a sharp, hissing sound as he landed on the cashier's counter, the sole of his right boot grinding glass

175

into the wooden panel, as if chewing on ice cubes, then both his boots hitting the floor on the other side, crushing shards into the carpet. And as he ran towards the inner door to let in Blue Three, then back towards the cashier screaming *give me the keys to the vault*, the voice he used sounded like the one he'd practised – and it worked. Fingers with red nail polish stretched up towards him, holding a set of keys.

'Ninety seconds!'

Leo was standing in the middle of the bank with six people at his feet: the young woman in the yellow quilted jacket who hadn't made a sound when Vincent stepped on her; a man in a coat and brown loafers who refused to lie down until he forced him to with the butt of the gun; an elderly lady pressed against the counter following him with her eyes, not pleading, not afraid, more like she wanted to record what was happening; two guys behind a big palm tree near the front window around Vincent's age, who would talk later of how they'd been there, in the middle of a robbery; and the woman holding a shopping bag, from which cornflakes and bread and a red container of baby formula had rolled out.

'A hundred and twenty seconds!'

From his station in the middle of the bank he was able to watch Blue Three open the door to the vault, shovel wads of cash from three shelves into his shoulder bag, and then shoot the safe open, and empty it of 500-kronor notes. Meanwhile, Blue Four moved methodically from till to till, knocking over the chairs that stood in his way, pulling out drawers and emptying the cash into his shoulder bag.

Jasper was acting perfectly. Vincent was acting perfectly.

Only Felix left.

'Blue One to Blue Two.'

He pulled the microphone on his collar closer to his mouth and looked through the window to the van, which still stood in the square with its engine running.

'Do you see anything?'

'I see something. You know the place next to the bank?'

'I mean . . .'

'The Ant Pizzeria. What a stupid fucking name.'

'Blue Two . . . do you see anything?'

'There are three men sitting in the window. They've each got a beer. They're staring at me and drinking and . . .'

'Damn it, Blue Two! Sirens, cops, do you see or hear anything?'

'. . . they keep glancing over at the bank. Eating pizzas, with canned mushrooms and ham. They seem to be having a very nice time anyway.'

A voice that often grumbled and questioned, but that you could always rely on. And because of that started talking about beer and canned mushrooms and three men in a pizzeria, calming his big brother who was standing on the other side of a display window, inside a bank, surrounded by terrified people, counting time.

'A hundred and fifty seconds!'

Time for Jasper to get out of the vault. For Vincent to finish with the cash tills. For Felix to start rolling the instant they came out of the bank. Leo would continue counting down, leaving the bank last and guarding their path to the getaway car.

'A hundred and sixty seconds!'

Vincent jumped over the counter, zigzagging between the bodies both on the floor and standing behind him. Felix hit the accelerator outside the window. And of course Leo stood still, watching, counting. Then one more shot was fired. Jasper. He should have been one step behind Vincent, but he was lingering in the vault, shooting the lock off the next safe, opening the next compartment packed with 500-kronor notes and stuffing them down into his bag.

'A hundred and seventy seconds!'

And the next safe.

'A hundred and seventy-five seconds!'

And the next safe.

'A hundred and eighty seconds!'

They had agreed to work together using a method that maximised profits without increasing risk – an agreement that Jasper was breaking. Again.

'Out!'

Leo took aim at the ceiling.

'Get out!'

And fired.

'Out out out!'

Two shots in the ceiling just above the vault. Drywall dust and plastic splinters fell onto the people hiding their faces on the floor. And it was as if Jasper suddenly understood – he dropped the box he'd just emptied, closed the bag's zip and ran towards the entrance and the square and the car.

32

IT WAS ALWAYS cold in the cemetery. But somehow, when it was covered with leaves, it seemed warmer, wrapped up, cared for and protected.

John Broncks wiped the water off a rickety bench and sat down.

One of thirty thousand resting places in one of Sweden's largest cemeteries. For a long time he'd avoided coming here. The headstone was beautiful. Black, smooth granite, not even twenty years old. He leaned over and adjusted a straggly brown plant that looked like heather, watered it a little. He wondered who'd put it there. He'd never done it. His mother? Why would she lay flowers on his father's grave?

Palm against the edge of the headstone. BORN. DIED. GEORGE BRONCKS. He'd been sixteen years old when the coffin had been lowered into its hole. And he remembered how heavy it had been on one side, that it had almost tipped over, and how his mother had stood nearby, weeping. Everyone else there was now a black mass in his memory – family, friends, and colleagues, people who John knew by name but whom he'd never met. The white tie had pinched his neck, and afterwards he'd untied it, burned it, vowed never to wear one again.

Mamma had wanted to go there the next day.

And he'd gone with her; he'd thought it was because she hadn't been honest during the funeral – afraid that the black mass would be able to see what she really thought about her husband. But that wasn't why. She still hadn't absorbed what had happened, had really happened – she'd accepted being beaten, controlled day after day. The few times John had tried to talk to her about it, about what it had been like, she didn't even seem to remember, *what do you mean*, as if it was held so far inside, *you know what I mean*, that his mother could no longer reach it, *John, I don't like it when you talk like that.*

They lay wreaths on the grave, said what you were supposed to say.

John had stood beside her, and she'd stared vacantly at the pile of gravel, and he'd realised the real reason she was weeping: not for his father's sake, but for Sam's sake, who unlike her hadn't surrendered, and it was probably at that moment that she'd decided to stop remembering.

A few more drops of water.

The car was waiting at the entrance, and he slowly left the stillness, heading along Solna Church Way towards the city. He was halfway to the police station when he heard the alarm for the first time.

'Bank robbery. Svedmyra.'

The other side of the city, too far away, so he drove on towards Kronoberg when the voice on the radio returned.

'Heavily armed.'

Something felt familiar.

'Military-grade weapons.'

Jafar. And Gobakk. He listened and changed direction, headed south.

'Getaway car located 150 metres from the crime scene.'

But this was strange.

'A car park next to the Svedmyra Tunnelbana station.'

Bank robbers don't drive 150 metres, park their getaway car, take out their tickets, and ride away on the Tunnelbana.

'The suspects have not left the car.'

John Broncks grabbed his radio and spoke into the microphone.

'Broncks, City Police, here. Repeat.'

'The suspects have NOT left the car.'

What hadn't made sense before, made even less sense now. After only a few seconds of driving, they'd parked at the nearest Tunnelbana station. And then stayed there.

Inside the car.

Just before the crossing, a policeman in a neon chartreuse police vest waved him to the side of the road. And there, just after the junction, near the crime scene, sat the rotating blue lights of two police cars parked diagonally across the road.

'Sorry, this road is closed. I'll have to ask you to either turn around or take the exit to the right or left.'

Broncks searched his inside jacket pocket for his black leather badge, an ID with a shield of yellow, blue and red.

'John Broncks, Detective Department.'

A young face, reflected in the light of the torch, examined his badge and nodded. Broncks was used to it. Every time he went through passport control, the officer would compare the picture with the real thing several times before being able to grasp his neutral appearance.

'They're apparently still there.'

'I heard that.'

'Heavily armed.'

'I heard that, too.'

He moved aside and shouted towards the other side of the intersection – *one of ours, let him through* – while Broncks rolled up his window and left the worried face of the young police officer behind, zigzagging between the slanted police cars, continuing down the completely deserted road. The Tunnelbana track, which at this time of day usually had trains barrelling down it every other minute, also lay deserted. That's what he'd just seen in his young colleague's eyes – everything that was normal had disappeared and his sense of security had gone with it.

He slowed down at a roundabout. Blue and white plastic tape swayed in the evening breeze in front of the bank on Svedmyra Square.

He parked on the cycle path and hurried through the wet grass.

'How many in position?'

The first policeman in uniform was waiting at the edge of the modest car park, taking cover between the large pillars. Broncks turned towards one of them, the same age, tall, someone he recognised whose name he couldn't remember, a sergeant from the Södertörn police.

'A team has been placed up on the platform. One team behind the kiosk, over there. One team on the walkway, by the hospital. There's a team on the large plot of land over by that house, there, with its lights on.'

The nameless man pointed in various directions, and John Broncks felt embarrassed. He should know his name.

'And in front of us there – a SWAT team is preparing to engage.'

There wasn't much to the parking area. Ten spaces wedged between concrete pillars. The sort of place he'd usually pass by without even seeing it. Badly lit by the streetlamps. Two parked vehicles. An older, brown Ford with the sort of frame that rattled every time it drove over a speed bump. And a Dodge van, yellow, or at least he thought so – the colour blended into the darkness, and the only thing that was clear were the huge letters that spelled out HEATING SOLUTIONS on both sides.

'Why the hell would you rob a bank and stay within sight of it?'

The nameless man stared at the getaway car. He'd been standing like that when Broncks arrived – as if he was being sucked inside it.

'John? Do you get it? It's so fucking ostentatious! Rob a bank, get in your car, drive 150 metres, park. And then . . . wait.'

John. He'd said his name. It was too late. Now it was Broncks's turn to say a name, to prove recognition, acknowledge that they'd met before.

'No . . .'

Guilt. Damn. In the midst of pursuit of four violent bank robbers? It felt as if he were marginalising someone who remembered him and his name.

' . . . I don't get it either.'

'Everyone in position.'

The nameless man had his radio on his right collar, a clear loud voice that should have been quieter to avoid being heard inside the van.

'Forced entry in five, four, three, two, one . . . now.'

Then out of the darkness men emerged one by one, in black, with helmets, flak jackets, guns cocked – eight bodies in a single motion. John Broncks had seen this several times before. And he'd felt it several times before. Getting into position for a confrontation with violence and force. He'd never seen a bank robbery in progress, but he'd examined the surveillance images later many times, and it was clear that the police in uniform circling the vehicle were guided by the same motivations as those wearing ski masks inside – meet my enemies, see if I have what it takes, find out if I can accomplish what I've been training for without suffering any losses.

Eight shadows moving forward.

One stayed at the concrete pillars and took aim at the driver's seat. Two knelt and aimed at the long windowless side of the van. Two continued to the other side of the vehicle and aimed at the rear doors.

He couldn't even feel the breath on the back of his neck any more. The nameless man had stopped breathing, as if with each inhalation and exhalation he'd been bringing the images from inside the van into himself, and now held them, frozen.

Two of the three officers from the SWAT team continued towards the vehicle, stopped one parking space away and peered into the cab. Empty. Whoever was hiding inside was at the back of the van and every weapon was aimed there.

One officer left.

One officer who crept up to the side door, shone his torch at it.

The van was unlocked.

He put his left hand gently on the handle, pulled the door aside quickly and threw himself to the ground.

No explosions flashed in the darkness.

No shots echoed against the concrete.

No screams, no hatred, just a voice over the radio.

'The van is empty.'

33

LEO SHOOK THE beautiful bottle and the cork popped. The Pol Roger champagne bubbled over the sides of the narrow glasses as they toasted their first bank robbery, singing and hugging each other. Anneli drank up and refilled her glass. Vincent, who hadn't said a word since they stood outside the bank, raised his glass and howled just as Felix had howled, out of the self-control that had kept them all together, which they could return to and draw strength from when needed. Jasper talked and talked about how he'd shot open every compartment in the vault and made another toast, voice bubbling over with champagne.

'Everyone in position.'

They fell silent, leaned forward, listening to the police scanner in the middle of the coffee table among half-full beer glasses and newly opened whisky bottles.

'Forced entry in five . . .'

A scratchy voice counted down as eight fully armed members of the SWAT team gradually approached the plumber's van.

' . . . four, three, two, one . . .'

Now the voice fell silent, just as the voices in this room had, and they perceived new sounds. Not words, but still a language.

the scrape of feet

harsh breathing

a car door squeaking

And then.

The most powerful and clear sound.

silence

The silence that occurs when a group stands close together, listening to an opponent who is defeated.

'*The van is empty.*'

And then, their laughter, which turned into more raised glasses and ceremonial toasts, requiring even more bottles to be opened and emptied. Leo looked around, from face to face. He didn't need to laugh; he'd shot the police's advantage to pieces, and now those bastards were outside the first getaway car with no clue how four bank robbers had made their way out of there.

Hit the bear's nose and dance, anticipate and wait for your opponent's fear, go straight to the centre, where he's strongest and therefore weakest – use violence to tear away his security and replace it with confusion.

And act in the gap.

The sense of security that people took for granted was just an illusion. Chaos and order were like two snakes coiled tightly together that changed places when you crossed a line they didn't even know existed. It was violence that created that gap. Time he'd frozen for those who lay on the floor of the bank, for those who'd shouted over their radios that the robbers were shooting indiscriminately – things that couldn't be understood because they weren't logical. And therefore it made them even more bewildered and gave him three minutes of freedom to act.

'Vincent?'

Among the hugs and champagne, Leo had been observing Vincent, who never seemed to put into words what he was thinking or feeling.

'Yeah?'

'Come with me, Vincent.'

'Where?'

'Just come.'

They left the scene of post-robbery celebration, diluted now by a mixture of expensive alcohol and thick cigarette smoke, and went into the kitchen to a single bottle of whisky and two glasses, pouring a few fingers in each. It was dark outside, and the kitchen of their neighbours' house was like an illuminated stage, as a young woman placed a glass bowl on a round table, a young man strapped a baby into a high chair and put a bib over the baby's chest, a spoon in his hand, and someone insisted on eating by himself.

'Do you remember? You always spat out your mashed bananas.'

'I still do.'

'But you liked the canned peaches. If I cut them into cubes.'

You were a year old. I'd just turned eight. A whole lifetime ago.

'You did well today.'

'No. I hesitated.'

'But after that. Not one mistake. You jumped up on the counter, took the keys to the vault, opened the door for Jasper, emptied the tills. All within our schedule.'

'I stopped. Hesitated. Everything could have gone to hell.'

'You solved the problem. Right? We were in control in there for three minutes. That's how you have to see it, Vincent – we were safe and everyone else wasn't. And that's why we had time to correct a mistake we hadn't anticipated.'

The family in the other house had started eating beef stew and salad. Leo raised his glass, waited for Vincent to lift his. They emptied them.

'Now, you have to let go of that. You hear me? You didn't stop. The only thing you should think from now on is that you did well – that's what you should take with you to the next time.'

They walked from the kitchen to the room above the Skull Cave and the bags that just an hour before had been hanging off Vincent and Jasper's stomachs as they shovelled in thick bundles of kronor.

'Over a million. Maybe one and a half. So . . . how does it feel?'

Vincent put his hand into a bag that held hundreds of thousands of kronor.

'Surreal.'

Leo turned towards the window and the kitchen table in the other house. The one-year-old no longer ate by himself; his father was beside him wiping off his shirt and hair, and then feeding him one spoonful at a time.

'It is, I know that. We robbed a bank. But they don't have a fucking clue how we did it. There's only one moment that absolutely cannot go to hell – the first vehicle switch. The transformation.'

34

THE GRAINS OF shattered glass looked different in direct light. The floodlight the forensic scientists had set up on the small square streamed through the bank window, creating a sparkling fog out of thousands of shards.

Broncks didn't look back as he walked away. If he turned round, he'd have to face microphones and cameras and even more questions from reporters. On his way in he'd managed to avoid the seven news teams that were already in place, and he intended to continue avoiding them.

In the middle of the bank, dust and splinters had floated down from the ceiling and settled on a red packet of baby formula. The woman had hidden her face against the cold stone floor, and her shopping bag had overturned near one of the perpetrator's boots. Afterwards she'd sat on a bench in a corner listening to Broncks's questions without being able to respond. He'd seen it before, the confused expression – the loud reverberations of repeated gunshots had damaged her hearing, cracking both eardrums, resulting in a sustained, intense whine inside her head.

Two cameramen were running behind him, shouting at him as he crossed the same pavement the getaway car had crossed. When he stepped onto the roundabout, still on the same path as the getaway car, they gave up and ran back towards the bank and other potential interviewees.

He'd lifted up the dusty packet of baby formula and handed it to the woman whose eardrums had burst. A total of nine witnesses. Three bank employees and six customers, all of whom had lain on the floor for three minutes that lasted a lifetime. Two were so shocked that they were unable to recount anything that had happened. The six who could speak gave reasonable, but not unanimous statements, and not even the two teenage boys who'd been standing close to each other by the window could agree on the perpetrators' appearance . . .

> Rickard Toresson (RT): blue jumpsuits . . . I think, like a car mechanic.
> Lucas Berg (LB): Not jumpsuits, it was more like jackets and trousers with side pockets.

. . . on who'd shot down the protective glass, who'd emptied the vault, who'd made the countdown . . .

> RT: They were wearing masks, covering everything except the eyes.
> LB: They didn't all have masks, I don't think so anyway. I saw at least one mouth clearly.

. . . just as every consciousness interprets events differently when faced with extreme violence. Fear distorted appearance, size, the passage of time.

> RT: I was at his feet. He was at least six foot five. I'm sure of it.
> They were all so fucking tall.
> LB: I was at his feet, and he was quite short, no taller than I am,
> and kind of overweight.

Only one witness had been able to calmly and reliably describe what she'd seen – a woman in her fifties who'd been behind cashier three when a masked man aimed his machine gun and fired about forty shots at her security window. She had small, sad eyes, and she showed him how she'd held up her hand with its red nails towards a voice telling her to hand over the keys to the vault, as all the while the shards of glass fell off her clothes, her hair, her skin.

> Inga-Lena Hermansson (IH): Swedish. No dialect. No accent. A
> deep, slightly strained voice, like it was almost too deep. And his
> eyes – it was like he was looking above me, through me, but
> never at me. The other man was waiting farther away and had a
> harness around his chest, like soldiers wear. And protruding ears,
> they all had those.

One who demanded the keys and one who opened the vault. And both of them, she was sure, had glanced several times at the one who remained on the other side of the counter.

> IH: He was counting down. Without having to raise his voice.
> Until the end.

Protruding ears – headphones. Quiet voice – a microphone.
   The leader.
   One who ruled and the others who were ruled.
   Broncks looked around from the middle of the roundabout, checked to make sure no one was following him as he crossed the other side of the road, back to the car park where the empty getaway van stood. A train pounded rhythmically over the bridge above his head from the reopened Tunnelbana line.
   Communication equipment. Load-bearing vests. Automatic weapons.
   A military operation.
   According to the plumbing company that owned it, the vehicle, a yellow

186

Dodge van with fluorescent text printed on both sides, had been stolen sometime during the night. Somewhere between thirteen and eighteen hours, Broncks calculated, before it was used as a getaway car.

The nameless Huddinge policeman was circling the rough pillars.

'Entrance to the Tunnelbana. Streets in front, behind and beside us. Bike rack after bike rack. We're standing in the middle of a damn junction!' he said. 'This is where commuters switch from train to bus, from bus to train, arrive or leave on foot or by bike, everyone's in motion all the time. And *no one* saw them leave the van!'

Broncks didn't answer, as he looked towards the bank, the square, the roundabout. Four roads to choose from. And each one, after a few kilometres, led to a new roundabout with four new roads. Four times four times four. Sixty-four options. As many routes as there are squares on a chessboard, and just as many ways to escape.

'John?'

The nameless guy had used his name again. And John couldn't – not again – refuse to answer, while pretending that he, too, knew.

'It's been forty minutes since we opened the first getaway van,' said Broncks.

Maybe he could keep talking, avoiding it, hoping to suddenly remember.

'In the perfect place to carry out a robbery.'

No. He couldn't.

'The search area is already too large.'

This colleague, who he'd worked with several times, kept catching his eye after every new reply.

'You don't know it, do you?'

'What?'

'Erik.'

'Excuse me?'

'My name.'

Erik let the statement hang, and turned back to the scene, sweeping his arm in a wide arc.

'What if they split up? If they left the car one by one and disappeared from here? If the first one took the Tunnelbana before we'd stopped it, went a few stations and got off? If the next one took the 163 bus in either direction? If the third one took a bike along the cycle path to the residential area up there and the fourth simply walked away from here and into that neighbourhood over there?'

Tunnelbana. Bus. Bicycle. On foot. Or sixty-four different routes by car. Broncks peered into the van.

'Erik?'

His colleague seemed pleased, he really did. But it felt uncomfortable to use a name he'd only just learned.

'They came here prepared for war – and nobody could leave here unseen carrying machine guns, body armour, load-bearing vests and communications equipment.'

Broncks knocked lightly on the side door of the hollow, empty van.

'Someone saw the car drive here. Someone saw them get out. Four full-grown men in black masks don't just disappear without a trace.'

———

A little greasy spoon restaurant was wedged between the pillars of the Tunnelbana tracks. Broncks had never liked the rancid smell of frying oil. It crept in underneath the mouldings and behind kitchen counters and clung there. He made sure to breathe through his mouth as he looked out of the window towards the van. The restaurant's owner had a clear view of the poorly lit car park – he was the only person who might have seen something. He was a scrawny man of indeterminate age – the kind of face that was asked to show ID at the off-licence even when he was the father of four children – wearing an apron that had once been white. That was probably why the smell followed them out into the tiny dining area, where three high stools stood along a counter.

'They get here in the morning and leave in the evening,' he said, pointing out into the car park. 'But that one, the Ford, the brown one in the middle, arrived at lunchtime. And the big yellow Dodge . . . it turned up about an hour ago.'

'And the yellow one – you didn't see anybody leave it?'

'Nobody.'

Broncks guessed there were no more than fifteen metres between the door of the greasy spoon and the getaway car.

'But that's not so strange,' the restaurant owner shrugged. 'Sometimes they just sit there. Waiting. For someone who's coming by bus or train. And then they leave again.'

'And today? You've seen *everybody* who arrived and left?'

'I see everybody every day,' he replied defensively. 'There are only ten spaces. And I'm standing here . . . the whole time.'

Broncks took two napkins from the metal holder on the counter and a pen from the inner pocket of his jacket. He drew ten oblong squares and wrote *brown* on the spot that corresponded to where the old Ford sat and *yellow* where the getaway car was.

'These are the ones here now. But do you remember any more?'

'More?'

'Cars that have been here during the last few hours.'

'Yep,' said the restaurant owner, pointing though the window. 'Over there, for example, a—'

'Write it down in the boxes.'

'There . . . in that space . . . an estate car. I'll write it down. *Estate car.* I don't remember the colour.'

'Good.'

'And over there . . . a dark blue Dodge. Exactly like the yellow one standing there now, but next to it. I'll write it down. *Dark blue Dodge van.*'

'And the other spaces?'

'Nothing. At least not near the end.'

The restaurant owner pushed the napkins across the counter, preparing to go.

'We're not finished yet,' said Broncks. 'I want to know which ones left after the yellow Dodge was parked.'

'After?'

'*After* the getaway car arrived.'

'I don't remember!'

'Try.'

Pen in hand, the restaurant owner glanced at the car park, then at the napkin, then at Broncks, and then put a big ring around the space in the centre, the estate car.

'That one.'

'When?'

'I don't know . . . maybe ten minutes later.'

'That's the only one?'

He tapped the pen absently against the counter, making an annoying sound.

'Then the other Dodge. The one that was dark blue.'

He drew a ring of ink around the box that said *Dark blue Dodge van,* several times, until it was thick and uneven.

'Maybe . . . yeah, it left about two minutes later. Or five. Or . . . around that.'

'That one?'

'Yep. The square one next to the yellow. Right next to it.'

Broncks examined the napkin. The square one next to the yellow van. He looked up from the drawing towards the real parking space. Dim light from the streetlamps seeped in and landed on the tarmac.

'You're sure? It drove away straight afterwards?'

'I'm sure. It didn't back out.'

'Back out?'

'Everybody who parks here drives in front first and has to back out. But that one was the opposite.'

Two cars parked in the parking spaces next to each other. Two cars of the same kind. One with the front facing inwards, the other front outwards.

Broncks crumpled up the napkin and threw it hard at the rubbish bin. And hit.

It was so damn easy, like when two people sleep head to foot. Two similar cars parked close to each other, turned in opposite directions, and therefore less than half a metre apart on their right-hand sides – their sliding doors.

Broncks nodded towards the man who owned the greasy spoon, and let out a defeated sigh as he went back out into the darkness into an ever-expanding search area.

———

Leo stretched up towards the opening of the Skull Cave, grabbed hold of the sports bag filled with 500-kronor notes, and placed it on one of the shelves on the far wall. The next duffel bag, containing notes of various denominations, he put next to boxes of ammunition.

They'd stopped there in the car park in the middle of rush hour and among all the commuters, with loaded guns and ski masks pulled down. Completely silent. Completely still. The Tunnelbana passed overhead. The bus stopped and dropped off passengers. The voices of two young boys, who'd gone past without realising that only the thin shell of a van sepa-rated them from four bank robbers on the run.

'The vests, Vincent, pass them to me.'

Vincent was kneeling by the hatch, unzipping one of the bags – guns, magazines, ammunition, load-bearing vests.

'Not that one – the other one.'

The next zip got caught, and he had to coax it a little bit. Bulletproof vests, large, round headphones, the thin microphone. One thing at a time through the safe into Leo's hands and onto the shelf above the bags filled with money.

They'd stayed there for sixty seconds. Until Felix opened the side door, reached over to the other van, which was parked in the opposite direction, pressed down on the handle and opened its side door. Two identical vans turned into one unit, two open doors opposite each other, hidden from view. A short leap from one getaway car to the next. Felix into the driver's seat, Jasper and Vincent carrying one bag each, and finally Leo who closed the doors to the two vans, now two separate entities again. The same movements as they'd made five minutes and thirty seconds earlier, when they'd been on their way to the bank. But in reverse.

'Vincent? Jumpsuits and ski masks should be kept separate – we'll burn those.'

Their first important car change. Just a few hundred metres from the bank they'd just robbed. The transformation. No one had seen them leave a yellow van, no one knew that they'd driven on in a similar blue van. And the circle had widened. The mathematical formula the police used in every pursuit – the time elapsed since the offence multiplied by the distance to the final getaway car – the circle that became the police's search area and indicated their chances of catching up.

One more kilometre until the next car change, another car park in another neighbourhood, sandwiched between a three-storey house and a copse of trees. Thirty seconds to change out of the jumpsuits and masks into work trousers and shirts, thirty seconds to move the bags and trunks through the copse, twenty-five seconds to climb into the last getaway car – one of their own Construction Ltd pickup trucks that would soon blend in with all the other contractors driving home at the end of the day, Felix and Leo in the front seat, Jasper and Vincent under the cover on the flatbed. Twenty minutes later they were in their living room, listening to the radio as a SWAT team crept and crawled towards nothing.

'Now I want what's in the other trunk.'

Leo took both the submachine gun and the AK4 through the hole in the floor, wrapped red tape around one of their barrels and placed the weapons on the bottom shelf.

'Leo?'

'Yeah?'

Vincent wanted to say it too. But it felt so strange. He'd never said it before.

'Just so you know . . .'

Leo took the last machine gun, which was much larger and weighed more, marked the barrel with red tape as well, and placed it next to the others that would never be fired again. Then looked around. Two hundred and eighteen automatic weapons left.

'What?'

It was so hard to say, it might sound false or artificial, even though it wasn't.

'. . . I love you too.'

35

JOHN BRONCKS OPENED the computer and clicked on the file labelled SVEDMYRA. It contained two documents. He put his cursor on the first, named CAMERA 1 – the surveillance camera above the entrance door. He clicked and slid a thin timeline to a sequence at 17.51, the time at which the three bank robbers in black masks had entered the building.

A total of five seconds of film. No sound, no colour. And jerky, as moving surveillance images always were.

The back of a head. That's what the camera sees first. A black head with a larger bulge at each ear, and which after the next step turns into a black neck.

Broncks moved forward one frame at a time.

The black head makes a half turn of his upper body, looking for the camera, raises his weapon, aiming.

Frame by frame. *You see me.* Moment by moment. *I see you.*

And in the eyes – no anger, fear, stress.

> Pia Lindhe (PL): They smelled. The boots. Like shoe polish. You know, petrol and toffee, they smell like that straight after you've polished them.

The woman who had just gone up to the counter to be served, holding

192

a plastic bag in her right hand and her number in her left. Then the shooting.

> PL: They were so shiny. When I stared at them, I could see . . .
> myself in them.

It's as if all of her bones and joints are gone. She goes down in the shortest possible time and lands flat on the floor. And even though she's so scared she can't understand what's going on, she turns her head again, up towards the masked face, because she wants to know.

John Broncks clicked on the timeline, froze the image.

Throughout the interview she'd sat in front of him leaning against the window of the bank, bleeding from one ear, from at least one burst eardrum. And afterwards she'd collapsed, her last resources exhausted, still weeping. They'd approached like a firing squad, carrying out an execution without considering who stood blindfolded in front of them – terrifying everyone into obedience.

'John?'

Sanna, at his door, like last time. Despite how late it was, she was still in the building.

'I've finished my analysis. Altogether a total of eighty-one cartridges were fired inside the bank. Which means, according to the available statistics, this was one of Europe's most violent robberies. Ever.'

She shifted, now leaning against the doorframe. She was going to stay there.

'FMJ, 7.62 calibre. Manufactured by the Swedish military. Karlsborg, 1980.'

'Yeah?'

'I can't determine whether or not it was the same weapon, the same suspects as in the security van robbery.'

'But you can't rule it out?'

'An investigator might see patterns indicating as much, John. But no facts.'

'You mean that we could have two groups equipped with Swedish military weapons, committing robberies in the *same* neighbourhood, in the *same* autumn?'

'That's *not* what I mean. But the forensic evidence doesn't rule it out.'

'Farsta almost forty shots. And now . . . eighty-one? First they shot up a security van, now a bank. Something must have come from the same weapon!'

'No.'

'No?'

'Nothing has been used twice. I've checked everything I can.'

'There is a pattern. Their behaviour.'

'Yes. But no facts.'

He looked at her.

'And if I wanted to hear one more time what Sanna thinks, not what the forensic scientist has been able to establish?'

'There are . . . movement patterns that recur. Camera Two. The moment before it was shot down.'

He turned his computer screen to her as she spoke.

'Legs bent. Low centre of gravity. Those were the security guard's words exactly, when you questioned him next to the security van. And now – see? That's exactly how the gunman is standing here too.'

Jerky and silent. But clear.

'And then, his finger, if you make the picture a bit bigger there . . . it's clearly above the trigger guard, perfectly straight along the barrel – as if he's pointing it at us.'

A few more frames, then Broncks stopped time again and zoomed in on a gloved hand. Sanna leaned in to look.

'Discipline, John. Never expose your men, every shot should be secure. This is a robber who doesn't put his finger on the trigger until right before firing – he thinks about weapons safety – so he's not self-taught. He's been educated. He's assumed the firing position thousands of times. He's been drilled.'

Just four kilometres between crime scenes. Just seven weeks between crimes.

Still – the forensic evidence showed something else.

These could have been carried out by different perpetrators.

———————

Ten past five. Still a long time until dawn. If he tried, he could hear Anneli snoring softly upstairs, and he knew she'd be asleep for many more hours; he was doing the opposite, avoiding sleep so he could fully absorb what had happened yesterday and prepare for the final phase of the robbery.

With the thirty-kilo case on his shoulder, Leo crossed the yard through the first snow of the season. Just a few centimetres of fluffy powder, and his shoes were covered with white without getting wet. A pleasant feeling in his chest. His deep breaths turned to clouds of steam. Several times during the night, he'd got out of bed to read Teletext and listen to the radio news – there were no leads. His plan and its execution had been perfect.

He unlocked the garage and turned on the lights. It was just as cold inside, and he pulled two heaters towards him, then grabbed the circular saw to start splitting the broad plank of plywood lying on the workbench into equal-sized pieces.

A car drew up outside. The garage door glided open and one of the company's cars drove inside with its windows down.

'Every single year!' yelled Felix. 'Fucking idiots don't change their tyres! It's chaos out there!'

Felix, dressed in work clothes, his hair messy, tired eyes avoiding the glare, climbed out of the car and went straight over to the compressor and the nail gun to fit together five equally long pieces of plywood into square boxes.

'Felix?'

Leo had learned to recognise the irritation, the dramatic gestures. Waiting was usually the best strategy, so he opened the trunk instead and took out three weapons marked with red – two from Svedmyra and one from Farsta – and started taking them apart, a total of forty-eight separate pieces.

'Come on? Felix? We robbed a fucking bank yesterday!'

Felix filled the mixer a third full with water and picked up a lumpy bag of cement, a wall of dust rising as he poured it.

'Felix? I can damn well see that something's the matter.'

'He needs to cut it out.'

'Who?'

'Just cut it out!'

'*Who?*'

'Jasper.'

Felix grabbed the bucket and emptied the mixed cement into the newly built boxes.

'He needs to just fucking stop picking on Vincent. All the time! Every single little mistake! If he stands wrong on the shooting range or stops for a few shitty seconds outside the bank. Or when we practise in here, he starts fucking shouting like he's Ivan.'

While the boxes were half filled, Leo flattened out bolt after bolt with a sledgehammer, and then pushed them down into the cement along with pieces of pistons and bolts.

'We're a team. And I'm trying to hold us together.'

'And he just talks so damn much. Running around in that leather jacket he dropped five thousand on and those damn boots he always wears, Fly High, or whatever the hell they're called, and . . .'

'Hi-Tec Magnum.'

'I don't give a damn about what they're called! He runs around in that fucking cop outfit, talking about how he's in the SWAT team or . . .'

'What did you say he did?'

'One beer in a bar, and after two fucking sips starts Jasper telling anyone who'll listen that he's working on some task force and . . .'

'In the same boots?'

The last box – weapon parts drowned in liquid cement.

'Felix? In the same boots as inside the bank – and in the security van?'

'In the same boots.'

Leo carried the heavy boxes to the truck bed, put the cover on, closed it again. And then looked up through the skylight into the morning darkness. It wasn't enough to plan meticulously – the seconds, disguises, movements, voices, getaway cars. Afterwards, without instructions or rules, when normality returned, he hadn't continued to control them. *The only tracks that exist, that should exist, are the ones I choose to leave.* He had to be clearer, require even greater devotion.

The air was crisp. The sparse snowflakes twinkled.

The good feeling was gone, and he had to get it back.

———

John Broncks hurried out of the building he'd lived in for so long, where he knew everyone's faces but nobody's names, a ground floor one-bedroom flat in western Södermalm. Cold, damp morning air. He passed the Italian café, as always nodding through the foggy window to the owner, who was grinding coffee beans behind the counter.

Seven weeks between robberies. Four kilometres between crime scenes.

And military equipment.

He'd reviewed every open case related to weapons theft at military installations again. This time he'd included an even heavier armament, the KSP 58, a machine gun that was extremely rare on the black market

– the theft of a weapon that powerful always caught the attention of the police.

Nothing. In any of the records.

The crossing at Långholms Street. Thirty thousand cars per day. Broncks usually tried to hold his breath as he hurried over, until he reached the snowy slope on the other side.

Three hours of sleep and despite that, he was still wide awake.

He had got home around three thirty a.m., lay down immediately, but kept his bedside lamp lit, comparing the five- and twelve-second loops of surveillance video from the bank with the twenty minutes it had taken to hijack the security van. Seven weeks ago, supposedly Middle Eastern men. Yesterday a disciplined group, military in appearance. It wasn't until he turned off the lamp that he'd realised that only one witness would be able to say if they were the same – and that witness spent his days in an apartment just a ten-minute walk from his own.

He headed down the hill, past a constantly red stop light and across the bridge towards Reimersholme, a sleepy and forgotten corner of Stockholm, where 1940s buildings stood on the edge of the canal. Swans were circling in front of two elderly ladies who held plastic bags of stale bread. Broncks appreciated all the many guises of the city – here, just three hundred metres from a major road so choked with exhaust fumes he'd felt the need to hold his breath, nature still reigned.

A small kiosk stood on the other side of the bridge, operated by a young man who'd grown up in Kuwait. He opened early every morning and was always friendly. Broncks stopped, purchased his breakfast of a Coca-Cola, a candy bar and a few newspapers.

He turned shortly beyond the kiosk and browsed the headlines as he passed – EUROPE'S MOST VIOLENT ROBBERY – the facts he'd told the press officer to release – 81 SHOTS FIRED – you have to give a little in order to keep most of it to yourself – MILITARY MACHINE GUNS – the balance between the secrecy a certain kind of police work required in order to move forward and the transparency demanded by the public who paid for that policing. After the headlines were theories on pages eight, nine, ten and eleven of both papers referring to important sources who were close to the investigation, which he knew often meant one reporter speculating with another reporter – the four robbers were mercenaries according to one source, or former UN peacekeepers, or unemployed soldiers from the former Eastern Bloc.

The house stood at the end of the street, near woodland and an area popular with hikers. Canoe racks lay covered in white under the first snow, as did the swimming and boat jetties that stretched out into the brackish water.

He entered the front door. A 1940s-style apartment building with banisters and lift original to the period. Fifth floor. Four doors in one direction, but none bearing the name he was looking for; four doors in the other direction and on the third, LINDÉN.

He rang the bell, waited.

Above the letterbox hung a stick drawing made by child in crayons and green paint. Two big circles, two small. Mum, dad, kids. Family.

He rang again.

'Yes?'

An elderly man in his seventies answered the door. Not one of the drawings.

'I'm looking for Jan Lindén.'

Broncks held up his badge.

'John Broncks. City Police. It's about—'

'I know what it's about. But my son isn't feeling very well. It would be better if you came back some other time.'

A man old enough to be his own father. Friendly voice, friendly face. He could *never* have been John's father.

'I need ten minutes. Then I promise to leave.'

The older man hesitated, but not for his own sake.

'I'll see if he's up to talking.'

He disappeared into what was probably the living room, where Broncks glimpsed a television and a glass coffee table. The room next to it had its door open, a children's room – a silvery robot stood guard on a plastic stool, there were drawings on the walls, and a pinewood bunk bed with large fish swimming on the sheets and pillowcases. According to his interrogation, Jan Lindén had taken two photographs from his wallet during the hijacking. One faded colour photo of a sweet child smiling at the camera with his football socks rolled down. And another child missing two front teeth blowing out the candles on a birthday cake.

'You can come in. But only for ten minutes.'

John Broncks took off his shoes and was about to step over the threshold to the living room when the older man stopped him.

'I'd like to hear you repeat it.'

'I'll leave in ten minutes.'

'Good. You can sit here in the meantime.'

The sofa was too low for him to sit up straight and the imitation leather made his back itch. The walls were everything that his own walls were not. Orange Dala horses next to authentic African masks made in China. He got up after a while, it felt wrong – only invited guests who'd been warmly welcomed should sit on the sofa.

Shambling, slow steps across the wooden floor.

'Hello. John Broncks. We met in Sköndal. Immediately . . . afterwards.'

'Afterwards?'

A man who two months later was still stumbling through his days, weeping, screaming, on medication. Broncks had met him before, or others like him. Some came back. Some were never again able to live a full life.

'At the ambulance. We spoke then.'

Bottomless eyes that looked at him without recognition.

'And now I'd like to speak to you again.'

The retired father was holding his forty-year-old son upright. His grey woollen socks were toeless, his tracksuit shapeless around the knees, there was sharp stubble on his chin, and his thin, unwashed hair hung over his troubled eyes – as if he were embarrassed, didn't want to be seen like this – the traumatised security guard.

'He . . . he said it.'

Lindén sank into the spot on the sofa where Broncks had just been sitting.

'The whole time. When he shoved the gun into my mouth.'

'He said . . . what?'

'Shoot. Shoot him.'

Darkness that turned to anxiety that turned to insomnia that turned to even more darkness. John Broncks thought he understood. At one time he'd lived like that himself.

'Here.'

An envelope containing two black and white photographs, frozen images from a surveillance camera. Broncks lay them down on the glass table. One to the left. CAMERA 1. Taken from above, an enlargement of the eyes and mouth. The second to the right. CAMERA 2. A wider picture clearly showing them in the firing position.

'The men you saw, did they resemble either of these two?'

Lindén pulled the black and white images closer with a trembling hand.

'What . . . is this?'

'Yesterday. At five fifty-one p.m. A bank robbery in Svedmyra. If you compare these two men with the two you met in Farsta – do you see any similarities?'

Lindén tried to pick up the two pictures, but the photo paper slipped through his damp fingers.

'Yesterday?'

He tried pulling the pictures closer, but they stuck to the glass table, so he gave up and crossed his arms over his stomach, as if to protect himself.

'When they were finished, one of them turned back. Not the one who took our name tags. The other one, the calm one. He wasn't at all in a hurry, and he walked over to the front seat and . . .'

'Jan . . .'

'. . . he moved his hand. I heard broken glass falling onto the floor. So you don't cut yourselves. He said that. "So you not cut yourself."'

'Jan, if you're not up for this, you don't need to do it.'

'He brushed it away so we wouldn't get hurt. Don't you see? First he says, "Shoot him." Then . . .'

'Jan, he's already been here for ten minutes. That's all we promised.'

'. . . brushed away the shattered glass? I don't understand. I don't understand.'

Jan Lindén's father couldn't reach him, his son didn't even hear him, so he leaned over to the table and knocked both photographs onto the floor.

'Take those with you and leave.'

'One more question. The robber who brushed away the broken glass. If you compare him with those pictures, is he one of them—'

'That's enough!' said the father, protectively. 'Those aren't shots from a movie! Can't you, as a police officer, see that? This isn't a damn video you rent and return late, pay your fifty kronor in late fees and . . . everything's fine again. This is real!'

'I know it's real. I live with it day and night. But your son is the only one who can help me to move forward, and stop these bastards so that no one else will have to go through what he's gone through.'

Both photographs lay near one of the legs of the low coffee table – they'd landed right side up.

Jan Lindén's father sat down on the sofa, next to his son.

'Please pick up your pictures.'

'One more question.'

'Pick them up.'

Broncks got down on his knees and peeled up the pictures that were now stuck to the rug.

'Thank you.'

The older man held out his hand.

'May I have them?'

He took them and held them in front of his son.

'Jan?'

Jan Lindén had closed his eyes for a while, gone elsewhere. Now he looked at the pictures in his father's hand.

'Look at them. Jan, do it. They can't reach you any more.'

Lindén looked. For a long time.

'Was it one of them, Jan, was it?'

Then he lifted a trembling forefinger, moving it slowly towards one of the pictures.

'Him.'

'You recognise him?'

'He was the one who aimed at me. I'm sure. At the beach, outside the car.'

'You're sure?'

'He stood like that. Sunk down. Held his weapon just like that. Had the same eyes.'

The security guard shuffled out exactly the same way he'd shuffled in.

John Broncks nodded a silent thank you to the father, then left the apartment and a man who would probably never live his life again without medication, who after years on disability would retire early, and who would be granted a small settlement of 29,200 kronor for the crimes committed against him. That was how it worked. A bank robber didn't just take the cash from the vault, he took something you'd always taken for granted, he took your sense of security. And that was the real crime they should be on trial for someday. The charge of *aggravated robbery* should be replaced by *theft of security*.

It was still snowing. Leo drove south on Ring Street, and every time he used the brakes, at every uneven patch of asphalt, five wooden crates full of gun parts banged against the walls of the truck bed. All morning he'd been trying to reach Jasper on the phone with no success, so he'd decided to go to his flat. First though, he was heading towards Svedmyra. It was a ten-minute detour, but he couldn't help it. And when he got there he did two laps of the roundabout.

It looked so different in the daylight.

The car park was cordoned off and the getaway car had been towed away. Police tape fluttered around the square and the bank, and there were a few people going into the pizzeria next door, but otherwise the place was deserted. Almost as if it hadn't happened.

He drove on through the small houses of Socken Road to the older apartment buildings of Bagarmossen, at the edge of a large nature reserve.

Up to the second floor of Jasper's building. The doorbell sounded muted, as if the metal bell had been unscrewed. He pounded on the door, shook the flap of the letterbox, leaned over and shouted.

It took a few minutes. A dishevelled Jasper in white underpants showed Leo in, happy and proud as he always was on the few occasions Leo came to visit.

A narrow hallway. Heavy boots sat on double shelves, but not the pair worn to rob the bank – and stand around in a bar. Jasper went into the kitchen and made coffee.

'With a splash of milk. How you like it,' he said, holding out a steaming cup.

A one-bedroom sublet. Black drapes separating the living room and a sofa, a table, and a television set. And the altar.

Suppressors Vol One Ruger MK I and Standard Model Auto Pistol.

Suppressors Vol Two Ruger 10/22.

They stood there in neat rows – thin books, manuals and booklets.

Suppressors Vol Three AR-7 Survival Rifle next to *Suppressors Vol Four UZI Semi Auto & SMG* next to the *Hayduke Silencer Book* next to *Home Workshop Silencers* beside *American Body Armor.*

The second half of the course literature, which Vincent hadn't yet received. Next to the books lay a bayonet and a green beret with a golden emblem, similar to the one Leo had been assigned – that was why Jasper had applied to that regiment, to do the same military service two years later. And then a photo in a gold frame, Jasper in a snow-white jumpsuit with a loaded gun under his arm.

Jasper's altar. A world that still meant so much to him, even though he hadn't meant much to it. His whole life had revolved around one day becoming an officer. But he hadn't been considered competent to lead and therefore had received a final grade that was too low to continue in the military.

His yearning sometimes got the better of him.

This morning's *Daily News* lay in the middle of the kitchen table. A double-page spread on a bank robbery in Svedmyra – good-sized pictures of the square filled with shocked witnesses. And there stood the black boots to the left of the newspaper. And to the right of the newspaper – tins of shoe polish and polishing rags.

'I sat up the whole fucking night waiting. And not a single picture of the security camera I shot down,' said Jasper.

Leo looked at him. He had to explain this more clearly.

'Jasper, you can only succeed out there if you become your job. The best artists don't stop being artists when they go home for dinner. The most important stockbrokers don't stop being stockbrokers at five p.m. You're a bank robber now. You have to be consistent. You're still a bank robber beyond the roadblocks. They're looking for us all the time.'

He turned the boots upside down and two silicone heel cushions fell out.

'You have to think and breathe like a bank robber all the time.'

'The inserts, damn it, be careful!'

'So you can't wear these, Jasper. OK? Never again. We have to burn them. And buy new ones.'

'What the fuck do you mean?'

'You wore them in Farsta. And yesterday. And you've been wearing them to bars. Damn it, Jasper! Whatever we use, we destroy afterwards. You know that.'

Jasper got down on his knees to grab the heel inserts, which had landed under the table.

'You know I . . . that these . . . I've broken them in!'

A person who wanted to be someone that he would never be. And just like the beret on the altar, he held on tight to what others didn't want to give him.

'I know you like them. I get that. But if they take an impression and then find your boots, then it's all over.'

Leo was still holding the boots and began pulling out one kitchen drawer at a time.

'I'm taking them with me. I'll burn them. Then you don't have to. Do you have a plastic bag?'

'I want to do it myself.'

'I'll burn them.'

Jasper squeezed the heel inserts inside his fists and opened a drawer filled with used plastic bags. He grabbed the boots and threw them inside, tied the handles together and handed the bundle to Leo.

'You're good, Jasper. Really fucking good.'

'What?'

'During a robbery. You never hesitate. Without you this wouldn't be possible.'

The smile he'd worn when he opened the door and realised it was Leo, or when he'd served coffee with just the right amount of milk, returned.

'But there is one more thing.'

The proud smile became unsure.

'What, Leo, what should I do? I'll do fucking anything, you know that.'

'When I say stop – *you have to stop.*'

Jasper didn't control the violence, he let the violence control him. He still carried inside him his dreams of a military career, and even though he hadn't measured up, he was still trying to prove they'd been wrong.

Jasper had no off button, and if Leo couldn't help him find it, he wouldn't just be shooting at safes and surveillance cameras. He'd be shooting at somebody's head.

'Leo, damn it, I took those safe deposit boxes for our sake! I made sure we got everything we came for, and all of this could have been avoided if Vincent hadn't stopped outside like a fucking fool. He slowed me down!'

Jasper pulled out a kitchen chair and sat down.

'I think about this all the fucking time, how we can get better, more efficient, make more money.'

His eyes were as sad as they were annoyed.

'This is my life now. You and Felix and Vincent. I share everything with you!'

Leo sat down in the chair opposite him.

'And *we* need *you.* I told you that. We could not do this without you. You know that.'

They sat in silence for a while. Until Leo stood up holding the boots in the bag. And Jasper smiled, again.

'Listen . . . *I've* also been thinking about something.'

'Yeah?'

'Next time. Ösmo. On our way home, after the double . . . we could fucking hit one more.'

'Another one?'

'Sorunda.'

Sorunda. Leo knew exactly where that bank was. Just ten kilometres from the two adjacent banks in Ösmo. It was one of the sites he'd scouted before he opted for Svedmyra. But then he'd been thinking of it as a single target, not as a third on their way home from Sweden's first double bank robbery.

'It's big, Leo. But it's possible.'

Jasper saw that Leo was actually listening and raised his voice.

'I know it's possible! If we just make sure the fucking cops are some-where else. If we *send* them somewhere else.'

36

SO MANY BEAUTIFUL homes. Äppelviken. Apple Bay. Even the name was beautiful. John Broncks had lived his whole life in Stockholm, but had never been here before. Just a few minutes' drive and you entered a different reality, as if the whole area were surrounded by an invisible fence.

Driving down the narrow tracks of the Nockeby tram as far as the school, then onto the smaller streets, and down to the water. Broncks checked the name and house number on the mailboxes and stopped in front of a house that stood right on Lake Mälaren. A thin layer of snow covered the lawn, and he nodded to the garden gnome that looked as if it was standing guard. It was surrounded by the footprints of two small children and one full-size man – perhaps from the ceremonial placement of a plastic gnome with a fixed smile.

He rang a doorbell, below which was a notice that said Welcome. He could smell home cooking inside.

'Hi.'

A little girl, who he guessed was the older daughter, the six-year-old. She was dressed in white with a crown of candles on her head, for the celebration of St Lucia's Day, like so many little girls her age all over Scandinavia.

'Hello. Is your dad at home?'

She straightened a sash of glossy paper.

'I'm Lucia. Who are you?'

'Well, then, well I'm . . . the Christmas Elf. Now then – is your dad at home?'

She examined him from top to bottom.

'You're not the Christmas Elf. I am.'

The younger daughter had just arrived. Four years old. Wearing sparkly pyjamas.

'You don't even look like an elf,' she said.

Then they both disappeared, and he heard the younger one speaking loudly and indignantly, *Dad, there's somebody here and he's lying*, and then heavier steps.

'John?'

His boss, Karlström, one of Stockholm's senior police chiefs, stood there in a checked apron with a kitchen towel hanging from one of its ties.

'Can we talk? Ten minutes. Then I promise to leave. This time as well.'

A hall filled with large and small clothes on hangers and hooks. Big and small shoes on the floor. Lucia and the Elf were sitting around a tin of gingerbread biscuits in the living room, and Karlström showed him towards the stairs.

'It's a bit quieter up here.'

They went up a flight of stairs to Karlström's office, an old desk, overflowing bookshelves, and a guest chair that Broncks sank into.

'Over a million kronor was stolen and forty shots were fired eight weeks ago.'

A beautiful view through the window – the frozen water facing Stockholm.

'Nearly two million kronor and eighty-one shots fired twenty-two hours ago. In roughly the same geographical area and with the same kind of weapons. The *same* group appears suddenly, then vanishes without a trace.'

There was music coming from downstairs, Christmas carols.

'And if we assume they won't need more time to prepare for a third robbery. Weeks? Maybe a month or so? Then that's how long we have to find out who these people are. So we can arrest them at home or on their way to work or at the gym or when they're leaving the store with shopping bags in their hands. Not when they make a mistake at the next robbery. Because with this pattern of behaviour, they won't hesitate to turn their weapons on us.'

'Pappa?'

A small hand opened the door, and the little girl dressed as Lucia came into the room.

'Yes?'

'What are you doing?'

'Working.'

'Working with what?'

'Someone's done . . . something naughty.'

'What have they done?'

'Grown-up naughty.'

'What's that?'

'Go downstairs now. To Mummy. I'll be down soon.'

Children. Family. Another world. Broncks wasn't sure, but it looked as if Lucia winked at him as she went.

'I sat down this morning with a man who's been robbed of his humanity. I don't want to do that again.'

He looked at Karlström.

'Forty years old. And he can't even stand up on his own. His father has to hold him up.'

And then at that beautiful desk. And out the other window, at the diametrical opposite of the decisions his boss faced every day – plastic gnomes draped with Christmas lights.

'The same group?'

'The same group.'

'And how can—'

'I was already sure. Now I have an identification.'

Karlström never sighed, he wasn't the type.

'As of tomorrow, John. Put all your other investigations aside. And investigate this until we stop them from robbing any more banks.'

Broncks nodded and walked towards the door and the stairs, already on his way.

'I said *tomorrow*.'

His boss knew him. John Broncks would head directly to Kronoberg and the department and spend the evening there.

'Now I've heard you out, and you'll get your investigation full time. On one condition. *You* have to do something for *me*.'

'Yeah?'

'Stay for dinner. Can you smell how good that smells, John? Thyme. Celery. Shallots. And good red wine.'

Later Broncks sat at one end of the dining table with his boss, an elf, St Lucia, and the boss's wife who he'd never met, but who was the kind of socially confident person who knew everyone's name at the party within a few minutes and made everyone feel important. It hadn't worked on him. He felt so uneasy sitting there pretending to be part of the family that it was hard to eat, or listen to the story of the St Lucia celebration at nursery, or even to answer how long he'd been acquainted with the two girls' father. He had declined Karlström's offer of a brandy and felt relieved as he said his thanks and started to open the front door.

'John?'

Karlström put a hand on Broncks's arm. And Broncks didn't like it.

'You stay late every evening.'

'Yes.'

'Searching and searching.'

'Yes.'

'And all your investigations revolve around extreme violence.'

'That's the way the world works.'

'When I finish *my* day I shut the folders on whatever investigation I'm working on and put them in my desk drawer, and I decide the next day if I want to pick them up again. But you open them right before you go, lay out the pictures of broken bones and black eyes. And read. For hours.'

'That's the way the world works.'

The hand on his arm felt as if it was weighing him down, pinning him in place.

'You're not reading those cases in order to solve them. Are you?'

'I don't know what you're talking about.'

'You want to get closer. To *him*.'

'Thank you for dinner. It was nice.'

Broncks turned the doorknob he'd been holding for so long and opened the front door. But the hand remained on his shoulder.

'I haven't finished.'

Karlström held on tight.

'John, you don't care about the people in those folders. What their names are, where they're going. You're just trying . . . to understand.'

A door held open between warmth and cold. The kind of cold that crept inside your jacket and the warmth of family.

'But you're never going to succeed. Or understand. If you don't go and see him. Someday. Right, John? Maybe you should do it now, with just a couple of weeks' head start. Go there.'

He shook Karlström's hand from his arm. It felt wrong. Karlström was his boss, not his fucking pal. He shook it loose.

'That's enough.'

Broncks stepped outside. It was snowing more heavily now.

Go there.

He knew his boss was right.

37

THE SNOW CRUNCHED beneath his tyres as Leo drove into the middle of some gloomy woods and parked a few kilometres into the Nacka Reserve, one of Sweden's largest national forests, where a wide track narrowed to a path. He unbuttoned the flatbed cover and carried the five heavy boxes to a rocky hill that sloped down towards a deserted shoreline.

In the shadowy illumination of his headlights, he threw each box onto the ice. A hole opened where each one sank, holes that would soon freeze over again – healing the membrane above a heap of sawn-up weapons encased in cement. In the spring, algae would grow over the hard surface of the boxes, and they'd become indistinguishable from the rest of the sea bed. Turning green like the glass of the aquarium that had stood between his bed and Felix's, and which they'd never cleaned.

Then he kicked a hole into the deep snow, tore up the earth and moss with a collapsible shovel, placing Jasper's boots in it. He doused them with lighter fluid and lit them. Shiny leather and solid rubber soles melted while black wisps of smoke stung his nose and eyes.

Not even Felix or Vincent knew where he was dumping these things. They'd never have to sit there and run the risk of being called snitches.

Not like he'd sat there with a fat cop in front of him demanding answers over and over again.

I didn't betray you. I didn't save myself. I saved you.

Through the park and then the city, steaming in the cold, and there they were, waiting for him in the middle of the yard as he drove through the gate. He'd called Felix and told him to meet him at home.

'What's so damned important?'

Leo could hear the alcohol in Felix's words; he'd always known how much had been drained.

'Let's discuss this in the garage.'

A taxi was standing some way off, the engine running.

'You're paying, brother. And it'll be more expensive if we go inside. We're going back to the bar.'

'Go inside.'

Leo knocked on the taxi driver's window and handed him two 500-kronor notes. The window wasn't even rolled up again before the driver turned his 'for hire' light on and the car disappeared.

'You can call a new one when we're finished.'

The garage was dark and cold. Leo lit the lamp, turned on the heater. Vincent followed him inside, while Felix made a point of staying outside. Until Leo unfurled a detailed map of Stockholm and its southern suburbs, *then* he decided to come in. Using a red marker, he circled an area at one end of the map, near a main road and not far from the open sea.

'Here.'

'Here, what?'

'Ösmo in about twenty days.'

'Are you serious?'

'Nobody's ever robbed two banks at the same time.'

'But, damn it, we already know that! Is this why we had to leave our window table and sit in a fucking taxi for forty-five minutes?'

'Felix, listen to me.'

'You listen to me! It's Lucia, we were sitting in a pub, eating dinner, having a beer . . . and now here I am, in a freezing cold garage? It's fucking Christmas soon! We have to have a few days off!'

'You can celebrate next year.'

Leo straightened the map.

'Nobody's ever robbed two banks simultaneously. So we're going to rob three.'

He drew a red line from the ring around the little town of Ösmo, west along Highway 225, and to a new ring around an even smaller town called Sorunda.

'On our way home. We'll pass through here. A small bank, completely unprotected.'

Felix looked first at his smiling big brother then at the map marked with red ink.

'Have I been drinking or have you?'

He snatched the pen from Leo's hand and drew a new, larger circle.

'There are no fucking escape routes from there. Right? And you think we should give them our position, one more time? Let them surround us?'

Leo grabbed the pen from Felix's hand, drew a cross outside the map – directly onto the wooden surface of the workbench.

'Not if they don't have any cops to surround us with.'

He looked at them and then pointed to the cross outside the map.

'That . . . is Central Station. The middle of Stockholm. Forty-nine kilometres away. And they'll have their hands full . . . defusing a bomb.'

38

A FLAT LANDSCAPE. White as chalk. It had been dark when he left Stockholm, but now it was bright, sun bouncing off the snow, blinding him as he drove the 220 kilometres to the Kumla Maximum Security Prison.

He could still feel his boss's hand on his arm. He knew he wasn't doing this because of Karlström, and yet, he was just as sure that Karlström was right.

Just like Sanna had been right.

They'd used all their contacts with any connection to the criminal underworld. No results. But there was one contact left – one that was his alone.

The grey wall, seven metres of concrete and barbed wire, loomed in the distance beyond the fields. It had been a few years since the last time he'd been here, but he had the same feeling as he got closer – were there really people inside, walking around and thinking and sleeping and eating and longing away huge chunks of their lives?

He parked near the gate, got out and rang the bell.

'John Broncks, City Police.'

The crackling speaker on the door did not work.

'John Broncks, City—'

'I heard you the first time.'

'To visit Sam Larsen.'

'You don't have an appointment.'

'I'm making one right now.'

'Six hours. Even for police officers.'

'This is not a visit. This is a criminal investigation.'

The click of the door unlocking and then a short walk to the guard post where a uniformed man sat surrounded by institutional Christmas decorations – a plastic star in one window and an ugly straw goat sitting on one of the monitors that transmitted images from fifty-eight surveillance cameras.

He showed his ID and received a visitor's badge; he was supposed to wear it on his chest, but put it inside his pocket. A guard escorted him to the visiting area and left him alone in a room with a conjugal bed covered by rough protective plastic, a simple table with two equally simple chairs, a sink with a dripping tap, and a view through the barred window of the wall outside. Here there was no Christmas, no holiday season for those who didn't have the luxury of counting out time.

Fifteen minutes later, the door opened and two prison officers came in with a figure, then exited, closing the door after them. They left the man they'd brought with them behind. He was two years, three months and five days older than John Broncks. And a couple of centimetres taller. And, nowadays, thirty kilos heavier. They'd been the same size, but eighteen years of lifting weights daily, a structure when all other structure was lacking, had changed that.

'Hello,' said Broncks.

They looked at each other. One in jeans, a jacket and winter boots. One in baggy trousers made from fabric that was simultaneously stiff and loose, a worn T-shirt with a prison logo on the chest, and slippers on his bare feet.

'I said . . . hello.'

Broncks sat down at the rickety table. Sam went over to the barred window and looked out.

'How are you?' Broncks tried again.

He'd visited occasionally in the beginning, those first few years the life sentence was being served, first at the Hall Prison and then at Tidaholm. That was before he understood that not being able to think in terms of time was the same as not being able to hope, not having a future. And when Broncks finally understood that this kind of life changes a person, he visited less frequently, and eventually not at all. And he'd probably never even been in this particular visiting room before.

'Listen . . . next time you come here, make a fucking appointment,' said Sam. 'Just like everybody else. Just like people who aren't cops. Next time I don't want any questions when I get back to my kitchen section about where I've been. You should know that as well as anyone – a visit from a cop without any explanation is about the worst thing that can happen to you in here!'

Sam was still standing by the barred window, his back to Broncks.

'I asked you how you were.'

'How I am?'

'Yes.'

'When the hell did you become interested in that?'

He turned his broad back around and looked at Broncks.

'And since you can't answer me – what the hell are you doing here, anyway?'

John Broncks pulled out the second chair from the table. It was going better than he'd hoped. They were talking.

'Two big robberies. Svedmyra. Farsta. By the same guys.'

But his big brother chose to remain standing.

'Mamma was here last week.'

'Heavily armed. Very well planned.'

'I offered her marble cake. Do you remember what that tastes like, John?'

'Do you think it could be someone you've done time with? It's surely—'

'And the time before that . . . muffins.'

'—being talked about in here, right?'

Sam leaned over the table, furious.

'You haven't been here for three fucking years! But you come here and think that I'm about to give you information! That you can use me in your fucking investigation!'

Sam was shaking as he walked over to the metal disc attached to the door, reaching for the red button.

'Fuck you, John!'

'Sam, you know I want to see you, too. You're my brother.'

'Even if I did know something, I sure as hell wouldn't say anything to you! But I don't. No one knows! No one in here has ever heard of them! Are you with me, bro? These guys are completely unknown. They've never done time. And they still know exactly what they're doing.'

Sam stared at him with eyes John couldn't reach, his finger on the red button again. He pushed it in and leaned toward the microphone.

'This visit is over.'

'You have more than half an hour left.'

'What part of *over* do you not understand? I want to go back to my section.'

They avoided looking at each other just as they had when they'd fought as children, when they would have done anything to see over and around each other.

'So Mamma visited?'

Marble cake. Muffins. Prisoners serving long sentences and who were considered a security threat always baked before a visit. Broncks smiled weakly.

'Do you know, Sam, that you have more contact with her than I do?'

Steps outside the door, then it was opened by the prison officers. Sam had already started to leave, one of them in front of him and one behind, when he turned round.

'You should see her. She's getting old.'

John Broncks watched his older brother disappear down the prison corridor, his broad back between a pair of scrawny men in uniforms, returned his visitor's badge, passed the central guard post and walked through the gate in the wall, then sat motionless in his car.

Seven-metre-high walls. Four hundred and sixty-three of Sweden's most violent criminals serving long sentences. One had been elected spokesperson for all of them, one of the few whom everyone spoke to.

His own brother.

And even Sam hadn't heard anything. The men Broncks was searching for were just as anonymous inside those walls.

He started the car and drove away. The sunlight still glistened on the snow.

39

STREETS THAT WERE white and clean outside the walls of the prison turned muddy and dirty 220 kilometres later as the E4 motorway to Stockholm became the Essinge Highway and then the garage entrance in the rock beneath the police headquarters at Kronoberg Park.

He was heading for the lift when he heard a sound from the little garage inside the garage, where the forensic technicians kept the vehicles they were working on. He walked over and went inside, and there was Sanna, just like last time. She lay halfway inside a van with HEATING SOLUTIONS written on both sides, an infrared lamp in her hand.

'First getaway car. A Dodge van.'

Sanna crawled out and went over to the next vehicle, switched to a lamp with ultraviolet light.

'Second getaway car. A Dodge van.'

The same mechanical voice. He wondered if she was aware of it, or if her voice was only like that when she talked to him.

'An older model. Stolen the night before the robbery.'

She held up an elongated tool, metal protruding from a wooden handle – aimed it at a small, black, square sticker sitting on the van door just below the side window.

'It's just as fast as using a key.'

She was done. Broncks recognised her way of turning her back when she didn't want to talk. She opened the computer that was on the bonnet of the car. Not even a goodbye. He said it, *bye*, but she didn't hear, and he was on his way out, halfway to the lift, when she called after him.

'John? I hadn't finished.'

He stopped, turned around.

'You hadn't?'

'One more thing.'

She turned the screen towards him, waited for him to come closer.

'This picture. I want you to look at it again.'

CAMERA 2. Twelve seconds in. From above. Robbers in blue jumpsuits, black boots, black masks.

'His microphone. I was trying to find out what make it was, so I enlarged it and concentrated on the collar, seconds before they went inside.'

She rewound, froze the picture.

'Four seconds in – fifteen frames per second. I want you to look at each one.'

Her voice wasn't so mechanical. She was standing closer to him. And he knew exactly how she smelled. How strange. As if it were another time. As if they could walk away from here together to the apartment they shared. As if ten years had never gone by.

'There.'

The first bank robber had only one step left to the door.

Then he stopped.

'His hand.'

She enlarged the image.

'Do you see?'

John nodded. He saw it clearly.

The one going in first, leading, stopped and turned round, lowering his weapon and putting his left hand over his collar, where the microphone was, covering it with his palm. He leaned forward and moved the other robber's headphones with his right hand.

'The movement . . . *there*.'

The hand over the microphone. The hand on the headphones. And then, Broncks was sure of it, he . . . whispered.

'It doesn't make sense,' said Sanna.

She zoomed in on the mouth and its thin lips, two light streaks in dark fabric as they formed words.

'The hand. The whispering. It doesn't make sense.'

Sanna, standing close, looked at John – just as the leader in the frozen film frame was standing close to his partner.

'Intimacy. As if he's putting his hand over his microphone, then raising the headphones almost lovingly. Do you see? Just before he's about to start firing live rounds.'

After two months of round-the-clock police investigation, he had no clues, knew nothing about them. But this. John Broncks could see and feel it. He *knew* something now. He wasn't exactly sure what, but for the first time in his search for shadows, he saw real people. And they were standing close to each other in a way that two violent bank robbers shouldn't.

Something he almost recognised.

'Can you return the picture to its original size? And play the same sequence again? The first four seconds?'

She did so.

'Stop . . . there. And enlarge . . . there. His face. Just that.'

Three robbers in a row on their way into a bank and Broncks's index finger on the screen. Pointing to the one in the middle.

'Do you see? He closes his eyes.'

Cursor on the timeline, she moved it manually, frame by frame.

'He hesitates. He's worried.'

The eyes in the mask remained closed.

'He's scared and that was . . . like a damn hug! The leader who's holding his microphone, he's being protective – they belong together.'

40

JOHN BRONCKS AVOIDED the lift. Sometimes he needed to keep moving, force his heart to beat faster, to squeeze every breath through his chest and into his throat.

He practically ran up the stairs.

And then into his office – he threw the windows wide open, let the damp chill from the inner courtyard of the police station hit the dry heat inside.

They'd looked so intimate. Bank robbers shouldn't look like that. The leader should have been in command – but the other robber's hesitation had been more important.

Something Broncks recognised.

One who was taller and one who was a little shorter. One who was broader across the shoulders and one who hadn't finished growing. One who was older and one who was younger.

Intimacy. Trust.

That was what Broncks recognised. The bond between them. Someone who had always been close by, who'd held him in the evening, who'd said everything would be all right, and then later that night had crept into their parents' bedroom and put a knife between their father's ribs. A big brother who'd held him and whispered to him and calmed him down, right before an act of violence.

A few deep breaths at the open window. John Broncks knew now.

For the first time since the beginning of this investigation, he actually knew something, and they were no longer completely faceless, there was an outline.

Intimacy. Trust.

They were brothers.

41

LEO STOOD AT the window, which was carefully decorated for Christmas, watching a grey, misty dawn. The weather had turned in the last few weeks. The snow was melting by Christmas Eve, and Christmas morning arrived with steady rain, the ground turning into a dirty mix of ice, snow, gravel and dirt. Leo had been hoping for this – a grey Christmas and snow-free roads. He hoped that it would continue – if the surface were dry it would simplify the getaway after the bank robbery.

Two plants on the windowsill, and between them a porcelain angel – most of the white paint on one side flaked off and only one eye – which had come from Anneli's childhood home, and now for a few weeks every year appeared in her kitchen next to the poinsettia. Things had popped up everywhere. One oversized plastic Santa by the fridge, another Santa almost as large under the hat rack in the hallway, a few smaller ones on the stairs to the second floor, and one under the Christmas tree in the living room. Things she'd brought into his life, that meant something to her. He could see her joy, her anticipation, as she chose where things went, rearranged them until she found the right place.

A porcelain angel with worn edges and a shitload of plastic Santas, thought Leo. It was just a date. Worth as much as the 25th of November or the 25th of October. Maybe she just needed something to hold on to as time slipped by: New Year's Eve, Easter, Midsummer, all just dates.

Someone else had made that decision, had used the calendar as a tool to control people's lives. What mattered was what you yourself decided and carried out. Creating your own calendar – 2 January, when the first triple robbery in Swedish history would take place, or 17 February, 11 March, 16 April, the other dates he'd chosen for robberies, and which therefore meant something.

He lifted up the porcelain angel, turned it round, tried to read the stamp on the bottom, put it down again.

Expectations.

Just as fragile, he'd had to find a way to gently lower hers, explaining that this Christmas wasn't really Christmas, that they'd celebrate properly next year when all this was finished, just like their neighbours on the other side of the fence, who she liked to watch through the kitchen window, joining them from a distance. She'd gone to the window several times on Christmas Eve. They'd eaten ham and cabbage and meatballs and Jansson's Temptation, and he'd given her the Christmas present meant for her son who she was going to visit straight after the holidays. They'd even lit candles, and watched a few hours of Donald Duck and Karl-Bertil Jonsson's Christmas Eve programme, like everyone else in Sweden, until he couldn't take any more and went down into the Skull Cave to continue working on his own calendar.

Plastic bag in hand, and carrying a tray of food, he walked out into the damp morning darkness. His thin shoes were soaked through by the mix of snow and rain on the asphalt. The garage was the opposite: dry and warmed by the pleasantly buzzing convection heater, well-lit by intense lamps. Vincent, Felix and Jasper were already waiting for him on wooden stools around a table of hardboard and two sawhorses. The map was open on top of it.

'Coffee and sandwiches,' said Leo, passing the tray around.

––––––––––

Right across the map ran a red, almost straight line. Starting in the neighbourhood of Kronoberg in central Stockholm, where the majority of Swedish police operations were based, and ending nearly fifty kilometres away in Ösmo Square where there were two banks sharing one wall. A line that cut through Stockholm and the towns of Huddinge and Haninge and Nynäshamn, and was the key to diverting the police and disappearing from the scene of the crime.

'Target One.'

A 10-kronor coin in the palm of Leo's hand. He placed it on one of the grey squares near the end of the red line, which indicated areas of dense population.

'Target Two.'

Another 10-kronor coin. On top of the first.

'And here.'

Just outside the window of both targets. The getaway car.

A toy car just as red as the line.

'That's you, Felix.'

There was much more where that came from. A cardboard box they all recognised. Three plastic, olive green soldiers that had once stood on the floor of their childhood apartment in Skogås. A few centimetres high, and they smelled just like they had then.

'This is Vincent. And Jasper. And there . . . here I come.'

He separated the gold coins, put the final plastic figurine on one of them.

'Target One – Leo opens the door. Target Two – Jasper and Vincent open the door. At two fifty p.m.'

Now, the Dinky car. A red Volkswagen model 1300, the Beetle, which they still kept in its original packaging, they'd never been able to throw it away, and which Leo had shoplifted for Felix at Toys & Hobbies in the Skogås shopping centre.

'And Felix takes care of the car. Just like in Svedmyra.'

Another larger box of plastic figurines, but these were brown with rounder helmets than the Americans and had different weapons.

'Russian soldiers.'

He dumped a whole handful of plastic soldiers onto the red line and lined them up there, and then put a few at the other three locations further away.

'Cops. Every single one. Most of them work here . . . at City Police HQ. Then a few here, the Huddinge police, and here, the Handen police. And the fewest here . . . the Nacka police.'

He made sure they all stood in the right place. And then he moved his arms around them, a giant capturing and slowly pulling them towards the point where the roads, railway tracks and Tunnelbana lines met – the well-connected, grey area that represented central Stockholm.

'And they'll all go there, together, to Central Station.'

He looked at Jasper, nodded.

'Because we'll have planted a bomb there – a real bomb in a locker.'

Vincent had been silent up to this point, as he usually was. Now he slammed his coffee cup down on the hardboard table and the soldiers who hadn't yet fallen, toppled over.

'Vincent, what the hell . . .'

'Are we terrorists now?'

'It's not going to explode. But they need to know it's real.'

Leo collected the pile of soldiers around Stockholm's Central Station.

'Our first diversion will be to close down Central Station. And while the cops gather there, busy defusing a real bomb, we'll be robbing two banks fifty kilometres away.'

It didn't help. Vincent moved half of the soldiers towards Old Town and the other half towards Kronoberg.

'And then what? What do we threaten to bomb next? The castle? Police headquarters? Or something bigger?'

A little annoyed, and a little proud, Leo smiled at Vincent, while patiently moving the soldiers back to the area around Central Station.

'Our second diversion – two red cars.'

The Volkswagen Beetle that for so long had lived by itself on the shelf above Felix's bed. Leo grabbed it with his thumb and forefinger and moved it across the map – from the banks onto the minor roads that led through the countryside.

'We're going to use a car that everyone recognises. And one that whatever cops are left south of the city will find . . . here.'

He moved the toy car from the road they would actually drive on to a larger road that lay on the other side of the banks, the motorway to Stockholm, which they wouldn't use.

'It will stand here. And the cops will therefore block the road. They'll think we've gone down that road.'

'I don't understand,' said Vincent.

'Vincent, it—'

'I don't understand how you could have sat there in that car, given me a bunch of books, and told me that we were going to rob banks.'

'And?'

'Building a bomb is not robbing banks.'

'*If* we build a bomb, and *if* we use it, it *won't* explode. OK?'

Vincent didn't move any more soldiers. But he also didn't look away.

'I don't understand.'

'Vincent, can't you—'

'I don't get why we're building a fucking bomb. Then painting ourselves into a corner – leaving the first getaway car, which everyone recognises, on the main road – where it's completely visible!'

'That's exactly what they should believe. But we'll be here, Vincent, we're on one of the minor roads, on our way to rob a third bank.'

A third 10-kronor coin on the map, along the minor roads and on to the even smaller town of Sorunda.

'I still don't understand.'

A tiny bit proud as he produced another car out of the bag.

'Do you know how long it took for me to find this? I went to every toyshop in the city – then I saw it in the window of an antique shop on Ring Street.'

An exact replica of the getaway car – a red Volkswagen Beetle model 1300 – and he set it down next to the new 10-kronor coin.

'We'll be in this car on the minor roads.'

Then he pointed to the other side of the map.

'And at the same time, the same car will be here, on the main road, surrounded by roadblocks.'

Leo looked at Vincent who had no more protests, not this morning.

'Magic, fellas. Four days left.'

———

Felix's shoulder bumped into the door every time he turned the wheel of the Beetle. And even though he'd moved the seat as far back as possible, his knees hit the dashboard when he changed gear.

It didn't have much in the way of horsepower and wasn't very easy to drive. But that wasn't why they'd chosen this car – it was because everyone who saw it would recognise it, and they'd easily be able to identify it later.

He waited for the garage door to roll up and then drove in, the headlights beaming towards the workbench and the map. Jasper, Vincent and Leo sat further inside the room at the other workbench, opening four cardboard boxes and four soft packages wrapped in thin plastic.

And now Jasper stood up and approached the car.

'A . . . fucking Beetle? Felix, those were just toy cars – you didn't actually think Leo was fucking serious?'

'Well done, Jasper,' said Felix.

'How the hell can we—'

'You don't know shit about cars, but you recognise it and you can name it. Just like everyone in Ösmo Square.'

Leo, a box in one hand and some plastic wrapping in the other, left the workbench and placed himself directly between Jasper and Felix, in the crack that had opened a few weeks ago and could not be allowed to get any bigger.

'But I'm riding shotgun. Right?'

Leo tapped lightly on the red metal roof.

'We need two that are identical. Make, model, colour. We'll start here in the south, and split up. If we can't find the other one here, we'll do what we did last time, and hit the northern half of the city. Three days left.'

———

It was basically a simple device. Purely mechanical. A long, narrow metal box half-filled with nails and screws and bolts and m/46 plastic explosive. The fuse was connected to a spring percussion detonator, which lay against one of the short sides of the metal box. When the short side is opened the percussion detonator releases the fuse and the contents of the metal box explode, killing every living creature in the immediate vicinity. A simple chain reaction.

Leo was sitting on the garage workbench, a red steel wire in his hand. He cut off exactly ten centimetres. Felix switched from the wood to the metal drill, the little hole should sit in the middle of the uppermost side of the box, a cover that hid the nails and explosives.

There was a knock on the garage door.

Leo opened it to Vincent, cold, clear air and a muffled bang in the distance.

'Eleven forty. You're late.'

'It was hell getting a taxi.'

Leo closed and locked the door and hugged his little brother, took a step back and whistled loudly – Vincent, who was wearing a dark suit and white shirt open at the neck under his jacket.

'Damn it, you almost look grown up.'

'Two thousand kronor. Bought it today.'

Vincent was holding a bag in his hand; he handed it to Leo and continued into the garage.

'Is that . . . the bomb?'

Leo emptied and folded the bag. Two bottles of Bollinger. There was just enough room for them on the workbench next to three champagne glasses.

'Yes.'

'OK. Then I guess that's what we are. *Terrorists.*'

Vincent stared at the grey-black box, could hear Felix pulling duct tape off a roll.

'Our mother could be the one who puts her purse in the fucking locker next to this!'

'I thought we were done talking about it.'

'You were, Leo. Not me.'

'We're *not* putting it there to kill someone. We're putting it there so they have to take it seriously. If we put a fake in there, they'll see through it.'

'But what if . . . if it explodes accidentally?'

Leo leaned closer and smelled alcohol on his brother's breath.

'Vincent? You weren't waiting for a fucking cab.'

And he sniffed several times, to prove the point.

'You were at home drinking.'

Leo tried to catch his little brother's eye, but couldn't, his eyes were on the box with a red wire sticking out of a hole drilled into its lid.

'Vincent? If you've got something to say to me, just say it. We're brothers! You don't need to get drunk before talking to me.'

'I've already said it. It doesn't feel right.'

'What do you mean "not right"?'

'It doesn't feel good. And if it feels like this again . . . I'm not doing it.'

'Vincent, listen to me.'

Leo angled up the lid, revealing several layers of nails, screws and plastic explosives.

'If this is secured . . .'

His index finger over the black tubular percussion detonator.

'. . . it *won't* explode.'

Then into the red wire loop on the other end of the igniter.

'But *if* I were to pull just a little bit more on this . . .'

He did so, looking at Vincent as he watched the wire.

'. . . then it would only take a movement of a hair – and that'd be it for us. But *only* if I pull the safety ring.'

He gently took his finger out again.

'Nobody gets hurt, Vincent. No one will die. Not even the lady who stores her bag in the locker next to it.'

Felix put a strip of duct tape over the lid to keep it on tight, then tore off another one and put that on too, just to be sure. He'd stood between his two brothers, listening without taking sides. He recognised this, even though it had never happened before. It was the first time Vincent had protested in the same way he himself usually protested. And it had ended as it usually did. The big brother he knew so well couldn't be persuaded; he could convince everyone else with his energy. So if anyone were to ever change course, it had to be the younger brothers.

'Then we're agreed. Right?'

Vincent nodded slightly.

'Good. Because it's ten minutes to midnight. Time to open these up.'

He folded his jacket, grabbed the glasses and bottles and started towards the garage door.

'One more thing,' said Felix, leaning over the workbench towards Vincent. 'I mean, since we have our little brother here. Who opened the door?'

Vincent didn't understand.

'That time . . . when Pappa turned up.'

'For fuck's sake, Felix – are you still stuck on that?' said Leo. 'It's eleven fifty-two. We're leaving now.'

Felix shook his head.

'No. We *are* going to discuss this. Vincent – who was it that opened the door when the old man came to our house and tried to kill Mamma?'

'What are you two talking about?'

'When Pappa got out of prison. After we'd moved to Falun. He drove out there.'

'Felix, damn it, he was . . . six years old. Is he a witness now?'

Vincent became very quiet.

'Seven. I was seven. When he tried to kill Mamma.'

Felix did what Leo usually did, and put his hands on Vincent's shoulders.

'Forget that we're your big brothers. Tell me what you saw. Did I open the door – or did Leo?'

Leo waved the champagne bottle towards his watch.

'Exactly. Tell us what you remember. Then Felix will be satisfied, and we can go out.'

He stood there. Felix with his hand on the door handle. Leo on his way.

'Come on! Vincent – what did you see? Was it me or was it Leo?'

He jumped. And couldn't reach. But almost.

'It was me.'

And then, he did it, reached, twisted.

'I opened the door.'

Leo laughed, not loudly, not from joy.

'That was a diplomatic answer.'

Felix didn't even laugh.

'It was *me*,' Vincent repeated. 'I remember it. I turned the lock and pushed down the handle and opened the door.'

Felix became flushed. He tried to understand how all three of them could have stood next to each other at that door, all three later believing that they had opened it.

'And where the hell was I? Wasn't I there? Leo jumped on his back and you opened the door and I . . . I sat on a chair in the kitchen, perhaps? On the toilet? Maybe I didn't even exist . . . maybe you two were the ones who spat in Mamma's face too? Were you? Which one of you was it then?'

'What's the fucking difference?' said Leo.

'It fucking matters. To me.'

The large garage, completely quiet. Outside, the sound of fireworks and firecrackers increased in intensity.

'You *were* the one. Who spat. But it . . . it was something else.'

Leo nodded to Felix.

'And it really doesn't matter any more.'

Three champagne glasses in Leo's hand and thirty seconds until midnight. He rolled open the garage door towards the tapestry of a night sky filled with shooting stars. He pulled off the gold foil from the neck of the bottle and pushed up the cork, which flew away and landed somewhere.

'Cheers.'

Bubbles in glasses in three hands.

'Cheers to Getryggen, to Farsta, to Svedmyra.'

He raised his glass to the sky, which burst with colour, fireworks blooming then disappearing.

'And cheers to next year – to Ösmo. In two days.'

42

NAILS, SCREWS, NUTS, plastic explosive pulled through his forearm to his shoulder, his hand gripping the suitcase handle. He walked at normal speed past people eating hot dogs, reading the evening paper, drinking coffee from paper cups, glancing up frequently at the electronic information board that covered an entire wall above the main exit. The bag was nylon and weighed about ten kilos; he wore it fairly high to make it appear lighter, as if it contained clothes and maybe a small toiletry bag, the kind a traveller would carry across the marble floor of Central Station.

A train station in a capital city is its own nation, has its own language; it's a place that both separates and brings people together. His job was to blend in, to look as if he was on his way either to or from Stockholm. A traveller in a black knitted cap and a winter coat, just like every other winter coat.

But there was no one like him. A shadow with only one purpose.

Find and open a storage locker. Deposit one bag. Lock it. Leave.

The short-stay car park under the bridge, opposite the Sheraton Hotel, was the only place close to Central Station that Leo knew for sure was outside the range of its roof-mounted cameras. He'd seen Jasper disappear through the main entrance a couple of minutes ago, melting into a sea of bobbing heads. He sat in the driver's seat of the company car with the engine idling. When Jasper came out again, they'd pick up Felix and Vincent at the abandoned petrol station, then continue south to Ösmo.

His mobile rang. It shouldn't have. Only six people had the number to this unregistered phone. Jasper who was inside the station, and knew very well that he shouldn't call. Felix and Vincent who were waiting for him, and knew they shouldn't call. Anneli at their home in Tumba, who also knew she shouldn't call; Mamma who was always asleep at this time of day since she worked nights.

'Don't hang up this time.'

And . . . Pappa.

'I *need* to talk to you.'

'I told you I didn't have time. I don't have time now either.'

Leo heard him breathing through his nose, as if the air itself were blocking important words.

'The envelope. I don't want to fight about the fucking money, but I started thinking . . .'

Heavy traffic on Vasa Street. A flock of pigeons on the roof of Central Station. A group of Japanese tourists with cameras and name tags outside the Sheraton. But no Jasper yet.

'If you can give me that much money, even though you don't think I'm owed it, that must mean you have even *more* money. Where did it come from? I work in construction too, and way off the fucking books, but I'm not paid that much. If you have that much money, Leo . . . then you got it some other way.'

'You don't know shit about my work.'

'No. I don't know.'

'And I've had enough of this. I'm not talking to you about it.'

'You have a company you run with your brothers . . . my *other* sons, Leo! That means your brothers are involved. You're responsible for them. If you're doing something illegal – it's your responsibility, Leo!'

That fucking breathing again, close to the phone, as if the old man was looking around to make sure no one was listening.

'If you have a problem, Leo . . .'

'Responsible?'

'If you have a problem, Leo . . . you know you can always talk to me, I've helped you before.'

'I don't have a problem.'

'You know, I've been alive twenty-seven years longer than you, Leo.'

'Didn't you hear what I said?'

'So I have a little more experience, Leo. I see things you don't see.'

'You?'

'Yeah?'

'You— *Pappa*?'

Inhalation through the nose – his father was waiting.

'I take responsibility,' said Leo. 'They depend on me. That's how it works – if you take responsibility, people trust you. Twenty-seven years? What the hell is that? Time! But if you don't do anything with it, that's all it is . . . time. Stop worrying about Vincent and Felix. They're doing just fine with the *snitch*.'

He searched the crowd outside Central Station's main entrance.

'And I will never fucking ask for your help.'

The storage locker had to be in the middle of the arrivals hall and at chest height, so the police would immediately have to evacuate the entire station, and so their bomb robot would have easy access. The woman to Jasper's right closed the locker door, turned her key, and a coin fell into the metal tray. She was already on her way, but Jasper averted his face just in case as he opened number 326. Her heels clacked along the marble floor, and she was far away by the time he gently pushed the bag inside. He looked at all the people around him, none of them looking at him. Not even the people in uniform with their knapsacks over their shoulders, passing just a few metres behind him, their dark green berets shining. He was suddenly unable to close the door, his arm went numb and his heart started beating so damn hard. Three golden prongs that gleamed at him in a row – one for Courage, one for Power, one for Strength. Commandos. Five men with buzz-cuts on their way to a northbound train.

They're walking past me. Their shaved heads, their eyes, all so fucking self-assured. They don't see me. But I see them.

I was one of you.

The bag was in, but the zip wasn't completely closed, it was stuck with a small gap at the far end. Jasper grabbed the chain and was about to tug it back when he saw the red wire loop shining inside those nylon walls, the safety ring.

Those slanted berets were behind him. Sitting so perfectly on those heads.

And then he felt it. Loathing.

Loathing in the face of men who had no idea that there were other groups that could invite you in, who made plans, carried out attacks, blew things up and fired weapons, just as precisely – and who, moreover, were true friends, brothers. Loathing of those who had no idea why he stood there.

I'm no longer one of you.

Finger through the opening in the zip and through the wire loop.

The safety ring.

229

If I pull this out. Then move the metal box inside this bag just a hair.

The crewcuts had disappeared into the crowd, becoming just like everyone else, looking just like everyone else on their way somewhere.

I'm so much more than you.

Seven minutes. Jasper should have finished by now.

The mobile phone was still in Leo's hand. Not a single phone call from *him* in years. And then twice in just a few weeks. The voice pecking against his skull, tugging at his brain, trying to get inside with a key that no longer existed.

I should never have gone there.

I should never have handed over forty-three thousand, shouldn't have shown him the car or told him about the company.

I should never have opened the door to our lives.

Now. There. Black knitted cap, long firm strides emerging from the main entrance to Central Station – Jasper without the bag. He was smiling – Leo recognised it from every incident that was like the nightstick and the broken wrist.

'You took your time,' Leo said as Jasper climbed in.

'I wanted to be sure that . . . no one saw me.'

Leo pulled away, and as they drove down Vasa Street towards the bridge, the people outside the station turned into a mass of small grey dots in the rear-view mirror.

'Leo?'

'Yeah?'

'Thanks. For trusting me.'

Across the bridge, Parliament on their left, then Old Town, and on towards Slussen, into the tunnel underneath Södermalm.

'Three minutes. OK?' said Leo.

'Three minutes.'

'Felix outside in the car. Just me at Target One. You and Vincent at Target Two.'

The taxi right in front of them slowed suddenly, as if it didn't know where it was going. Leo, who'd been driving too close, hit the brakes and switched to the outer lane next to Skanstulls Bridge.

'Nothing is allowed happen to my little brother – do you understand that? *Nothing.*'

43

JASPER WAITED IN a telephone box in Gullmars Square, the cold receiver pressed against his ear.

'This is the police.'

'You listening?'

'I'm lis—'

'At the following location – the arrivals hall of Central Station, locker number 326 – there is a bomb.'

Jasper could hear other officers in the background at the emergency call centre.

'I repeat. In the arrivals hall at Central Station. In a locker. With the following number . . .'

His voice was disguised without sounding made up, serious, a somewhat intimidating drawl. A voice he liked. It resembled Leo's, controlled and clear – screaming wasn't so frightening. Leo rarely raised his voice, but when he did everyone noticed because you didn't know what might happen.

'. . . three . . . two . . . six. 326. The bomb will detonate at fifteen hundred hours. This is *not* negotiable.'

He hung up and left the phone box.

Slightly hunched over, hands deep in the pockets of his jacket, he walked across the square towards the building with the 7-Eleven store and the waiting car. The engine was running, and Leo had the police scanner on his lap.

'The alarm's gone out several times. Bomb threat at Central Station. They're already on their way.'

They were careful not to drive south either too fast or too slow. Soon they met the first police car. Then another, and then three more, all of them heading north at high speed, blue lights flashing, in the direction of central Stockholm. They'd sat in silence surrounded by another world of voices. A news bulletin coming from the radio on the dashboard – '*Stockholm's Central Station has just now been cordoned off due to a suspected bomb threat*' – and from the police scanner on Jasper's lap, the warning from the commanding officer – *'explosives, confirmed*' – while the arriving patrols helped to evacuate and cordon off the area, temporarily closing parts of the Tunnelbana and stopping all regional and national trains.

Everything had gone exactly as planned, but still his father's fucking voice kept pecking at his head and pulling at his brain.

If you have a problem, Leo, I've helped you before.

He increased his speed – unaware of Jasper repeatedly asking him to slow down and of the police scanner, which reported that a bomb squad was about to open the locker.

Only another ten kilometres to the exit. He stayed in the outer lane doing seventy kilometres per hour.

I'm twenty-four, not ten!

A hundred and ten kilometres per hour.

You have no other sons! But I have two brothers!

A hundred and forty kilometres per hour.

You failed! I succeeded!

It wasn't until Jasper pulled hard on his arm and screamed loudly that he slowed abruptly. While trying not to miss the exit to the back roads, he'd temporarily lost control of the car, and the police scanner had fallen out of Jasper's lap.

They were on a narrow, winding road through woods and meadows and past the occasional lake. Outside, the fields had turned from white to mostly brown, dirt and grass, after a week of above-freezing temperatures, a dirty, irregular blanket. The petrol station was on the only short straight section of the road, closed after the construction of the nearby motorway. He slowed down and drove into the hidden area behind the building – yellow blinds and petrol prices still at 76.40 kronor – and parked the company car next to the stolen Mercedes that Felix and Vincent had arrived in.

They broke the padlock on the rusty metal door with a pair of bolt cutters, replaced it with a new one, and put all their equipment on a worn counter next to a half-open cash register. In silence – other than the creak of the faded Caltex signs swinging in the wind – they changed from one uniform to another. Leo helped Vincent tighten his bulletproof vest around his thin bare chest.

It would never change, thought Leo, no matter how many banks they robbed – the body he was strapping into this bulletproof vest was the same one that had once worn a green snowsuit zipped up to the chin, so no snow could get in. And it was only when Felix asked for the third time, *what the hell's the matter?*, and he answered for the third time, *nothing*, that he stopped pulling on the straps.

———————

The two wristwatches on Leo's right arm were on a little tight, because it was important for the jumpsuit fabric to stay put underneath. The first one was old with squat, red, ugly hands, but he'd replaced the strap with a new light brown leather one. He'd bought the other watch as an adult: a Rolex with a watchcase of brushed steel, a face with luminous hands, and clockwork that ticked the seconds loud enough to hear them.

Leo, according to his handwritten note, had to keep track of six different time frames.

Stage 1. 12 minutes. Change clothes.
Double car switch. Approach to Bank 1 and Bank 2.

This phase held the least amount of risk. From construction clothing into their robbery outfits at an abandoned petrol station and their first car change to a Mercedes. Drive nine and a half kilometres to the second car and switch to the stolen Volkswagen Beetle. Drive two kilometres to Ösmo Square.

Stage 2. 3 minutes. Double robbery.
Stage 3. 7 minutes. Move to Bank 3.

And this part would be the riskiest. They would have just committed two bank robberies. They'd be driving down minor roads with little traffic between Ösmo and Sorunda, first in a stolen Volkswagen Beetle that witnesses would see and the police would be able to identify, and then in a stolen Mercedes. But a bomb would also have sent large sections of the police force to attend Stockholm Central Station fifty kilometres away.

Stage 4. 3 minutes. Bank 3.
Stage 5. 6 minutes. Move. Change clothes. Change cars.

These phases had an elevated, but manageable level of risk. From the third bank they would head back to their starting point, the abandoned petrol station, where they would switch from their robbery gear into their construction clothes, from the stolen Mercedes to a company car. And that was what he was using the older watch for: to keep track of the total time – *31 minutes* – during which they could be captured.

Both of Leo's watches read 14.51. One minute left of *Stage 1*. They arrived at Ösmo Square via streets of villas, townhouses, apartment blocks. And in the distance there was a roof below which a lonely old man was eating onions and smoked pork.

The Beetle took the final turn past a library and an indoor swimming pool and into the car park in front of a U-shaped shopping centre.

'Down, *now*,' said Leo. 'Twenty seconds to go.'

Combat pack and bulletproof vest on, a heavy weapon balanced on his thighs, Leo pulled the ski mask over his head, straightened the holes at the eyes.

'Ten seconds.'

Slow breaths.

'Five seconds.'

A gentle bump and the car left the road and rolled across the square towards those big store windows and the two banks that shared a wall.

'Exactly three minutes. Two of them – simultaneously. Then we'll meet here again.'

```
Police Unit: Crime          Police Unit: Crime
Offence: Robbery            Offence: Robbery
Witness: Hansen, TOMAS      Witness: Lindh, MARIT
Loc: Handels Bank Ösmo C    Loc: SE-Bank Ösmo C
```

```
A lone gunman rushed in      Two men in black ski
wearing a black ski mask     masks rushed in and
and shouted 'Down! Get       shouted 'Lie down on the
down!' and fired several     floor!' and both fired
shots at one camera on       about twenty shots at two
the ceiling and one on       cameras.
the wall.
```

Hansen was standing in the customer queue, and a woman screamed she had to get out and ran towards the door. The robber then grabbed hold of her jacket.

———

The woman continued screaming as the robber pushed her to the ground. At that point one of the bank staff told her to be quiet and lie still.

———

After what Hansen describes as 'a moment' the screaming woman stood up. He then observed how the robber and a cashier went into the vault, while another robber stood outside the window and took aim at him.

———

When the lone robber left the vault, he was carrying a large bag over his shoulder. He passed the woman on his way out. As Hansen remembers it, she was frightened and screaming the whole time.

———

Lindh watched as one of the robbers jumped over the counter and asked 'Who's got the keys to the vault?'

———

Lindh took the key lying on her desk, pressed the button to the bank gate and opened the inner vault.

———

When the robbers were in the vault Lindh heard the buzzing sound, which meant that the cash drawer units were being opened. They emptied them one at a time. She was encouraged to lie down again and noticed that they were wearing identical boots.

———

A loud voice said 'Five seconds left, out out!' before both robbers disappeared. Lindh adds that during the robbery she could hear the shots and screams coming from the bank next door.

————

Leo ran out into the snowless winter cold after 170 seconds, with ten seconds to spare. A woman's cries followed him, full of agony and fear and panic. Just as his mother *should* have screamed back then.

Why hadn't she?

Leo straightened his shoulder strap, threw his bag in the boot and nodded to Felix, who was waiting in front of the car.

He'd fired six shots at each camera. He had eight left.

That was when everything stopped.

First he noticed the frightened but fascinated gazes of the people behind the supermarket window. Then the frantic barking of a German shepherd bound to one of the lamp posts in the middle of the square, throwing herself back and forth with slathering jaws. Gazes and sounds that seized him, just like a woman's eyes and screams, making it hard to breathe.

All she'd had to do was lie down, be still and stay quiet.

He'd prepared himself for some idiot male customer or staff member to play the hero, or for a showdown with the local police – prepared himself to take aim and fire to prove to them he was willing to use violence. He had sometimes imagined a life and death situation involving heavily armed police intervention. But this, a woman breaking down and crying and just wanting to get out, he'd never even considered that.

A woman protecting herself from a man using violence.

'Two minutes and fifty-five seconds! Fifty-six!' barked Felix, standing beside the Beetle. 'Fifty-eight! Fifty-nine! And out . . . out . . . out!'

Jasper and Vincent ran out of the other bank's door, threw one full bag each into the boot and themselves into the back seat. Felix jumped into the front seat, pushed the clutch and revved the engine, ready to drive.

But Leo stood there, completely still. On the square. Next to the car. He didn't hear Felix shouting.

'Black One – it's been three minutes!'

He was surrounded. Everything pressed in on him. The weapon around his neck. The screaming inside the bank, her cries replacing those he hadn't heard as a child because they never came.

A cursory glance at the roof in the distance.

He started walking back.

Felix hit the gas, without letting up on the clutch, and shouted after him.

'Black One – it's time, damn it!'

But Leo kept walking.

His black-clad body disappeared into the bank.

Leo's gun lay steady in his hands when he took aim.

When he fired into the room.

Eight shots.

He hit his target with extreme precision.

When his gun was empty, Leo lowered it and turned back to the door, and stepped outside.

It was silent. Just as he remembered it back then.

Nothing surrounding him, nothing pressing in on him.

No one was screaming and screaming and screaming.

He didn't hear the child running in fear from the tobacco kiosk across the square, nor the dog at the lamp post gnashing her jaws, nor the birds that landed on the roof, nor even the scrape of his own boots as they hit gravel and asphalt.

He moved in silence.

And now he felt what he'd felt before, that calm, peaceful breathing from deep within.

44

JOHN BRONCKS RAN through the tired corridors and dark staircases of the police station, over yellow plastic carpets and grey cement floors, past the pale-green metal door that led to the garage.

At 14.52:15 a civilian operator working on the front lines in the vast hall of the municipal emergency call centre had received an alert that a robbery was underway at Handels Bank in Ösmo Square.

At 14.52:32 another operator a couple of chairs away had received an alert that another bank, SE-Bank, was being robbed, and at exactly the same location.

At 14.53:17 Karlström had stepped into Broncks's office without knocking to say that what they'd predicted had now come to pass. Four robbers in black masks. Extensive gunfire. Swedish military weapons. Exactly three minutes.

It's you.

Broncks kept running through the underground garage. In the past month there had been three bank robberies in the Stockholm area, and he'd been on call for every one. The Savings Bank in Upplands Väsby – three men in an Opel with a gun and an axe, arrested the same evening at an illegal club. The Cooperative Bank at Norrmalmstorg – an armed, middle-aged man arrested only an hour later in his childhood room at his parents' home, with both the loot and a converted starting pistol under his bed. A security van on its way to the main post office – two men armed with shotguns, still at large.

But none of them had given him this feeling.

It's you.

He started the car and passed the crime tech cage, where just a few weeks ago he'd seen something on a computer screen that didn't make sense – a bank robber whispering, shielding his colleague, taking responsibility, on his way to one of Europe's most violent bank robberies. The garage door automatically slid open, and Broncks drove up the incline towards the lowered barrier and the daylight.

Two brothers.

And now they'd struck again. This time it was two banks at the same time. They were taking bigger risks and would take even more.

Every time you rob a bank, I get a little closer.

The heat of four adult bodies trapped in a cold metal shell had turned into a milky fog covering the interior of the car windows as everyone breathed quick and heavy all around Felix, still with their black ski masks pulled down.

'What the fuck was that?' he asked Leo, not taking his eyes off the road, hands gripping the wheel tightly. A constant speed of eighty kilometres per hour.

'You saw for yourself.'

'No, I did not! What the hell were you up to?'

Leo also stared straight ahead. Facing the trees, which multiplied as the houses became more sparse.

'You're the one with two fucking watches on your arm and six separate timelines! You're the one who's always preaching about time, time, time!'

Leo's shoulder collided with Felix's as the car left a narrow road for

238

an even narrower one: a rugged, bumpy track fit only for tractors. His knees knocked against the bottom of the dashboard at each new bump. His jumpsuit was soaked with sweat by the time they stopped at a mound of stones at the end of a snowless path.

'I had time.'

They all knew the drill. Out of the Beetle. Open the boot. Lift out three bags full of cash.

'You went back!'

On to the next car, the Mercedes.

'You went back into that bank and started shooting like a fucking idiot. You put us all at risk!'

Open the boot. Drop three bags inside. Jump in. Take the track out again towards a country road.

'We're sitting here. Aren't we, Felix? If you want to whine, you can do it when we get home.'

Leo turned round.

'And *now*, masks off.'

The fabric was pulled off, revealing four young men with damp hair glued to damp foreheads. In an oncoming car, a woman with a baby in a car seat drove by without reacting.

Jasper leaned forward from the back seat, tapped Leo's shoulder lightly and whispered.

'Front page.'

Felix turned towards the back with a jerk and the car swerved across the line. He didn't whisper.

'You shut your mouth back there.'

Leo continued to stare straight ahead, gun on his thighs, ski mask ready.

Five kilometres to the next bank.

The car in front of John Broncks stood completely still, as did the car in front of that. When he drove up onto the pavement to try to get a clearer view, *all* the cars were standing completely still, blocking every metre of asphalt from the City Hall to Central Station.

He rolled down his window, searched under his seat and grabbed a bubble-shaped light – the magnet stuck to the car roof and a blue light started spinning as his siren ricocheted between the buildings. He forced his way out, scraping bumper after bumper, crossed the solid line, zigzagging between oncoming cars trying to find space that wasn't there.

The whole of Stockholm's inner core was off balance.

The streets around Central Station were either cordoned off or carrying heavy, redirected traffic. According to his radio, someone had planted a bomb in the heart of Stockholm – initially suspected to be a dummy, they had just upgraded it to a live bomb, and the bomb squad, bomb dogs, and a remote-controlled bomb robot had just arrived. Microphone in one hand and steering wheel in the other, Broncks made sharp turns as he passed the City Hall and drove out onto the equally backed-up Central Bridge.

'I'm driving in the direction of Ösmo. How many officers on site?'

'*One.*'

'One?'

'*Another unit on its way from Nynäshamn.*'

'Two. *Two* patrol cars?'

There were multiple lanes in both directions on the short Central Bridge, but with oncoming traffic separated by a concrete ramp, he was forced, despite his blue lights and siren, to slow down as car after car tried to move aside for him.

'*That's all we have … So far.*'

'That's not enough. We need a SWAT team, dogs, helicopters . . . we're talking about two fucking banks – at the same time!'

Old Town and Slussen and then, somewhere in the Söderled tunnel, the traffic finally started to ease up.

'Did you hear what I said?'

A commanding officer in Nynäshamn's precinct came back.

'*I heard you. And who – to use your own words – the hell are you? And why exactly are you heading here?*'

'John Broncks, City Police.'

'*That says nothing to me about who you are or why you're on your way to a district you don't have anything to do with.*'

'The bank in Svedmyra, the security van in Farsta . . . this is the same group. I've been investigating them for almost three months.'

The tunnel traffic was much more spaced out. He increased his speed slightly, towards the daylight and the long bridge in the distance.

'They're heavily armed – and prepared to use their weapons. Two patrol cars? You need backup!'

'There isn't any. The rest of the police force in this county are all crowded into a few blocks close to where you're coming from. And you know very well why they've been ordered there. But there are more on their way from other districts.'

Daylight. Johanneshovs Bridge. And a strange sight. The water covered by shimmering blue ice far below and trains stationary on the parallel bridge. And between the railway and the road, hundreds, maybe thousands of pedestrians were streaming in both directions, wearing coats and jackets, legs melting together, becoming one, like insects moving, people who'd stopped hoping a train would come.

At the other end of the bridge stood Gullmars Square – platforms and stairs and even more stationary trains, and throngs of people crowding into chaotic lines trying to get onto hastily summoned shuttle buses. He had just reached the stadium and was about to pick up speed on a less busy road when a new voice broke the radio silence.

'It's exploded!'

It didn't happen very often. The professional voices communicating over these frequencies every day became difficult to tell apart, using the same emphasis, volume, detachment.

'The whole fucking thing . . . blown up! The robot is scrap!'

Occasionally when something unexpected happened, when threat and danger combined to become tangible, these voices became sincere, immediate.

'One of ours . . . he's down!'

The voice slashed through the radio like the knife that had slashed through Leo's jacket, when Vincent was too young to remember.

'One of ours . . . he's down!'

The frightened, hunted, furious voice on the police scanner stated that a bomb had exploded, that the police officer steering the robot had been hit by shrapnel in the blast.

Then he fell silent. No information about whether the police officer had survived or not.

'It wasn't supposed to go off!' yelled Vincent, leaning forward to Leo. 'You promised me, damn it!'

Leo lowered the volume of the police radio and the monotonous beeping disappeared. Straight ahead, a blue sign on the edge of the road and field, SORUNDA 3 km – they were almost there.

'We can't do anything about that now.'

'But what if he's dead!'

'We don't know what happened. We don't know why it went off. But I'll figure it out. Later. When we're done with the next bank.'

In the distance was a tractor with a trailer next to a snow-covered barn. A few inhabited farms, children's bikes and skis leaning against the walls. A truck at a lay-by, its driver peeing behind a tree.

Felix adjusted the rear-view mirror to look hard at Jasper in the back seat. Jasper wouldn't meet his eyes.

'Did you take out the safety ring? Did you?'

'What the hell are you talking about?'

'Look at me, Jasper! Goddamn it, did you arm the fucking bomb?'

Jasper met Felix's gaze.

'I sure as hell did not.'

And he stared long enough for it to become uncomfortable.

'Someone's been hit. They could die!' shouted Vincent.

'And what the hell does that have to do with me?'

Felix was still driving at a steady speed, despite the fact that he was looking backwards as much as he was forwards.

'You're lying, Jasper! I can see it!'

Leo had been silent. Until now.

'Stop it!'

'I helped build the damn thing,' said Felix. 'I know that it couldn't—'

'Just drive, goddamn it!'

In the twilight outside everything melted together, but Vincent noticed a difference in Felix's eyes in the rear-view mirror. Leo seldom raised his voice, they all knew that, but it was even more rare for Felix to accuse someone if he wasn't absolutely sure.

The exit to Sorunda, a suburb with a single bank, their third target. And Felix drove straight past.

'What the hell . . .'

'Like you said, Leo. We're going home. We're gonna "figure it out".'

'This isn't the way to . . . you're driving too far!'

The road was so narrow that oncoming traffic had to slow down to avoid a collision. But Felix hit the accelerator as they approached the next car, driving at over a hundred kilometres per hour.

'Turn round!'

'If you want to continue, go ahead. Without me!'

Felix's neck had gone a blotchy red, which spread upwards to his cheeks

242

and temples, and Vincent knew what that meant – it was taking everything Felix had to contain his rage. Vincent should have started to feel uneasy, but all he felt was heat in his chest. *If it feels like this again I'm not doing it.* He'd said it and meant it. And yet, so calm. Because if they all died in a crash at the next bend, if the policeman who was down in Central Station was dead, if the bomb had exploded because somebody had wanted it to explode . . . It didn't matter. It really didn't. For the first time in his life Vincent realised where Leo went when he disappeared into himself. To a calm where there was no time. No future, no past, and therefore no worries. Just now. Now. And the only thing he could do something about was what was happening right now, in this car, with his brothers.

———

Two banks shot up.

A bomb detonated in the heart of Stockholm.

John Broncks had driven thirty kilometres on the main road and there were twenty to go. The last suburb south of the city went by outside his window, and then the landscape flattened out into vast meadows punctuated by clumps of trees.

According to the operational chief in place at Central Station, the bomb technicians had determined that the safety ring had been designed so that the bomb would explode when it was taken out of the locker, with only one purpose – to maim and kill.

Two separate events, nine minutes apart, that were somehow related to each other.

Dusk approached with each passing kilometre; with twenty still left, it would be dark by the time he arrived.

'*Broncks?*'

The two-way radio – the officer in Nynäshamn, now more welcoming.

'*Where are you?*'

'Eight kilometres away.'

'*We've found the getaway car. A red Volkswagen. Registration GZP 784. On the same road you're driving down now, right at the exit. You'll see it and one of our cars in just a few minutes.*'

One of only two patrol cars in place.

'You found it . . . at what time?'

'*15.09.*'

John Broncks was thinking about a circle.

A search area expanding with each minute that passed. In Farsta and in Svedmyra it had grown rapidly, becoming too large.

'Any road barriers?'

Now it had been restricted.

'Two patrols from Handen have cordoned off the main road north and one from Nynäshamn has blocked traffic south – we're closing the road completely along the coast. More patrols on their way from Huddinge and Södertälje, which have been blocked off inland – west and north.'

Broncks counted quickly.

14.56 – a Volkswagen with four masked men leaves the crime scene.

14.58 – the same car parks three kilometres away.

14.59 – they continue in a new car.

A search area that was no longer widening – for the first time they were close to each other.

The exit to Ösmo. A few hundred metres later a sparse wall of trees – a thicket, and red paint shining through the bare branches. The air colder and rawer than in the city centre, the kind of cold that bites into your cheeks and neck and stiffens your fingers.

Broncks walked through the snow towards the abandoned car, avoiding the tracks that were already present. A red Volkswagen Beetle, parked with its front end against a pine, almost driven into the bark.

'Witnesses?'

The young man had fuzz on his upper lip that was trying to become a moustache. He wore uniform and greeted Broncks with an equally cold hand.

'No one saw anyone leave or arrive at the scene.'

'And . . . this?'

'We're confident that it's the car they used – same model, same registration that several witnesses saw outside the banks.'

The number plate at the bottom of the boot.

GZP 784.

Broncks went round and peered in through the passenger side window. On the floor a beer can next to a burger wrapper, in the ashtray three or four butts. In order to make his way forward he had to press through tightly packed tree trunks and thick branches. It was even colder here, the thin crust of snow gave way and snow tumbled into his shoes.

He saw it as soon as he reached the front of the car, despite the bark that obscured half the plate.

BGY 397.

Another number plate.

One number if seen from the front – another if seen from the back.

————————

The car braked abruptly on the asphalt behind the abandoned petrol station. The right headlight was crushed against the rusty iron railing near the entrance, and the right mirror hit a tap sticking out of the side of the building.

Felix ran, which was something he rarely did, the torch in his hand pointed at the metal door and padlock.

'Felix!'

Leo caught up and started pulling on his upper arm.

'We still have time!'

Two kilometres earlier. The exit. And Felix had driven past, interrupted their double robbery before it could become a triple robbery.

'We *had* time. We don't any more. Because time has run out.'

Leo pulled harder on Felix's arm.

'We're going to the bank in Sorunda *now*.'

'You're going without me, in that case.'

Torch under his armpit. Light on the metal door and the key towards the padlock. The faded Caltex sign at the gas pump was creaking as usual. It was always windy here.

'Felix, what the hell are you doing?'

Leo grabbed the hand that held the key.

'Let go of my hand. I'm going in here. I'm going to change my clothes, and then I'm going home.'

'Get back in the car! We have one bank left!'

'There will be no more. You wasted twenty seconds going back to do some more shooting – we hit two banks and have three kilos of banknotes in the trunk, that's enough for today.'

The two shadows on the metal door in the gleam of a single headlight turned to three as Jasper placed himself between them.

'We've been planning this fucking robbery for weeks!'

He was holding the black ski mask in his hand. Now he put it on, rolled it down over his face.

'This is what we're going to do, Felix – we're going to go and get three more kilos of cash!'

One set of keys still in hand, Felix found the car keys, handed them over.

'Then you can drive.'

'Are you serious? You're quitting? What we agreed on? What *we* agreed on!'

'We also agreed not to detonate a fucking bomb.'

Felix directed his torch into the eyeholes of the fabric.

'I *know* it was you.'

And Jasper raised his arm to protect them, squinted.

'You don't know shit.'

'*I know it was you.*'

Jasper knocked the torch out of Felix's hand, and it went out as it fell to the ground.

'I'm not gonna fucking take this any more. Leo? I—'

'A helicopter!'

None of them had heard Vincent at first. Not when he opened the car door, not when he ran over to them, the police scanner in his arms.

'They've got a helicopter!'

———————

'*Broncks?*'

'Yeah?'

'*You've got your helicopter.*'

The wind was blowing. John Broncks pushed the two-way radio receiver close to his cheek and cupped his palm over it, as the tall pines swayed back and forth. The wet snow had started to soak through his thin socks and run down into the soles of his shoes.

'*The Eleventh Helicopter Division has volunteered. They're on their way now.*'

The commanding officer in Nynäshamn was starting to sound as hopeful as Broncks was beginning to feel.

'*You'll hear it in a couple of minutes, it's heading in your direction, and it's going to concentrate on the area around the main road.*'

'Good! I—'

'*Broncks, wait a minute, I'm getting a message from a colleague.*'

In the middle of a thicket of trees, the faint glow of streetlights in the distance. The earpiece was silent, but if he concentrated, Broncks could hear people talking quietly to each other, then steps, then someone moving their microphone.

'This may sound strange, but the getaway car has been found. Again.'

'Again?'

'Same model – same number plate. Except . . . on the other side of town . . . along a country road.'

'I'm not sure I follow.'

'Volkswagen 1300. Red. GZP 784. At the end of a tractor path near a cairn. It's as far west of town as you are east.'

Broncks checked the plate at the back of the car. GZP 784. Then he trudged through deep snow a second time, in order to squeeze his body tight between the branches and check the plate up front. BGY 397.

'Do you have someone in place over there?'

'Yes.'

'Ask him to walk around the car.'

His colleagues were speaking faintly in his ear. He waited until the crackle and the voice came back.

'It has a different number on the front.'

'BGY 397?'

'Yes.'

They'd stolen two identical cars. Switched the number plates. And had two identical cars with the same numbers on front and back for witnesses to report.

One search area had suddenly become two.

Now they had to double the number of barriers, double the number of adjacent areas, double the number of surrounding districts.

The wind on the ground was increasing, even though the tops of the trees were swaying less than before. John Broncks looked around in the ebbing twilight. Then he saw them. It wasn't the wind picking up – it was rotor blades, cutting through the air.

'The helicopter!'

'Yeah?'

'It has to be rerouted! It has to leave the coast and the main road and go west instead, search the minor roads inland!'

45

ROTOR BLADES. AT first faint, then louder, closer. Leo looked towards a sky that should have been black as a searchlight cut through the darkness above the trees.

'Felix! Vincent!'

They were standing outside the locked door of the petrol station wearing the clothes they'd just robbed two banks in. With three kilos of cash. The Stockholm police had two helicopters, which had been deployed in the area around the bomb threat. But this, a military helicopter – he hadn't counted on that.

'The tarp! Over the cars!'

If they were to be seen from the air, if their current position was revealed, then he had only one real solution. Open fire. But a military helicopter has ballistic armour, bulletproof plates that protect vital engine parts and personnel – there would be almost no chance of taking it down before the crew reported in.

Felix had reached the company car, and was moving the driver's seat forward to uncover a folded tarpaulin, while Leo ran towards the other car and gathered up four automatic weapons from the seats and floor, hanging one around his own neck and handing one to Jasper.

'Watch the helicopter!'

Jasper braced one shoulder against the wall of the petrol station, sank down on his knees and assumed a shooting position, aiming towards the light.

'Tarp all the way over the cars!'

It rustled as they unfurled the wrinkled olive-green plastic. In its folds there were dry, brittle brown leaves from the forest around the bunker.

'Helicopter incoming!' Jasper screamed, but was drowned out by engine noise.

A sharp jerk and the tarp blanketed the two cars.

'Into the petrol station – everybody in!' shouted Leo, running towards the locked door. 'In, in!'

The key to the padlock – Felix searched his jumpsuit, chest pockets, back pockets, front pockets, cargo pockets. It wasn't there.

He searched again. The damn pounding came from above, harder and harder.

He'd had it in his hand ready to unlock when Leo grabbed his wrist and Jasper had knocked his torch to the ground.

'I can't find the key!'

'Felix, damn it!'

'I can't find it! But the bolt cutters are in the car, under the passenger seat, I . . .'

'There's no time!'

That damn awful pounding. That fucking light.

'Should I, Leo?'

Jasper. Kneeling beside them, gun pointed up towards the light sweeping across the partially snow-covered ground, the butt pressed against his shoulder.

'Leo, I'm waiting! Give me the order, and I'll shoot!'

Leo waited. The helicopter's light was like a long silver eye just a few hundred metres away. If he said *fire*, Jasper would shoot. If Jasper let loose and didn't aim just right, this would be it.

'Under the cars!'

He ran towards the tarpaulin, folding up the edge like a cave opening.

'In!'

Vincent crawled under. Felix crawled under.

'You too!'

Jasper stood up, ran two steps with the gun in his arms, threw himself to the ground, rolled under the cars. Leo followed him, as the helicopter searchlight probed its way towards the gas station, the asphalt yard, the tarpaulin.

Stomachs pressed to the ground, backs pressed against the exhaust system and oil sump.

It was there. Above them.

The rotating propeller blades pushed air against the tarpaulin and it quivered, then started to dance to an irregular beat. The spotlight filtered through it, a sharp shade of green.

Afterwards, they lay there, breathing in silence. Leo's shoulders were pushed up against Felix. And he knew what his little brother was thinking.

If Felix hadn't stopped him. If they'd robbed the third bank.

The helicopter would have been there before them, would have found them.

Eye, eye, nose.

A little further down, five holes next to each other, in a semicircle.

A mouth.

And it was smiling.

John Broncks counted. Eight shots fired. Into the shatter-resistant glass above the counter.

He was in the middle of the evacuated bank – customers and staff had been relocated to the library reading room across the square, to its calm and warmth, to be interviewed by the local police. A young woman had been taken to hospital, silent despite testimony describing her incessant screaming, one dislocated arm and a couple of external wounds, physical damage that would soon heal. But the screaming would return.

Security cameras on the floor. Shards of glass. And in the bank on the other side of the bullet-riddled internal wall – the same.

Three minutes, a double robbery, before disappearing in a car that would be found in two places.

Roadblocks – no results. A military helicopter – no results.

And you – you're outside our search area.

`The protective glass of a single bank teller's desk had`
`bullet holes in the shape of a face, and these measure-`
`ments can be found in a separate register.`

Broncks went closer, lifted his hand slowly towards eight holes.

An eye. An eye. A nose. A mouth.

He looked at the face, and it stared right back at him.

It didn't blink, didn't move its lips – empty eyes, a stiff mouth that would never stop smiling, a nose that sat wrong, too much in the middle. And the rest resembled skin, ugly wrinkles from hundreds of small criss-crossing cracks in the glass radiating from every bullet hole.

Broncks turned towards the entrance.

You were done. You'd left the premises. Then you turned back, made this smile, shot by shot.

A mark.

What the hell does it mean? Why are you smiling at me? Because you've vanished without a trace – again? Because you've committed

Sweden's first double robbery? Because you're going to do something even bigger next time?

He stared at the face and it stared back.

———

It was late afternoon, but dark outside. From far away it was easy to see Vincent and Felix as they walked from the kitchen to the living room, illuminated by the bluish light from the TV.

Leo and Jasper remained outside.

The wind cooled their hot cheeks, while their tense bodies slowly relaxed. They'd stripped off one layer of their robbery uniforms, their jumpsuits, and now the next was evaporating: their sweat.

After the helicopter's rotor blades had slowed down and the spotlight faded, they'd crawled out and pulled off the tarpaulin. They'd broken a padlock for a second time, changed and driven away in the company car, Felix in the driver's seat and Leo, Vincent, Jasper under the truck bed cover behind a wall of insulation. They hadn't said a word to each other. Eight shots into protective glass and a detonated bomb stood between them.

'I promise.'

Jasper shifted anxiously in front of Leo.

'The safety ring was intact when I closed the door. Leo? I swear on my life!'

On the other side of the fence, a panorama of rush-hour traffic, people on their way home after work.

'I built it, Jasper.'

Leo looked at the house. Felix was standing up now, the remote clearly in his hand.

'I designed and built it. And Felix built it. And he's right. It could not have detonated by itself.'

'Fuck, Leo . . . do you know how this feels?'

Jasper shook his head and beat his fist against his chest, several times.

'Do you know? When you stand in front of me and don't believe me? It fucking . . . hurts. Hurts!'

Now Felix sat down on the sofa. And it seemed as if Vincent was sitting down next to him.

'Explain to me then. How did it happen? How could it have gone off?'

Fist against his chest again, but not as hard.

'Damned if I know. *I* didn't build it. Leo . . . I swear! I only did what I was told to do.'

The rush-hour traffic would continue, maybe get even heavier – it would be a few more hours before most people arrived home for the day. But *he* did so now. Came home for the day. Into the hall and living room, while Jasper disappeared into the kitchen.

Leo went upstairs. Felix and Vincent were on the sofa next to the round table, police scanner in the middle, surrounded by glasses and bottles. They sat there just as they had after the Svedmyra robbery, but this time there was no laughter, no eager voices, and silent sips of whisky in large tumblers instead of champagne and bubbles.

'Turn on the scanner,' said Leo.

'No.'

'Felix? I want to hear what they're saying.'

'The news will be starting soon.'

Leo sank down into one of the armchairs and poured himself a few fingers of whisky.

'Stop sulking – there's over two million kronor in those bags out there.'

Felix didn't answer – instead he pointed the remote at the TV and raised the volume.

'Give it up, damn it.'

'Give it up?'

Felix held half a glass of whisky. He emptied it.

'You went back – had you planned that or was it just a fucking whim?'

'It wasn't a *fucking* whim. I just thought it . . . seemed to fit.'

'It didn't fucking fit me! You were on your way to the car. We were on our way out of there.'

The sound of the TV changed as the news programme began a more measured report.

'Can you turn up the volume a little?'

Jasper came out of the kitchen, four bottles of beer between the fingers of each hand.

A bomb planted in a storage locker at Stockholm's Central Station detonated shortly after three o'clock when a police robot tried to disarm it.

Vincent, who was sitting furthest away on the sofa, leaned forward to see and hear better. He saw long camera shots of the train station in the capital city. He heard a muffled bang.

And then a hasty, shaky zoom in towards the black smoke pouring out of the entrance hall, rising upwards, thinning out.

But that wasn't what he wanted to see and hear, not what he'd been carrying with him. He wanted to see images of someone who'd been hurt. Maybe blood on a white sheet or black asphalt. Maybe on a stretcher, maybe a paramedic. Nothing. The news only showed piles of rubble on the stairs and in the arrival hall and waiting areas, more barricades, long lines of travellers.

A bomb-disposal technician was slightly injured by shrapnel and was taken to Sabbatsbergs Hospital.

Now. Finally. A picture of an ambulance.

Vincent crumpled into the sofa. The policeman wasn't dead.

And he laughed a little. It had all been so weird. All of this, the last few months, hadn't felt real. More like a movie they'd talk about afterwards. But now he knew that it was real.

Felix filled his glass halfway again with the light single malt, then drained it again.

'Are you proud, Jasper? A bomb. In the heart of the city. Does it feel . . . good?'

'It's not my fucking fault that you built it wrong.'

'I know it was you!'

Felix got up off the sofa, grabbed Jasper's shirt, yanked him up.

'Let go!'

A shirt button bounced onto the floor. Savage breaths. Jasper grabbed onto Felix's hands, which in turn gripped even harder.

'Sit down, damn it!' yelled Leo, pushing his hands against their chests. 'What the hell are you two doing? *Sit down!*'

'I know he's lying!'

'Sit!'

'I won't sit in the same room as this bastard!'

Felix let go of Jasper's shirt collar, and Jasper released Felix's wrists and started to do up whatever buttons were left.

'Felix – be quiet now.'

Leo looked at his little brother, whose neck was flushed and his jaw clenched.

'I believe Jasper. He looked me in the eye and swore.'

'So you *believe* him?'

'I believe him.'

'He's completely fucking unreliable. He put his gun in that security guard's mouth, and he stayed too long at Sköndal and Svedmyra and kept shooting and fuck . . . today . . . it seems to be spreading, right, Leo . . . I don't trust him any more. And we have to be able to fucking trust each other!'

'But I trust Jasper when he says he didn't do it.'

'Then you can go to hell too!'

Felix overturned one of the armchairs and walked towards the hall.

'Listen to me, all of you – it doesn't fucking matter at all.'

When Vincent had seen the bomb for the first time three days ago, he'd challenged the man who'd taught him to walk. He knew he was probably the one who'd started this.

'It doesn't matter any more, Felix. No one died.'

He'd started this. Maybe he was the only one who could finish it.

'Let's forget it. Never talk about it again. And you two . . . stop arguing.'

He looked at Felix who was standing in the doorway, at Leo righting the overturned chair, at Jasper who, losing patience with the missing buttons, had taken off his shirt.

'Vincent's right.'

Leo bumped into the table, bottles colliding with glasses which collided with the police scanner, and pointed at the TV, where scenes of chaos from Central Station were replaced by scenes from a small town south of Stockholm – police tape and curious onlookers in front of two bullet-riddled banks whose vault doors stood open.

'It doesn't *matter*. The only thing that matters is that we're here together. And that they're out there still with no idea who we are or what we're going to do next.'

A black horse. With a thick and streaming mane. And when it rises on its hind legs it watches him. Vranac. A label on a wine bottle.

That's what other people see. But this horse is free and can't be tamed. He can see it. And all the while, other people think they're just drinking affordable red wine that tastes like plums and earth.

Ivan was sitting on a bench next to his kitchen table. He'd been doing this most of the day; sometimes it happened like that, cold outside and too much time on his hands. A firm grip on the cork as it came out, poured half into the pan over a couple of tablespoons of sugar that would melt slowly, then into a big coffee mug that was almost clean. A typical day. But not really. After the first ten Keno tickets and the first bottle and the first cigarette, he'd called his eldest son. It was only the second time he'd called him in several years and without his address book he wasn't sure he had the right number. It was. But not the right voice. Irritable and short and *I don't have time.* Then an extended news bulletin on the radio about a bomb in a storage locker in Stockholm that had exploded while they were trying to disarm it. A bomb in the middle of the city. He'd been living in Sweden for three decades; bombs were something that happened in other places, places he'd left behind. And then, twenty more Keno tickets, and maybe half a bottle more, quite a bit of tobacco, and Radio Stockholm on talking about a bank robbery, about two bank robberies, right here, in Ösmo, just five hundred metres from his window.

A typical day. But not really.

A black horse rearing up. He remembered a white horse that he'd been given by eight-year-old Leo on his pappa's thirty-fifth birthday. A white porcelain horse that lay down, resting. His son had seen the label on this bottle so many times, he'd thought it was the horses that Ivan liked.

More sips. Earth and plums. And warmth from his throat to his chest.

The window had been open, but he hadn't heard any shooting, he knew what it sounded like – the sound was easy to distinguish from a firecracker, a gunshot petered out so much faster. He should have heard it if someone was shooting.

Above the narrow radiator in the bathroom hung four socks that he'd washed by hand. The wine had neutralised the pain in his knee and helped now against the dampness of his socks as he slid his feet into his worn-out shoes.

Two jackets on the hat rack. He wavered between the light grey and the dark grey one. Light grey.

Hands jammed into his jacket pockets, the fabric stretched across his back, he went out and down the stairs and through the gate. The envelope filled with cash still made it difficult to button the shirt breast pocket, though it had become thinner. Pocket money. Forty-three thousand that was now twenty-nine and a half thousand. Rolling, Rizla, Vranac and a lot of Keno.

Down a sleepy street past villas and townhouses, down the hill and round the bus shelter outside the library, and there he met the first police car. Then the cordoned-off square, where cops in uniforms and ridiculous hats were walking around, talking to anyone who would talk to them under the Christmas lights shaped like snowflakes and Santas and Christmas trees. Fucking Christmas. Gluttony. People fattening themselves up – dead pigs fed to living pigs. Manufactured joy, everyone laughing until their children started to scream. But for once those Christmas lights would be put to good use, illuminating the scene of a crime. The largest Santa shone the brightest, its light landing on all those self-important faces; they had a story to tell that was unique and for a moment it made them unique.

Ivan stretched his head above the crowd. He saw them more clearly now, the fronts of the banks, and people moving around inside.

The busybody.

There he was. He was one of *them*. Ivan was sure.

That busybody who'd waved his fucking badge in his face, trying to insinuate that Ivan Dûvnjac was a fucking little rat who sneaked into other people's homes.

He pushed his way through the curious onlookers and watched as the little busybody walked around the bank premises looking at fallen security cameras and overturned chairs and upside-down cash boxes. Next to him, on her knees, a woman dressed in a solid white plastic jumpsuit with plastic gloves was picking up cartridge cases. Ivan waited there until the busybody turned and looked at the people looking at him.

You should recognise me. You sought me out, provoked me. And now you look at me like I don't exist. Because you didn't come round looking for me to ask about fucking burglaries.

Then the busybody moved behind the counter and into what Ivan guessed was the vault. And he saw what the cop had been standing in front of, looking at without understanding it.

Eight bullet holes in a security window.

And together they formed a . . . face. With two eyes and a nose and a mouth with a crooked smile.

A fucking sneer. At that busybody and his colleagues.

Ivan stood there in the late afternoon darkness outside the bank and looked at a face among the shards of glass and bullet casings, and he tried not to listen to the people around him, talking and talking about what they'd seen, which had already started to change and expand. And he thought about the clusters. Events that didn't seem like they belonged together, but they did, just like the number sequences on a Keno ticket. He thought about that busybody and the envelope in his breast pocket and two banks robbed just five hundred metres from his home and a smile that was a sneer, smiling at the people who were in pursuit, but also at the people standing there looking on right now, at him.

He broke away from the crowd and with every step the feeling of being watched grew stronger, two hollow eyes that never blinked lingering on his back.

then

part two

46

THEY'RE STILL STANDING in the confines of the lift, motionless, in the kind of light that hurts your eyes. They're still looking at each other in the narrow gap at the very top of the mirror, where the layers of spray paint are a little thinner. And once in a while, but just for a moment so Pappa won't notice, Leo glances at the Mora knife in his father's hand, still visible even though Pappa is gripping the wooden handle so hard that his knuckles have turned white.

'I'll be damned. You actually did it.'

Pappa's voice is trembling from within. And Pappa swallows it, just as Leo usually does.

'I could have lost you.'

'Pappa, everything's going to be fine. I thought everything through. They followed me here. And you saw it all. Saw me hit them on the nose, like this, in the middle.'

'Open the door.'

'Don't you want to see? Like this, in the middle—'

'Are you ever going to open the damn lift door?'

Pappa's voice almost sounds normal. He isn't trembling quite so much inside.

Leo opens the lift door, then the door to the apartment.

He knows that it's the same four-bedroom flat on the seventh floor in the middle of Skogås – the one he left not long ago. He knows that, of course. And yet, it's as if the rooms are smaller.

Cramped. Tight.

It feels as if he has to crouch down not to hit his head on the ceiling when Pappa tells him to take off his jacket and sweater. He's cold enough to get goose bumps from his stomach to his neck as Pappa inspects the rip in the sleeve of his jacket and then the hole in the shoulder. Then the scratch on Leo's shoulder just where the clavicle ends, which isn't bleeding any more. Pappa runs his fingers over its dry, uneven surface.

'It doesn't hurt at all, Pappa, it barely even touched . . .'

Pappa has already gone into the kitchen. He turns on the stove, heats up his wine and sugar. He sits down at the kitchen table, pours himself half a glass.

Leo watches his back; he'd like to sit down beside him, show him the scratch again, the blood that's turned brown and which he can't feel. He walks down the hallway that used to feel so much longer, stops at the open door – Vincent, who has placed all his soldiers on the floor in one big group, crawls under his bed and retrieves a new tennis ball from among the clumps of dust, then turns to Leo with a smile.

'Look, Leo, it's a bomb. Everybody'll fall over at the same time.'

Then Vincent drops the ball on his soldiers again and again, fetching it after each drop, until all of the soldiers are lying down, together.

'We're going to take it down, Leo,' Felix whispers right behind him. 'The punchbag. We're going to go in and shut the door.'

Felix moves the three-legged stool to the middle of the workroom, climbs up, stretching towards the hook in the ceiling, though he can't reach it.

'There should be a lamp there. The one Pappa took down. If it was still there, then Kekkonen would never have stabbed you with Pappa's knife . . . and you would never have almost died.'

'Nothing happened. Felix? I beat them. Both of them.'

'It will never be OK. Never! You hear me?'

Felix tries again, in the middle of the stool, on tiptoe, arms shaking. His hand stretches just a little higher and his fingers touch the hook, but he can't get the punchbag off. He sits down on the stool, biting his lip, like he does when he's crying and doesn't want anyone to see.

'Are you sad?'

He's seven years old. If you're only seven years old you can't take down a damn mattress from a hook on the ceiling.

'Nuuh.'

A severed, half no.

'I hear you.'

'It's not me. It's the stupid bag. And that stupid ceiling hook.'

Felix gets up and punches it, punches it again and again, until he tires himself out. And then he watches as Leo reaches up, pushes the punchbag up towards the ceiling, until the loop slides off the hook and the mattress falls to the floor. Then Felix hands him the lamp, and Leo puts it in place on his first try.

They leave the room, already the smallest one in the apartment, but now it feels even smaller, too small to enter ever again.

Vincent's room is larger. They each sit down on one corner of a rug that depicts a city, watch as their little brother stands up all the soldiers, then releases a tennis ball from each hand, two bombs at the same time.

They have been sitting there for quite a while when they hear sounds they know well coming through the walls – *tooot-toot-toot-toot-toot* – then again – *tooot-toot-toot-toot-toot* – then again – *tooot-toot-toot-toot-toot*.

'Come on!'

Vincent leaves his soldiers standing, lined up, unbombed, runs to the window and climbs up on the box full of Lego.

'Leo! Felix! Come here!'

They stand on either side of their younger brother, looking out of the window. The light-blue ice cream van that's honking so loudly stops outside building two – the building Jasper lives in, whose father throws condoms off the balcony that land in a tree on their way down and hang there like white leaves – then outside building four – where Marie lives, who Leo almost fooled around with once – and then at house number six – where the Turkish family lives, Faruk and Emre and Bekir – and then honks again as it drives towards their front door, where it will stand as long as customers keep arriving.

'Boys!'

That stupid honking. That was why they hadn't heard his heavy footsteps in the hall.

'My boys!'

It's hard to know whether Pappa is angry or not. The voice doesn't sound it. But he has those eyes.

'Ice cream! Damn it! My boys are going to have some ice cream. Get your jackets!'

Vincent runs again, from the window to the hallway to the front door. Felix moves more slowly, but follows him. Leo remains where he is, the soldiers at his feet and both tennis balls in his hands. He lets go and they fall over, all of them.

Then he goes to help Vincent put on shoes that were once his and the snowsuit that Felix loved so much, zipping it all the way up and then putting on the hat that had only ever belonged to Vincent – while Pappa empties the last of his bottle of wine into two squash bottles with pictures of blackcurrants on their labels.

It was almost winter as he was riding the lift with Pappa less than an hour ago. Now, when they open the door, it's spring – the birds, the trees, the sun. And there is the ice cream van, waiting in exactly the spot where the Mora knife was dropped.

'Boys, have whatever you want!'

Pappa has a 100-kronor bill in his hand. He looks different. He's been drinking his black wine, but that's not it. He's trembling again. Even though he's smiling. Even though he's drinking from one of the blackcurrant squash bottles. Pappa is trembling. Inside.

'That one.'

They choose.

'Maybe . . . that one.'

Actually, Vincent chooses.

'No. That one.'

The green ones that taste like pears, a whole box of them.

'Now, boys, let's go for a walk. We're going to have some ice cream and go for a walk!'

Pappa is tall, even compared to the other fathers. And when he puts Vincent on his shoulders, he's quite a way from the ground. Leo walks next to him, Felix a few steps behind. They each have their own green ice lolly in their hands, and Pappa drinks from the second blackcurrant bottle. They walk across a large car park, towards a field and a football pitch with new goalposts and new nets, then on to a wood near the shore of the bay, where you can hear the cracking sound of ice breaking up.

47

THEY'RE ON A peninsula, a solid area of land sticking out into the water, making the coastline less even. Huge boulders lying on top of each other, a jigsaw with edges that don't fit together properly. There are only two trees on the entire peninsula, pines, not very tall, with branches that are darker at the bottom from the moisture trapped there as the snow rapidly melts.

Drevviken Lake is almost three hundred metres across. Next summer Leo will swim all the way from one side to the other. He tried last year.

He swam as far as the middle one evening when the surface of the water was smooth. And he would have made it. He's sure of it. But he turned round because Felix and Vincent were screaming from the top of a stone slab so loudly it echoed off the bluffs, telling him to hurry back because he'd just eaten and he'd sink like a stone if he kept swimming. He wonders sometimes if that's really what would happen; it's deep out there.

It only takes half an hour by boat to get from here to the beaches of Sköndal, where his grandparents live. Maybe when he's bigger he could swim all the way to their house some time, if he sticks close to land where the waves are smaller and he doesn't eat beforehand, and if he has some dry clothes tied onto his back in a plastic bag.

Pappa is sitting under one of the pine trees swallowing loudly. When Pappa makes a noise, at least you know where he is and what he's up to. It's when he doesn't make any noise, that's when you feel your whole body preparing.

The second blackcurrant bottle is almost empty now, a few drops more and then all gone, and Pappa puts it down on the ground. It rolls down the embankment towards the ice and the thin strip of meltwater that has appeared along the shore.

'Pick up your lolly sticks.'

Leo searches the ground for lolly sticks dropped into the wilted grass and brown leaves. They've eaten so many that his stomach still feels bloated.

'Every single one! And then come here. Holding your sticks.'

They count to eleven, and then walk over to the two pines, and Pappa stretches out his hand.

'Give them to me.'

They're supposed to sit around him, like three Indians around their chief.

'Good. Now, you each take one back.'

'One each?'

'One stick for each of you.'

They grab them and sit down as before, holding three lolly sticks, waiting.

'Now you're going to break them.'

They all hear what Pappa said, but they don't understand him.

'In the middle. Break them.'

Break it. Take it apart. A lolly stick?

265

'Leo?'

Pappa's voice is impatient, annoyed – the tone that means anything can happen.

Breathe in, breathe out.

The lolly stick lies like a bridge between Leo's hands, and he pushes on it, breaking it into pieces. So easy.

Felix then does the same thing as Leo – the two ends, one in each hand. It hurts as the stick presses against the skin and bones. Again. Again.

'Felix?'

Felix presses again, doesn't pay attention to the pain as the edges dig in deep. And it breaks. Soft ribs protrude like antennae from each fractured edge.

'Vincent?'

A three-year-old body with three-year-old legs on his way to the water, the wind in his thin hair, he gets down on his knees and picks up something from the shore, then comes back with a stone that dwarfs his hands. He puts the lolly stick on the uneven surface of the bank. Three-year-old arms high above his head, he brings the stone down hard on the stick. He repeats this several times.

It begins to splinter, at least on one edge.

'How did it go?'

They're gathered in a ring, and Leo and Felix hold out the two pieces of their lolly sticks.

'They're broken?'

'Yes.'

'Completely?'

'Yes.'

'Good. Now, Leo, you're the strongest. Here. You take these five sticks from me. Break them in half. At the same time.'

'With my hands?'

'Just like you did before.'

He looks at Pappa, who has finally stopped trembling inside. He's going somewhere with this but won't say where.

Five lolly sticks. A much thicker bridge between his hands. Leo strains his shoulders, arms, fingers. And he can't do it. The palms of his hands are sore from trying to break stick after stick, and from the resistance of five of them.

He just can't do it.

'I . . .'

He doesn't dare look at Pappa. He can't look into those eyes, that have the same stare Pappa used on the blond curly-haired parasite and his long-haired buddy outside the shopping centre.

'. . . can't do it.'

Five thin sticks. Leo drops them and they bounce off the rock. He closes his eyes. Pappa's hand touches him, and it doesn't feel angry, it just rests lightly on his shoulder.

'That, boys, is our family. Our *clan*.'

Pappa picks up five sticks, slowly holding each stick up one at a time in front of their faces.

'This stick is Vincent. This is Felix. And this one is Leo. And . . . Mamma. And . . . Pappa.'

Then he bundles up all the sticks.

'A clan always sticks together.'

The sticks now lie between his own huge hands.

Vincent. Felix. Leo. Mamma. Pappa.

'*We* are a clan. *You* are *my* clan.'

And he tries to break them, several times, without success. Not even he can do it.

'If a clan can *stick together*, it will never break. Sometimes Mamma doesn't understand that. She doesn't understand what real solidarity is.'

They're sitting close to each other now. His breath smells like the wine in those squash bottles.

'A clan is small – but it can never be destroyed. A clan has a leader who leads – and who will hand over responsibility to the next leader. Do you understand?'

They all nod at Pappa, who is watching them. He is mostly looking at Leo.

'Do *you* understand that, Leo?'

Pappa's eyes are the same as in the lift. Only now there's no mirror in between them.

'Even large armies have tried to crush small clans but haven't succeeded – because a clan is a family that always supports each other!'

He looks at them, and they realise that he's said something important. And they try to respond.

'Like . . . Indians?' suggests Felix.

'No! No, no, no! Indian tribes are like . . . just ordinary communities, I'm talking about clans, family ties, that . . . like Genghis Khan. Or, like the Cossacks.'

Pappa rises and wobbles slightly on the rock.

'The Cossacks have no country . . . they have only their family and their friends. They're nomads with no homeland – they can go anywhere because they will always have each other.'

He crosses his arms over his chest with one hand on each shoulder, sinking down with legs bent like a frog, and starts kicking, throwing up one leg at a time, and now he's not a frog any more, he's more like a grasshopper, and he sings something that sounds like *kalinka*. He kicks until he stumbles and is no longer a Cossack, his huge body falling backwards towards the rocks, and he hits his head, but laughs out loud in a way he rarely does.

'In a clan, *a real clan*, we never hurt each other.'

After a while he sits up again.

'In *a real clan* we never snitch on each other.'

The smell of wine on his breath mingles with the smell of sweat from his tight work shirt.

'In *a real clan* we always protect each other.'

Leo knows it's probably not the case, but still it feels as if Pappa is speaking only to him.

'Otherwise . . . we'll lose everything.'

48

THEY STAYED THERE for a long time, with Pappa alternating between sitting and lying on the bank. Leo had always thought it was strange that Pappa could dance and sing *kalinka* one minute and then retreat into himself the next. And when he withdrew he would say things that Leo didn't understand, about when he was little and when he grew up and came to Sweden.

They walk one by one in a long line down the narrow woodland path. The afternoon is a little colder, and Leo hugs the quilted jacket more tightly around his body. They're not moving very fast, even after Vincent stops abruptly with his head tilted pleadingly, and Leo agrees to carry him. Pappa is at the back of the line, singing something that doesn't have any words. He's crept out of himself again and the silence has not returned, not once during their whole walk back along Drevviken Lake, through the woods, past the football pitch and the field and the school and all the way to their front door.

There's always another bottle.

The wine rack under the sink is empty, but behind it there is one more, the one that is always kept there so they'll never run out. Pappa takes the bottle and heads for the bedroom, lies down on the unmade bed, and Leo waits until he's asleep to close the door. It's important for Pappa to go to sleep, for the calm to return, so they don't have to feel on edge for a while.

They hang their coats on three hooks in the hall, and Felix stands there, scrutinising the large holes slashed in Leo's coat. He runs his middle finger and index finger along the frayed edges, exposing the white lining, which spills out; he tries to poke and push it back in, but it springs out again just as fast.

If he turns the knife hole on the shoulder against the wall you can see the knife hole on the arm. If you turn the knife hole on the arm towards the wall you can see the hole on the shoulder.

And Mamma will be home any minute.

Mamma mustn't see it.

Leo tiptoes past Pappa's intermittent snoring behind the closed bedroom door and into the kitchen, grabs a roll of tape from the top drawer under the workbench, and tears off some short pieces in order to put the holes back together, but instead they get bigger. Felix finds a few needles, but no thread that's the right colour no matter how many boxes and glass bowls he empties out on the hallway floor. Then they find a dry tube of glue on the desktop that neither of them can get anything out of even though they push until their fingertips hurt.

'This won't be good, Leo.'

'We'll turn the holes . . . like this . . . against the wall.'

'She'll see them!'

'Well . . . then I'll tell her it was from thorn bushes.'

'That's a stupid—'

'What if Faruk kicked a football into some thorn bushes. And when I leant over to pick it up a couple of the thorns got caught and tore the sleeve in two places. Does that sound OK?'

Mamma comes home.

They sit quietly in the kitchen, listening. They hear her put her bag down on the chair and a bag of shopping on the floor, hear her hang up her coat in the hallway.

And she hurries straight past. Without looking. *She doesn't see the knife holes.*

She goes into the kitchen, and when she hears Pappa snoring from the bedroom she asks what they had for lunch and dinner. Before Leo can answer, Vincent shouts from inside his room *ice cream*, and Leo adds that he made pancakes afterwards. And for a moment it seems she believes him.

'Pancakes?'

Her eyes search the kitchen for the frying pan, which isn't on the stove or the drying rack, for plates with remnants of strawberry jam.

Now Leo answers. Before Vincent.

'Yes.'

'Yes?'

'Yes.'

She doesn't get annoyed very often. But she is now. Every time the abrupt, anxious, drunken snores push their way through the bedroom door and flood the apartment, Leo can see it on her face.

'I washed up. And put everything away. Everything. The frying pan. And the plates.'

She opens one of the cabinet doors. But not to the pans or plates. The one under the sink. She pulls out the rubbish bin, and they both see it at the same time. Empty bottles. And the wine rack, just as empty.

She *is* annoyed. But not at him or his lies.

'OK. What do you want for dinner?'

She puts her hand on Leo's cheek. Her skin is always so soft.

'What do you say? Pancakes?'

'Pancakes.'

He helps her by getting out the flour and eggs and milk and salt. And a bit of Pappa's smoked pork, which he cuts into thick slices with a long kitchen knife and eats with onions.

Oven pancakes.

'When did Pappa go into the bedroom?'

'When we came home.'

'Home?'

'Yes.'

'From?'

From the ice cream van. From two blackcurrant bottles. From lolly sticks that couldn't be broken, just like a family can't be broken.

'From?'

'School.'

The hand gently on his cheek.

'From?'

The words in his mouth won't come out, which is why he runs down the hall so fast when someone rings the doorbell. Anything that gets him out of the kitchen and away from having to answer Mamma with more lies.

'Is your mother or father at home?'

He's never seen the man standing in the stairwell.

'Who are you?'

He's tall. Almost as tall as Pappa. But has short hair. And kind eyes.

'Are they? Are your mother or father at home?'

It doesn't seem as if he's selling anything. He's not the caretaker, here to complain about them running around in the cellar or broken lamps in the car park. He might be a Christian, here to show them flimsy magazines with brightly coloured drawings of children playing with lions. Drawings that aren't comics.

'Mamma. She's at home.'

No. He's not here to talk about Jesus and he has no magazines in his hand. They usually come in pairs.

Leo's stomach aches a little. Deep inside, below the ribs. It's good that Pappa's asleep, because this is surely one of those people who come here asking for Mamma or Pappa to discuss whatever Leo or Felix or Pappa has done. And who Pappa should not be awake to meet.

'Thank you.'

Leo goes into the kitchen, listening: Pappa is still snoring. And he makes sure to stand with his back towards the bedroom when talking to Mamma, who's stirring the pancake batter with a whisk, round and round in a plastic bowl.

'Someone wants to talk to you.'

'Who?'

He shrugs.

'Someone.'

She washes her hands in warm water under the tap, dries them on the towel hanging on the oven door, and walks down the hallway to the front door.

'Hello.'

The man holds out a skinny arm.

'Hello, I'm Hasse's father.'

Hasse? Hasse and Kekkonen? The ones who hurt my son?

'And I'm Leo's mother,' she says, taking his hand. 'And I'm glad you're here. I'd been planning to contact you.'

The tall man nods and sighs.

'I understand that. And appreciate it. Because . . . this is unacceptable.'

Mamma nods and sighs and opens the door a little more.

'Come in. So we don't have to talk in the stairwell.'

Hasse's father steps in, but stops on the hall carpet. And she sees how he sees it, as if it were two hallways. Her wall. And Ivan's. Her side with wicker baskets and drawings Felix has made for her. Ivan's side with the long rows of old tools and that sabre that always has to be adjusted and moved so that it hangs exactly in the middle.

'You have to understand – I'm not here to accuse you of anything.'

As he talks to her, he bends over trying to make himself shorter.

'I'm here because I want to make sure that you speak to your son.'

Mamma changes her position, not just leaning on her right leg, but balancing on both, as if preparing. No one else can see it. But Leo can, he knows her. He knows that when she stands like that she's mustering her strength.

'And *I* would like to make sure that *you* speak to *your* son.'

'I've already done that. We've had . . . plenty of time today. Four hours in Accident & Emergency.'

'A&E?'

'Yes, they—'

'Today?'

'Comminuted fracture. The result of "high-impact violence", they said.'

Mamma turns to Leo, looking at his face, which has gradually turned from very swollen with dark blue patches to just a little swollen with golden brown patches. And her expression changes as she realises that *a week ago* has just become *today* and things have changed. That *your* son has become *my* son.

Leo looks down and listens and realises that the snoring has stopped.

272

'A broken nose.'

'I know that. I work in healthcare.'

Listens to the bedroom door being opened.

'If I hadn't been home today. If I hadn't taken him straight to A&E. It might have been visible for his whole life.'

To the heavy steps coming closer.

'They raised the nose. And straightened out the nasal wall.'

Mamma turns to Leo again. And only at that moment does she see Pappa, the sides of his hair tousled.

'In that case . . . I am extremely sorry. I will speak with Leo shortly. And we'll sort this out. And then we can go to yours. And we'll talk all this through together. You and your son, me and my son.'

The heavy steps.

'Sort this out?'

Pappa.

'Sure as hell we'll sort it out!'

Pappa passes Leo and goes over to Mamma, then passes her too, places himself between her and the visitor.

'Right, Britt-Marie?'

The visitor is about to leave, his hand on the handle and the door halfway open, when Pappa takes a step closer.

'Hey, don't go. Come in. Come in! We're going to *sort* this out.'

And he winks at Mamma.

'Or maybe you'd prefer it if we invited you to dinner? Britt-Marie? We have a guest. Hasse's father! Dinner!'

The tall visitor seems confused, he was about to go.

'No . . . it's really not necessary, the only thing I wanted was to discuss . . .'

Mamma smiles weakly at him. But not at Pappa.

'Ivan – Hasse's father and I have already talked about this. I can explain it to you later. When Hasse's father leaves.'

Pappa smiles.

'Done? *I'm* not done. Leo is *my* son too. So . . . just come in. Join us, Hasse's father.'

He grabs the door handle and pulls the front door shut with Hasse's father still on the hall carpet. One arm gestures towards the kitchen and simultaneously stops Mamma from moving.

'You wanted to sort this out.'

They sit at the kitchen table. Pappa at his spot next to the ashtray and Keno tickets, Hasse's father in Mamma's seat.

'Yes.'

'Sort out what, exactly? That our sons have been fighting? That my ten-year-old son hit your thirteen-year-old son this time? That they're even now?'

Hasse's father looks round, looking for Mamma, who isn't there.

'Even? Well, if that's what you want to call it. My son came home this morning with some very serious injuries. A broken nose, and he—'

'Wait.'

Pappa holds up a hand in front of Hasse's father's face. And nods towards the hallway, to someone hidden in the doorway.

'Leo?'

Leo steps across the threshold.

'All the way.'

He doesn't go all the way, but comes a little further into the kitchen, to the refrigerator.

'Leo, my son, this is Hasse's father. He says you hit Hasse on the nose. Did you?'

The fridge seems never to have hummed as loudly before.

'Yes.'

'Once?'

'Yes.'

He stands in a kitchen that has become a courtroom and the jury looks at him, one half smiling, the other half nodding seriously. Then the half that's smiling takes some money out of his trouser pocket.

'Here.'

And hands Leo a 50-kronor note.

'The next time you need to get even you hit him twice. Then I'll give you a hundred.'

Fifty kronor of Pappa's money. Leo takes the note, running his fingers over it. It's wrinkled and he flattens it out.

'You can go now. Go to your brothers, Leo.'

Pappa then winks at Hasse's father, as he did at Mamma.

'So. They're even now. Your son hit my son first. Then my son hit your son. Now they're finished with each other.'

Pen in hand, he pulls the Keno coupons a little closer.

'But *we're* not finished with each other,' he continues, placing a cross at a time in different patterns. 'Because you came here, into my home, and blamed everything on my son. When it was your little hooligan who started all this! And therefore, as you surely know, it's you and me that will have to finish this. At this kitchen table. I promise you, I guarantee you . . . that every time your little hooligan hits anyone from now on, *anybody*, I'll find *you*, and beat *you*. Every time.'

Hasse's father stands up quickly from his chair.

'Are you threatening me?'

'You bet your life I am.'

'I thought we could talk about this.'

'We are talking. For now.'

Hasse's father just stands there, silent. His face red.

'You're threatening me. You know I can report you for that. You understand that, do you?'

Pappa laughs, quietly, or seems to.

'Good. Do it. Report me.'

Louder now, really laughing.

'The fucking cops will thank me. Thank me! Because from now on they'll know who your little hooligan is.'

And then it all happens so fast, just like at the table in the restaurant with the glass of orange squash. Pappa stands up and grabs Hasse's father by his collar and presses him against the wall between the humming refrigerator and the door.

'Don't forget. That every time your little hooligan hits someone else, I'll hit you. Every time!'

Pappa raises his voice and the door to Vincent's room opens. Felix and Vincent peek out as Pappa pushes Hasse's father against the wall, and then down the hall towards the front door.

'Goodbye, Hasse's father. Say hello to Hasse for me. Take care of his nose, squeeze it tightly, and shake it a bit, and say hello from Leo. From *Ivan's son*.'

Britt-Marie is still standing in the hallway as the door closes and steps disappear down the stairwell. Her legs try to bend and her body wants to collapse on the floor, as if they just can't take any more drunken aggression. But they don't. Because she's decided that they won't.

'Leo. Felix. Vincent. Go to your rooms.'

'And why should they do that?'

'Because I want to talk to you, Ivan. Alone.'

'You? Do you know what our son did today?'

Now – when Pappa holds it up – she sees the jacket, one shoulder of which was facing the wall with a broad scarf hanging over it. The hole is even bigger now. Even Pappa's fingers can fit through it.

'He defended himself. Us. Our honour. Leo stood there – facing a knife! For our sake. You can speak, Britt-Marie. Do it! But then you speak to us. All of us. We're a family. If you believe that your son did the wrong thing today, you tell him. In front of all of us.'

'Leo didn't do anything wrong, Ivan.'

Her legs won't give way because she's made a decision.

'*You* did something wrong.'

'Me?'

Pappa drops the jacket. But not his hand.

'*I* taught our son to defend himself!'

'And if Hasse's father reports this to the police?'

He moves closer.

'For what?'

'You threatened him, Ivan.'

'There are no witnesses. Right?'

He looks at her, at their three sons.

'Did anyone here hear me threaten Hasse's father? Any of you? Or is my wife the only cop in here?'

He looks at his eldest son the longest.

'Leo, did you? Did you hear that?'

And waits until he gets an answer.

'No, Pappa. I didn't hear anything.'

'But *I* heard it, Ivan.'

Mamma is standing close to Pappa. Close to Pappa's hand. But she doesn't care.

'I heard you threaten him. And I can repeat *exactly* what you said.'

'Are you . . . going to snitch on me?'

He moves his hand closer until it is almost touching her face.

'Snitch? Is that what you're going to do?'

'No, Pappa!'

Felix runs towards Pappa and Mamma, and the hand that shakes in front of her face.

'Pappa! You can't! Pappa . . .'

He screams, pulling on the pockets of Pappa's trousers, until he lowers his hand.

'You will *never* turn against my family again.'

And then it's as if everything is suddenly in motion.

Leo watches as Pappa goes through the kitchen and out onto the balcony and leans over the railing. Mamma rubs her hands against her eyes and goes to the bathroom, closes the door and turns on the tap. Felix follows her and tries to grab her and stands knocking at the door wanting to get in. And Vincent runs towards his room to his balls that are bombs, sobbing loudly as he releases them.

Everything is in motion, nothing is still.

Except Leo.

He's the only one who remains, who doesn't raise a hand or scream or cry.

And he knows now.

That Pappa is trembling in the apartment that has become smaller. But this time *both* outside and inside.

49

SHE ACTUALLY LIKES the dark. The long nights at the nursing home, the silence, someone coughing in the room for patients who need special supervision, someone who needs to be turned in bed, or someone waking up from a nightmare who needs comforting – a pillow under the head, a gentle hug, a glass of water. The darkness hanging beyond the window of their bedroom is different – it is hunting her. She's been tossing and turning until she ends up on her right side, watching him as he snores just a caress or a slap away, both his hair and the pillowcase plastered with sweat. He'll wake up in a few hours full of anxiety and look at her and ask her forgiveness without putting it into words.

She hears footsteps in the apartment, and moments later the front door opens and closes. She sits on the edge of the bed, searches under the bed for her slippers with tassels on them and then goes out into the hall.

No one is there.

Kitchen, living room, workroom, Vincent's room. Everything looks as it should. Until she enters Leo's and Felix's room and realises that one of the beds is empty.

She rushes to the kitchen, the balcony. She knows that if someone's gone down the stairs, then they should leave through the front door.

All of Skogås seems to be asleep. And the door is still closed, no shadows under the streetlamps.

She goes back and sinks down into the abandoned sheets. Bedspread on the floor and the three pillows on top of each other.

Felix.

He screamed at Pappa to keep his hand away from her face and pounded in panic on the door of the bathroom, and he had disappeared before when words turned to threats. But never like this, at night. Maybe that's why she's freezing, even though it's not really cold. And doesn't feel the hand on her right shoulder, even though it's been there a long time.

'Mamma?'

She jumps. Leo. He's awake.

'You need to sleep, sweetheart.'

'I'll look for him.'

She takes him in her arms. He's getting big. His ten-year-old body barely fits.

'You *have to* sleep, it's me and Pappa who . . .'

'I know where he is.'

'He didn't go out by the front door.'

'I know – he went out the back.'

Her eldest son is putting on clothes from a messy heap on the chair – jeans, sweater, jacket, shoes – and the apartment door slams shut for a second time that night.

She stands alone in the kitchen. In here the clock is round and ticks too loudly – no matter where she is in the flat it consumes seconds. She moves the full ashtray and the Keno tickets, and stares at the walls of a home that used to be hers.

One bed with a man snoring, a sweaty brow, anxiety.

One bed empty because someone's run away.

One bed empty because its occupant is searching for the one who ran away.

And one bed empty because she's resting her elbows heavily on the kitchen table and wondering if he ran away because he heard the phone conversation she had with her mother just before midnight, whispering, but with a sharpness and clarity that comes from having made a decision.

50

THE MOON IS nearly full tonight, and its light scatters in the clear sky and trickles down onto the back of a seven-storey building in a Stockholm suburb.

Leo breathes in, breathes out. In front of him is a steep hill where they like to play, which separates the housing estate from a forest that shrinks a little every year.

He gets ready to run just as he always does, his back against the building's rough walls, and then full speed towards the hill, and then up it, and he feels the crevices and stumps on his feet, which he uses to brace himself to get even further up. His heart pounds against his ribs and neck. Breathes in, breathes out. The crevice, the stump, the bulge – and he's up. The rocky hillside soon turns into an actual defensive wall, built for some war. They often play here; the walls are steep and angular and pitted with small cavities that resemble caves. He moves quickly along it, a snake winding through the dark forest terrain, patches of snow on the ground.

He knows that he's gone at least another hundred metres every time he passes a new cavity in the wall, squares that were dug out during the war and that Leo, Felix, Jasper and Buddha usually hide in when they themselves are playing war with air guns amid the low-rise buildings. Jasper always wins – he's best at camouflaging himself. One time he even cut off his hair and taped dry, yellow grass to his head.

After four hundred metres, there's a cavity that empties into a copse – the crooked trees where Greger's father hanged himself. After six hundred metres he passes the crag that Little Billy fell off last summer – his mother ran a hair salon in building ten; she closed it after that, wandering around Skogås until, eventually, she just wandered away. Leo still remembers what the body looked like, but he decided then never to think of it again.

'Felix?'

Over there. By a cliff like a precipice. He comes closer, stops, listens.

'Little brother? Where are you?'

His little brother is sitting at the very edge.

'Felix! I see you.'

One more step. As close as he dares to go. The moonlight makes Felix appear a little bigger.

'I want to be on my own.'

'You can't stay here, Felix. It's the middle of the night. You have to come home.'

'No.'

'Mamma's up. And she's worried.'

'I'm not going home.'

Leo takes one step at a time, small ones, so Felix won't notice. And then he's there.

'Why?'

Only one more step, one *short* step, and he'd walk right over the edge of the cliff and fall towards the rocks below, just like Little Billy did.

'Cos it's gonna be bad.'

'Bad?'

'I heard Mamma.'

'Yeah?'

'I heard her say she was leaving.'

Leo sits down. Not too close. But almost.

'She's not leaving.'

'I heard her.'

Darkness. Silence. And something that cracks, crackles, just like the ice did earlier today. It's the wind grabbing hold of bare branches and damp leaves.

'You heard . . . what?'

'She made a phone call. After we went to bed. When she thought we were asleep.'

'And?'

'To Grandma. She had that voice.'

The grey rock is cold, Leo notices only now how the chill penetrates his body from below and crawls up and then out of the holes on his jacket.

'She said: "It's not working any more." Loads of times.'

'She's said that before. She always comes back.'

'I heard it! She's not coming back! Not this time.'

The cracking. It's louder now, you can hear it more often as the wind strengthens. But there's another sound, too. The cars driving along the old road on the other side of the forest. He's never thought about how many people there are moving around at night.

'It's cold, Felix.'

'No.'

'You don't have a hat or gloves.'

'Because it's not cold.'

Leo searches his coat pockets and finds the red-and-white striped stocking cap. He takes it out and puts it on Felix's head.

'You lose eighty per cent of your body heat through your head.'

'What?'

'That's just how it is.'

Felix readjusts the striped hat, which has ended up too low on his forehead. Then they sit there, close to each other, looking at the bright round moon.

'Leo?'

'Yeah?'

'I'm thinking about Pappa.'

'Yeah?'

'He doesn't know.'

'And?'

Felix's legs are dangling over the edge, as they have been the whole time.

'Should we tell him? That Mamma's leaving?'

now
part three

51

HE'D ALWAYS LIKED April. Life – a whole world waking up around him.
It made him want to sit down in the bilberry bushes, on the moss-covered
rocks, and let the sun warm his forehead and cheeks as it streamed through
the treetops in narrow, bright strips of light.

He leaned back against the car that had taken him here for many years,
a beaten-up Volvo hatchback whose bolts were so corroded by rust they
barely held it together. This was probably the last spring it would get
through. Maybe a summer too, if he was lucky. Then he'd be ready to
take it to the scrapyard, and say goodbye.

The short stretch of unmade road led between the sharp bend and the
lowered barrier. That was where he parked every night, lit a cigarette,
and waited the five minutes required by his work manual.

Six-month inspection.

Here they came. A green van carrying two uniformed members of
Defence Area 44's security service, who greeted him with a firm handshake
that always lasted a little too long. One of the security officers nodded
at his left hand, the burning cigarette that would soon reach its filter.

'I thought you'd quit?'

'Does it bother you?'

'No . . . but didn't your wife . . .'

'Listen, I'll smoke any damn time I want to.'

A deep inhalation, straight into the bottom of his lungs, then he stubbed
out his cigarette in the same place as he'd done last night and every other
night, just above the first U on the boom's square sign, NO ACCESS FOR
UNAUTHORISED TRAFFIC.

'OK. OK. I hear you,' said the security officer with a rare smile. 'In
that case . . . where do you live now?'

'Probably in the same damn neighbourhood of studio flats that you
do.'

The other went over to the barrier's thick padlock, the same sort found
at the approach road to every arms dump.

The key didn't work.

The security officer tried the next. And the next.

'It . . . they . . . don't work. None of them.'

They examined both the key and the padlock. No damage. Nothing looked out of place. He tried them all one at a time, sixteen different keys.

'I guess we'll have to walk.'

'I do that every night – 150 metres there, 150 metres back. Ten armouries. It adds up to quite a bit of exercise,' said the inspector, patting his stomach – sixty years old, he was still slim – and set off.

They were both panting behind him, twenty years younger but completely exhausted after walking through the forest for just a few minutes. Right before they reached the top of the hill, he lengthened his stride just enough for them to still be able to keep up, while also leaving them breathless.

The inspector arrived at the cube, its walls easily two and a half metres wide, stopping in front of what looked like the door of a safe. He held up the same bunch of keys as before; after a few seconds of shuffling he found the right one, and turned it.

'Well, this one works anyway.'

The door swung inwards. The first security officer stepped inside – and stopped abruptly.

'What the *fuck*?'

His companion stepped in past the inspector – but didn't say anything. He just stood there, completely still.

'What is it?' The inspector twisted from side to side behind their broad backs trying to see what they were looking at.

He took a slightly crouched step forward, pushing his way through the doorway and the narrow opening between their shoulders.

And now he met his worst nightmare.

There was a big hole in the floor just beyond the threshold. More than half a metre wide. The rebars that had once sat within the concrete had been cut, forced up, like a broken ribcage.

One of the men in uniform grabbed hold of the wooden box that sat on top of the stack closest to the door, with **KSP 58** stamped on both sides, and lifted the lid. Empty. He opened the next. Empty. The next – empty. The next – empty. His colleague chose one from the pile on the far wall, opened one after another.

A total of twenty-four empty boxes.

'Everything . . . everything's gone!'

Now they looked at him.

'You've been here every night since the last inventory.'

Suddenly, he wished he had a cigarette.

'I . . .'

'Every night!'

The inspector rarely felt afraid. At this age, there wasn't much left that scared him. But now he was, because he didn't understand, and what you don't understand scares you.

'It's . . . it's intact on the outside. You can see that for yourselves! And yesterday, it was—'

'You must have fucking well seen *something*!'

'You went along with me. You saw the same thing. You—'

'Somebody's been in here, and they've taken every single weapon with them! Two whole companies' worth of weapons . . . *gone!*'

The inspector sat down on one of the empty crates and looked around the confined space.

'It must have happened late last night. I haven't . . .'

The expressionless soldier had got down onto his knees, and was bent over the hole, shovelling away the porous concrete debris and gravel. He grabbed hold of a broken rebar, rubbed his thumb along where it had been cut, letting loose a great deal of rust.

'This was cut a long time ago.'

52

EVERYTHING HAD GONE to plan since the beginning of the year.

February: the renovation of an apartment in Old Town, a week and a half, 37,000 kronor excluding the cost of materials; then a robbery in a small town, Rimbo, about sixty kilometres north of Stockholm, that was different from the others: they'd dressed in jeans, cheap bright jackets and trainers with Velcro straps, black stockings pulled over their heads, had used fake guns, and only Leo and Vincent went inside the bank. It was an experiment in changing their identity and breaking patterns, in case variations in their behaviour and performance should eventually become necessary, 556,000 kronor.

March: the installation of heating coils and parquet flooring in a basement in Älvsjö, one week, 10,000 kronor; then a bank robbery in Kungsör, a smaller city 140 kilometres west of Stockholm. Thirty-four minutes after their escape, the police had located the getaway car on an unmade road through woodland, but there all leads ceased. They'd continued on foot in the dark, compass and map in hand, towards a hole they'd dug in the ground earlier, stocking it with food and sleeping bags, covered with hardboard reinforced with studs and insulated with foil, and layered with dirt and moss to blend in with its surroundings, simultaneously serving as protection from the cold and from helicopters with infrared cameras. The next day they'd walked to a petrol station and rented a car, and when the roadblocks were removed, they drove home with 812,000 kronor, excluding the cost of materials.

The latest job was a 1930s house a few kilometres from Leo's home in Tumba. He'd put in a bid low enough to undercut any other firms. Gabbe had probably wondered why, but didn't say anything. Not much profit in it, but it wasn't about that; with each new bank robbery their cover became more important.

The two banks had given them 1,368,000 kronor to finance their next robbery – the biggest one so far.

Now it was 4 April: inspection day. The day Leo been living with since that dark night spent pressed against the moss and bilberries. The night everything had changed.

The police would discover the missing piece of the puzzle that linked together a series of robberies, a gang whose arsenal was bigger than all the other gangs in Sweden combined.

Leo drove slowly past fields dried out by the sun after the winter. New grass was sprouting in the verge, and in a few weeks it would push away everything yellow and lifeless.

After a long, sweeping bend, he came to the military area and the locked barrier.

He slowed down a little. And then he recognised it: the car he'd watched night after night, a beaten-up Volvo, owned by an elderly inspector who usually stood in the dark smoking a couple of cigarettes. But he recognised another vehicle too – a van with military licence plates.

Now. Now he knew.

They were there. They were going to open the door, perhaps already had opened it. They would discover what had happened, and it would terrify them.

A few minutes past ten, still plenty of time to spare. The train from Falun wasn't due to arrive until 10.37.

53

THIRTY-SIX VIOLENT ROBBERIES in three months all across Sweden. Twenty-two banks, eleven security vans, two exchange offices and a pawnshop. A dramatic increase without precedent – and the gang *he* was trying to capture was certainly not responsible for them all.

John Broncks was standing in a brightly lit corridor, digging coins from his right back pocket. There were always more there than he thought.

Twelve bank robberies a month in such a small country created a state of constant, feverish anxiety and fear – this world was unfamiliar and as long as nothing changed, as long as there was no cure, they'd all sink further into the sickness – a crime pandemic. By mid-February the security vans were being given police escorts, but the banks, too numerous and too scattered, were impossible to protect from infection. Their work had been reduced to waiting for the next alarm and the next investigation.

Broncks pushed coin after coin into the vending machine.

A pandemic has a source. In this case, eight shots shaped like a smiley face in shatterproof glass. And he still had no leads, except for piles of cartridges that couldn't be linked to any specific weapons and several wounded psyches that would never completely heal.

Smile, you bastard.

A time of change had turned into a time of confusion – which always happened when a new conceptual model was introduced, when a system fell apart and gave way to a new one, and this new model had spread almost instantly among those who were willing to take risks, those with nothing to lose. The four masked bank robbers had not only changed how the police protected likely targets, they'd changed the behaviour of the entire criminal world – other criminals looked up to that fucking smile, read the newspapers and watched reports on TV and were inspired to copy, committing more robberies, using even more extreme violence as a tool to get more loot. An escalation between us and them. Violence had torn apart the moral compass of the criminal landscape. If we're armed, you have to be armed, and then we need even more guns to stop you. In ten or twenty years researchers would say that this was when the banking system had been forced to change how it managed its cash handling and when ruthlessness became an admired tool, Broncks was sure of it.

He pressed the square buttons and waited while the metal spring released the first marzipan and chocolate cake. Then another one. Sugar and silver tea during the day and takeaway pizza at night. That's how it had been since he'd joined this search that was leading nowhere. Long, aimless walks through Stockholm early in the morning and late at night to let off some of his restlessness and energy – then in the middle of the night, visits to the police station's gym. Alone in a big room at three o'clock in the morning, he fought with dumbbells and barbells and treadmills and punchbags in order to avoid fighting people. He tore open the plastic, shoved in more green marzipan and chocolate, and swallowed, feeling a creeping disgust for the sweet goo in his mouth. But he had no choice, he had to fill the hollow inside to keep at bay the mirror image of a gaunt, pale, wiry body.

A homogeneous and close-knit group. No connections to the criminal underworld, and hence none to the network of informants that Broncks and his colleagues worked with. The group's four members might not have a criminal record; if so they would be anonymous until they made a mistake, and they didn't make mistakes.

The newly polished linoleum glistened in the bright light streaming through the office windows. Restless and so tired that he was wide awake, he headed towards the exit for his second walk of the day, even though it was only late morning. He zipped up his lined leather jacket; it was too warm for the spring sun, but he hadn't yet had time to take down a thinner spring jacket from the attic.

He'd started to feel a different kind of anger in the last few weeks, an anger he didn't recognise. He'd been watching him almost every day, a few seconds at a time, on jerky black-and-white surveillance films. The leader. The one who performed the countdown, who shot smiley faces into shatterproof glass, who was able to direct excessive force in order to get what he wanted. That was probably what it was about, this anger. It wasn't just violence. It was violence combined with playfulness, and that was what Broncks couldn't relate to. The man in those pictures solved his problems like a child in an adult world, and that was why he was successful – thinking in ways they didn't and getting around their road-blocks using the kind of magic tricks you'd find wrapped in a box under the Christmas tree. The police knew how to deal with adult criminals, but not this, an inventiveness as fascinating as it was unpleasant.

He wanted to peer inside that head, talk to it, understand it.

He headed downstairs, through four locked doors, using first his plastic card and then the key to the gate. It was brighter outside than Broncks had expected, so he closed his eyes, breathing in the mild, spring air, and set off east, towards the city centre.

Thirty-six aggravated robberies scattered the length of Sweden had taken place since the double robbery at Ösmo, and he had examined them all carefully. He was struck by two. One that followed this group's MO to the letter, and one that was quite different.

The first in Kungsör, a sleepy little town an hour's drive from Stockholm, a bank robbery taken straight from their manual. The leader – Broncks had started calling him *Big Brother* – always went in first and shot down the camera above the door. Then came *Little Brother*, always armed with a submachine gun, who would either jump over the counter or run around it to empty the tills. Then the third, the *Soldier*, who moved into shooting position as if the robbery were a military engagement, urban warfare, a tactical course in which he'd been given a mission. The Soldier was always armed with an assault rifle and shot down the second camera before going behind the tills to the vault. The fourth Broncks called the *Driver*, who took them to and from the site, who guarded the bank premises from the outside, and who, according to witness testimonies, drove with restraint, neither too fast nor too wildly.

When Broncks first read the witness statements and technical descrip-tions from the second robbery – Rimbo, north of Stockholm – he'd put it back in the folder, dismissing it as unrelated. Only two men on the bank premises. Jeans and jackets. Stockings over their heads. And they didn't shoot down any cameras – so he'd been able to follow the entire robbery, every movement, from entrance to exit. They'd been very calm, polite to the staff, never raised their voices. They'd walked in, shown their weapons, taken the money, and left the scene in a stolen Opel Kadett.

Nothing that resembled their earlier actions. It was only after Sanna had shown him a short sequence caught by the camera on the bank's exterior, just as she'd done once before, that he opened the folder again. Just before going inside the first man had turned round, as if checking on his colleague, put his hand on his shoulder and said something, and they had shared a lingering look. One who protected and led. *Big Brother*. One who was protected and who followed. *Little Brother*.

'John!'

Broncks, squinting in the intense sunlight, was nearing Scheele Street when he heard hasty steps behind him.

'Wait!'

He'd never seen his boss run before. And definitely never here. They met each other every day, but only in the corridors, or occasionally at a crime scene, except for the evening he'd visited Karlström's beautiful home in Äppelviken.

'A hundred and twenty-four m/45 submachine guns!' shouted Karlström, breathless and triumphant. 'Ninety-two AK4 automatic rifles! And five model 58 machine guns!'

'Yeah?'

'Quite a few, right?'

'Depends on which war you're fighting.'

'What if you're robbing banks and security vans?'

Broncks had just started an aimless walk in order to burn off nervous energy. Now he no longer needed it.

54

THE FOREST ROAD climbed sharply for a couple of hundred metres, dissolving at the top of the hill into a gravelled plateau where a crowd of people mingled – uniformed policemen, soldiers in green uniforms, some in civilian clothes, and one technician in a white jumpsuit glowing in the sun. Then he found it. A small, cube-shaped building. It was around this the crowd had gathered.

Broncks greeted his colleagues from both the City and Huddinge police, representatives from military security, and an older man smelling of cigarettes who introduced himself as the inspector, and whose anxious eyes followed him as he continued towards the building.

The white jumpsuit. Kneeling in front of a closed door of thick metal. She heard his footsteps on the gravel and turned round.

'Hello,' said Broncks.

'You noticed the lock down there? At the barrier?' said Sanna.

'Yes.'

'Intact. At least, it looked intact. The original had been removed and replaced with an exact replica. Even the serial numbers were the same. The key fits, but can't be turned.'

There was a large hole in the ground at Sanna's feet.

'Just like here. Everything looked intact.'

Sanna nodded towards the civilian with anxious eyes.

'He's been inspecting this bunker every evening and hasn't spotted anything. From the outside.'

She strained against the heavy security door as she opened it. She moved slightly to the side to let Broncks look in.

'This is how the perpetrators got inside. A tunnel underneath the building. It was completely filled, we've just dug it up again now.'

She went inside and he followed her into the cramped, sealed space. He thought of his big brother.

'They did a good job.'

Olive-coloured boxes, all opened and stacked on top of each other along the walls. On the part of the floor that was still whole, the lids had been stacked in a high pile. **AK4, submachine gun m/45, KSP 58** in black, slightly sharp type.

'They made efforts to hide what they'd done, and they succeeded.'

'So this is where it began,' he replied. 'The unknown variable.'

'What variable?'

He crouched down, a layer of cement and dust on the knee of his trousers.

'Farsta. Svedmyra and Ösmo. Rimbo and Kungsör.'

'What variable, John?'

He put his hand against the edges and bottom of the hole. The starting point. For the late nights, early mornings and long weekends, and always he was still running behind, arriving too late. With his arm deep in a void of damp gravel, he was just as impressed as he was pissed off.

'If you've never been to jail, if you have no weapons, nor any criminal ties to get weapons through, but you want to build your own criminal operation – what do you do? You simply get them from an arms dump.'

'Never been to jail? John, did you visit him?'

John Broncks didn't respond. He didn't need to. They knew each other in a way that made hiding something like that impossible. And they smiled, quickly, at each other, before he broke away and went outside.

According to the forensic investigation of a total of five aggravated robberies, the group had never fired any weapon more than once. Broncks had been assuming that after each bank robbery their weapons had been scrapped and replaced by new ones so that the crimes they committed would never be linked technically, and so *if* the perpetrators were arrested none of them would be linked to more than one robbery.

But now he had the missing variable: 221. If they continued using an average of two automatic weapons for each new robbery, they would have enough weapons to commit 110 bank robberies.

That is unless someone caught them.

A beautiful, arched ceiling. Infinity. Leo always got the same feeling when he found himself in a vaulted stone hall like that of Central Station – the feeling that it went on for ever.

He proceeded towards platform seven, where trains came in from the north, and made his way under the sheltering roof. He'd always felt most at home in buildings that echoed and stretched out, buildings with open spaces, and he often stopped and leaned his head back to look upward, something people rarely did. Every time he did, he thought of the very first time – when they'd visited Stockholm Cathedral. Mamma had wanted them to see the statue of St George and the dragon, but he'd already discovered the vaulted ceiling, and was standing on tiptoe, trying to touch it even though Mamma kept pointing to the large pedestal of St George in shining armour, a sword raised above his head and a roaring dragon under his horse's hooves. A moment frozen in time. The moment before it was all over. When the dragon might still wriggle away and tear down the weakling hiding behind his armour and horse.

He'd also frozen for a moment.

He'd stopped time, right here, in Central Station. Travellers had been kept waiting behind wire fences, while most of the police in the Stockholm region manned the barricades and guarded the bomb robots. A moment that had stretched out for several hours, as the system shuddered to a halt both before and after an explosion that should never have happened. And now it was as if it never had.

He wasn't sure that Jasper hadn't actually taken out the safety ring, but he'd decided not to ask again. He didn't want to risk getting the wrong answer. He wanted to keep the ever-widening fissure between Felix and Jasper from growing any further. He'd stepped in between them and stayed there, forcing them to treat each other professionally while simultaneously minimising the number of occasions they needed to work together.

In the distance a train rolled in and came to a stop. All the doors opened, and the passengers swarmed out with suitcases and buggies. He could see her, a woman in her fifties, with strawberry-blonde hair that had grown a little greyer and a step that wasn't quite so light. He waited there watching her, and after a moment of searching she looked at him too. But didn't keep walking. Instead, she took out her phone, and his rang.

'Where are you?' she asked.

He smiled.

'I'm standing here. Right in front of you.'

'I can't see you.'

There are people between us. But I'm here, I can see you. And you can see me.

'I'm waving.'

He raised his hand until she saw it, lowered her phone and walked towards him. They hugged. Then she took a step back to study him.

'Dear lord, how strange! I didn't recognise you.'

'It's only been a year.'

'More like, I recognised you, but I didn't see you. It was as if . . . I was looking for someone else.'

'Mamma.'

He hugged her again, and she examined him again.

'You're older.'

'I *am* older.'

'It's not a bad thing. I don't mean it like that. It's just . . . I don't know, maybe just time.'

He tried to take her bag, but she held it up to show she could manage by herself and set off along the platform, through Central Station, towards his car outside – when she stopped.

'Was it here?'

In the middle of the arrivals hall. In front of the long row of lockers.

'I saw it on TV. There was police tape all across the hall, and people waiting for their trains.'

She looked at him, remembering other police tape, fluttering in the air around a much smaller house after a different kind of bomb. A basement and her father running back and forth as the flames grew, and in the midst of everything her ten-year-old son had looked at her through the window, so scared.

'Fucking idiots!'

She put her hand on Leo's arm. He couldn't look at her, so he took hold of her bag and wouldn't let go until she let him carry it.

'The idiots were lucky, Mamma. No one died.'

The company truck was waiting for them not far from the exit, a parking ticket under one wiper. He tore it up and dropped it on the asphalt, while his mother walked around both the vehicle and him, nodding proudly at the logo on the door: CONSTRUCTION LTD.

'You built this, Leo. Just you. You made sure you had a job. And that Felix and Vincent had jobs, too.'

She hugged him again.

They drove south through Stockholm. He hesitated for a moment at the exit after Hallunda with his mother in the seat next to him, but then switched to the right-hand lane and left the E4 for the old main road – he wanted to drive past, to slow down just before the barrier.

The shabby blue Volvo and the military van were still there. And beside them, four cop cars. Three in official livery and one unmarked. Blue-and-white police tape hung like another gate and two armed police officers stood on guard in front of it.

'Something's happened.'

His mother had noticed him glancing in that direction, and she knocked on her window and pointed.

'Leo, do you see it? That plastic tape . . . that always means something bad has happened.'

He increased his speed again and the cars, the uniforms, even the police tape faded away in his rear-view mirror.

Now everyone knew.

Broncks looked at the growing crowd, which still consisted mostly of policemen and soldiers.

'That guy there, Sanna, in civilian clothing. Who did you say he was?'

'The inspector. He's followed every step I've taken. As if this was . . . personal.'

Broncks zigzagged between uniforms and walked his way with his hand extended.

'John Broncks. City Police. We met briefly when I arrived.'

'Joachim Nielsen. FO 44. And I know what you're thinking.'

The smell of cigarettes was stronger when he stood closer to him.

'And what am I thinking?'

'That I should have seen it.'

'Should you have?'

'I have followed protocol to the letter. All the instructions that are part of my job description.'

He stopped. From the woods, just behind them, two people were approaching. A woman and a man with a camera in hand. Broncks recognised the woman. A journalist. A pretty good one. They must have made a wide circle around the roadblock. But she shouldn't be here, not yet, it was too early.

'So much for secrecy.'

'Excuse me?'

'Always somebody who tips off the media to make an easy ten thousand.'

They waited while the journalist and the photographer were shooed away, not roughly, but firmly.

'So who was it? Whose hands are the weapons in?'

Broncks shook his head slightly.

'I don't know who they are. But I know what they've been using them for.'

The crowd was getting larger. Another four men had climbed up the steep hill and onto the gravel. Two in suits and two in uniform. From the National Bureau of Investigation and the security department of the Commander-in-Chief. They nodded to the inspector, who seemed much less anxious, as if this was what he'd been waiting for.

Broncks shook the inspector's hand – he would probably be redeployed very soon – then went back to the empty storage space and the smell of gunpowder.

They'd broken in sometime between the fourth and the nineteenth of

October, between the previous inventory and the hijacking of a security van in Farsta.

Nearly six months ago.

Where the hell do you hide a whole regiment's worth of weapons for that long?

———

Late morning light lit up the spacious garage. The floor was stained with oil and paint, and the large workbench on which they'd sawn apart a safe and built a bomb was now covered by cardboard boxes filled with nails and a small pile of tools under a couple of metres of rounded oak mouldings. Leo let his mother step in first, walk down the strip of light in a room that never seemed to end.

'We do quite a bit of preparation here,' he said.

'Preparation?'

'Structures, models, that sort of thing.'

She looked proud.

'I'm so glad you're doing well. And that you're taking care of Vincent and Felix. And all this is yours?'

'Ours. We need a lot of space, Mamma. The company is expanding.'

She pushed the oak mouldings aside and picked up a hammer, twisted and turned it, a screwdriver, a wrench, and then picked up what was underneath – a packet of cigarettes.

'What's this?'

'You can see what it is.'

'Do you smoke?'

'Sometimes.'

'But not Vincent?'

He smiled at her, putting his hand against her cheek.

'It's good to see you too, Mamma.'

They heard a truck coming across the asphalt yard, and moved aside as Felix drove into the garage and parked next to them, a bale of insulation and a couple of ten-litre buckets of paint in the back.

'Another company truck?'

'I told you, Mamma. We're expanding.'

Felix nearly jumped out of the driver's seat, arms outstretched.

'Mum!'

He lifted her up in a big hug and spun her around twice, while the dust from yellow house paint whirled off his work clothes.

'Now, Felix!'

She laughed, and Leo thought how it was so lovely when Mamma laughed that you wanted to join in with her.

Felix let her go, and now her youngest son opened the truck door.

'And Vincent!'

She hugged him a little longer than the others. He didn't really look comfortable, but tried to hide it with a smile.

'You've grown . . . so big!'

'Well, I am eighteen years old.'

'You're seventeen.'

'Soon.'

She took a half-step back without letting go.

'Vincent – you smell of smoke.'

'Mamma, it's *me* who smokes,' said Felix.

'So now both of you are covering it up,' she said, looking at Leo with a smile. It was hard to know whether it was sincere. Felix decided that it was.

'Sometimes it's better for mothers not to know everything. Right?'

The warm spring sun was only shining in the yard now, and she looked around as they walked towards the house, perhaps looking for a lawn, though she didn't say so. She linked her arm with Felix's.

'How long are you staying?' he asked.

'I'm leaving early tomorrow morning. To see Grandma. But you can come with me? All of you? To Sköndal. Leo, how far is it from here?'

A place they'd visited not so long ago. One brother had driven by the little house that belonged to Grandma and Grandpa in a hijacked security van, one had been lying on a hill ready to shoot, and one had landed a getaway boat at the jetty.

'We can't, Mamma. We've got so much . . . you know.'

'I know. You're *expanding*. Shall we go in?'

Anneli had watched them from the kitchen window, all four in the open garage. They'd hugged and laughed. A togetherness that left no space for anyone else.

She'd seen how Leo headed for the house first, like a surrogate father taking responsibility. Then Felix, who in front of his mother always seemed a few years younger than he was, transformed into the one who made her laugh, a role they both seemed to need. And Vincent just behind them, always the baby, no matter how hard he tried.

She should have known.

The front door opened, and Anneli greeted this woman she'd never really understood. They talked, of course, but not about anything specific. Leo's mother never said what she was really thinking – and certainly never straightforwardly. She forced you to search for answers by asking her questions, and every time Anneli did so, it felt as if Leo's mother saw through her – as if she'd done something wrong. Leo could be like that sometimes; they scrutinised every question looking for its intention, preparing themselves to avoid being hurt – as if it were something more than just a simple question.

'Can you look after Mamma and show her round?'

Leo could hear the television in the living room, as it showed footage from the empty arms dump.

'I'd like you to accompany me the first time your mother visits us.'

So he did. He tried to rush through the house tour, which took so much longer than he'd hoped because his mother stopped in every room and wanted to know more, be told more, and Anneli, every time she got the opportunity, reiterated how this was only temporary, *I know, Britt-Marie, it's not much of a garden, but it'll be better in a year*, explained that they'd buy a much bigger one when the company had grown. First floor and the last room, their bedroom, and he could finally leave them at the window overlooking their neighbour's apple trees and lawn, *something like that, Britt-Marie, that's the sort of home I'd like.*

Felix and Vincent sat at opposite ends of the living room sofa waiting for a breaking news bulletin that was about to begin.

'Do they know?' asked Felix.

'Yeah. I drove past,' replied Leo. 'There were loads of people there.'

The TV host had sat there since they were little, voice calm and face neutral whether he was reporting on the stock market or a death.

> The greatest weapons theft in Swedish history was discovered this morning in a military armoury in Botkyrka, less than thirty kilometres south of Stockholm.

Short scenes from a patch of gravel in a forest with a small grey building at its centre. The camera aimed through the open door at a brightly lit, confined space. An unsteady movement, sometimes out of focus as it searches for a big hole, it's as if the entire camera is tilted forward and pulled down into the image of blackness.

According to the report, the police are searching for perpetrators described as being well versed in military tactics and knowledgeable in the handling of explosives.

Leo felt the calm again, almost a kind of happiness.

'But look, Leo . . . that's it, that's what we drove past on the way here!'

Mamma. He hadn't noticed that she'd come into the room.

'I told you so. Every time they put up that police tape, it means something bad has happened!'

She squeezed onto the sofa between her younger sons. Felix felt her shoulder against his, but said nothing. He was the one who usually made Mamma laugh; now he had no idea what to say. She didn't know, of course, but she looked at him as if she did, a look that forgave everything, even his dreadful betrayal of her years earlier. He grabbed the remote and lowered the volume until it was silent. Maybe he should do it now. Maybe he should look at her and say, *Mamma, we were the ones who stole all those guns on the TV, and then we robbed five banks with them*, and maybe she would lean over and hug him.

'Felix? What's wrong? What is it?'

More pictures from an empty arms dump. And everyone except his mother knew that what should be lying there was lying under their feet instead.

'I'm thinking about leaving the . . . construction company.'

Leo had been quiet since their mother came into the room. Now he jumped a little.

'You're thinking about . . . *what*?'

Felix didn't look at him. He looked at his mother.

'Because I don't think . . . you know, I'm not really sure I want to be in the building trade.'

'No?'

'Mamma, I think I want to start studying.'

Felix felt Leo's questions and eyes, but pretended not to notice them. He just looked at Mamma, who smiled at him.

'What fun, Felix, of course you should study.'

She hugged him, and then turned to Leo.

'Right, Leo? Doesn't that sound right?'

———

301

The garage inside the garage. John Broncks knocked and waited for Sanna to ask him to enter.

'John – you don't need to knock. You've never knocked before, come in.'

'The Military League. That's what they're calling them now.'

When a criminal or a group of criminals were first connected to a pattern of crimes, they were given a name, a label. Military weapons, combat harnesses, boots, precision, communication. The name had seemed so obvious after those first published pictures of an empty arms dump just a few hours earlier.

On the workbench in the forensic scientists' little nook lay fragments of plastic and hardboard spread out in a sooty puzzle.

'Right now,' said Sanna, 'you're looking at the plate they used to build the bomb. The plastic explosives were divided into twelve piles and linked together with pentylstubin. And in order to make a hole with a diameter of sixty centimetres, the weight of the explosives would have been around half a kilo.'

'It must have made a helluva bang.'

'The plate of explosives lay *under* the foundations. The sound was muffled by the building. And besides – they were far out in the forest.'

She looked at him, tired after a long day of work, eyes that he'd once fallen in love with. She reached for the jacket hanging on the back of the chair.

'We can carry on talking about this if you walk with me.'

Through the corridors of police headquarters and out onto the street. Beside each other on a deserted block, not talking at all. It was a few hours before midnight, and even colder now.

'Big Brother. That's what I call him. The leader. He's addicted to robbery. And in order to get the same high, the rush, he'll need a little more and a little more. When he planned the hijacking of that security van in Farsta, sitting in a wheelchair waiting for them to come . . . that was enough, then. Sitting in a van outside a bank in Svedmyra . . . that was enough, then. But afterwards . . . he needs to increase the dose. So he plans to take two banks, simultaneously, one by himself while two of his partners take the other.'

Hantverkar Street ended, and Broncks nodded towards the bridge at the edge of Riddar Bay, and she nodded back and followed him.

'So next time, he'll need to do even more. Maybe rob more banks, maybe do more shooting, maybe . . . in order to get high, to get a rush, he'll have to raise the stakes. And for this kind of addict, it won't stop – not until death stops him.'

The water on the right-hand side was still, the ferries across the archipelago all docked until tomorrow, and the railway tracks to the left peaceful and deserted.

'Big Brother?' she said, meaningfully.

He stopped. There was a bench in the middle of the bridge and he leaned against it as he watched her – she who knew him in a way very few others did. Or she *thought* she did.

'I know what you're thinking. But it's not that fucking simple. If you think I'm putting my brother's face to someone, then you're wrong. They aren't . . . they don't have the same motivations.'

'How do you know? Two big brothers who use violence.'

'But this . . . he's doing it for personal gain.'

'So your brother killed for someone else's sake, is that what you're saying?'

He stared coldly at her.

'Sanna?'

'Yeah?'

'Sometimes I don't understand what the hell you're talking about.'

They walked quietly past Riddarholmen, an island of beautiful buildings where no one lived, then on towards Slussen and the contours of Södermalm, which stood up to greet them. Took the stairs outside the hotel to a spot with railings and a gorgeous view of a city about to go to sleep. Looking out over Stockholm, over the rooftops and alleyways, her voice was no longer mechanical, it hadn't been all day.

'We . . . walked past each other once,' she said. 'Did you know that, John? On King Street.'

She looked at him in the way he'd hoped she would again someday.

'I saw you. From afar.'

I saw you.

'It was summer. I don't know, a couple years ago. It was a Saturday. Loads of people on the street. I tried to catch your eyes when we passed and you, John, you looked away.'

You saw me. And I chose to look away.

He'd imagined this conversation every day for ten years. Several times a day. She'd been there all that time. When he woke up. When he went

303

to bed. And he wished he could explain why he'd asked her to move out on that long-ago Thursday, why he'd told her to be gone by the time he came back. He wanted to tell her about the panic attack that had hit him as he approached, that the closer he got, the more overwhelmed he'd been by the thought of what was no longer in the apartment, and how desperately he had fought for each breath. And then that terrible walk through rooms with bare walls, how afterwards he lay on the floor in the hallway with his heart racing, so fucking frightened, two days at the hospital and EKG tests.

And now she was standing in front of him, almost touching him. And if he moved, the moment might be lost. She leaned closer and kissed him, and he only kissed her back when he was sure she meant it.

He wept.

He held her and wept and couldn't stop. He hadn't even cried at his father's funeral, because you can't cry if you haven't forgiven.

'I saw you, too.'

'What?'

'That day. On King Street. I saw you but—'

'You saw me? But you didn't show it?'

He thought that maybe he should be asking her questions about her life now. About what it was like for her these days.

'Just like you didn't show it when we lived together?'

He should ask her about her sister. And if she'd ever bought the house she'd wanted to buy. Ask her why she'd applied for a position in the City Police. And who else had stood this close to her.

'John, do you remember . . . do you remember the last time?'

She's screaming.

'No. I don't remember.'

She screams, 'You're so fucking hard.' She screams, 'You're so fucking hard,' once more, then closes the door and disappears.

'You don't remember why you packed up my things in a fucking IKEA bag? You . . . haven't changed! You're still the same, John, as you were then, and you don't remember. It's still impossible to reach you.'

She wasn't crying, he was. But she walked away towards the bus stops and the taxi rank, and he didn't turn round this time; he didn't want to see her disappear.

Leo stood in the window and looked out at the hollows collecting rain-water in the yard. His mother behind him in the room on the edge of the sofa bed in a nightgown so different from the ones Anneli wore, lifting off decorative pillows and throwing them in a pile on the chequered floor.

He pulled down the blinds and turned round, gently moving her away from the bed.

'I'll do it, it's a little bit tricky.'

He pushed down on one corner and grabbed the handle with the other – and jerked. The mattress gave in. It folded open, and he pulled it out to its full length. The bed covered four floor tiles, two white and two black, which in turn covered the safe and the entrance to the weapons store. Then he undid the straps holding the quilt in place, and ran his hands several times over the sheet to smooth it out.

'To be honest, Leo, I expected this.'

'Expected . . . what?'

'That when Vincent came to me and said he wanted to move to Stockholm, to you . . . that you'd take care of him.'

She held his hand and stroked it, and he shivered even though it felt familiar. It was the same this morning, when they'd walked through Central Station.

'Vincent takes care of himself.'

'I know for a fact that he doesn't. Not entirely, anyway. You've always taken care of him. And of Felix. And even me and your father.'

He shook his head, as if he didn't want to hear any more.

'Mamma . . .'

'Leo, if you hadn't intervened, I would have died. He would never have stopped hitting me.'

She saw the guilt in his eyes, but she didn't care.

'I'm so proud of you. You take responsibility. You *always* take responsibility.'

'Mamma, stop, please.'

She grabbed his other hand now and put it between hers.

'You've succeeded at what he failed to do. You started a company that's expanding instead of going out of business, which gives your brothers jobs. You're more a father to them than he ever was. Or . . . he was like you. In the beginning. Caring. Loving.'

She fell silent. And when she continued, her voice had hardened.

'You're more like me. Do you know that? We can take a lot, you and me, Leo. You might not be able to see it, but it's there inside us.'

She'd surely see through him soon, realise that what she thought was guilt was actually shame. So he smiled and hugged her.

'Goodnight, Mamma.'

As he left he switched off the overhead light without turning, and went out into the kitchen.

She thought she was sleeping on a solid floor laid by her youngest sons, when what was beneath it would have shattered her. She believed that her eldest son ran a construction company, one which gave all her sons a job. She thought exactly what he wanted everyone to think. Even she saw what he wanted everyone else to see.

And yet – it didn't feel good.

He looked in the window for the image of someone she thought was like her, someone who took responsibility.

Breathed out, slowly, until the windowpane blurred and his reflection disappeared.

Just one more. Just one more, and it would be the biggest yet. A triple robbery. Fifteen million kronor. Then he'd sell back the weapons, and Felix would be able to start studying. Then he'd be like her again. If they stopped after that no one would ever know.

55

NOTHING WAS ALLOWED on the coffee table when his programme started except a brand new notepad, each page white and empty. He'd bought it when he was buying the newspapers at Jönsson's kiosk. He rarely read the news, but for the last week he'd walked down to the square around four o'clock every day in order to buy the morning and evening editions, all of which lay in a pile on his sofa now. The cutting board, knife, ashtray, onion and wine were gone, even the remnants of tobacco and the thin red rings made by his glasses of wine had been wiped away and dried.

He moved closer to the pile of newspapers, flipped through it uneasily without knowing why: he'd already read every article several times. But the TV show he was waiting for always had the latest images from current crimes, ones the newspapers didn't yet have access to, information that the police chose to present; it was as if the pigs thought they were doing something important, even though they just sat there like they were part of the studio furniture.

He wasn't worried. He was impatient. It was crawling so insistently inside him, he just couldn't sit still. He pulled his reading glasses out of his pocket, and they got caught on the envelope that now contained nineteen thousand kronor in 500-kronor notes. Not as thick as it had been on that autumn day when Leo came here for the first time in four and a half years and handed him forty-three thousand as if it were Monopoly money in order to pay a debt he felt he didn't owe.

Ivan swapped the newspaper on top for one below, which showed a picture of a black-clad robber aiming his weapon. He'd stood in a queue at the supermarket down in the square that moved so slowly he wondered why they didn't open another cash register. While he waited his eyes had landed on the newspaper rack, and there from a distance he'd seen two words, **MILITARY LEAGUE**. And then, when it was his turn, he saw the rest – according to the article, whoever had stolen a shitload of weapons from a military armoury had used them to carry out a robbery in Sköndal near a summer camp for the handicapped that Britt-Marie had worked at for several years, and two robberies just five hundred metres from his own home.

Sköndal. Her domain. A place the police described as so obscure that you had to know about it in order to choose it.

Ösmo. His domain. And the paper pointed out the brutality of eight shots forming a face.

He had gradually stopped caring about what they wrote, focusing instead on the pictures, in particular two black and white ones, that appeared in all the papers, of the man they called the leader. Slightly blurry photos, and yet. Broad shoulders. Eyes behind the mask as if she were standing there looking at him. And a mouth with thin lips stretched into a tight line, an expression he himself often wore.

Ivan adjusted the notebook and lifted his pencil.

It was starting now.

SWEDEN'S MOST WANTED. According to the newspapers today's whole programme would be devoted to the Military League. A special that would highlight every aspect, every detail, in the hope of generating responses from the public.

He flattened out the pages of his notepad and watched the host standing in front of the cops, talking about the biggest weapons theft in Swedish history, and about the six aggravated robberies that the group might be linked to.

Six robberies.

He wrote that down. The newspapers had only written about four.

Rapid pictures of the insides of bullet-riddled banks. Shattered glass on the floor and open doors to empty bank vaults. A security van in Farsta. Handels Bank in Svedmyra. Handels Bank and SE-Bank in Ösmo. Savings Bank in Rimbo and SE-Bank in Kungsör.

He started writing again. New information.

Rimbo. Kungsör.

Then several seconds of a panning shot taken inside Stockholm Central Station. Where a bomb had exploded. Terrified people pushing each other behind a high fence.

Bomb?

He wrote it down, but couldn't really see it. He understood the weapons, he did. And the robbery. But not the bomb. The word 'bomb' didn't belong with the rest. It didn't fit into the pattern.

The host now spoke about the members of the group. About their military knowledge. About how they were athletically built, spoke perfect Swedish, and probably had no criminal record.

Perf. Swed.
No record.

And then. Brand new images. Moving.

They hadn't shown anything like this before. Shots from various cameras just before they were shot down. Short snippets angled from above and often only a few seconds long, depicting a clear leader described as between six foot two and six foot four, weighing between 80 and 85 kilos.

He dropped the pencil and heard it roll across the table and onto the floor. Despite the fact that this was exactly what he was supposed to be keeping tabs on. Height. Weight. All the things he didn't know. All the information that was new. That was why he'd bought this notebook.

But he didn't need to write it down.

He could see it clearly, though it was just a few seconds of footage: the pattern that is repeated in everything, from the smallest element to the movement of our limbs, a driving force inside millions of cells present even in the unique rings of small ridges on our palms and fingertips.

Ivan reached for the wine bottle that stood on the floor at his feet, untouched. He opened it and drank until he had to stop to catch his breath.

Now he knew.

56

THEY DROVE ACROSS Sweden for six hours to reach the starting point of their very last robbery, setting up camp a kilometre or so outside the small town of Ullared. It had only a couple of thousand inhabitants, but was also the location of the largest outlet store in Sweden, a place people from all over the country made pilgrimages to. Especially in a week like this – Easter. Free time to burn, one of the year's commercial peaks. And with the outlet store on one side of the town's central square, the vaults of the three banks on the other side would be full right now.

Spending the night in a patch of forest, they brought camping beds and sleeping bags, freeze-dried food and water which they heated over a camping stove. First, they made the final adjustments to the vehicle they'd arrived in, creating a secret wall in a small truck they'd rented a week earlier. Rented because it had to be obtained legally, as it was the vehicle they would pass any checkpoints in later. Then, when darkness had fallen, they'd gone to Varberg, the closest town, to steal the truck they'd use during the robbery.

After they came back, they took turns standing guard while the others got a few hours' sleep. But Felix hadn't slept at all, and gazed up at the stars, white specks in a blue-black sky, as the moisture forced its way up from the ground. Something didn't feel right.

All night it was so quiet in the woods. The only sound was the occasional barking of dogs. A kennel, that's what it sounded like.

They woke up at 5 a.m. Breakfast was a thermos of coffee and ready-made sandwiches.

They started the day by refilling the fuel tank from the four cans they'd brought with them from Stockholm – you couldn't trust a stolen truck to have enough petrol. Then they sat down on their adjacent camping beds, laid out aerial maps like art prints and went through the three parallel robberies. Leo would rob Bank 1 by himself, Vincent and Jasper would take Bank 2, and then they would all rendezvous at Bank 3 and rob it together.

During the entire process Felix would keep watch over the town's entry and exit points through the hatch in the roof of the truck. Cutting out the hatch was the last element of preparation, one he was now trying to finish – the delivery truck was now missing a large circular chunk of its ceiling. The sweat ran down his forehead and into his eyes, started to sting.

'Vincent? Can you give me a hand?'

His little brother pulled the creaking door to the side and stood up on the seat, pressing upwards on the nearly loose sheet of metal. Together they prised off the hatch and threw the remains into the ditch.

'Felix?'

'Yeah?'

'This isn't going to go well.'

Vincent's anxiety was the same as had kept Felix awake last night.

'It's never felt like this before, ever.'

'I'll be behind the wheel. And as long as I'm there, everything will turn out fine. OK?'

He wanted to believe it. But he didn't.

One last time.

This was their destination. Three banks at the right time. Ten million, fifteen, maybe even twenty. Then we'll have enough. That was what this had been about. Getting enough money. And doing what no one else had done.

'One last time, Vincent. Then we disappear. And no one will ever hear from the Military League again.'

––––––––––

The light was different. In the forest, it had been muted, greener, but sitting here, with the car parked diagonally in front of the three banks, the daylight streaming in through the hole in the roof, it seemed changed to Felix: sharper, making everything look more distinct. It felt as if he was seeing the machine gun for the first time. Even though it had been down in their armoury for over six months, he'd actually never been this close to it. An 11-kilo machine in his hands, cartridges in long metal strips hanging down the sides, fangs ready to tear apart whatever got in its way. The automatic rifle he'd always had lying across his thighs during a robbery, waiting in the getaway car, was small and petite and invisible; this was a beast, like comparing a pike with a great white shark. He folded out the tripod, twisted his body in the cramped space trying to get a good grip on the ungainly gun, lifted it over his head and through the sawn-out hole and placed it on the roof. The ammunition flapped, rustling like chain mail, and he seized it with his forearm in order to silence it.

A war zone: that's what he thought it looked like. Like something from a TV news report, a civil war where a guerrilla fighter lay on a hill, firing on a village. Now he was the one, sticking his head up through the hole and looking down the barrel of the gun at the people in the square of a typical Swedish town.

The three banks sat in adjacent buildings just off the central square. To the far right, Jasper and Vincent had already stepped into SE-Bank, and Felix could hear Jasper shouting at the staff and customers to *get down on the fucking floor*. At Handels Bank, in the middle, a cashier had heard the gunshots next door, and when she looked out of the window she saw Felix, guarding every road in and out of the square with a machine gun. Her eyes shifted and then she noticed another man dressed in black and wearing a mask. But he didn't stop at her bank: he ran on to the next bank, so she locked the front door and hid behind the counter.

As he went past, Leo heard the cashier locking the door of the bank that they'd all be robbing together in exactly one hundred and eighty seconds. But this one, the Savings Bank, on the far left, this one he'd take on his own.

'Listen to me very carefully,' he shouted as he opened the door. 'I'm going to rob this bank. So everyone in here needs to lie down on the floor. On your stomach with your arms out. And if you treat me as politely as I'm treating you, then you can stand up again in five minutes and go home to your families.'

He looked around and realised that practising the robbery of *one* bank in the garage was the same as practising for all banks – they didn't differ much, with the counter at the front, the desk that handled loan applications a little further in, and the vault in the same section as the cashiers' desks.

The only thing he could never really foresee was how many people he'd find inside and how they would react.

He counted three customers – two young women around Anneli's age and one older man with a grey overcoat similar to the one their grandfather always wore in the spring. Then there were four bank employees – three behind the counter and one who'd just returned from getting a cup of coffee.

And they all did as he said.

They lay down and stared at the shiny stone floor.

'You, with the coffee.'

The cashier had carefully put her still-steaming coffee cup on the desk before getting on the floor.

'Take this bag and put all the money from the tills into it. Do it quickly. But don't be nervous. I'm just here for the cash, nothing else. And then you and I are going to go into the vault and, when the bag is completely full, you'll never see me again.'

It was the second time he'd robbed a bank on his own. And it was so quiet. He couldn't even hear them breathing. Just the ventilation system rumbling above his head. Not like Ösmo – with the woman who screamed and screamed – this was perfect: he was in control of every ticking second.

He'd even chosen the right cashier. She steadily and confidently emptied the money from cashbox after cashbox. And when she glanced at him, her eyes were not judgemental – he was calm, and therefore she was calm. It was that simple.

'You're doing a great job. You're not putting these people in any unnecessary danger. I really appreciate that.'

They walked side by side towards the vault. Her badge said her name was Petra. And while she unlocked the vault, he checked his watch to see how much time had elapsed.

'Petra?'

She looked at him as she pulled open the vault door.

'This is how it is – things are going well. You've got plenty of time.'

Two and a half, maybe three million kronor stacked on the shelves. A little less than he'd anticipated. But they had two more banks to make up for it. Petra was methodical as she filled the bag with perfectly wrapped bundles.

One last glance towards the bank premises.

They were all still lying there with their arms outstretched.

TV screens – that was how Felix had always seen the robberies from the outside, and how he saw them now as he turned the gun from bank to bank. A TV report about a war, with three televisions tuned to different channels. Three square bank windows, each lit with soft yellow light from inside. Three boxes where three parallel scenes played out.

On the TV to the left, the Savings Bank, a lone masked man in black, Leo, was following a bank cashier while she filled a bag with money from the tills. On the screen to the right, SE-Bank, were two masked men in black, Vincent and Jasper, one taking care of the tills while the other held a gun to a bank official's back on their way to the vault. And last, the TV in the middle, Handels Bank, which they would rob last, together, and where the staff were retreating as far into the bank as possible.

In Svedmyra and Rimbo and Kungsör there'd been just one screen. In Ösmo two. Here there were three televisions broadcasting a show directed by his brother. None of it was real.

Then, suddenly, for the very first time, it was.

The parallel films now featured new stories that he hadn't anticipated: new lines, new scenes, new characters acting outside the script. Three chance interruptions that shattered the illusion. It was no longer possible to reduce what he saw to a drama on a TV screen. The people existed. They were stepping out of the picture. And if they were real, they were also vulnerable. And here he was, standing with a real machine gun in his hands, which shot eight hundred lethal rounds a minute.

First, an elderly hunter left his car with his wife still in the passenger seat. Wearing a camouflage jacket and a hat with reflectors, he opened the boot and pulled out a case with a hunting rifle inside. He then walked purposefully towards the machine gun, which Felix was pointing in his direction. Right up to him.

'What the hell do you think you're doing?'

And Felix aimed a war machine at him.

'Get out of here, now!'

But the old man just stood there, staring defiantly into the barrel and cocking his own gun.

It was him or the old man. He had no choice.

They were aiming at each other, and Felix knew he was about to shoot. That was when the wife got out of the car and began shouting at her husband, pulling on his jacket.

'Please, stop, Bengt, come back, come with me right now!'

It had been so close. And it had been *real*.

Then Leo left the bank, walking the way he did when he was feeling on top of the world . . . until suddenly he stopped, fear filling his face.

The bag in Leo's hand exploded. A dense, red cloud of dye pushed its way through the open teeth of the zip, staining his thin leather gloves, and kept rising into his mouth and nostrils and eyes.

A damn fucking dye pack.

Two million, probably even more, destroyed.

I was in control. Of the whole place. We had an agreement. And she ruined everything.

He kicked open the glass door, holding the steaming bag in front of him like a time bomb, and stepped over the customers who were pressing themselves to the floor.

'I told you! Everyone in here could go home to their fucking families if you just did what I said!'

He knew exactly where in the room she was – under the second cashier's desk.

'Petra!'

The still-warm coffee cup was standing there.

'Petra, get up!'

She did, and when she looked at him, her eyes weren't at all like before. Now they were filled with contempt.

'You sneaked in a fucking dye pack! I trusted you – and you betrayed that trust!'

'I did my job.'

Although her voice betrayed her fear, still she spoke without hesitation.

'You are responsible for their lives! This is your fault!'

And then he started shooting. Without aiming. Just held the trigger in for as long as it took to empty the whole magazine. Into the safety glass, chair backs, desks, walls, ceiling. And all the while she stood there looking at him. Weeping. Convinced that she was about to die.

'It's your fucking fault!'

Then he left with the bag in his hand, while the red smoke slowly petered out. One bank to go.

Felix had never seen Leo like this before, not when it was important for him to keep his composure – he'd just lost it in the bank, firing wildly, out of pure anger, completely out of control. Like Ivan, Felix thought, Leo had lost control when a woman betrayed him, and he'd turned back in order to punish her. From the roof of the car, it was difficult to see if anyone had been hit. He didn't think so. But the reality that had arrived with the old man and his hunting rifle moved even closer now: he saw its pores, experienced it with all his senses.

Then came his little brother.

It was Vincent who reached the third, middle bank first and arrived at the now-locked bank door. He used the butt of his gun and the barrel to break down the window, splintering the TV screen, and ran inside. He ordered them to *lie down* as he was supposed to, and everyone complied.

Except for one elderly lady.

She walked towards him with her hand outstretched as if asking for something, perhaps to be let out. An outstretched hand that was mis-interpreted. Felix watched as Vincent turned round and cocked his gun in one movement, before realising that the old lady wasn't a threat. With the gun pointed at her, she started pleading so loudly it could be heard all the way out in the car.

'Don't shoot, please, don't shoot!'

A single finger-tap away. His little brother had almost killed someone. And reality had never been as present as it was when Vincent stood motionless with his gun pointed at the ground trying to understand what he'd almost done.

Then, just as suddenly, the three parallel films returned to their prede-termined course.

The robbers left the third bank through the sharp gap in the broken TV screen, rushed towards the car, threw in the bags and pulled open the side door, while Felix took down the war machine and sat himself in the driver's seat.

Moments later, they were zigzagging between passing cars frozen in fear on the road.

Vincent guessed they were going at a hundred and twenty kilometres per hour on a very narrow road. Cold air blew in from the hole, and the entire roof rattled. In front of him, Leo furiously searched around in a bag full of red bills.

'Fuck! Fuck fuck fuck! Two million! And all of it's red!'

Vincent could still feel the tension of his finger on the trigger as he looked at the woman's wrinkles and grey hair, could still hear her pleading to leave.

She'd been brave, he thought. And the cashier had been just as brave when, despite her terror, she did as she'd been instructed to do, sneaking a dye pack in among the money that the robber was demanding.

'That fucking bitch, everything's red!'

Leo continued to scream and Vincent looked up at the treetops through the sawn-out hole. The forest was becoming denser. A few kilometres outside town and only one or so left to the forest road Felix would turn onto.

'And you two? How much did you get?'

'Don't know,' replied Jasper.

'Guess, damn it!'

'Max . . . four hundred. Altogether. The vault in the first bank was completely empty.'

Wrong answer.

The bag ricocheted off the wall when Leo threw it into the back of the van.

'Four hundred thousand lousy kronor!'

The treetops were no longer one mass, Vincent was able to discern individual trees. They'd slowed down, left the road, and Felix accelerated again as the uneven surface started to beat against the chassis.

Not far to go until the protective darkness behind the wall. The forest road stretched out and started to slope upwards. And they were halfway up that hill when the first thump sounded. Vincent heard it and felt it. A clear blow. The next blow was even more powerful, as if made by a wooden mallet. It was then they started to lose speed. And he knew right away what was wrong.

There's a very particular feeling when an engine gives out.

The van was on a steep incline as Felix put on the handbrake and hopped out.

'It's . . . completely dead! It won't start!'

With torch in hand, Felix was under the stationary van.

'The fuel line, Leo. It's completely broken!'

'You're sure?'

'Yes.'

'That fucking dye pack and now this . . . *Fuck!* . . . fuck fuck! . . . we'll have to push it the rest of the way up, then roll it as far as we can. And walk the rest. We'll be at least twenty minutes late!'

Eight young arms pushed a heavy van up the hill, each metre taking a little more of their remaining time. When they reached the crest, Felix jumped in and steered until the wheels almost stopped and turned straight into the woods. Two kilometres left to their rendezvous. They started running.

The truck was standing where they'd left it nearly an hour earlier, at the edge of the turning area, surrounded by trees and stones and a small pile of timber. If someone had gone by, become curious and opened the doors, they would have seen just what Vincent and Leo and Jasper saw now as they pushed the rear doors open. Bales of scratchy, rough, fluffy insulation. They jumped in, pushed their way through and up to the wall that backed on to the cab, and loosened it. An illusion. A detachable wall that exposed a secret chamber, which they'd built the previous week in their garage in Tumba. It was there they'd stay during their ride to Gothenburg and the next vehicle change.

'Twenty-seven minutes late,' said Leo.

The police had had time to set up roadblocks now.

Felix was nearly finished; he'd changed out of his robbery gear into his work clothes, because he'd be doing the driving.

'Knock twice on the wall if we need to turn the safety off on our weapons. OK?'

Felix nodded and straightened out the fake wall.

It was completely dark in that small space.

———————

It was a squeeze, and Vincent was sitting very close to Leo, almost on top of him, as they bumped from the unmade road to the asphalt. Jasper was just as tight on Leo's other side. They sat in complete blackness, the kind of darkness that was living, organic, a tissue growing out of the wall and into the cab where Felix sat. Every time Leo exhaled in short, intense breaths, Vincent could feel the warm air caress his cheek.

And every time the truck slowed slightly, they were inhaled by the darkness, the movements of the truck rocking around inside his chest.

But not this time.

Felix stopped for real.

They heard the first knock. Then the second.

Vincent felt Leo shift his body in order to turn off the safety on his weapon, and Jasper followed his lead, a clicking sound that bounced around the cavity. Vincent realised that this was what he'd been waiting for all night and all day.

This isn't going to go well.

He knew what a roadblock looked like. Two police cars with rotating blue lights. Four officers – one of them holding up a sign that said POLICE on it, requesting vehicles to stop.

Felix hadn't slept either. He hadn't said anything, but Vincent had seen it in his eyes. He'd been awake for thirty hours.

He rolled down the window; they could hear everything through the thin wall.

'Can I see your driving licence?'

It was not an old voice. Barely older than Leo. Then silence. Felix kept his wallet in his breast pocket, and was probably taking it out now.

'Where are you going and where have you come from?'

'Come from?'

'Where have you been?'

'Has something happened?'

It was quiet again. Vincent imagined the policeman examining Felix's licence while his colleague waited a short distance away.

'I asked where you've been and where you're going.'

'A summer cottage in Tylösand. On the coast, white sandy beaches, pretty as hell. I rent it out. The first tenants arrive from Stockholm in a month, and they pay damn well. I'm putting in some insulation in one of the rooms for them. The materials are in the back.'

'Could you please step out of the vehicle?'

The door was opened, and there was a thud as Felix landed on the ground.

'And please open up the back.'

Steps along the side of the truck. He recognised Felix's. The policeman's steps were lighter – maybe he wasn't so big. Then the doors were opened, angled outwards. The policeman could now see straight in.

And light started to seep through the gap at the top where the secret wall met the ceiling. It was possible to see the policeman's shadow as he moved around.

Vincent held his breath. Closed his eyes. He tried to focus only on Felix, who might be talking to the other policeman.

In his mind, he saw her grey hair again, her wrinkles like tree rings that made him think she was probably wise, her outstretched hand appealing to him.

The bales of insulation on the other side of the wall were pushed aside. The plastic surrounding them scraped against the floor. He was close now, the policeman. The fabric of his jacket got caught as he turned, scratching against the wall.

Anything could happen. Any time. Jasper would shoot if the police found them. Leo, too. But Vincent hadn't turned the safety off. Not yet.

Someone was leaning against the secret wall. The gap up above let in a little more light. Leo and Felix had built it, and they usually did a good job. But what if . . .? What if the weight of a body caused it to give way?

'What are you looking for?'

'There's been a robbery.'

'A robbery?'

Get out of here.

'A bank robbery. And not one. Three.'

Away from the wall. Now.

'I get so tired of this,' Felix said.

Vincent opened his eyes. He could see him shaking his head.

'I mean . . . why don't those fools just get a job like the rest of us?'

The policeman wasn't leaning against the wall any longer. It sounded as if he was moving away, his clothes rubbing against the plastic around the closely packed bales.

The policemen hopped down from the back of the van. The two doors were closed.

The darkness enveloped them again, alive like before. There were foot-steps outside, Vincent could just make them out, and Felix saying some-thing to the officers about doing a good job. Reality had shattered for a few minutes, millions of shards falling like broken glass behind his eyelids. Now he put them back in place again, piece by piece. But they wouldn't fit.

The truck's engine started.

The shards could never be put back in their proper places again.

He was sure of it. The only thing he really was sure of. And he felt their speed increasing, as they found their way back into his chest.

57

VINCENT DRANK THE contents of the glass so slowly it turned lukewarm and then stale. He was being careful not to get drunk. Not here. He'd been on the verge of falling asleep several times, and a night without rest had left him with only the remnants of extreme focus and fear. Just a little longer, then they'd be on their way home, the thumping of the tracks would rock him to sleep and the images of a triple robbery would blur – the moment he'd almost stopped being a robber and become a murderer. A single moment that had split reality into two distinct alternatives.

He looked out the window of the bar at the back of Gothenburg's central train station.

Jasper.

Walking out of the 7-Eleven opposite the bar with bouncing steps, even though he too hadn't slept, carrying newspapers that shouted **TRIPLE ROBBERY, MILITARY LEAGUE**, accompanied by a picture of Jasper in a black mask caught by a surveillance camera right before the moment he shot it down. Jasper was flushed, and he threw the papers onto the table then went to the bar for a third beer and a third shot of Jägermeister that he downed at the counter.

'Have you seen? The late edition's arrived!'

'Ten minutes till departure.'

'Three fucking banks, Vincent, can you imagine? Fucking madmen!'

He held up the papers. He was talking too loudly. And looked around to make sure other people were paying attention to him.

'Jasper, stop,' Vincent whispered softly.

Jasper laughed, hoarsely and incoherently after so much alcohol in such a short time, while he picked up one of the papers and pointed to a large picture.

'Have you seen this guy?'

'There are cops out there! I saw them. Several of them! At the station! And they . . . stop for fuck's sake!'

Vincent didn't want to sit here with Jasper. He wanted to talk to his brothers, with Leo driving the truck somewhere along the E4 motorway or with Felix who was about to take off from Landvetter Airport and would land in Stockholm in forty-five minutes. He needed them, here, now.

Splitting up afterwards was another way of not attracting attention, yet here was someone doing just that, spattering his aggression all around him in an attempt to be provocative, as if the robbery hadn't let go of him and had to be let out somehow.

'Listen . . . everyone's talking about this. What do you think Grandma over there is reading about? And that guy there, sneaking Smirnoff into his coffee, don't you think he's seen the reports on TV? It's not weird if we are too. It's fucking weird if we *don't* do it! Just relax, little brother.'

Little Brother.

'Did you see Leo's eyes? When he realised that more than half of it was red? *I* saw them. *I* know exactly what he felt. Me and Leo . . . we planned this together. Then that fucking cashier puts a fucking dye pack in his bag! It's all red, and it's fucking worthless now. It'll have to be burned.'

'Jasper – shut up.'

'But we would have got a lot more money, little brother, if you hadn't wasted so much time talking to the staff like a fucking wuss! A bank robber doesn't need to coddle the staff! We could have fucking got a few more million!'

Coddle.

That bit and took hold.

Vincent had to get out of here. He stood up, grabbed the bag under the table and slung it over his shoulder, felt the outline of a gun on his hip. He headed towards the platform and the train to Stockholm, with Jasper running behind him.

'Little brother, coddling the staff.'

'Hey, I got the keys. Didn't I?'

'*Get* them? You *take* keys. Press the barrel against their foreheads until they're in your hand.'

He hadn't been able to resist. But no matter how long that fucking idiot talked to him, he would just lie down on the train seats and sleep. He would not, could not answer Jasper again.

'But listen. Leo explained that we're a real company. And in that case Leo . . . he owns the company, like a CEO, and I . . . I'm more like a supervisor and you, Vincent, are just a teensy little trainee, an intern, that's why you coddle the staff. Leo knows that. So he has me to take care of it. To be hard on the staff. And I am. Hard. Not like you, little brother.'

Vincent climbed up into the train carriage and walked along the narrow corridor with his hand behind his back, holding the bag in line with his body – he didn't want to poke any of the other passengers with an automatic rifle as he passed by. There was just one private compartment at the far end of each carriage. He drew the curtains, closed the door and put the bag on the luggage rack, then sank down across three seats with his jacket over his head.

As he lay there the thump of the joints between the rails moved upward and into his body, a pulsating lullaby in the same rhythm as the colours and small flashes of light that ran smoothly behind his eyelids. But within ten minutes the conductor came in to check their tickets, then Jasper stood on his seat and lifted the bag down and pushed a reinforced-steel-toed boot against Vincent's ribs.

'Want one?'

Jasper put the bag on the floor, took out a beer and opened it with his finger through the metal ring. Drops of beer spurted out and landed on Vincent's face.

'Please don't open that in my face.'

Jasper looked into the bag again, the folded wooden butt of the gun clearly visible next to the plastic bags filled with red-stained bills. He fished out another can and handed it to Vincent, who shook his head.

'What did I do to make you hate me so fucking much? Eh? Little brother?'

'We're not brothers.'

He'd answered again. And he could see it satisfied Jasper. But his head was so heavy . . .

'I'll call you little brother if I want to call you little brother. You're the youngest, right? And that's why you don't know shit about what Leo and I used to do – because you were just a puny, snotty whelp.'

Vincent wanted to be able to think clearly, but his eyes were itchy and dry, and the hair on the back of his neck felt charged with electricity.

'At every robbery, little brother . . . Leo goes first, I go last, and you're in the middle, the safest place. We protect you – Leo and I discussed that.'

Jasper started squeezing the empty can in his hand to make the annoying sound of a dent being pushed in and then popping out again.

'We get off a shitload of shots, but we always keep some in reserve in case any fucking cop starts getting ideas about following us. Haven't you ever wondered, little brother – where all the ammunition comes from?'

The dent on the can. In, out. A ticking second hand. Jasper moved it closer to Vincent's ear.

'If you only knew how much I've done for you, Vincent. Every day for six years. And you lie there with your fucking attitude. For fuck's sake!'

He was being provoked. He knew it, felt it.

'Six years . . . what the hell are you talking about?'

'What am I talking about? Where do you think we got the plastic explosives and pentylstubin to blow the floor out of the bunker?'

Vincent hurt all over. Sleep was all he'd wanted.

'Military service. First, Leo took what we needed. Then I did.'

But now it was as if his strength were slowly returning as he listened.

'Final excercises, little brother. It starts with them transporting a whole fucking truck full of sealed boxes and setting them down next to the road, in the middle of the snow. Weapons. Explosives. Ammunition. And after a while it's impossible for them to keep track of everything, but Leo knew and I knew that it was only when the exercise was over and everything was about to be driven back that the crates were inventoried.'

The louder the bloody idiot spoke, the more sure Vincent became that they would never rob a bank together again.

'And then, little brother, at night when we stood guard, we brought black bin bags with us. We had three hours in the snow to take out cartridges or pentyl or hand grenades. Black bin bags that we buried before going back to our stations.'

Nothing else existed except Jasper's mouth, with which he talked and talked about Leo, as if Leo were Jasper and Jasper were Leo.

'And we knew that after that exercise there would be a complete inspection, and they'd turn the whole fucking regiment inside out.'

As if Leo were Jasper and Jasper were Leo.

'Literally inside out, like a house search, they go through everything. But they didn't find anything. Nothing, little brother.'

You are not my brother.

'Do you understand? We've been planning this for six years, little brother – me and Leo.

'It's weird, you know . . . even though you're his little brother I know him better than you do. When we go into a bank, Leo and I have a bond that you don't have. We each know exactly what the other will do.'

Vincent stood up suddenly, in the middle of the swaying carriage. He wanted to hit those moving lips, empty out whatever energy his weary body had left.

'Me and Leo. We can do anything. We stopped the entire police force with a little fucking bomb. Imagine what we can do next time!'

'A bomb you pulled the safety ring out of, Jasper!'

He felt his fingertips pushing hard into the palm of his hand.

'I know it was you! Just like Felix, I've known all along!'

Jasper shook his head just like he'd done every other time. But then it was as if he changed his mind. And smiled.

'I knew the police would send in that bomb robot.'

'So it was you?'

'I know what I'm doing, little brother – nothing serious could have happened.'

'It was you who took out the safety ring! You denied it!'

'Nobody died. Right?'

'You lied! You lied to Leo! He trusted you! But you don't understand because you're . . . alone, you don't have any brothers!'

Vincent sat down, straightened out his fingers, which had gone white at the tips, and it was finally quiet in the train compartment. Something felt lighter inside.

'So I'm . . . alone?'

'Yes.'

Jasper was still staring blankly at him, as he unzipped the bag to take out one more beer. But that wasn't what he held up now. It was a submachine gun.

'And I have . . . no brothers?'

'No brothers.'

Jasper straightened out the butt of the gun, ran his hand down its barrel.

'Little brother? Do you know what I could do right now? Something that can be done alone. Without brothers.'

He left the seat so fast that Vincent didn't even understand what was happening, not until Jasper was down on one knee, pressing the gun to his head. It chafed against his temple, and Vincent slid gradually backwards until he sank into the headrest.

'Then I'll explain it to you, little brother. Listen to me now. With this I can do whatever the hell I want to.'

Vincent had never been this close to death before.

He realised that he'd become the security guard in an armoured van or the bank cashier behind a counter, that he'd changed places with them.

'Jasper, you have to—'

Jasper pressed harder, and it started to bleed where the barrel of the gun cut into his skin.

'I didn't lie to Leo, do you understand that?'

He held it there while someone passed outside their door. Someone else was laughing and talking loudly on the other side of the thin wall.

'Do you understand that? *Little brother?*'

Vincent wasn't sure if his head was moving, his body wasn't responding, but he tried as hard as he could to nod. Jasper lowered the weapon as calmly as he'd raised it, folded it up, put it back in the bag and zipped it up.

More steps outside. More voices.

Vincent sat perfectly still.

Nine robberies. And he hadn't realised it was that simple: you can take what you want if you've got a gun in your hands.

58

A GROUP OF inmates sat on a bench in the gravel courtyard, sucking at cigarettes in the cold April wind, a short break from their places on the assembly line in the prison workshop, where they would cut out and assemble square wooden blocks for eleven kronor an hour. They were dressed in stiff and ill-fitting quilted coats, which reminded John Broncks of old prison movies about the Gulags.

This is where you'll be sitting when I catch you.

He looked around. Though he lived alone, he never felt alone anywhere but here. There was nothing in the world that felt more futile than waiting for someone in a visitors' cell. Shut off. Prison visits weren't about happiness – they were about control and security.

He heard a bell, grating and metallic like the one on the front door of the flat where they'd shared a room until John was fourteen years old, the beds pressed close together, which never felt strange, even though none of his friends had had to share. Then a rattle of keys, two mechanical clicks, and hooks sliding out of a reinforced frame.

Slippers and blue shorts. White T-shirt with the Swedish Prison Service logo on the chest. And a guard half a step behind him.

Sam had become broader. Even more fury had been turned into muscle. His face revealed nothing, it was lifeless. The most difficult thing was living in the present, without being able to experience it.

This is where you will sit. This is how you should act.

And this will be you, Big Brother.

'You applied in advance,' said Sam.

'Yes, I—'

'But I didn't bring any cakes with me this time either. You're not here for a visit.'

They both leaned against the wall. There was no way to be further apart.

'I ate on my way here.'

John pulled out one of the chairs and sat down.

'Last time I was here they'd only robbed a security van and a bank. Now they've robbed a security van and eight banks, and set off a bomb in Central Station, and they have a stash of over two hundred automatic weapons.'

Sam smiled faintly.

'Damn, seems like they're doing pretty well . . . what was it you called them . . . the Military League?'

John rested his elbows on the table. It was just as wobbly as the chair.

'There are four hundred and sixty-three long-term convicts in here. And after eighteen years, Sam, you know them all. And they know everyone.'

'Listen . . . we've already talked about this. Right? *If* I knew anything I sure as hell wouldn't tell it to a cop.'

'But this isn't like last time any more. Sam – forget about the banks. Before this group went on a rampage there were exactly thirteen stolen military automatic weapons unaccounted for out there. Now there are enough to equip every criminal organisation in Sweden that you eat lunch with in here every day. Every little wannabe gangster may soon be on the loose with a weapon of war. And then this won't be about bullet-riddled cameras any more – a shitload of innocent people will end up in the way, and not even someone who "doesn't want to talk to a cop" could think that's a good thing.'

The ironic smile disappeared, and Sam's expression seemed to soften a little.

'I will never accept it, Sam. Hurting the innocent.'

It was only for a moment.

'I don't get why you're so fucking obsessed with this.'

'I told you why. I will never accept that some people solve their problems with violence. When a security guard shows them photographs of his children, and they push the gun further into his mouth to get what they want.'

'But he was a security guard. If you choose to be a security guard you have to accept the risk. Security vans get robbed.'

'What about the bank cashier they pushed to the floor then? Lying down with lacerations on her cheek? She'll never sleep without taking a pill again. Her eyes – if you'd seen her eyes, they looked like our mother's, back then.'

Sam finally left the wall for the table where John was sitting. The veins on his forearms looked like a road map and he squeezed the back of his chair, as if he was trying to crush it.

'She worked in a bank. She chose to work there. She knew that banks are robbed.'

Sam hadn't been a criminal when he was sentenced to life in prison. He'd become one inside these walls.

'So you . . . you think what they're doing is fine?'

'I've been here for eighteen years – what the hell do you think?'

Sam's grip on the back of the chair relaxed slightly, and his hands returned to their natural colour.

'You sit there on your fucking visitor's chair. And I'm sitting in here. You chose to hold his hand. I chose to fight back.'

Sam looked at him in a way that John recognised, without irony, contempt, hatred or guilt.

'They tried to get me to go and see a fucking therapist once a week. So some idiot could tell me I stabbed my dad because I'd had a bad childhood. That it wasn't . . . my fault.'

He sat down opposite Broncks, laying his thick-veined forearms on the table.

'Fuck that. I was the one who chose to stab the bastard. I'm the one sitting here. Talking about what happened back then is like talking about a fucking cassette that is playing over and over and over. He's still here, whatever we choose to be like. Whatever you and I do. No fucking therapist can change that. *Accept* it.'

John suddenly wanted to touch those arms, lay his hand on them, but it had been many years since he and his brother had had any physical contact.

'I didn't come here to talk about him.'

'No, you came here because you want me to be your snitch.'

He remembered the last time when he'd put a gentle hand on Sam's shoulder, and he had pulled away as if John had struck him.

'I heard you sat with him.'

'And you're sitting here, Sam.'

'You held his hand.'

'You have to know who's doing these things.'

'Mum told me that. You sat next to the hospital trolley holding his hand. That devil's hand which . . . beat you.'

'Sam, you *must* have heard something. A name. A weapons cache. Somebody always talks. You're my brother, it'll stay in here, you surely know that?'

'You held his hand. But you come here, *brother*, and think I'll run around in here asking questions on *your* behalf?'

Sam pushed the button on the wall, calling for the guards.

'The visit's over.'

'*Already?*'

'Already.'

Just like last time. Sixty minutes, after several months, was too long. And silence fell. They avoided looking at each other until John couldn't stand it any more.

'They're brothers. At least two of them.'

Two guards arrived to escort Sam from the visiting room, one walking in front of him and one behind. They were halfway to the staircase to the lower floor when Sam turned round.

'John? I never want to see you again.'

59

LEO GENTLY TOOK five dripping 500-kronor notes out of a bowl filled with liquid and hung them on a clothes line he'd stretched between the walls of the garage. The wet paper was heavy, and they'd dry into rigid U-shapes that would need to be ironed straight one at a time.

The clothes line crisscrossed the whole of the large garage, a roof beneath the roof made of dangling kronor in various denominations – no longer worthless.

The plastic bag he'd carried fifteen hours earlier had weighed nothing, filled as it was with pieces of paper that had lost their value. That's how he'd treated its contents when he closed the door to the garage.

Their value couldn't be lost a second time.

If he'd considered it for what it really was – over two million kronors' worth of red-stained money, real money that couldn't be used – he would never have found a solution. His anger, his fury at the cashier who'd ruined their haul by sneaking in a dye pack disguised as a roll of money would have hindered his creativity, and the stained banknotes would have ended up being no more than just bits of meaningless paper.

He'd started with a 500, stretched between his fingers, red dye splashed across a dead king's face. When he'd rubbed his thumb on it, the dye had stayed on the paper, just as permanent. He'd been sure he'd have to burn the whole bag.

Then he'd seen his thumb. It didn't look the same any more. There was a coating over the skin, a faint red film.

One-part dye.

As anyone with any construction knowledge knows, anything that is one-part hasn't reacted to another component and is therefore not permanent.

He still hadn't dared to think *two million*, not yet, but he'd opened the metal cabinet holding inflammable liquids, taken out the plastic bottle of benzene, and squirted a few drops on the 500-kronor note. The red had dissolved immediately. After only a few seconds, the original print had dissolved as well. But it *was* possible. The red dye did go away. Now, it was just about finding the right kind of solvent.

Renol. Methanol. Methylated spirits. He'd even experimented with acetic acid before realising that the most accessible solvent – chemically pure acetone – worked best. Just like benzene, it dissolved the original ink and the ultraviolet security printing. But not so fast, not so annihilatingly. Time. It had been about finding the precise number of seconds. And he'd tested it on low denominations, 20-kronor notes and sometimes 50s.

The right amount of time. And the right balance between acetone and water in bowls of liquid.

Acetone, which could be bought in any local shop! He'd instructed Anneli to take the car and buy fifty litres, spreading her purchases – half a litre here, half a litre there – while he continued mixing, measuring, weighing.

And at last he succeeded.

After 114,400 obliterated kronor, the very first banknote came out perfect. Given acetone, water and time, two million in stained notes would be washed clean.

He was hanging up the latest round of 500-kronor notes when there was a knock on the door.

'It smells like a paint factory in here,' said Vincent.

'You need some ventilation, Leo, this isn't healthy,' agreed Felix, just behind him.

Leo was wearing sticky plastic gloves and his sleeves and chest were wet, so the hug he usually gave them would have to wait.

'I've solved it. Can you believe it? Solved it!'

On the workbench lay a huge pile of red banknotes. In front of them, lined up, stood three large metal bowls half full of clear liquid.

'First you bathe them – pure acetone.'

Yellow gloves grabbed a stack of notes.

'500-kronor notes. Twenty at a time.'

The red trickled out while Leo watched the clock. Five seconds. Then he quickly moved the money to the next bowl.

'Half acetone and half water. They stay here for ten seconds.'

330

The liquid turned a light pink as the last of the red dissolved, and the wet paper was moved to a third and final dish.

'Clean water stabilises the bills. Three minutes.'

They waited, mutely, studying the underwater text that read SWEDISH NATIONAL BANK. Everything seemed to be preserved. Leo fished out one of the notes and let the wet paper lie in the gloved palm of his hand.

'You see?'

He hung up every banknote after its swim in the last bowl.

'Is Jasper here?' asked Vincent, and Leo could hear worry in his voice for some reason.

'No.'

'Is he coming here?'

'Why would he be?'

Leo searched his little brother's face.

'What is it?'

'Nothing.'

Nothing?

This was more than *nothing*. He'd ask him later.

One step back. The room full of money was a beautiful picture: he'd succeeded. Because nobody but him said when it was over. It may have taken 114,400 kronor to solve the problem, but the pinkish notes that lay in a bucket could still be used.

'These got fucked up when I was experimenting, but they work at unmanned petrol stations. I've already tested it. We just have to be careful to spread out where we get petrol.'

Felix stirred his hand around in the bucket full of discoloured paper.

'It's idiotic to put these back in circulation – they'll end up with the cops.'

'On the contrary, they'll see that no matter how hard they try to stop us, they won't succeed. Not even with dye packs.'

He giggled, the acetone vapours wrapping his brain in drowsiness.

'That fucker Jasper isn't even coming here?' asked Felix, glancing at Vincent.

Leo pulled off his plastic gloves.

'Why do you keep asking about him? What's this about? He's not here. He's not coming here. Satisfied?'

'No, I'm not satisfied. And Vincent isn't satisfied either. But sure. Why would that idiot come here? I bet he's fucking hungover today, he drank enough on the train journey home.'

'Drank?'

'Yes.'

Leo turned to Vincent.

'Vincent, was he drinking?'

'Yes.'

'Around other passengers?'

'Yes.'

'Fucking hell . . . we drink here! Afterwards. Not around other people. We don't want to be noticed.'

'He was noticed. Right, Vincent?'

It was clear. There was a pressure behind Felix's words trying to break free.

'Right, Vincent?'

Vincent didn't look at Leo, or Felix. He just looked straight ahead.

'I don't know what you're talking about. Knock it off.'

Leo waited, but Felix didn't say anything more. But he would later, Leo was sure.

He poured the contents of the three metal bowls into the sink, flushed it clean, and filled them again, in the same way.

'I've been thinking about the next robbery,' said Leo.

'The next robbery? We were going to stop after this. A triple robbery. Then we were done,' said Felix.

The yellow gloves were on again. And a new handful of red banknotes taken from the pile.

'We were. But our yield wasn't as much as we expected. What we need to wash in here, and what we have in the weapons room, will support us for a couple of years max with all the expenses.'

'Then we'll get a job, like everyone else.'

Felix had a way of being sarcastic that pierced his defences.

'We don't need to. Because we're going to redo it.'

'Redo . . . what?'

'Ullared. We'll take the same banks, all three, again. A repeat. We've already made all the mistakes. We won't make them again. Between ten and fifteen million!'

The first dip. The pile contained ten 500-kronor notes and ten 100s.

'I'm serious. Everything's already planned. In a couple of months.

Not a single cop in Sweden will be expecting it. The same fucking banks!'

Five seconds. The notes needed to go to the next bowl.

'We were stopped at a roadblock,' argued Felix.

'Which you took care of nicely!'

'And what if they'd taken out the insulation bales and realised it was a fucking fake wall?'

'They didn't.'

'But if they had?'

'I would have put a bullet in their legs.'

'If you missed, if they—'

'Felix, damn it, we rob banks, we're armed, we have live ammunition. If they take out their guns, someone could die, and I'm gonna make damn sure it isn't us.'

'What if something happens to us, Leo, if something happens to you or me or Vincent?'

'Then we'll take over a hospital. Take control of a ward. Or we'll take a doctor with us.'

The third dish. He had plenty of time again.

'Leo, damn it, are you high on acetone?'

'Before every robbery I always check for the addresses of any surgeons living nearby, and I'll continue to do so.'

'Surgeons?'

'If one of us gets shot, we can't go to A&E, can we? So we'll bring someone to us. We'll go there, throw the doctor in the boot, take whatever medical supplies he has at home. We've always had needle and thread with us in the car, and disinfectant for cleaning entry wounds.'

The paper had stabilised. Perfect. Again. He held out the bowl to Felix, who stood closest.

'I'm not here to hang up money. Neither is Vincent. Because we're not doing this any more.'

Leo handed the bowl to Vincent instead, who shook his head like Felix.

'What do you mean . . . not doing this?'

'We're not doing this. As in *not* a part of it,' said Felix.

'What are you talking about?'

'I was lying on a hill when we did that first robbery. I'd hardly ever held a gun before. I lay there and took aim when you went by in the security van, squeezed the trigger at the car behind you. I'd almost

333

decided to shoot two people who just happened to be driving in the wrong direction.'

'But you didn't.'

'And now . . . this last time, sticking out of a roof with a fucking machine gun in my hands! In the middle of the day! Everyone could see me. I was ready to shoot whoever the fuck got in my way.'

'But you didn't.'

'And Vincent? Our little brother. Who almost shot an old lady who just needed help! Our little brother!'

'He didn't.'

'I'm there. Vincent's there. Right on the line. And when you're right on the line, the next step you take . . . you step over it. If the cops had decided to take a long hard look behind those bales and found you there . . . do you understand?'

'Felix? Look at me. Repeat after me. They didn't.'

'Our luck's run out. Next time, hell, the bullet's been on its way for so long. It'll hit something, Leo. Them. Or us.'

Leo still had four soaking wet notes in his hand, but Vincent stood in his way.

'Leo, we – Felix and I, that is – we're moving to Gothenburg.'

It was so seldom Vincent looked at him that way.

'We've rented a flat.'

He waited for him to continue, but it was Felix who spoke.

'You took the car to Stockholm. Vincent was on the train with that idiot, who I am going to have words with you about later, no matter what you say, Vincent. And I flew from Landvetter Airport. I did it then. I changed my ticket. There were several flats in the *Gothenburg Post*. Expensive as hell, and they wanted three months in advance, but they're in the city. A two-bedroom flat. One room each.'

A puddle was forming on Leo's shoes, trickling onto the floor. He hung up the last four notes from the batch.

'I don't give a shit how many bedrooms there are.'

And as he hung them up, he was able to turn away from them.

'So what the hell are you going to do in Gothenburg?'

'Study. I'm going to take a few courses at Chalmers. And Vincent, he's going to take some school courses.'

'You can't be serious?'

'This weekend. We're moving.'

'Are you? Both of you? Seriously? Are you kidding me?'

'We're serious. So now you can do what you said you were going to do.'

'Do what?'

'Sell back the weapons. You said you'd do that when this was all over. So you can get rid of that shit and get your cash and you'll be fine.'

'But we were going to do that together! That was our finish!'

'Now that's not going to happen.'

'You go . . . behind my back? Is that what we do? We're supposed to trust each other. Always, always tell each other everything? You go behind my back and don't say shit and arrange everything. And *then* you tell me! When I can't . . . when I don't even have a chance.'

Vincent looked down at the floor.

'You would have . . . got in the way. Convinced us.'

'In the way?'

'Yes.'

'*In the way?* Well in that case . . . what the hell, go ahead. Go behind my back! Why are you standing here? I bet you have a lot to pack, right? And I have a million more of these to wash.'

A new pile of notes. Fifties and twenties. He didn't hear them leave.

60

ANNELI HELD HER phone in her left hand and a cigarette in her right. It was nice to stand outdoors talking, the sun on her face, and if she leaned against the wall she was protected from the wind completely. And then, the echoing, gnawing hole. Every time he hung up.

She missed him so much.

She inhaled the smoke deep down into her chest and let it stay there, filling a void, then she felt calmer, knew that everything would turn out all right if she could just stand the waiting. Just like on the very first day. At the hospital, the fragile oxygen tube on the wall had fallen apart when the midwife pulled on it, so it was up to the woman to run down the hospital corridors with her son in her arms – not breathing, the water still in his lungs – and for several terrible minutes she was sure that he was dead. She'd smoked then as well, on the hospital balcony next to a giant ashtray filled with hundreds of cigarette butts.

The midwife had come out on the balcony then. Sebastian had cried for the first time, taken his first breath, the water in the lungs had gone away. In the evening he'd lain next to her in a plastic box filled with oxygen, and she'd looked at him, and she was pretty sure he'd looked at her too.

Sebastian had been everything to her. And she'd abandoned him. Now they talked on the phone three times a week and met every other weekend.

She had met a much younger man, a 21-year-old who was everything Sebastian's father was not, full of energy, madness, strength, a man who made other people's dreams come true.

She had been in love. She was still in love. And things would be like they were before, in a year, she and Sebastian together again. When this was over. Then they would be a family, a real one. She just had to be able to stand the waiting.

'Hello.'

She was blinded by the spring sun. The woman from the house next door was standing at the chain-link fence, looking through it at her. Her baby was on the grass some distance away. They'd never spoken to each other, but she'd often seen this woman from her window, and would watch her rake leaves or throw a big yellow ball with the little one.

Like Anneli and Sebastian. Before.

'Hello.'

She put out her cigarette with the sole of her shoe, then went over to the woman, who lifted her child and held him in her arms. Anneli would be able to caress his cheek; half her hand could fit through the holes in the fence.

'My name's Stina.'

'Anneli.'

'I've seen you here for a while now, across the yard, and I thought, well, you're our nearest neighbours, would you like to come over for dinner?'

Sometimes it takes very little to make everything feel different. This was one of those moments. Asphalt and chain-link with barbed wire at the top couldn't obscure the view. The person on the other side of the fence had an ordinary life, and she wanted to share it with Anneli. Maybe she would become a friend, somebody to talk to about whatever girlfriends talk about. She didn't even need smoke in her lungs – the calm came anyway. And then, after just a few moments, she felt like dancing. No one had shut her in here. That wasn't the case. It had been her own choice to stay in this ugly little house, she'd chosen to be here in order to be close to him, and she was prepared to wait for *their* ordinary lives. But in the meantime, here was something she hadn't even thought possible! *Hello, what does your husband do, oh, he's a teacher, my husband robs banks.* But it was possible. Nobody knew. Leo was in the building trade. And she could be an artist. Or unemployed. Or on disability for a bad back. They would have dinner. And then a coffee now and then. Maybe watch her kids for her. An ordinary life.

Anneli hurried inside. She threw open the front door and ran into the kitchen, threw her arms around Leo's neck, making his coffee splash onto the table, but she didn't care and hugged him even tighter.

'We're going out to dinner!'

He looked at her; he'd been somewhere else.

'There! The woman there, see, the woman on the lawn, she's invited us to dinner. On Friday.'

'Dinner?'

'Yes.'

'Anneli . . . I have no interest in neighbours with buggies and small dogs. I'm here for other reasons and . . . do you even know their names?'

'Her name is Stina and her son is Lucas and her husband is—'

'I don't care what their names are.'

He knew he was hurting her. But he wanted to finish things, not start them.

'They invited us. You're out there in that garage all the time! I need to meet people!'

'Anneli? Look at me. Stina will understand. When I'm done, when I've fixed what I need to – then we can start thinking about whether or not we'll have dinner with people I don't care about.'

Anneli let him go.

She looked at this man sitting in the kitchen with his back to her, and wished he was still beside her in a car on their way to Farsta, that they'd never robbed a bank, and she realised that at that moment she'd crossed a line and would now always be on the other side of it.

'Should I go over there now, do you think? And say what? That we can't come next Friday because my husband has a little problem he needs

337

to solve, that his brothers don't want to rob banks with him any more? Your brothers . . . your fucking brothers, it's always about them!'

She'd crossed that line because she thought it was better to be a part of it, to be there and to know. But her fear hadn't diminished, it had got worse – every time they took a risk and managed to succeed, she knew they'd take another risk.

'Don't you understand? I have no friends any more. I don't socialise with anyone.'

'Is that really my fault?'

'I can't invite anyone here. I can't . . . hell, not even my own son.'

He didn't understand fear, didn't carry it around like everyone else. Leo was never afraid. Or, he never allowed himself to be. Like the time she'd lost sight of Sebastian – the only time it had happened – in the middle of Sergel's Torg, Stockholm's biggest square. Her little son had been next to her and then he suddenly wasn't. That's how quickly he had disappeared. That's how fast you lose control over time and space. She'd trembled, run around and shouted, picturing Sebastian somewhere by himself, or walking into traffic, or next to a stranger holding his hand on the way somewhere else – a single image that meant she'd never see her son again.

'I do things for you, Leo! All the time! Every day! Things I might not want to do. I do it – for your sake!'

Leo didn't work that way. Leo had grabbed her there in the middle of the crowd and said *you go that way, I'll go the other way, we'll meet here in five minutes and split up again.* He'd transformed fear into action – searching became his 'now' instead of letting it take over space and time as it had for her. That's what he did, every time. And that's probably why he didn't really understand the need to have dinner with the neighbours; for him ordinary life was just a façade. He saw the practicality of everyday life but not the need, because he'd simply decided there was no room for it, just like he'd decided that there was no room for fear.

'I've never forced you to do anything.'

'I want you to do this for my sake!'

'If you don't want to do something, Anneli, just tell me. If it's not convenient – don't do it. Just like I'm not doing this.'

'Did you ask me if I wanted to live in this house? I hate it! This ugly stone house and those fucking barracks where you practise robbing banks all day and . . .'

She didn't cry often. Now she did. Anger turned to tears.

'You'd already decided that *you* were going to live here because it suited *you* – not us! The cave in the guest room that reeks of gun oil, and this fucking kitchen where you have more meetings than we have real dinners! The only positive thing about this house, *this fucking house*, is that fence, because on the other side of it lives a normal family that's invited us over for dinner because they want to get to know me. Us! Don't you understand that?'

She stood in front of him crying and he ought to comfort her, but he couldn't. Not now. Felix had moved to Gothenburg. Vincent was on his way. And Jasper was about to come through that gate any moment. He'd comfort her later.

He kissed her on the forehead and walked out. The woman next door was still in her garden. Leo looked up and their eyes met, and he nodded because that's what neighbours do.

He walked slowly to the garage. He wanted to meet him somewhere he could lock the door.

If I see that fool again . . .

That was the last thing Felix had said before he left, as if handing his rage to his big brother. They had been out in the yard, Vincent having gone inside to say goodbye to Anneli, and Felix had whispered to Leo something Vincent had forbidden him to tell, about a train journey.

If I see that fool again, I'll kill him.

Felix had handed Leo his rage and left. Now Leo carried it alone. Soon he would pass it on again.

He fetched the toolbox and there, amidst hammers and screwdrivers, was a piece of aluminium he'd ripped from the camping bed he'd slept on in the forest the night before Ullared. He'd made ten different prototypes, tested each one, and for a long time believed that insulation muffled sound best. Until he simply wrapped a long strip of the aluminium blanket around the barrel. It wasn't perfect – but it was good enough.

A silencer.

He lay the gun down on the workbench and waited.

A knocking. At first hesitant, then harder.

Leo rolled up the garage door.

Jasper looked tired. Worn down. Then he smiled an apologetic smile, as if not sure what he was apologising for.

'You wanted to . . . talk to me?'

'Come in.'

The uncertain, apologetic smile stayed on his face as he stepped inside, and Leo rolled down the garage door behind him without saying a word.

'Holy shit, Leo, you've got the dye off.'

Jasper came further into the garage and stopped under the clothes lines stretched between the walls. He moved his palms along the floating 500-kronor notes, laughed as if tickled, and the apologetic smile turned into adulation.

'Leo, you're a fucking genius, you can—'

'You took ten thousand. Of the clean money.'

'Yes. But it was—'

'Tell me. How is it possible to blow ten thousand in four days?'

It was as if Jasper exhaled. Now he knew why he was here – money.

'How? Leo, hell, have you forgotten? Well, you invite a girl to a bar, have a drink beforehand, that's three hundred right there, and then an appetiser and main course and a bottle of wine and . . . there goes a thousand . . . then a nightclub. Taxi. And then . . .'

'Good. Then you can take some more with you.'

He held an empty plastic bag in his hand – and handed it to Jasper.

'Take it, damn it! It's your share.'

Jasper threw up his hands, not so amused any more.

'When we divide what's left into four.'

'But . . . next time? It costs a lot to plan and . . .'

He hadn't been interrupted this time, but he still stopped talking and looked at what Leo now held in his hands.

An AK4. But it wasn't that. It was what was on the barrel. A rolled-up strip from the camp bed.

'Fuck . . . you kept on with that?'

'It works. If I fire a bullet in here, no one will hear, not even the neighbours out there.'

Leo nodded towards the wooden panel under the clothes line.

'I'll show you. One shot. So you know what it sounds like.'

He cocked, aimed, fired. And the sound that should have deafened them was sucked up by the homemade silencer.

'I know you pulled out the safety ring.'

'The safety ring?'

'The bomb, Jasper!'

The apologetic, meaningless smile.

'No . . . no, Leo . . .'

'I was the one who built it. And like you said – I worked out how to get the dye off the money, worked out the silencer. And the bunker. And the secret room. Do you think I'd build a bomb that wasn't safe, that could explode at any moment, and then send one of us walking into Central Station with it in their bag! First you lied. Now you insult me.'

Leo lifted the gun slightly, with the barrel down.

'Leo, listen, I thought . . . I thought . . . hell, Leo, you have to understand—'

Jasper stopped short. But Leo nodded, in a way that meant *go on, damn it, I want to hear this.*

'—and I thought that . . . we could create more chaos and confusion if we really used what we had. Right? Extreme violence, Leo! You usually . . .'

'Is there anything else you want to tell me?'

Jasper glanced at the silenced gun.

'Something else?'

'Yes. What happened on the train home from Gothenburg?'

'Nothing much.'

Leo's open right hand landed hard on his face, the kind of slap that holds more humiliation than pain. Jasper rolled around, floundering, which is what happens when you don't understand what's happening, when someone you trust strikes you.

His arms and shoulders were braced against the wall as he stood up, with unsteady legs that hadn't yet regained their balance when an open palm hit his other cheek and he fell again, the back of his head hard against the floor.

'Humiliation, Jasper? Do you think it's fun? Well?'

Jasper lay there trying not to look up, everything gathering in his face. Confusion. Disappointment. Hate. Grief. An animal considering striking – but with its throat exposed.

Leo waited until Jasper stood up for a second time. That was when he raised his weapon. Turned it. And handed it over. Jasper took it without really understanding. Not even when Leo grabbed the barrel and brought it to his own forehead, pressed it onto the anger oozing through his temples.

'You humiliated Vincent! My little brother!'

Jasper tried to drop his arms as Leo grabbed his right hand, spread his fingers and put his index finger on the trigger.

'Stop, Leo. Stop!'

Leo slammed a cheek that was already marked with wide red streaks.

'If you threaten my brother you're threatening me!'

He pressed the barrel against his forehead and took a step forward, forcing Jasper backwards.

'You humiliate Vincent, you humiliate me!'

Jasper's back hit the wall, the dried kronor on the clothes line hanging between their faces.

'If you're going to kill him, you have to kill me first!'

The look that had been full of disappointment and hatred and confusion vanished, was replaced by something that came from within, something Leo had never seen before. Terror.

'I'm sorry. Leo . . . I'm sorry.'

They stood like that for a long time, opposite each other.

Leo let go.

'Now take your money. And leave.'

He removed the weapon from Jasper's cramping hands and put the safety back on.

'Leo . . . *Leo* . . . I'm sorry! Never again! I swear! It won't happen, it'll never . . .'

The last blow wasn't delivered with an open palm. And Jasper didn't fall, he slid down the wall, which caught him.

'I swear . . . fuck . . .'

A string of saliva and blood dangling between his lips.

'What you know about me and what I know about you stays here when you leave,' Leo told him. 'And you and I will never see each other again.'

He waited until the garage door had closed. He was alone again.

It could have been over.

But it wasn't.

Not yet. Not for him. *Not yet.*

It was him against them, against every fucking cop out there. He would challenge the entire police service and defeat them all – now it was his turn to make demands, and they'd listen and give him the answers he wanted.

61

JOHN BRONCKS NEVER let go of something that mattered. He couldn't.
Not people, not investigations. Nor anything else for that matter. It could
be a strength – never giving up or backing down, walking around with
a motor in your chest that never turned off. And it could be hell – collecting
and carrying, but never dropping anything.

Now he was close to doing just that. Week after week, month after
month. And he still knew nothing.

They didn't exist.

So many times he'd been on his way to tell Karlström he couldn't do
it any more. And every time he'd turned back in the corridor.

They were out there, somewhere. But this time he'd decided to argue
that this case should no longer be a priority, that he should take on other
investigations in order to re-energise.

'Hello,' said Sanna.

She no longer stopped at the threshold and held on to the doorframe,
no longer looked at him listlessly, but also never spoke of the only thing
he could think about when he saw her: a long walk and a kiss that could
have been a new beginning.

'Do you have a minute?'

He nodded, and she sat down opposite him on one of the cardboard
boxes, as she'd been doing once a week lately, always with new pages to
add to the forensic reports. This time she brought two plastic pockets
and a brown envelope, and she lay them on his desk.

'The letter was in your mailbox. And here's 14,400 kronor.'

She pushed the envelope aside and concentrated on the plastic pocket
on top. There were notes inside in denominations of 500 and 100. All
pale pink.

'We've been getting these from petrol stations. Unusable in a shop, but
the machines can't tell any difference.'

Broncks had often seen banknotes stained by dye packs, and they'd
always been completely red.

'I'm pretty sure that these were in the robber's bag when he walked out of the Savings Bank at Ullared,' she continued. 'We've analysed the dye, and it matches the contents of the vials left at the branch – which we've also activated and tried out on discarded notes with the blessing of Sweden's Central Bank. And the red, John, comes from the same manufacturer, same shipment.'

A pile of three or four documents. Orderly, neat, as always, as she presented the analysis and the results.

'But this is where it gets really interesting. I found traces of acetone on each bill. I've never heard of anything like that. Plain acetone! How do you even begin to investigate? I tried it myself, and with the right mixture of acetone and water . . . John, it's not visible at all, the red dissolves completely!'

Broncks opened the second plastic pocket and took out the notes, examined them, felt them. They were genuine. They looked normal.

'The ones you're holding were stained just a few days ago by dye from a vial I triggered myself. Now they look completely normal. If the robbers also succeeded in finding the right mix . . . then they've got away with almost all of their last haul, and the banking industry will have to change their routines. Again.'

She was done and on her way out, just like every other time. As if nothing had happened.

'Hey?'

She stopped at the door.

'Yeah?'

'Do you want . . . to go for a walk? Have a beer?'

'No.'

'No? But . . . last time?'

'Last time?'

'You know what I mean.'

'It was just a kiss.'

'It was anything besides just a kiss.'

'Sometimes, John, it's no more than that.'

She came back into his office, cheeks turning progressively redder as they used to whenever she was gathering strength from deep within.

'John?'

That was how she'd looked when she told him that she loved him.

That was how she'd looked when he'd asked her to go.

'Yeah?'

'You know I've thought about you too. I've thought about you over the years. But now that we've met again, worked together . . . how can I explain this . . . it's just memories. Now it's like I never knew you, as if nothing ever happened, I don't remember any of it any more! Did we live together? Did we touch each other, have breakfast, assemble furniture . . . did we laugh and cry? You're like a . . . photograph, John. Sometimes when I see a picture of myself taken long ago, it's as if it's of someone else. And every time I see you, John, I feel even more like that. You're someone who doesn't exist.'

He noticed she was shaking a little, as if she was being drained.

'The kiss wasn't something I planned, it just . . . happened. Do you realise you never gave us closure? If you'd really dared to stay until it was over, then you wouldn't miss me. You would have been able to let go at some point.'

He couldn't bear much more of this, her voice rising as she went over to two packed-up cardboard boxes and it seemed as if she was about to hit them.

'Closure, John! Like these fucking boxes – just something else you never let go of. Please, please, please, John, let go! Of anything at all! I live with someone, you know. I'm on my way home to him. Someone who exists, now.'

He sat there for a long time afterwards. Pale pink banknotes next to the completely clean ones in the middle of his desk. A 41-page notice of stolen weapons on one side, 3109 pages of preliminary investigation reports on the other. And the brown envelope she'd brought him.

John Broncks slumped in his chair, braced his feet against the legs of his desk, pushed the chair backwards and rolled until he hit the wall.

He didn't give a damn about the clean banknotes, the investigation or the letter. He didn't even care that she was living with someone *who exists, now*. For the first time since he'd stepped into this police station, he wanted to get out before night fell, before he gave himself permission. He turned off the reading light, and had taken his first step away when he stopped. PERSONAL, read the envelope that she had brought from his mailbox in the corridor and put on his desk. And then his name, Detective John Broncks.

Personal.

Nothing in this fucking building was personal.

He wormed his index finger into the gap where the glue didn't quite stick, and ripped it open hastily.

And started reading.

```
                    Dear Mr Broncks

After contacting the twenty most dangerous criminal
organisations in the country, according to your
classification, and receiving a great deal of
interest in our stock, we have decided to extend
the opportunity to buy our goods to your
organisation as well.

Thus we have the pleasure of offering you the
following equipment.

Submachine gun m/45 - 124 pcs
AK4 - 92 pcs
Machine gun KSP 58 - 5 pcs
```

Broncks searched through his top desk drawer. A pair of plastic gloves.
He pulled them on, he should have had them on from the beginning. And
then proceeded to read the last thing he'd ever expected to receive.

```
Here are a few details from our high-profile
advertising campaigns, known only to us and you,
for reference purposes.

Svedmyra 12/11: An MP58 used to fire 7 shots from
below, at the corner camera. The lid on the
freestanding safe jammed, only the upper tray was
emptied.

Ösmo 1/2: Two identical escape vehicles used to
avoid detection. One cash register in Handels Bank
never emptied due to time locks.
```

For six damn months he had searched, hunted, lived with them, without
finding a single trace. And now this. Direct contact with the lead detective.

```
We have left a sample for you at the following
location.

Old Södertälje Road.
Stop at the barrier. Face the barrier.
```

```
Go 7 metres to your right. Follow the path 35
metres to the summit.
On the top of the hill there will be a pile of 5
stones and a young spruce.

Under the spruce you will find your samples.

Sincerely, Anna-Karin
```

Broncks quickly wrote down the directions in a notebook and gently put both the letter and the envelope in a plastic pouch.

Just a moment ago he'd decided it was over. But they'd made contact, and he would continue to devote all of his time to them.

They were out there somewhere.

And he wouldn't let go until they were stopped.

62

JOACHIM NIELSEN. THAT was the name of the armoury inspector who stood by the red and yellow barrier, smoking. He seemed calmer now, radiating a certain power. Given enough time, everything got better.

'The worst part is, they must have been watching me for weeks.'

One more drag.

'Take me here,' said Broncks, holding up his notepad with its hastily jotted down directions.

'Why?'

'We're going to do a little digging.'

The inspector shrugged and strode into the woods on the first seven-metre stretch. He stopped on the path to read the instructions.

'Thirty-five metres. Then I know where we're going. A small hill.'

The soft path led deeper into the dark forest.

'They knew how I moved, when I moved, where I moved. They made sure I wouldn't be able to see it.'

The anxiety was gone, thought Broncks, but he continued to dwell. And even though he himself had not directly experienced any violence, it would continue for the rest of his life.

They jumped over a fallen tree trunk, heard an owl hooting.

'Here.'

They stopped by five stones, a young spruce. Broncks unfolded the shovel and scraped away a layer of moss. The soil was like a sponge. Someone had recently been digging here. After a huge shovelful he hit something that sounded like metal. He took a new pair of plastic gloves out of his pocket; kneeling, he put his hand into the loose soil and grabbed hold of a black plastic bag.

'They've done everything right. Until now,' said Broncks.

The knife was in his other jacket pocket, and he used it to cut through the bag, exposing the contents.

'They want to negotiate, so something has happened. The group has changed. As everything changes.'

He handed a gun to the inspector and lifted up the next.

'They've decided to stop robbing banks.'

He'd thought there would be more people, that Broncks would have taken other cops with him, maybe some forensic scientists.

Leo adjusted the binoculars and moved slightly to one side to see better; thick pines stood in the way now that they'd started digging. He lay comfortably in soft moss at the highest point of the forest, sheltered by shrubs and two large rocks. He had picked out both sites with care – the one where he'd buried the weapons, and where he'd have a good view without taking any risks.

Broncks seemed to be ten, maybe fifteen years older than Leo. Thirty-five, maybe forty. He walked vigorously, might have been an athlete at some point, but not any more. His clothes resembled Leo's own, jeans, leather jacket, formal shoes; typical plainclothes cop, inappropriately dressed for both a forest walk and for digging holes.

He knew he was taking a chance coming here, but he felt calm. He watched without being seen. He planned without anyone knowing. And this, the cop digging up the weapons, who would soon be reading more instructions, was just the next stage of the sale.

Three AK4s and two submachine guns. All well-oiled and wrapped in plastic.

Broncks still didn't know if this was serious or if he was the victim of an elaborate prank.

'There's something in there.'

The inspector had unpacked the last weapon and turned it over. A string was attached to the trigger guard, with an envelope tied at the other end. It was the same size and style as the previous one, but this time with flowers and hearts drawn on the outside, and a red circle around the address.

Broncks opened it. And read.

Dear Mr Broncks

```
We are pleased that you have now seen some of our
samples.

Taking into account what the sale of our stock to
other potential buyers would mean for you, we've
set the price for the entire consignment at 25
million SEK.

Please indicate your acceptance of our offer by
inserting the following message in the Daily News
under the headline MESSAGE and PERSONAL on May 4:

I miss you, Anna-Karin
```

'Anna-Karin,' Broncks muttered to himself. 'They have a sense of humour.'

'Humour?'

'I lost an old girlfriend yesterday. Now I've apparently got a new one.'

'Oh wait, Anna-Karin!' said the inspector with a sudden smile. 'Ingenious!'

'Pardon me?'

'That's what they call them in certain Swedish regiments. You know? AK4. Anna-Karin.'

John Broncks looked around.

A strange feeling of being watched.

He spun around again, but there were only trees and the hoot of an owl.

63

NOW – NOT a soul around. Now – a small clearing in another beautiful wood, 140 kilometres northwest of Stockholm, in an area between two small towns named Sala and Avesta that he'd chosen on the map. The last dwellings he'd seen were a couple of ramshackle summer houses he had passed half an hour earlier as he crossed the lake in a small rubber boat. This was where the police service would give him twenty-five million kronor.

Leo pushed nails into bark. It was easier than he'd imagined; they stayed in place as if sucked into the tree. He took a step back in the soft moss and looked at a bent sheet-metal case that contained screws and plastic explosive, wrapped in brown masking tape and with a short piece of cord sticking out at the bottom.

A homemade landmine. About half a kilo of scrap metal and explosives. He'd built fifteen of them in the garage and stored them in the Skull Cave.

He looked around again. The trees should be standing neither too close together nor too far apart. From inside the helicopter, they'd have to be able to see the signal flare Leo would fire, and then the slowly sinking light would lead the pilot to four more light sources on the ground – where the bag of cash should be dropped.

The cops would have to wait for a last letter of instruction and would therefore be unable to plan their countermove. Only when he had twenty-five million kronor in his hand would they gain access to the weapons.

The helicopter would have to fly round and round using the given coordinates of a circular 200-kilometre route. He'd drawn that out on the map too. The circle consisted of five small airfields where the helicopter could refuel. He would choose both the departure time and the speed of travel, and would thus know when the helicopter passed this location.

They wouldn't know where or when the drop was to happen, but he assumed that every fucking cop in central Sweden would be on call and in position near the route. And the moment he chose to shoot the red flare into the night sky and signal the helicopter in this direction, they would all go into action.

Sunlight streamed through the treetops and the transparent fishing line glittered as he gently threaded it around the spring percussion detonator. The mine was ready to go. He walked backwards, gradually releasing more line, stopped after ten metres and tightened it. He was truly alone. But with a weapon that could kill ten, twenty, maybe even thirty people.

He'd been alone for three days, sleeping under the stars. No one to talk to or laugh with. No brothers to share the excitement.

He tightened the line a little and the detonator resisted, like a fish taking the bait.

Tomorrow the paper would arrive. The answer. The enemy had an unremarkable face and name, John Broncks, and in a few lines he'd express his desire for Anna-Karin.

He was convinced that they would go through with it. And that it wasn't just due to their fear that other criminals could be armed. There was another carrot – himself.

They would do anything they could to arrest him. So he was preparing himself for everything.

The police would send their best. Their elite anti-terrorist force.

Twenty trained Jaspers.

And he could beat them all with a network of fishing line.

He put on ear protectors and pulled lightly on the line attached to the test mine hanging on a pine tree ten metres away. The sudden bang was enormous – it smashed through anything alive a metre up from the forest floor, and even a glade of birches sank to the ground with a creaking wail.

An even greater effect than he'd bargained for.

Now it's up to you, Broncks. Do you want peace or chaos?

Leo looked around one last time at the vast forest that had already swallowed one explosion. He was surrounded by birdsong and a breeze. Time to go home and change out of his camouflage clothes into jeans, jacket, and a shirt with light brown coffee stains he'd made on purpose, the occasional spot you would expect on the white shirts night-time taxi drivers wore.

He walked through the empty glade, heading towards the company of those who never slept, to wait for the answer to a personal ad.

64

AT FOUR O'CLOCK in the morning most of Stockholm is asleep – the last customers heading home from the bars and the morning commuters still in bed. But not here. An all-night café on the edge of Gullmars Square filled only with taxi drivers. Loud conversation, coffee in plastic mugs, ink-stained fingers flipping through the newly arrived morning papers.

Leo was sitting in a corner booth, and had spread out the *Daily News* across the pine table. He wasn't interested in the news, culture or sport sections. Just the classifieds. He hurried past the ads for cars, houses, buggies, then leaned in close enough that he could smell the fresh paper. There. **ANNOUNCEMENTS.** And a bit further down, **Personal. Inger and her children Fanny and Mia. Please contact us immediately. Anita.** There were only two ads today. **I'll be waiting for you at the ferry. B.**

Someone named Anita. And someone who was meeting someone else at a ferry.

That was all. That was all!

He tore up the paper.

No brothers. No group. No more robberies. A house that Anneli hated, with more than two hundred weapons in its cellar.

And that fucking bastard didn't respond!

He ran past the Taxi Stockholm and Taxi Courier drivers dressed in blue, out of the café and into the chilly dawn. There was a telephone booth out on the square, the one they'd used to make the bomb threat, one he'd hoped to avoid calling from again. He stepped into the glass booth and dialled the number of a mobile phone. Six rings. Then he was sent to the answering machine.

He called again. Six more rings. And then – six more.

'Hello . . .?'

'The sample.'

'What?'

'Wasn't it to your satisfaction?'

'Who . . . is this?'

A voice that was almost naked, that had just been asleep.

'The woman in your life.'

John Broncks heaved himself over to the edge of the bed, put his feet on the cold floor and walked towards the window. He wanted to make sure no one was watching him.

'Who?'

'Your very own little Anna-Karin.'

A man's voice. Not old, but hard to say how young. Neither high nor low, somewhere in the middle register.

'And you want . . . *Anna-Karin?*'

'This morning's paper. You didn't answer.'

'I don't look for women in the personal ads.'

Broncks left the window, rushed towards the hall and the tape recorder in his jacket's inner pocket, pushed its cord into the phone.

'If *you* don't buy them. If *you* don't take them off the market . . . there are others who will.'

'I dug up your sample. And I've examined it. They were indeed stolen from a bunker in a place called Getryggen south of Stockholm. But there's no way for me to know that you stole them.'

'If you don't buy our stock, it will end up in other hands. In the hands of other criminals. Who might not be as . . . disciplined as my little group. You know, that organised crime you're always talking about. Platoons of Hell's Angels armed to the teeth.'

'Your sample doesn't prove that you have the rest of them.'

'It shows that I replaced the barrier's padlock with an identical one that had the same serial number. It shows that I saw the inventory list dated October the fourth, so I knew it would still be hanging there six months later, because I did such a good job covering my tracks that that sixty-year-old inspector in his decrepit blue Volvo never saw a thing. Do you want any more details that only the person who stole the weapons would know?'

Broncks stretched in order to see the kitchen clock. Ten past four. He wouldn't be going back to bed.

'In that case, Anna-Karin, I just want to know one thing.'

'Twenty-four hours.'

'I want to know . . . why are you doing this?'

'You have one day if you want to buy them.'

'Have you really decided you won't need those weapons again?'

'Twenty-five million.'

'Anna-Karin, my dear . . . you've made a terrible mistake. You should never have contacted me. You should have buried those weapons in a field, thrown them into a lake, but you should *never* have contacted me. If you'd just let it be, you would have been able to keep whatever you've stolen so far, and you *might* even have managed to get away with it.'

The tap on the sink jammed at first as it always did, and the water was lukewarm. Broncks let it run – he wanted it cold.

'And by the way, if your name is Anna-Karin—'

'What the hell are you up to?'

'I'm getting a glass of water. If *your* name is Anna-Karin, what do you call your brother?'

He drank, filled it again, drank half a glass more.

'Your brother. You know, the one you rob banks with.'

'An answer in the next twenty-four hours. A personal ad. Same place. That starts with "Dear Anna-Karin".'

'I have a brother, too. So I know how brothers look at each other, touch each other. Even when I see it on the black-and-white film taken by a camera on a bank wall. And you . . . you're the older one. So you whisper into your younger brother's ear right before he fires a weapon in the middle of a crowd for the first time.'

'And then, on the next line, it should say "I miss you and want to see you again."'

A grey hoodie hung over a chair in the hall. It was still cold on this spring morning, so Broncks pulled it over his bare chest.

'Listen, Anna-Karin. I don't like violence.'

'And once you've answered, then Anna-Karin will reply again with a new personal ad that will tell you exactly how we can continue to have a good relationship – how you'll make payment, and how we'll deliver the rest of the goods.'

'And do you know why I don't like it? I grew up with it. I know how it works – you either choose to hate it or you repeat it. Right?'

'Twenty-four hours.'

'A day is too short.'

'That's all you're getting.'

'Then you won't get anything from us. I need time to run this past the Commissioner.'

John Broncks walked through the small apartment, listening to the silence. The caller was still on the line, it wasn't that kind of silence, he could clearly hear the sounds of the street and someone breathing – thoughts were being weighed, maybe re-evaluated.

'OK.'

And the voice on the telephone grew deeper, articulated more clearly.

'A week. May the eleventh. The *Daily News*. If you don't want to date Anna-Karin any more after that . . . all hell will break loose.'

Then it truly was quiet. Whoever had called had hung up.

65

JOHN BRONCKS YAWNED. He hadn't gone back to bed. Instead he'd had a cup of tea in his kitchen, bare feet on the cold wood floor, before going for a walk along the northern shore of Södermalm and around the island of Långholmen.

He'd made the right decision in not sending a personal ad telling Anna-Karin how much he longed for her, treating her as he'd once treated Sanna. It had worked. Better than he hoped. He had forced out a voice – for the first time he'd made direct contact.

Now he had seven days to make the next decision.

That was why he was now in the police station's huge, dank underground garage, waiting for Karlström. He didn't want to disturb him at home again, or wait until he was sitting in his office, and he knew his boss's routines. Every weekday Karlström drove his younger daughter to nursery school, then his older daughter to school, and finally his wife to work, a slow farewell to the family he'd return to a few hours later. He arrived at his designated parking place never earlier than eight fifteen, never later than eight forty-five.

Broncks wasn't hiding, but Karlström didn't notice him waiting by a rough pillar, and jumped when, the moment the car stopped, the detective opened the rear door and climbed in.

'I've made contact with Big Brother. He called me early this morning.'

It took Broncks ten minutes to walk his boss through the story, and it was another minute before Karlström spoke.

'When *exactly* did you dig up these five weapons?'

'Eight days ago.'

'And *now* you jump into my car and decide to tell me everything?'

'I wanted to be completely sure how he would react. If I'd told you before, more investigators would been called in, and there would have been more agendas in play. We wouldn't have reached this point. Do you understand? Now he's made contact with me personally. It's just us two.'

Chief Superintendent Karlström stared at the grey wall and the sign that bore his name.

'OK. So why do you feel you need me now? What can I do for you that you can't do by yourself?'

Twenty-five million kronor.

'John, did you hear what I said?'

Pay. Leave Big Brother without any weapons. Make sure Sweden's most violent bank robber of all time never robs again. And at the same time – be the kind of police service that after months of hunting, gives them the chance to pull back, disappear for ever, to become a faceless chapter in the history of Nordic crime.

'John. What do you need from me?'

Or don't pay. Force Big Brother to keep going, robbing more banks, hurting more people. But also have the opportunity of capturing him someday.

'I need something that only people with their own parking spaces have access to.'

'I'm not sure I follow.'

'Twenty-five million in cash.'

66

'YOU'RE NOT MY dad.'

Trapped as he was between sleeping and waking, Leo's reaction started as disbelief, but quickly transformed into the most recognisable emotion

– fear. The words burrowed inside and took over, like the shrieking whistle of a runaway train or an air-raid siren.

But what he heard, deep within, was no whistle. No siren. It was a voice, calling out across the distance of time, yet still so clear.

'You're not my dad.'

He shouldn't have said it. It wasn't right. But the words came again, this time seeming to fill his own mouth, causing disgust to well up from his stomach, forcing him back to the present, to realise that what he'd experienced had been and gone.

This isn't Felix, and the words are not his.

Far from having Felix's dark hair, this figure is blond and dishevelled, almost angelic, his tone playful rather than accusative.

'You're not my dad!'

Sebastian.

And the feelings of disgust and fear turn into annoyance. He's spent five days in the woods planning escape routes and placing his homemade landmines – just three hours of sleep a night all week, and now he has been woken by this teasing.

'You're not my dad.'

'No . . . but I could be your extra dad,' said Leo, raising himself up groggily.

'No!'

'Yes! That's what you call someone you see once every six months, you little hoodlum!'

Leo lifted him up, threw him over his shoulder. Sebastian shook his head and laughed until his curls got tangled.

'Didn't your mum tell you it'd be only porridge for you, if you wake King Leo without his permission!'

'I hate porridge!'

Down the stairs and into the kitchen, and Sebastian laughed and screamed that he didn't want, didn't want, didn't want any porridge, until Leo dropped him and he ran out into the hall and hid in one of Leo's jackets, pretending to be afraid of being served porridge.

'Sebastian?'

Anneli was already sitting at the kitchen table with a cup of coffee and a cigarette.

'Now listen to your mum, little one – it's time for you to get dressed. If you do that, we'll soon be going.'

She stubbed out her cigarette in an almost full ashtray, lit another and looked at Leo.

'What is it?'

'Nothing,' he replied.

'Leo – I can see something's wrong.'

'I just need a cup of coffee, and I'll be fine.'

There was just one cup left in the coffee pot. The last drops ran along the porcelain rim.

'We're in a hurry, get dressed.'

'Is that why you sent the hooligan to wake me up?'

'I don't like it when you call him that.'

'And I don't like it when you smoke indoors.'

He snatched the cigarette from her mouth, walked over to the open window, and threw it out.

'Especially right now – do you really need to smoke when Sebastian's here so little?'

He opened the other window, wide.

'I probably can't go with you today.'

Anneli looked as disappointed as he'd guessed she would, and she glanced towards the hall and whispered.

'We had an agreement. And now he's getting ready.'

'Sorry.'

'Has something happened? You came home late last night. Again. Where were you? What are you up to?'

'I was working.'

'And why can't you come with me now?'

'Because I have to keep working.'

'Work? Do you understand how disappointed he'll be?'

'Damn it . . . he's your son, he doesn't care about me.'

Leo searched through his pocket and pulled out a 1000-kronor note – from the Savings Bank in Ullared, the one he'd taken alone.

'I can't go with you.'

Sebastian waited at the front door, fully dressed, his eyes shining with expectation. Leo opened his little hand and put the money in it.

'But have fun today.'

Anneli did not look happy. And she wasn't trying to hide it. What Leo had just done was on the verge of insulting, and he rarely made her feel that way.

'That's enough for every ride, little fella!'

Leo ruffled his blond curly hair, and Sebastian looked at the 1000-kronor note lying in his palm.

'Ride them . . . all?'

'Fun, right? You can do whatever you want all day without any boring grown-ups stopping you.'

Anneli's gaze burned into Leo's neck, while Sebastian nodded without really understanding. She whispered again.

'We'd decided.'

'But I have some complications. A job.'

'What "job"?' she said, miming air quotes.

Leo hated it when she did that, and she knew it. Idiots used it when they were unsure of what they wanted to say and felt the need to reinforce it with some sort of theatrics.

'The "job" that's going to pay for the "house" you "want",' he mimicked her. He was still as annoyed as he had been before and last night and every other day since that phone call.

'If your name is Anna-Karin . . .'

That bastard had known. He'd known something he shouldn't know.

'. . . what do you call your brother?'

And even though Leo hadn't actually said one word too many, Broncks had got him to say too much. He'd informed on his brothers, confirmed something that fucking cop couldn't have known, and if they ever got hold of him, they'd arrest his brothers too.

Leo heard her close the door without saying goodbye. He changed into his carpenter's clothes, it was important that everything should appear normal.

One more cup of coffee and he felt himself slowly becoming less irritated. That fucking detective, he was just like the fat cop who'd once sat at the kitchen table. You drive a lead pencil through the hand of a man like that – not even a child has to sit quietly and be controlled.

Because what you don't get, you have to take.

Reclaim it.

And never, ever let go again.

67

THE POLICE STATION'S cafeteria was half full. People sitting together during their free time, without much to talk about besides the one thing they had in common – work. John Broncks usually avoided eating here, conversations that felt natural during an investigation became strained at the long identical tables. He filled a cup of warm water from the machine without paying.

Karlström sat at a small table close to the window overlooking the courtyard. A fork in his right hand, his left hand leafing through the pile of documents. Broncks had never seen that before. His boss usually gave all his attention to his food.

'Hello.'

A plate of overcooked chips surrounding a tough piece of meat. Not really Karlström's style either. But he looked up from the stack of papers, took a drink of iced water and swallowed – at least that fitted, he never talked with food in his mouth.

'John. I'm glad you could come.'

Broncks sat down while Karlström wiped his hands with a paper napkin.

'It's done. There's a black bag on the floor behind my desk. Twenty-five million kronor. Cash. Used notes.'

Shared laughter from a group a couple of tables away. Staff from the Emergency Call Centre. They seemed relieved to not be answering the phone.

'You now have everything you need to make the exchange. Weapons for cash. But it's not enough.'

'Enough?'

'I had to run this past both the national police and the minister for justice. They aren't content with just taking the guns off the market. They want to see an arrest.'

'And what the hell do they think I want?'

'Weapons. *And* an arrest. Do you understand? And I need to be informed about everything that happens.'

'Of course. Everything.'

'So I want to know when, where and how the exchange will take place.'

'We're not there yet. Just communicating.'

'And when they make their demands and tell you what they want you to do, then you should give them *your* demands. So we can plan our countermove.'

'I'm not sure it'll work like that.'

Broncks studied Karlström. After ten years of working together they knew each other well, at least here, inside the walls of the police station. And he could see that Karlström knew they might be heading in different directions.

'It will, John. If we plan properly.'

'These guys have bombs and guns. They never shy away from violence. Their actions are always well planned. A single mistake during the exchange and . . . people could die.'

'That's exactly why they need to be apprehended.'

'If they butcher our colleagues, and then escape, then we won't know a damn thing more about who they are – *nobody* knows who they are! They're invisible. And willing to do anything to stay that way.'

Now it was Karlström who studied Broncks. And his face changed colour. Broncks's boss was rarely angry, he wasn't the type. But he was losing the self-control he'd nurtured until it became part of his personality.

'John?'

'Yes?'

'You *know* how this fucking works. Only time earns trust. The kind of trust that gives you the possibility of asking for favours. But you only get so many. So you have to choose when to use them up. I've done that now. Getting hold of twenty-five million without any guarantee of anything in return, taking the risk that some shitty criminals might manage to blackmail the government, which could become common knowledge later . . . our country's highest officials went along with it, because I've earned it. Because I used up one of my few opportunities and demanded it. John, damn it, make sure it's not in vain!'

Broncks leaned across the table, over the plate of leftovers.

'Karlström – they *have* no contacts. I know it. They *have* no criminal history, and if they try to approach someone out there to sell those guns . . . our informants will know it. So they won't. Not because they're afraid, but because they're smart.'

'And you're absolutely sure of that?'

'The only thing I'm sure of is that if we force them to keep robbing banks then our chance of catching them increases. So if we don't contact them, don't come back and explain that we want to buy back . . . Karlström, they'll get desperate. They'll have to do another robbery. And if you're desperate, you expose yourself.'

Karlström rearranged the silverware on his plate. First the bad food. And then this.

'How long . . . *damn it, John*, how long have you . . . been heading in that direction? To that decision? To this approach? *Not* paying?'

'Since the first letter.'

'And you let me run around begging for money for nothing!'

'Not for nothing. I need to know that it really exists, I don't want to stand there and lie – Big Brother can't have any doubts, he should hear in my voice that there's twenty-five million kronor on my desk, see pictures of it if that's what he wants.'

Broncks pushed back his chair, about to stand up.

'And . . . *if* I'm wrong. *If.* Then I'll use it. If that's our only option. If that's the only thing keeping all hell from breaking loose.'

He got up to go, but Karlström – just as he'd done at their last meal together – reached out and put his hand on Broncks's arm.

'John? Are you interested in what I think?'

Broncks pushed away the feeling of wanting to break free, nodded and listened.

'I believe in making the sale *and* an arrest. We have more resources than they have. But the most important thing is to end this madness. To be able to show everybody that we took them when we had the chance and not by luck. And after that . . . fewer bank robberies, fewer victims.'

Karlström still held onto him. Just like last time.

'One more thing.'

And Broncks felt equally uncomfortable.

'When this is over . . . I want you to take some time off. Do you understand?'

'Sure.'

'You hear that, John? Not a single case. *Free.*'

'Later. When this is over. But I have a few things to do before that. For example, for the first time in my life I need to write a personal ad.'

68

THEY'D HAD A six-year-old in the house for a week, but Leo had barely been there. He knew that Anneli was disappointed, it was so rare for her son to visit his second home, but she'd understand. He knew that too.

When this was over.

Now Anneli was asleep, now Sebastian was asleep, when suddenly Leo heard the lid of the mailbox being opened and closed, a metallic rattle in a beautiful, warm May dawn – the newspaper arriving and with it, the beginning of the end. He filled a large porcelain cup with coffee and put it down on the kitchen table.

All his planning had led to this moment. He went the few steps to the gate and the mailbox. Later today, he'd post the last letter, instructions the cops would use for the actual exchange.

Then it would be *over*.

All the planning, all his preparation had boiled down to this reply. He opened the newspaper near the middle, flipped, skimmed.

Page thirty-seven.

Leo stopped. His rage became an icicle, dripping from the top of his skull and cutting through his chest.

He wasn't going back to the house and his coffee steaming on the table, he'd sit down in his car and drive while the day woke up.

He hated that fucking cop.

John Broncks hadn't slept. Hadn't even tried. The bed was still made, the bedroom door closed.

Three cups of coffee at the kitchen table, and he never drank coffee. But the blackness and bitterness seemed appropriate for a night of waiting.

The phone, lying next to page thirty-seven of the newspaper, the classifieds, rang for the first time. Then moments later it rang again while he was reading. And again.

Personal.
Anna-Karin,
I don't give a damn
about you and don't want
to see you any more.

He watched the phone as it rang for a fourth time, a fifth. Then stopped while Broncks counted the seconds to himself, like a child counting the time between the sharp flash of lightning and the muffled rumble of thunder.

Seven seconds. Then it rang again.

He let it ring three times this time.

'Hello . . . Anna-Karin.'

'You've made a big fucking mistake!'

So this was how his voice sounded when he was under stress. Neither powerful nor thin, and still absolutely no accent or dialect. It went well with the black-masked body he'd seen so many times.

'You think so.'

'Now listen to me, you little son of a—'

'Are there many people there? Around you, there on Gullmars Square? Yes, I've had your last call traced. I can send over a patrol car if you want.'

'We've been talking for fifteen seconds. I have thirty more seconds before you fail to trace the call. But first you need to understand one thing – you've just started a fucking war. You've put the weapons of the state into the hands of criminals.'

Broncks tried to catch any background noise. Completely quiet. Either he'd covered the receiver with something when he wasn't speaking, or this particular phone booth was at a traffic-free site.

'Big Brother . . . you know just as well as I do that's not the case. Right? You have no record. Even though you might be the most dangerous bank robbers I've seen. How the hell does that work? It works because you can think. And therefore you *won't* contact any other criminals.'

'You shut the fuck up and listen closely, you little son of a bitch! I don't need any contacts for my weapons to fall into the hands of others! I'll just bury a few boxes and send a letter with red hearts on it, giving directions. Maybe you recognise the style? Forty automatic weapons in each box – one to the Hell's Angels, one to the Yugoslavian mafia, one to those fools in the suburbs . . . and that'll be your damn fault, *yours*, because you wouldn't buy back what I stole!'

'Listen. You know what? Right now there's a black bag containing twenty-five million in used kronor on my desk at the police station. Your money. Which I was supposed to exchange. If I hadn't decided to fuck all that.'

There was silence.

'Because the only thing you're really good at, Big Brother, is robbing banks. And you're gonna rob again. And again! You hear that, Anna-Karin! You'll be robbing banks again, you motherfucker!'

'Broncks . . . John . . . you're forgetting one small detail. You don't know who I am or what I look like. But I know who *you* are and what *you* look like.'

Then the silence changed. No background noise. Big Brother had hung up. When Broncks put the phone down on the table, he realised he'd stood up during the call without noticing it.

Now he just had to wait for Big Brother's next move.

It was eight o'clock by the time Leo rolled onto his property and parked. A coffee at one of the open cafés and a few hours' aimless driving through the southern suburbs trying to calm himself hadn't helped. The feeling that his plan had been a big, fat failure could not be dislodged.

He got out of the car and walked towards the garage. His persistent irritation was only increased by the sound of a bouncing ball. Sebastian was already awake and pretending to be a professional footballer, kicking the ball against the garage door, commentating on every shot in pretend English.

'Hello, Extra Dad. Where are you going?'

'Why aren't you asleep?'

'Wanna join in? I need a good goalkeeper.'

Leo opened the door beside the gate.

'Sebastian? Go in to your mum.'

The six-year-old managed an unexpectedly powerful kick with his right foot, and the garage door shook.

'She just sleeps all the time. Sleeps and sleeps.'

Leo picked up the half-inflated ball, and drop-kicked it far across the vast concrete yard towards the house.

'Play over there.'

A disappointed look from Sebastian as he ran after the ball and his extra dad went into the garage, turned on the lights and shut the door behind him.

It still stood under his workbench. He picked it up, put it down in the same place as before.

The typewriter.

Everything moved quickly then. A few steps towards the wall, to a sledgehammer. He raised it high above his head and swung, pulverising the heavy iron casing and slender keys, a loud scream ripping through his throat with each blow.

'What are you doing?'

The damn kid had opened the door and was peering inside.

'Get out!'

'It's so loud.'

'Now!'

Leo didn't even stop, raining down blow after blow as Sebastian closed the door behind him, and kept swinging until the typewriter was reduced to splinters of metal and plastic. It would never be used again! No fucking cop would be able to link it to those extortion letters! That was John Broncks's decision, and Leo wanted nothing more than to complicate life for him, to fool him again and disappear before his eyes.

69

SEVEN MONTHS AGO the envelope had been entirely white and had contained eighty-six 500-kronor notes. Now it was dark from being thumbed open and closed, and just four of those notes remained.

After years of silence, Leo had come to his home and waved it around. *I've just completed a major construction project in Tumba, the Solbo Centre. Seventy square metres. Commercial property, good money.*

As soon as his eldest son had driven off in his shiny fucking company car, Ivan had rushed inside, looking for a pen under some Keno tickets, and had quickly written down what he needed to remember. He'd known it even then, forty-three thousand handed over like it was fucking Monopoly money.

That thirty-five grand you thought I owed you. And five thousand in interest. And three thousand more . . . One for each rib.

Ivan balanced the envelope against the beer glass on the table, yellow plastic just like the chair he was sitting on, while heat streamed from the wide pizza oven. He sipped a little more beer from his glass – but not too much, he had to be sharp when he left.

He turned his head to the window. The busy road outside quaked in the early summer warmth – he was surrounded by heat.

He had called twice and tried to ask his son if he was up to something he shouldn't be, without getting any answers. Until recently, there had still been a slight possibility that he was wrong. That was until just now, when the hot-tempered fat man finished his beer and left the pizzeria. He was a construction manager named Gabbe who, Ivan had discovered after many phone calls, was the entrepreneur behind the job he'd written down on the envelope. He'd presented himself as a carpenter with his own business who'd received an offer to work with a builder named Leo Dûvnjac – and therefore was seeking references.

And the conversation had started out well.

The shrill foreman confirmed that indeed he *had* hired Leo's company as a subcontractor, so the money *could* have come from a construction job. But then, halfway through his beer, the foreman had leaned forward and given him a piece of advice: *Be vigilant when they put in the bid. I'll be honest with you. He won't suit you. He dumps prices. It suits me 'cause I'm buying from him but for you, who'll be working with him . . . they're so far underpriced I don't understand how they survive.*

And now he knew. His suspicions had been justified. The foreman Gabbe had, without realising it, confirmed what Ivan had long suspected – that he recognised the masked robber on the television screen: it was his eldest son.

On the other side of the road stood a little house with a big garage.

The one the construction manager had pointed out.

Leo's house.

Ivan drank up and put a fifty on the table. Everything would turn out as he'd thought it would during those long sleepless nights when the wine started to taste bad. First, he and Leo – the core – would unite in a small father-and-son firm that would gradually grow. Then he'd solve his problems with Felix and get to know Vincent, and they'd all sit and talk to each other in the evenings.

All four of them. Working and building a family business. A clan.

He set off. Across the main road. Towards the strange little house enclosed by fences with barbed wire spirals around the top – it looked more like a fortress than a home.

Hand against his breast pocket. He didn't feel it – he'd forgotten the envelope at the pizzeria. No, there it was, close to his chest, a constant reminder of when he'd last seen his eldest son. It lay near his heart, just as it had month after month.

He was anxious to meet Leo, and he'd never been afraid of seeing anyone, ever.

Over the busy main road and onto a much smaller one and then around a proud wooden villa. Sweat slid down between his shoulder blades and stayed there, soaking the fabric of his shirt. He trudged past the villa and through an opening in the fence which reminded him of a small prison gate, and which led to an empty yard, almost completely covered in asphalt.

He went into the yard. Someone had done a poor job; the asphalt was uneven and crunched under his shoes.

He was passing the garage on his way to the house when he saw the door being rolled up. Someone was standing inside in front of a rotating cement mixer. A back he recognised. He'd seen it dressed in a black jumpsuit on the TV in his living room.

'Leo?'

He peered into the dark garage, until the cement mixer was turned off and the figure turned round.

Only one meeting in four and a half years. Never here. And yet his son didn't seem surprised – as if he'd been expecting him.

'Hello, Pappa.'

'Leo – we need to talk.'

His son looked much older than the last time he'd met him. Even though it had been less than a year. But he'd carried out nine aggravated robberies since then.

'Sure. Talk.'

'Can we go there?'

Ivan nodded towards the house he'd never visited as Leo pressed a button on the wall, and the garage door started to slide down. A hasty step inside as the door closed behind him.

'Leo?'

'Yeah?'

'You and I belong together.'

Ivan patted his breast pocket, a rhythm only he could hear.

'Because there are no secrets between us.'

He waited for a response that never came. So he continued.

'You understand . . . I know it's you.'

'Know . . . what?'

'That it's you. And your brothers.'

'What do you know about me and my brothers?'

It felt so strange to put it into words. He'd never imagined that. That it would be so damn hard to look at his own son and say it, just lay it out, and then wait for his reaction.

'That you and your brothers are the ones the pigs are looking for . . . the Military League.'

He got no reaction. Leo's face was blank.

'It doesn't matter whether or not you're wearing a fucking mask. I can see straight through it. Through you. I recognise your movements, Leo, I'm your damn father.'

'You don't know anything about me, and you know even less about my brothers.'

'You think you can fool me? You can fool the pigs – but not me!'

That damn blank face. It was still there.

'*Pappa*, if you believe that, that it's me and Felix and Vincent . . . if you believe it, go and snitch on us.'

And then it was as if all his nervousness subsided.

'What?'

He didn't even need to keep his hand on his chest any more.

'Go to the police, Pappa, and turn us in – tell them you think your sons are the Military League.'

There was a homemade wooden box on the bench, as big as a banana box. Leo picked up a plastic bucket and emptied the contents into the mould. First, something that looked like a black cylinder. And then long metal arms with letters at the end – a typewriter. In pieces.

'Do the same thing – snitch on me! – like you claim I did to you.'

The cement mixer had small wheels that squeaked. Leo pulled it towards the table and tipped it until the grey goo completely hid the parts.

'We belong together, that's what you said, we don't have any secrets from each other, just like when you explained to me exactly how much petrol should be poured into the bottle. Right, Dad?'

Leo rolled up the garage door and left, while it slid down behind Ivan's sweaty back for a second time.

'I would never go to the cops. And you know it.'

Leo started walking towards the house, and Ivan followed, hurrying to keep up.

'Leo, listen to me.'

He walked straight ahead.

'Don't do it again.'

Without even looking at the man talking beside him.

'If you need my help, Leo, let me know. We can work together. Build together again. We'll put the past behind us and move on.'

Until he stopped. And looked at his father.

'*You're* going to help *me*?'

He stepped up onto the porch and opened the door to the little stone house without turning round.

'You found your way here, so you can find your way out again.'

then
part three

70

SHE IS LYING close to him. The scent of his hair wafts on his peaceful breath, and she contemplates the naked body as it moves, turns over. Hand against his cheek, she caresses it, kisses it.

Vincent's cheek. Skin that has been in the wind and cold and sun for only three years and is still smooth, soft.

First Britt-Marie settled into Felix's empty bed, her son who screamed at his father's raised hand and pounded on the locked bathroom door to be heard over the water running from the tap, and then sneaked past her bedroom door and fled into the darkness. Then she lay down in Leo's empty bed, who was ten years old but for a moment had been an adult when he ran into the same darkness after him.

Vincent's bed gives her some kind of peace. She doesn't sleep, she can't, but her heart beats a little more slowly.

She is lying there, her nose in his thin hair, when the front door opens. *It's them.*

And then it feels like it always feels when something bigger than herself, something she risked losing, returns. She is flying. She's singing. She's laughing.

She gently moves her face away from the back of Vincent's head, rolls over carefully, shuts the door and then checks the next door, the one to the single bedroom from where the snoring can still intermittently be heard.

Leo and Felix, her beloved sons. She holds them tightly in the narrow hallway, and Felix's mouth moistens her ear as he presses himself against her and whispers.

'I know you're going to run away.'

Leo hears, just as she hears, and he doesn't whisper.

'And *I* know you're not going to. Right, Mamma?'

She's careful to hold them both, simultaneously.

'Everything will be all right.'

'But . . . *I* know you talked to Grandma. I heard you. When, Mamma? When are you going away?'

She looks at them, into eyes so similar to her own.

'I'm still here, Felix. Right? Now go and wash. And I'll make some breakfast. You have to go to school soon.'

The boys are on their way down in the lift when she opens the cupboard in the hall. A light-brown leather suitcase stands at the back, half-filled with her stockings, panties, dresses, trousers, shirts from the last time she decided to leave but didn't – fragments of a life in her hands – and then she continues to Vincent's room and fills the other half with *his* clothes. That's when she hears it. Running water in the kitchen. Ivan is awake. And she stands still.

The clink of a glass being put down in the sink. He's on his way back to the bedroom. The door creaks and closes.

She waits, listening. Silence.

She sneaks past with suitcase in hand and puts it down by the shoe rack, returns to Vincent's room, lifts up his still sleeping body and walks back gently.

Hand in her jacket pocket. Car keys. They're not . . .

In the kitchen, they're right there, on the kitchen table.

Vincent in her arms, she hurries towards them and her shoes make a little noise; the keys are next to the ashtray, and she grabs them and turns round.

'What's this?'

Ivan. He stands in the doorway with the brown suitcase in his hand.

'What the hell am I holding?'

He whispers as he turns it upside down, tipping out the contents. A white slip lies on top of the pile in the doorway between the hall and kitchen. He bends down, grabs it with two fingers, lifts it as if it were dirty, and throws it behind him without looking away from what lies beneath.

'Where do you think you're going with my son?'

A small red T-shirt. Meant for a three-year-old.

'You take my son to his room and put him back to bed without waking him. *Now.* Do you understand what I'm saying, Britt-Marie?'

He stands in the doorway, still whispering, his huge body filling the space. She walks straight up to him; he moves slightly and she forces her way past, towards Vincent's room and Vincent's bed. She wraps the blanket around her son's arms and legs, and they move uneasily as she readjusts his pillow.

She returns to kneel on the hall floor.

A pair of panties and a green dress with yellow stripes on the sleeves are the last things she replaces in the leather suitcase, and she holds it tight as she walks towards the front door.

'And where are you going?'

He hurries after her, standing on the hall carpet between her and the door.

'Sweetheart?'

He holds out his arms, an embrace wider than hers, that kind that captures and destroys.

'Let's go back to the kitchen, to our kitchen table, sit on our chairs. The ones we bought together.'

And destroys.

'We'll talk. Just for a bit.'

'There's nothing to talk about.'

'Of course we need to talk, Britt-Marie. You and me.'

'Don't you hear me, Ivan? Don't you understand what I'm saying? There's nothing to talk about any more.'

He raises his hand as he raised it last night and shakes it in front of her face.

'We have three sons. Right? Three fantastic sons! And I have a good job. And you have a good job. And we . . . Britt-Marie, we have this, we live . . . here.'

The rough palm caresses her cheek.

'It's *you* who doesn't understand what *I'm* saying. Britt-Marie? My love? That it's important for me, for us, that our sons are able to defend themselves.'

He now caresses her cheek with the back of his hand, which is softer.

'What is it you really want? I don't understand. Sweetheart? What do you want me to do? What would you change? Why do you want to . . . destroy all this?'

'I'm not the one who's destroying it, Ivan.'

He gently pushes her long hair behind her ear.

'Maybe I went . . . a little too far yesterday. But you understand why. Right? You know what that was about. I love our sons. I love Leo. I love . . . *our* son.'

His voice changes, the whispering becomes a hiss.

'I was just so fucking angry! Hasse's father stood outside our door and . . . made demands. That *we* should apologise! You surely understand, sweetheart, why that pissed me off. Sweetheart?'

He slides his index finger down over her lips.

'Next time. I'll calm down. Control myself. I will. I promise.'

She looks him in the eyes.

'I'm . . .'

And holds on a little tighter to her brown leather suitcase.

'. . . going now.'

'What do you mean . . . going?'

She unlocks the front door.

'What'll happen then? If you *go*? What'll happen to my family? To my boys?'

'It's too late.'

'My darling, I—'

'I'm leaving now, Ivan. You have to understand that.'

Then everything changes. He grabs her arm, tugs it away from the handle, and lashes out verbally.

'You think you can go? You think so, eh? And what the hell are you taking with you? Nothing! Not from here! You're not taking anything with you!'

He grabs her arm and pushes her against the hallway wall, holding her with one hand and hunting through her jacket pockets with the other. He pulls out the car keys, and they glitter in front of her.

'You're not taking any fucking car. Do you understand! Not from here! Because you don't own anything. Nothing!'

Her other pocket, her purse, he empties out all the notes and all the change.

'Nothing! It's not your money!'

'Half of it is.'

'You don't own any of this!'

'Half of the car is mine. Half of that money is mine.'

Ivan releases her, she sinks down a little, and he runs to his wall – full of tools, and as any visitor would notice, so different from her side of the hall, with its wicker baskets for mittens and the two paintings Felix did for her – and takes down his sword from its place of honour. He draws the shiny blade.

'Half?'

The blade of the sabre shines like the car keys, and he thrusts it forward, then up, down, up.

'Half, you say?'

The wicker basket on her wall. He thrusts the blade towards it, through it, and two pairs of gloves and a hat fall at their feet.

'Let's do that. If you leave . . . we'll split it all—'

He holds the sword in front of him and runs down the hall, past their bedroom and into Vincent's room.

'—in half.'

She doesn't understand yet. But she knows something is wrong. And she runs after him.

'Split it. Everything.'

He pulls off Vincent's blanket and throws it to the floor. A naked three-year-old body rolls over on its side and Vincent curls up slightly, scratching his cheek and nose, yawning.

'*Everything.*'

The curved blade. Above the three-year-old body. Above her Vincent.

'Leave, Britt-Marie, and you'll make me split everything.'

She can feel his breath, violent and erratic, full of fear and aggression.

'Half for you. Half for me.'

'You're whispering.'

'We'll split everything, Britt-Marie, just like *you* want, like *you* choose.'

'You're whispering, Ivan. Why are you doing that? Because you don't want to wake him. If you really wanted to cut him in half, you wouldn't be whispering.'

He is sweating, trembling, the edge resting on Vincent's bare skin.

'You were the one, Ivan, who ran downstairs barefoot when you saw that knife – you were afraid of losing one of our sons.'

She is no longer looking at Vincent, who yawns and turns onto his other side; she's looking at someone even smaller.

'You won't do it, Ivan, because I know you love him.'

As he sweats and trembles more violently, he loosens his grip a bit.

She doesn't look at him as she leaves the room, the flat, the building, she can't hear him as he sinks to the floor slowly, as the sabre falls from his hand, as he cries like someone who's never cried before.

71

LEO IS SITTING on one of the long wooden benches next to the fourth years' brick wall, a gumdrop in his mouth. He looks through the bag for a yellow one, the kind that's sour at first, then sweet, then salty and good to chew on for a long time.

He looks around in the same way he has done for the last few weeks, like an Indian on the mountaintop looking over the valley below. The secondary school playground and, near the middle, the flagpole and smoking area. There's a group without any coats on, despite the chilly March wind – year sevens, three girls and as many boys. He doesn't know any of them. The two he's really looking for haven't stood there for a while.

Hasse and Kekkonen.

He wonders if Hasse's father is still shaking. Pappa had been shaking inside, and when Hasse's father arrived, the shaking stopped. That's what you do – you give the shakes to someone else.

It begins.

The ugly, annoying ringing that goes on and on.

Leo brushes the brick dust from his coat, and even though he walks quickly he barely makes it.

The first years' door almost slams open, and his little brother runs out.

'Felix? Wait!'

They look at each other just long enough for their eyes to meet, and Felix keeps running, across the playground and over the street to the other side. Felix is fast, but not as fast as Leo, who manages to catch up by the time his brother stops at the far end of the car park.

'She's still here.'

He walks over to Mamma and Pappa's red and white Dodge van, shrugs off his gym bag and jumps up, peeking in through the window on the driver's side, jumping again.

'She would have taken it? Wouldn't she?'

He looks at his big brother for the first time, waiting for the nod that means, *you're right, she would have taken the car.*

'Here, choose whatever you want.'

Leo holds out a bag of sweets. Gobstoppers and gumdrops and Sour Patch Kids and ones that taste of raspberry and ones that look like rats and marshmallows.

But he doesn't nod.

Felix kicks his stupid gym bag and starts running again, through the thorn bushes and up the pavement and into the lift, and Leo catches up with him just as the door is about to close.

'Take one. Whatever you want. I bought them with the fifty Pappa gave me when I hit them on the nose.'

Leo smiles as he pretends to punch Felix's nose and then hands him the bag.

'Felix?'

A bag full of sweets, and he doesn't even look at it.

Out of the lift and into the flat, and Felix stops in front of the hat rack, like he did at the car just now, looking, jumping, jumping again. Mamma's black shoes aren't there. Nor is her coat, or her gloves, or the thin scarf she bought when they went to Åland, which she often ties around her head.

'Mamma?'

The kitchen is full of dirty dishes and open packets of sugar and there are empty bottles on the stove. In the bedroom the beds are unmade and the blinds pulled down.

'Mamma!'

In the workroom a rice-paper lamp hangs from the ceiling, and Felix and Leo's own room is just as it always is.

'Mamma!'

Vincent's room. Vincent and Pappa are on the carpet, surrounded by soldiers and piles of Lego. They're building something. Pappa has a cigarette in one hand and with the other he gives Vincent one piece of Lego at a time, which Vincent presses into a long line on a square base.

'Boys?'

Pappa's long arm cuts through the thick cigarette smoke, cuts out small cubes and creates space, fresh air to breathe that soon turns smoky.

'Come on in, boys. Sit down. Here, next to me.'

'Where's Mamma?'

'Sit down.'

'I want to know.'

'When you sit down, Felix.'

He sweeps his other arm and knocks down whatever soldiers haven't yet fallen, and a piece of a house on the Lego base.

'She's not here.'

'Where is she?'

'She's not living here any more.'

'Where, Pappa?'

'I don't know.'

'Where's Mamma?'

'She's hiding.'

He puts his arms around them, his upper arms with the big muscles, one around each neck, something he only does when he's been drinking red wine and melted sugar.

'And I don't know where. Where do *you* think she's hiding? Did she say anything before you went to school? Did she? To you?'

Felix turns his head away, his eyes on the carpet at his feet.

'Felix? Do you know something?'

Felix who screamed *no, Pappa* and knocked on the bathroom door, desperate to get in.

'You can't lie to me. Felix? You know that, don't you. It never pays to lie to your pappa. And I can see that you know.'

The first tears.

'Don't cry now. Felix, not now.'

It gets worse.

'Look at me, Felix. She's betrayed me. Mamma's betrayed me!'

They just keep coming. Even though they shouldn't.

'She's left us. Do you understand? So *we* don't cry. Because she should be the one to cry. Now, you tell me. And we'll go and get her, and bring her home. You and I and Leo and Vincent. Together.'

Leo was the most surprised of all when he spoke, but when Felix sat like that, he couldn't stand it any more.

'She's gone to Grandma and Grandpa's house.'

72

PAPPA'S MOVEMENTS ARE muddled and uncoordinated when he sits down in the front seat and starts the car without Vincent, who stands by himself in the car park, and just as confused when he realises after a moment why his other sons are shouting *stop, Pappa,* and he backs up at high speed.

No one speaks as they drive – to talk is to risk getting even closer to the other side of the road and the oncoming traffic. They keep quiet when Pappa stops at another square called Farsta, and goes to the off-licence, and they're quiet when Pappa gets back in the car and opens a bottle with the black stallion on it, and they remain quiet the rest of the way to their destination over the bridge crossing Nynäs Road and past a high hill that seems like a good vantage point for Indians, down the other side and right up to the sign on iron posts that gives the area's name, Stora Sköndal.

Finally they stop.

Pappa winds down his window, lets the wind hit his face as he empties the rest of the bottle then throws it out, to make a loud bang when it hits the sign. Leo opens his eyes at last, now the journey is over. Pappa is next to him, staring out of the window at the empty bottle in the tall grass; Felix and Vincent are still behind him with their eyes pressed shut, and about twenty-five metres away is a row of small houses with small gardens and small lace-curtained windows and potted plants.

Grandma and Grandpa's is roughly in the middle, behind a raspberry hedge divided into three short rows, and Leo likes it very much. There he is never shouted at, the radio plays public radio or classical music, the rooms smell of candles and crumbs get stuck in the tea towels.

A plastic bag lies on the floor between Pappa's legs, near the accelerator pedal. Another bottle. Pappa opens it, taking three, four, five, six sips.

'If she doesn't come home with us, then you know what to do.'

He turns the rear-view mirror to look hard at Felix in the back seat.

'Because this . . . Leo can't do this. Do you understand? He's too big. Neither can Vincent. He's too small. So *you* have to do it.'

Felix stares into those eyes for as long as he can, and then lowers his head.

'Look at me.'

If he just keeps staring at the car mat he won't be able to hear what his father says.

'Felix?'

Pappa waits until the mat turns into a backrest, then into a headrest and then a father.

'Look at her. Just like I'm looking at you now. And ask her the same question once more. You must always do that. Give a person one last chance. And then, Felix . . . get close to her. And do it.'

Pappa snaps his fingers, thumb against middle finger, and nobody snaps louder than he does.

'If you don't do it, Felix, *exactly* like I just told you to, she won't understand that we belong together.'

He turns to the passenger seat.

'Right, Leo?'

Leo doesn't move, nor does he respond.

'*Right*, Leo?'

Eyes that won't give up. Will never, ever back down. Until Leo nods.

Ten, eleven, twelve more sips, and Pappa opens the car door and steps out.

He's wearing a carpenter's shirt over carpenter's trousers, a red-handled Mora knife sticking out of one pocket and a folding ruler sticking out the other. His brown shoes slip as he staggers across the road, waving his arms to his sons to follow close behind him, over the ditch and into the garden past the tall, bushy cherry tree Leo liked to climb to the top of, and then between two of the leafless raspberry hedges.

'I'm staying here.'

Pappa grabs onto the fragile raspberry twigs, and they break every time he's about to fall.

'You go on.'

Vincent clutches Leo's hand. Felix hunches over a little.

'Leo? Felix? Vincent? You go on now. You do what we decided.'

The house is white. Five steps to the top of the porch and the wooden door with its small window of wavy opaque glass and just below it, edge to edge, a thin metal plate that looks like gold that Grandpa fixed there, with AXELSSON written on it – Mamma's maiden name. The doorbell is friendlier than most, two repeated notes, not at all like their own or the bell that penetrates your skull at school.

No one opens the door. Vincent holds onto Leo's hand. *She's not here.* Felix breathes heavily on his neck. *She's not here!*

They all run down the steps, and Pappa waves his arms from the raspberry bushes to signal that they have to go back up, ring again.

Nobody opens the door. The doorbell. *Nobody opens . . .* Two repeated notes. *Nobody . . .*

Somebody opens the door. Grandpa. His eyes aren't happy like they usually are.

'Is . . . Mamma here?'

Grandpa looks over their heads, scanning.

'Where's your pappa?'

And steps outside.

'He's in the car, Grandpa.'

And closes the door behind him.

'In the car?'

'We want to talk to Mamma.'

Grandpa looks around again, whispering.

'Come in.'

'Out here. We want to. Please, Grandpa.'

Grandpa doesn't really understand. Just as they themselves don't understand. He looks at Leo, the oldest, who's trying to say what Pappa wants him to say. At Vincent who's holding his big brother's hand and seems so small as he moves even closer. At Felix standing some distance behind them, staring down at the ground with both hands buried in his coat pockets.

'Please?'

'Out here. OK. Wait a second.'

He shuts the door carefully, and goes inside. Time moves slowly. One hour. Another hour.

Leo checks the ugly hands of his wristwatch.

Two hours. It feels like that. Two minutes.

Then he hears it.

Someone slowly climbing the stairs, the ones from the room in the basement with an extra bed so big that usually all three sleep in it, stairs that are slippery and sound hollow when you walk on them.

Mamma. And she smiles, happy and scared at the same time. She does as Grandpa did, looks around and takes a step outside.

'He's not here, Mamma.'

She hugs them, one by one.

'Mamma?'

Leo concentrates on saying what Pappa wanted him to say. If he does it, she won't hear what's stuck in his throat.

'Yes?'

'Come home.'

She shakes her head, her blonde fringe falling down over her forehead and eyes.

'I can't.'

'Please.'

'Not now. Everything will be all right. Later.'

'Please, please, please, Mamma.'

'Leo? Listen to me. Everything *will* be all right. And you *will* live with me. In a few days. Do you understand?'

She squats, holding onto Leo and Vincent, hugs them for a long time. But not Felix, who steps back so she can't reach him. He's the only one who can do it, because Leo is too large and Vincent too small.

He runs to his mamma, who is holding her arms wide, clears his throat, looks at her . . .

And spits.

He weeps and spits again. Warm saliva he's been saving for a long time runs from her forehead and cheeks down onto her neck.

Felix stands in front of her and closes his eyes, shaking and crying. And she puts her arms around him and hugs him too. He spat in her face twice, and yet still she hugs him until he pulls away, away from the saliva on her face and chin, and he can hear Leo and Vincent running away, his brother's clogs clattering as he runs across the road to the car with Pappa's face staring out of the window.

73

IT IS NIGHT, or at least Felix thinks so. Time seems far away when he wakes up. There are neither curtains nor blinds on the window. They usually keep it like this – a window no one can see through on the top floor of the seven-storey building. During the winter, or like now when winter is coming to an end, the sky is blacker and the stars and full moon brighter by contrast; lying in bed, it's like being close to them, and Felix feels as if he could open the window and stretch up to touch them.

Felix likes looking at the sky. But he doesn't like himself.

He doesn't like lying here not being able to sleep. He doesn't like sweating like this or breathing like this, gasping for air. But what he likes least is how he can still feel Mamma's arms holding him. She just held him when she should have beaten him! He should have hit her! He hits his own body, hard, and the arms he can still feel wrapped around him. He feels absolutely nothing, so he scratches his forearms with his sharp thumbnails. He's trapped between waking and sleeping, but he can hear the voices coming from the kitchen: Pappa talking in that way he does sometimes that makes it hard to understand what he's saying; Leo responding occasionally with a few short words.

He creeps out of his bed, across the floor to the hall and the threshold of the kitchen, and peeps in.

Pappa is sitting with his back to him on a chair. Leo has his left side to him. All the lights are on, even the bright one above the stove and sink that stings your eyes if you look into it.

On the kitchen table stands a petrol can, sickly green and with its lid on. Beside it stand two empty wine bottles. Beside those a plastic funnel and a cigarette lighter.

He's never seen those things on the kitchen table before, not at the same time, and he creeps closer, his elbows on the threshold as he tries to get a better look.

That's when Pappa gets up and comes towards him.

Felix plunges into the dark hall and stays close to the wall, holding his breath. Pappa goes past without seeing him.

'Leo?' calls Pappa over his shoulder as he passes.

Felix stretches his upper body, his neck. In Mamma and Pappa's bedroom, near the edge of Mamma's bed, Pappa holds her pillow in his hands as he pulls off the pillowcase.

'Leo, the plastic wheel? Have you been listening?'

Pappa holds the pillowcase under his nose, where Mamma's initials are embroidered in one corner. He pushes his head into it, smells it, breathing deeply, never noticing that someone is lying quietly in the dark, watching.

'That should go down into the neck of the bottle. You push until it stops.'

Pappa's long feet almost step on Felix as he heads back to the kitchen table, then he lifts up the bottle and shows Leo in that expansive way that only he has.

'We did this when I was little, not with bottles but with geese. My brothers and I pushed food down their narrow fucking birds' necks, and they grew big and fat and delicious.'

Felix bumps the threshold with his elbow, and the sound echoes through the apartment. He holds his breath like before, closes his eyes. Pappa should turn round. But he doesn't. Even though it's echoing.

'You don't know about that sort of thing, Leo. You don't know things like that. But I know and I'm going to tell you, that's what I'm going to do. Four thousand years ago the Jews were the first to tend geese. They were slaves. And they worked for a Pharaoh of Egypt who loved goose liver. All he ever wanted was foie gras foie gras . . . and they were forced to find a quick way to feed those fucking geese. Right? That's when they started pushing the food down. Pushing pushing pushing. With really long sticks. Because the Pharaoh, he just wanted more and more. Then, there was this Spaniard, and he loves his geese – he talks to them, gives them fruit from his garden. Heaven for geese! But every autumn, when the other geese are heading to Africa or wherever the hell they fly to, *his* geese start walking around on the ground honking. *Honk honk honk!* And the geese up in the air stop – this is true, Leo – and they fly down and land and stay there, in Goose Heaven.'

Pappa's hands fumble as they feel for the cap of the petrol container, tremble as they unscrew it and pull out the spout, until the bottle is resting on the edge of the plastic funnel.

'He gives them love. Just like me. He creates a clan. And then . . . then you stay there.'

There's a strong smell of petrol immediately.

'Hold it here, Leo . . . like this . . . a firm grip, on the bottle. With both hands.'

Leo holds the bottle in both his hands. The black horse on its label rears on its hind legs while Pappa pours, checking now and then to see how much space is left.

'No more than half. That's important.'

Pappa is satisfied with the amount of petrol in the wine bottle. He smells Mamma's pillowcase again – his breath fills up the whole kitchen – then holds it with two hands and rips it apart, putting strips of equal width into a pile.

'Strips this size.'

He folds one of the pieces into a square with Mamma's initials in the middle, then dips it until it's damp with petrol.

'A narrow fucking bird's neck. Now press again. In goose hell there's no protesting.'

Pappa pokes down the fabric a little at a time and stops before it touches the petrol in the bottle.

'See? Never push it all the way down. If you do that, and then light it . . .'

Pappa uses his hands and makes a sound to simulate an explosion.

'. . . it'll go off too soon. You hold it firmly and when the cloth is burning, don't tilt the bottle. And you throw it forwards, with your whole shoulder and arm, like when you're throwing a punch.'

Pappa walks round the kitchen table, twice, holding the bottle with a straight arm, chin and lower lip jutting out, hissing as he usually does when he's drunk and somewhere else.

'Because we are no Axelssons.'

He washes his petrol-soaked hands under the tap, and then lights an untipped cigarette as he opens a new bottle. This one is for drinking.

'Do you understand that? You'll never be a fucking Axelsson!'

He drinks even more quickly than usual.

'It *was* like this. When I met your mother, I didn't really want her. She was beautiful, she was, but I told her. I said, "I don't want you," I said, "love is just betrayal."'

Pappa is carrying the newly opened bottle in one hand and the can of petrol in the other, as he walks towards the hall, close to Felix, and stops in front of the hat rack.

'Do you know what she said, Leo? She said, word for word, "I will never betray you, Ivan."'

The jacket is hanging on one of the hooks, the shoes are on the doormat.

'Word for word! Just that. And then I said, "And how can I be sure of that?" Do you know what she answered, Leo? Can you guess?'

Leo's jacket is on the next hook. Pappa throws it at the kitchen table where Leo is still sitting on his chair.

'She said, "If I betray you, Ivan," word for word, "you can kill me."'

74

LEO COUNTS THE seconds. Six seconds from their sudden deceleration before the gearbox malfunctions, twelve seconds between Pappa screaming at the car in front of them for driving too slowly and the bend that's sharper than Pappa remembers, nine seconds between someone honking their horn several times behind them and suddenly swerving out of the left-hand lane.

They stop. The same place they stopped this afternoon. And even though it's dark, he can just make out the squat chimney of Grandma and Grandpa's house, which seems so small under the branches of the cherry tree, partially obscured by the overgrown raspberry hedge. They sit next to each other, silent, scouting the area, as if they'd climbed up a hill and were looking down.

The plastic bag lies in his lap.

It's not very heavy, but it forces him to sit as still as a stone because the bottle has to remain upright.

The smell is the worst part. Petrol fumes creep into his nose, his brain. He didn't know what a Molotov cocktail was before this.

The shaking belongs to him now. Pappa has given it to him, just like he gave it to Hasse's father.

'Whatever happens, Leo, I want you to know that I love you.'

The shaking he's so afraid of.

'Pappa?'

'Yes?'

'Do we have to?'

He doesn't blink once. It almost makes his pupils hurt.

'Yes.'

'But what—'

'We'll talk to her first.'

'What if she doesn't want to talk?'

'Then she's the one who's decided what's going to happen.'

Pappa opens the door and climbs out. The first step goes awry, and he staggers, before grabbing the rear-view mirror and regaining his balance. He waits for Leo to climb out too.

But he doesn't.

Instead he stares at his watch and its ugly hands. Sixteen minutes and twenty-four seconds past one. He knows that's how it works – if you just keep track of time, look at the clock, you won't feel so much. He always does that when he races Felix up and down stairs with leaflets in his hand – counting the seconds keeps away his exhaustion.

Pappa doesn't say anything. He doesn't have to, he just holds out his arm until Leo gets up and moves the plastic bag a little, pressing it against his chest while he stands up. He doesn't remember Pappa's hand being so rough; he hasn't held it in years.

It feels like a long walk to the house. Pappa keeps moving in that jerky way, tripping and stumbling. Still they make it to the back of the house. In the darkness, on the path between the raspberry bushes Grandpa is so proud of, raspberries that are larger than other raspberries, of a warmer red, some old variety that tastes especially sweet.

'Britt-Marie.'

Pappa squeezes his hand and chases away the silence. But not the dark.

'Britt-Marie!'

Leo twists his left arm towards the brightness of the porch light and looks at his watch, the ugly hands. Nineteen minutes and fifty-two seconds past one. He checks again when the first light is turned on inside the house. Grandma and Grandpa's bedroom. And again, when one of the living room lights goes on, the standard lamp with a flowery lampshade.

'Go away!' shouts Grandpa. He's opened the window, and they look at each other. 'Ivan, it's the middle of the night, just go!'

And then it's Leo and Grandpa looking at each other, until Leo looks away.

'Britt-Marie! Come out, Britt-Marie! You don't belong here!'

'I'm calling the police, Ivan.'

'You? A fucking Axelsson?'

'If you don't get out of here!'

'Britt-Marie's coming with me. She's going home. To her family.'

'I'm going to close the window. And if you don't leave . . . I'm calling them. You hear that, Ivan? I'm calling the police.'

Grandpa closes the window, turns off the light. Pappa lets go of Leo's hand for the first time and raises his fist to the house, towards Grandpa.

'Britt-Marie! Don't sit there like an Axelsson! Come out! To *your* family! Your kids! Me!'

The window stays closed, the house stays dark. Pappa grabs the plastic bag Leo holds pressed against his chest, lifting it right out of Leo's arms, and takes the bottle out of the bag.

'Come out now! Otherwise I'll burn you! I'll burn down the whole fucking thing!'

Pappa holds the bottle, hands it to Leo. Leo's arms just hang there, useless.

'Leo – aim at the basement window.'

Arms still not moving. He doesn't take the bottle. And he doesn't look at Pappa, he stares down at the ground and the grass.

'We're going to drive her out with fire. Do you understand?'

He takes a cigarette lighter from his front pocket, puts the flame to the mouth of the bottle, to the fabric soaked in petrol and pressed far inside, like a goose with a skinny fucking neck being fattened up.

The fabric flower petals turn yellow and orange.

'Britt-Marie! You're making this decision! It's your choice! It's . . .'

Pappa's movements are slow, as movements are when even as they happen you know you'll always remember them, even as they melt into the bare branches of the swaying cherry tree. He hits the basement window, the room where they usually sleep during those visits they never want to end. It takes almost a minute from the glass pane shattering – Leo is sure of it because he's counting one second at a time – until the fire really starts to burn. That muffled sound. And the small flames growing and spreading and taking over.

Pappa isn't screaming any more. He's not going anywhere. He's not even trembling.

The entire room is illuminated. A different shade of light from the lamps, yellower. Fire eats both the chairs and the bed.

Then the basement door opens.

Grandpa throws a large rug over the flames and then another one. Grandma and Mamma are carrying green and blue plastic buckets and throw the water onto the fire.

'Let's go, Leo.'

They are still running around inside. In and out of the laundry room filling buckets.

'Now.'

Two ugly hands. It's been four minutes and forty-four seconds since Leo stepped out of the car and into the raspberry bushes, which Pappa is falling into right now, and since they first passed the clothes line that Pappa just now cut his cheek and chin on. It's not much.

Leo closes his eyes as they drive home and keeps them closed the whole way back, and it feels like a long journey, as if they're on their way to the other side of Sweden.

75

HE SEES THE police car as soon as Pappa parks, the moment he opens his eyes again.

Near their front door. Black and white. Parked diagonally in front of the high-rise, clearly visible under the streetlight.

He's never seen a police car this close to home before.

They usually park further away, or in the car park, and then walk from there. Never like this, right outside, as if blocking the exit.

'Everything will be all right.'

Leo curls up a little more tightly in the back seat.

'We're a family. Right, Leo? And if we stick together like families do, then everything will be all right.'

The front doors of the police car open simultaneously. And there are two of them. An older man, even older than Pappa, and a younger female cop, he's not seen that many female officers before. They go straight to the car, towards Pappa.

'Ivan Dûvnjac?'

They can be heard clearly even though all the windows are shut, and they knock on the glass until Pappa rolls it down.

'Yes?'

'You're coming with us.'

'What the hell are you talking about?'

'You know what we're *talking* about.'

Pappa shakes his head and makes an effort to speak clearly; he doesn't mumble, and he moves his lips.

'No. Not a clue.'

And turns to the back.

'Do you have any idea what they're talking about, son?'

Pappa leans close, his alcohol-laced breath as intrusive as the smell of petrol and smoke on the sleeve of his jacket.

And they *see* him.

'No, Pappa. I don't know what they're talking about.'

The older policeman nods towards Leo as he speaks.

'Ivan – there are children here.'

The woman moves around the car, handcuffs in her hand.

'So come with us now. Voluntarily.'

She waits there until Pappa, after an eternity, shrugs.

'Leo?'

'Yes?'

'Go home and take care of your brothers.'

'Pappa, I—'

'Do it! Go home. Take care of your brothers.'

The police officer holding the handcuffs opens the door and Pappa stretches out his hands, palms up. The two cops in uniform stand on either side of him as he walks towards the police car and the back seat. That's where he sits as the black-and-white car drives away, and he turns around, and they look at each other, not long, but long enough.

76

LEO PRESSES THE door handle gently, takes off his shoes and creeps inside, without turning on any lights. Vincent is lying upside down in bed as he sometimes does; he says something unintelligible and continues sleeping. But Felix wakes up. Or maybe he was already awake.

It's hard to explain – at least in the middle of the night – that Mamma is not coming home. And then, after explaining that, it's hard to explain that Pappa isn't coming home either. Leo does it anyway, and Felix listens, and just when he's finished explaining, Mamma calls. She asks if everyone is there, and when he answers that they are, she says she's changed her mind, she's coming. Right away.

He hurries into the kitchen, opens the cabinet under the worktop and pulls out two paper refuse sacks.

Mamma will be here right away and when she gets here the kitchen table should look like a kitchen table.

A petrol can. The remains of a pillowcase. Two bottles of wine.

Cigarette butts, Keno tickets, sugar packets.

He cleans away one thing at a time and puts the refuse sacks under the sink.

When the can and the pillowcase and the bottles are gone, and the kitchen table is a kitchen table, they don't need to talk about it.

He wipes the table for a second time with a sponge and rinses out a saucepan, sniffs it and rinses it again until the smell of wine is gone. Just before Mamma arrives. And it feels so good in his chest and stomach. And he's heading towards her when he sees two others.

'Leo, these are . . . they're police officers.'

There is no question. That's why he doesn't answer.

'Do you understand? They're here to look at the flat. And then . . . they'll want to talk for a little while. To you.'

In our flat there is only us.

'I'm tired.'

Vincent and Felix and Mamma and Pappa and I live here.

393

'I understand that, love. But this will only take a few minutes.'
Those two . . . they don't belong here.
'Then they'll leave. Leo? OK?'

They're everywhere: the hall, the kitchen, Vincent's room, his and Felix's room, Mamma and Pappa's room, the workroom, the living room, even the bathroom and the balcony. They open and close cabinets, drawers, cupboards, move shoes and soldiers and paintings and flower pots. They examine a homemade punchbag and then the golden mount on a sabre carelessly stuffed into a blue velvet sheath above a wide range of obsolete tools. Leo stands on the threshold between the hall and the kitchen the whole time. Even when they open the cupboard under the sink and lift out two paper sacks, pieces of cloth torn from a pillowcase that still smell like Mamma.

'Hello, Leo,' says the larger policeman, trying to smile at him. 'It's just as your mother said. I work as a police officer. And I want to talk to you. Just for a moment.'

Leo has never met a police officer who doesn't wear a uniform. He wears a long coat like Pappa's except lighter, and he points to the newly cleaned kitchen table.

'You're not . . . in trouble. And it's not your fault. Nothing that's happened is your fault, Leo. I just want to ask a few questions. I just need to know what happened when you and your pappa were out driving around.'

He pulls out a kitchen chair, Pappa's chair, and sits down, holding a small spiral notebook and a pencil above it.

'Tell me, Leo. You sat in the car. And Pappa was driving. Where did he drive?'

'I don't want to say.'

'And . . . why don't you want to?'

'Because I don't want to.'

'Try.'

'Because I don't want to.'

'Leo? I'm talking to you.'

'Because I don't want to.'

Leo looks down at the floor until the terrible cop goes out into the hall and comes back with his winter jacket and puts it on the shiny kitchen table. He notices how big the cop's hands are, but he knows that however strong they look, they couldn't snap five lolly sticks held together.

'It smells of smoke. Can you smell it?'

This is ours.

'There's a can of petrol in one of the paper sacks. In the other one there were some empty wine bottles and shredded rags.'

Not yours.

'Do you know what that means? Altogether?'

We live here.

'Do you know what your pappa's made here?'

Not you.

'A Molotov cocktail. That's what it's called. It's a bottle full of petrol. And when it's smashed the petrol turns into flames, spreads, destroys, kills. A fire bomb used in war.'

We are a clan.

'Your grandfather saw both you and your father at the house when it was burning. And your grandmother did too. And your mother. And five neighbours. All of them saw you – and all of them saw your father.'

A clan always sticks together.

'Your grandfather also saw you holding a bag. What happened then? Did you throw it? Or was it your father?'

A clan can't be broken.

'Leo?'

No matter what happens.

'Now I want you to listen to me.'

In a clan, a real clan, we never hurt each other.

'Your mother could have died. And your grandmother. And your grandfather. They could all have died.'

In a real clan, we never snitch on each together.

'Look at me, Leo. Do you understand what your father did, that he meant it?'

In a clan, in a real clan, we protect each other, always, always, always.

'You don't need to protect your father – he's the one who's done something wrong. He's the one who should take care of you.'

'I'm not a lolly stick!'

It comes out so suddenly that even he isn't prepared for it.

'Do you hear what I'm saying! I'm not!'

'Tell me now exactly what your father did. For your mother's sake, for your brothers. Leo? Tell me.'

He hasn't thought about his mother crying. But maybe she's just started?

She is somewhere behind him, he can't see her eyes, but he can hear her – she's not afraid, not of what happened or could have happened, this is directed at him, at her son standing in front of a detective, answering questions that no one else has anything to do with, that's why she's crying.

'I'm not a fucking lolly stick you can break in two!'

The pencil on the spiral notebook is lying there as he rushes up to the table, snatches it away and, with all the fear and all the anger collected in his ten-year-old arm, stabs the grey point of the pencil into that huge right hand.

Then he runs away, chased by the howling detective and by Mamma, who tries to grab hold of him, and the other detective who almost collides with him in the hall. Leo locks the bedroom door from the inside. Vincent is still asleep upside down in his bed, and Felix is sitting on the floor next to a pile of Lego.

'Leonard!'

He hears Mamma pounding on the door.

'Come out of there! You hear me! You *have to* talk to them!'

It's hard to understand how Vincent can sleep through all this commotion.

'Open the door!'

And that Felix can sit on the floor surrounded by hundreds and hundreds of Lego pieces.

'Leo? Do as your mother says. Turn the key and open the door,' shouts the tall detective.

'Was it him?' Felix whispers as he points to the door. 'Was it him? Did he . . .'

'He was the one who screamed. Whose hand got hurt,' answers Leo.

Voices rumbling. He doesn't hear it. If you decide to not hear something, you won't. He does that sometimes, goes into his own room and locks the door. His room is even smaller than this one, and inside it's only him, his body, everything exists inside, nothing exists outside.

'Leo? You know we can open this door anyway, don't you? Leo? Your mother doesn't want that. So open up!'

Then his youngest brother wakes up. Tousled hair, tired eyes.

Leo picks him up and walks back and forth between the door and the window.

'Vincent? They don't exist.'

He stops near the door and the rumbling that's telling him to open up, come out.

'They don't exist.'

The tired eyes aren't tired any more, they're watching him, listening.

'You hear that, little brother?'

'Yes.'

'They don't exist. And we're . . . going to go straight through them.'

The three-year-old is trying to understand. And then he smiles.

'Straight through?'

'Straight through.'

Mamma and the two officers are still outside. Pappa is being driven along some other street with two police officers.

He walks around the room for a long time, a big brother holding his little brother behind a closed and locked door.

And he's probably never felt as calm as he does right now. With Felix and Vincent. In a place where he decides who exists and who doesn't.

now

part four

77

DECEMBER CHANGED ITS clothes during Leo's three-hundred-mile ride west through a countryside decked out for Christmas; ice on Lake Mälaren and a capital city where people walked quickly with their eyes to the ground were replaced by Gothenburg, a city of pedestrians in their autumn jackets. So Leo did the same as they did – buttoned up his jacket and strolled.

He got a bottle of water at a kiosk and a hot dog at a grill opposite Valands Art School, where he was supposed to turn off the avenue and follow the tram lines to Vasa Park. From there it wasn't far to Erik Dahlberg Street. To them. His brothers. He hadn't seen them once since they'd moved here. He hadn't felt it so much this autumn because he'd decided not to, but he did. Now that he was so close he felt the tug of expectation.

He'd decided to leave them be, yet somehow it still felt as if it were they who were keeping him at arm's length. They'd always been in contact. Never judged each other, or got in each other's way, never ever needed to ask each other for help. Now they spoke two, maybe three times a month, stiff conversations about the weather and the price of taxis and some new movie the other should see. Not a single word about the abortive weapons sale. He hated it. It was just like his mother and her siblings, the way people who had nothing in common talked to each other.

His little brothers lived in an apartment in a beautiful 1920s building. On the board inside the door a piece of tape with their names had been affixed over someone else's. Third floor. He rang the doorbell and knocked, just to be sure. He could tell just from the sound of approaching feet that it would be Felix, before he even opened the door.

His hair was longer – Felix had always kept his hair cut short – but it looked good. They hugged each other in the doorway, as if everything was normal.

'Hungry?'

The smell of food. He followed Felix down a narrow hallway to the kitchen where Vincent stood next to the refrigerator. He looked older. Older than just the few months that had passed. Stronger – physically more like a man. And his eyes, just as intense, were more piercing and distinct. Another hug. It was hard to say if the distance and chilliness were just in Leo's head, something he'd imagined.

'So . . . nothing here is yours?'

'Nope.'

A table he'd never seen before. Chairs he'd never seen. A microwave oven, a toaster, a radio, all unfamiliar. And a Salvador Dalí poster on the wall. He wondered if they even knew who that was.

'Just like when we were little, and you got all my hand-me-downs,' said Leo.

'Second-hand. The whole lot. Furniture, kitchenware. They even left us some shampoo. But Mamma liked it.'

'She said she'd been here.'

Bolognese on the stove; Felix was making dinner.

'She said it was going well. At the university, with your courses. And she was so proud of you, Vincent, that you'd already got through the first year of your school studies.'

He was anxious. He couldn't hide it, and he could tell Felix could see it.

'You should see his marks. Every single exam, perfect. He's only eighteen, Leo, and our little brother can do anything he wants to.'

Felix winked at Vincent, who smiled shyly – that was still the same at least – and then took out the plates, glasses and a bottle of wine.

'How long are you staying?'

'The train leaves in four hours.'

'Four hours? Here I thought you came to hang out for a while.'

Leo didn't say anything. *Fucking superior, stubborn little brother.* He was here to heal the breach, not make it worse.

'Just a simple financing robbery. Everything's ready. A little bank in Heby. The day before Christmas Eve. A few million.'

The bolognese was almost ready. The water on the other burner was boiling.

'Then we'll have enough money for a big job. And after that . . . you can study whatever the hell you want to.'

'That's what we're already doing,' said Felix, taking out a packet of spaghetti and dumping it all in at the same time. 'I thought you knew that. That we're already studying what we want to.'

'I need you.'

'We've quit, Leo.'

He'd decided he'd stay calm no matter what. But that didn't last long. Leo slammed his hand onto the table, the silverware and plates shook.

'Do you think you're normal now because you're at college? Because you're sitting on a fucking wooden chair behind a fucking wooden counter?'

Felix poured wine into his glass up to the top.

'I'm not studying in order to be normal, I'm studying to get an education.'

Leo took a small sip.

'What about you, Vincent?'

His youngest brother looked away.

'Vincent, damn it!'

'It was easier to be part of it than to not be,' Vincent replied. 'To find out if everything was going to go to hell.'

Leo laughed, not kindly. He took another small sip of wine.

'Go to hell? Vincent – it *won't* go to hell. Ever. Come over here, sit down.'

Vincent did as he asked and sat down on the chair opposite Leo.

'But *if* it does?'

'It won't.'

'If we end up at a police roadblock again, and they figure it out? That it's you? That it's us?'

Another small sip. The wine didn't just look cheap, it tasted cheap.

'Is that what you're sitting here doing – imagining things?'

'Listen to what he's saying!' shouted Felix.

Spaghetti strands had collapsed into the boiling water, limp now. Felix stirred them with a plastic fork, a little too vehemently.

'Leo – you need to fucking understand what it is he's trying to tell you!'

'Him? Or you?'

'OK. OK, Leo. Why are you doing this?'

'Doing what?'

'Robbing banks.'

'So *we* can be financially independent.'

'You have the weapons. Sell them. You said you were going to.'

'I almost did. I did exactly what I planned to – contacted the cops, recce'd a place for a handover, built fifteen fucking landmines. Everything was ready. Twenty-five million in a bag on some cop's desk.'

He stopped.

'And . . .?'

'And then that fucking cop started provoking me. Consciously. Tried to knock me off balance, wanted me to make mistakes. I wrote nine letters. The cop replied in five personal ads. Before I realised they were just stringing me along. That they'd never pay a fucking penny, that they were just trying to flush me out. That's when I broke it off, completely.'

Felix was listening, but he still had the same expression on his face.

'OK. Then I'll ask you again. Why are you *doing* this? Robbing banks?'

'Why am *I* doing it? And here I am thinking you did it too. Or am I mistaken, Felix? Weren't you there? And if you *were* there – why did *you* do it?'

'That's exactly what Vincent's trying to explain to you! Because it's easier to be a part of it than not to – if everything went to hell, at least I'd know. This anxiety, you don't get it, but I feel it, Vincent feels it. The only one who doesn't think like that is you. You think . . . this *won't* go to hell.'

Felix poured the water from the pan into the sink, the steam softly enveloping his tense face.

'Because it won't.'

'You said you'd never seek out our father again. I felt calm after that. But you did it anyway! And I can see it. You're turning into him! Nothing else exists for you except the next robbery. And the next. Nothing except that. You treat me and Vincent just like Ivan did when you broke with him.'

'What are you talking about?'

'You're just like him. And I know exactly when it happened. Then . . . when he almost killed Mum. When you jumped on his back and she ran away and he stopped, and I saw how you looked at each other. You just . . . took over.'

'Settle down now.'

'And after that? Do you remember what happened next? You don't, do you? You waited until he'd left and was back in his car, and then you fucking mopped up all the dried blood in the stairwell. When you were done you came back in and looked at me and Vincent, and from then on it was all your way.'

'Are you finished?'

'No! Not until you understand. You said "independent". You stood there in the window, staring out over Skogås, talking about how no bastard would have any power over us. But the opposite has happened. Robbing banks has only made us more dependent on each other. It's just as important to you as it was for that old bastard. Stick together. Stick together! Shall we try to break some ice lolly sticks too?'

'Are you finished yet?'

Leo looked at the two pans steaming on the table. They looked like the wine. Cheap. Junk.

'I'm not the one who's like Ivan. You are, Felix. You go on and on about how much you hate him. You are fucking fixated. You dwell on shit just like him. And he couldn't do any of the things I've done!'

He dug into the pans anyway, spooning brown sauce over a pile of white pasta. On his own plate, onto Felix's and Vincent's.

'One more time, Vincent. And if Felix is right . . .'

Leo put his hand on Vincent's arm.

'. . . then you should be part of this – now! If it's . . . *easier*. Not just sitting here and worrying the day before Christmas Eve.'

'Enough, Leo, can't you see he doesn't want to come with you!'

'What the hell do you know about it? I'm talking to Vincent now.'

'I can feel he doesn't want to!'

'Really? Felix? You can *feel* it?'

The saucepan of meat sauce stood between them. Felix suddenly grabbed hold of it and threw it against the wall. It splattered across the kitchen.

'I spat in my own mother's face! I will never do anything against my will again for the sake of someone else, ever!'

Warm bolognese ran down the white walls and Leo's white shirt.

'You're talking about yourself, Felix. I'm talking about Vincent.'

Vincent had been staring down at his plate; now he looked up.

'Can't we just stop?'

Now he was the one who put a hand on Leo's arm.

'Can't *you* just stop?'

There were napkins in an ugly little wooden dispenser in a corner of the kitchen table. Leo grabbed them all, crumpled them, and wiped the trickle of meat sauce off his shirt.

'And do what? Sit on a fucking wooden chair at a fucking wooden counter, pretending we're normal?'

They had never needed to ask each other for anything. Leo did it anyway.

'Please, I'm begging you. Have I ever begged you? Have I? I'm doing it now. I'm *begging* you. I need you. One more time. One last time.'

He looked at one little brother whose hair was longer, at another who was quickly becoming an adult.

'Please?'

One at a time. And he didn't recognise them.

'Felix?'

No reply.

'Vincent?'

No reply.

'*I'm begging you.*'

Felix met his eyes. Vincent looked down at the table and his plate. Silence.

'Well then. I'll do it alone. If I don't have a family, I'll do it myself.'

78

SOMETIMES THE NIGHTS never end. Sometimes you sweat and freeze and sweat, waking up every ten minutes just to fall into another incoherent dream that leads nowhere.

It was that kind of night. Again. All week, since being turned down by the two people he was closest to. Six nights of fucking loneliness lying beside him in bed, between his body and Anneli's. If they'd been dead it wouldn't have felt like this – then he would have understood why they couldn't be together. If they had said they hated him, it wouldn't have felt like this. But they were alive. And they still loved him as he loved them. Yet despite that – they weren't going to carry on. Two brothers who had been so close were now so far away.

Leo pulled the sweaty sheet from his back, went downstairs to the kitchen. He opened the window wide, even though the temperature was eight below zero, and let his face meet the cold, breathing in, out, in.

The last few days he'd been going over the three elements all these robberies had in common, again and again. Planning. Execution. And the most crucial – escape – the transition from robber to civilian.

One element always remained the same – the execution. They had never left their target with exactly what he'd expected. The ten million kronor in the security van had ended up being only one million. At every single robbery there had been less money in the vaults and safes than he'd expected. At the double robbery, he'd been convinced they'd take at least eight million but it ended up being three, and at the triple robbery the fifteen million he'd hoped for had ended up being only two, mostly drenched in red.

He ran his hand over the window ledge, gathering up the recently fallen snow and pressing it into a fistful – a pleasant chill as it melted into water.

He pulled down the window and wiped his hands dry with a kitchen towel, walked out into the hall and into the guest room. Nine robberies, and that fucking cop Broncks had no idea who they were – so if he just kept choosing the right date, continued to plan and escape properly, then sooner or later he'd get the execution right and receive the maximum return.

The tenth.

A small town outside Stockholm.

The day before Christmas Eve – payday.

And it would *not* be carried out by the Military League.

Because the Military League no longer existed; no one would ever write a line about that group again. The phantoms were disappearing and taking a new shape. That was exactly what he had rehearsed in the bank in Rimbo: a robbery that would differ from the others – casual clothes, black stockings over their heads and no shots fired. It had been preparation for changing their identities and breaking his pattern, if one day it were to become necessary. Now it was.

He lifted the floor tiles, pulled up the hatch and opened the horizontal safe, watching the black velvet fall away into the darkness. He climbed down and lit the lamp hanging above the rows of automatic weapons.

Next to the bulletproof vests lay a black sports bag.

The triple robbery had netted 2,137,000 kronor. 227,000 had gone on various expenses; 195,000 hadn't been ruined by the dye; they had divided the rest into four piles, 428,750 kronor each. His pile had shrunk considerably since then: 75,000 left. The bills barely covered the bottom of the bag.

He unzipped it and gathered up ten thousand in various denominations – he would give it to Anneli for Christmas gifts, Christmas food, a Christmas tree and some Christmas lights she had seen, the same as the ones the neighbours had in their apple trees. Then he separated off ten thousand for himself – leaving 55,000. He closed the bag and sat down on a concrete slab, lost in the fiery glow of the lamp, listening to the sump pump growling under his bare feet.

If he climbed out of the hatch, if he closed the safe and never opened it again, no one would ever know.

Feet on the cold, black and white vinyl floor. Steps. Her steps. She was standing up there now, and the light on the underside of her kneecaps, that was all he saw.

'Leo?'

'Yes?'

'What are you doing?'

Anneli squatted down. She was freezing in a thin nightgown.

'Come up and join me. Let's go back to bed. Try to sleep.'

'Fifteen million. That's what we were supposed to take home from the triple robbery. And we ended up with almost nothing.'

She hunched down and crawled through, her bare feet balanced on the slender rungs as she climbed down, then stroked his cheek, her hand warm even though she was cold.

'Leo?'

They were surrounded by neat lines of weapons, sunk into the walls like large fossils. He'd threatened to donate his collection to Sweden's criminal elite, but refrained. He cared as little about them as he did about that cop he'd threatened.

'Leo, I love you. I'm the only one who knows all about you, about this.'

She sat on his lap, she was really freezing, bare toes rubbing against each other and avoiding the floor.

'I know what Felix and Vincent mean to you. I know that. But I left my son for our sake. And you have to let go of your brothers. For our sake.'

She looked at him, his eyes close to hers. She had met someone who shone and had fallen in love with his light. Now that light was gone.

'I know you took care of them. But a brother shouldn't be a father to his own siblings.'

She kissed him, and he looked at her. And maybe he glowed; it had been a long time, but he did, at least a bit, she was sure of it.

'What is it?'

'Anneli?'

'What?'

'Do you think you could drive the getaway car?'

She thought she hadn't heard right at first.

'Can you do it?'

'Me?'

'You.'

She'd helped them into their disguises and dropped them off at a robbery. Then she was always supposed to leave, go home, wait without participating.

Now he wanted her to be a part of it, for real.

She'd be driving the getaway car, like Felix.

She kissed him.

'*Me?*'

'Yes. *You.* I'm serious. You're a damn good driver.'

She snuggled into his arms, skin to skin, laughed, kissed him.

79

IT WAS EARLY morning, still dark, the streetlamps spilling light onto the pavements, which found its way between Bagarmossen's 1950s three-storey apartment buildings. After three hours asleep in Anneli's arms, Leo felt thoroughly rested again. He had deliberately parked some distance away and walked now through leafless bushes across a deserted playground on his way to the rear of the building. He didn't want Jasper to see him, and he knew how he peered through the kitchen window every time a car parked out front, ready to flee if the cops got close.

Leo keyed the four-digit access code into the back door and hoped that it hadn't changed. A muffled click and he stepped into the stairwell, holding the door as it closed again.

Jasper had planned his escape in detail, Leo knew. Opposite the house, across the car park, stood the Nacka Reserve national forest, and just inside, between two large rocks, Jasper had buried a plastic container that held clothes, a knife, cash, passport and a pistol – a Beretta he'd bought in the United States three years earlier and sent home in pieces. But he wasn't going to be allowed to escape now, nor arm himself and hide. Both remembered the blow so hard it had knocked Jasper to the floor, leaving him staring upwards with hatred, disappointment, confusion, sadness.

The stairwell walls were painted a suffocating green colour. Leo made his way cautiously to the door and rang the bell.

He didn't hear a thing, but he was sure that the door's peephole darkened.

He knocked. Continuously. The flap of the letterbox swung upwards.

'What do you want?'

'To talk.'

'About what?'

'Open the door, for fuck's sake.'

It was quiet for a long time. Finally, the door slid open until the chain was fully extended.

'Hold out your hands.'

Jasper's eyes loomed in the gap between door and frame, and they weren't jumpy so much as uncertain. Leo held out two open palms. Then the chain rattled as the door opened completely.

Jasper was wearing a pair of creased brown trousers and a beige shirt. He was freshly shaven and his hair had been trimmed. It was six thirty in the morning; at this time Jasper used to look like an unmade bed, and that's what Leo had expected – more than that, perhaps, someone who was broken and lost – not a face that had colour in its cheeks.

But the uncertainty remained. And he kept his right hand angled back, as if wanting to make it clear that he was hiding something along his forearm.

Prepared to expose his throat. Ready to strike.

Leo stepped inside and Jasper simultaneously stepped back, careful to maintain the same distance between them – close enough to be able to attack and far enough away to avoid being attacked.

'There's no need to be scared of me.'

A shake of the head was Jasper's only response.

'Jasper – put away that crap behind your arm.'

'Put it away? Leo, you and me . . .'

Jasper swallowed saliva down a dry throat.

'. . . know way too much about each other.'

'But you don't need to be afraid of me.'

'No? An armoury? Nine bank robberies? Central Station?'

A step forward. And like before, Jasper took an equally long step back.

'Maybe you're here to . . . do some cleaning up. Perhaps you and your brothers have decided to close down the whole operation. Don't you think I realise I could just . . . go up in smoke in that case? Like a pair of boots.'

Leo was about to take another step when Jasper held up his left arm. 'No closer.'

'You don't need that knife – put it away.'

'Take off your jacket.'

They stood there, both of them maintaining the same distance. Leo took off his leather jacket and held it up, turned it back to front and back again to show there was nothing there, nothing hidden.

'And the shoes.'

Leo bent down and untied them, held them up, put them on the shoe rack next to a pair of glistening black boots that looked new. Combat boots. Just like the ones he had burned – but this year's model.

'Can I have a cup of coffee now?'

'After you roll up your trousers.'

He did so, and threw his arms wide.

'Look, just socks and hairy shins. And the coffee? Now?'

The uncertainty remained. Jasper looked at him, silently, as if he couldn't quite decide what to do.

'Fucking hell, Jasper . . . if I wanted to get rid of you, I sure as hell wouldn't do it in your flat. Right?'

A short pause. Then Jasper nodded, bared his right arm, revealing a long, sharp kitchen knife.

They walked down the short hallway to the kitchen, Leo quickly glancing into the living room. The altar was gone. The green beret. The photo of Jasper in uniform at the Norrland Rangers final manoeuvres. The course literature. The bayonet. Everything that had been so important, taken away. Only the table stood there still, but on it was a vase that held no flowers and a candlestick with no candle.

In the kitchen Jasper put coffee into a filter, while Leo sat down.

'OK. Why are you here?'

'Just wanted to see how you were doing.'

'How I'm doing?'

Jasper smiled, or rather smirked. And that was when Leo saw it for the first time. On the other side of the table. Hanging over a chair. The same brown material as the trousers. And with a badge on the right sleeve half-covered by a fold.

'What are you wearing? What the hell's that hanging there?'

Leo nodded towards the back of the chair and a uniform jacket on which the first three letters of a company's name were visible. SEC. He already knew what the rest of it said, the letters that had disappeared into a fold, but he didn't understand why that jacket was hanging on Jasper's kitchen chair.

'It's mine.'

Leo looked first at the jacket, then at Jasper.

'Yours?'

'Yes. I got fired from my last job, right?'

'OK . . . well, in that case . . . what do you do there?'

'OK . . . well in that case . . . what are you doing *here*?'

Jasper turned his back to him while doing something with the coffee, which hissed and bubbled. He wasn't so unsure any more.

'I'm here because I need you,' said Leo.

He turned round, a little too fast.

'Need me?'

'Yes. We're going to do the tenth robbery.'

Jasper's body relaxed completely. The threat which had existed earlier was gone. And with it the hostility and suspicion.

Seven months of longing. And here they were. Together.

'The tenth?'

'The tenth.'

'I thought you'd never ask,' said Jasper, smiling broadly.

He poured two cups of strong coffee.

Leo unfolded the uniform jacket. All the letters were visible now: SECURITAS. Sweden's largest security company.

'What the hell are you doing there?' he asked.

'Turning off alarms when they go off, checking out broken windows at schools or storage units that have been burgled, driving around industrial estates . . . that kind of thing.'

Jasper opened the refrigerator and took out a carton of milk, pouring a splash into Leo's cup.

'They talk about us all the time at the office,' said Jasper, his smile still filled with longing. 'The Military League. *What will they hit next? A bank? A security van? A depot?* And there I sit, listening.'

He looked proud. It was easy to imagine him in that staff room, about to burst from not being able to tell anyone.

'In a few months I'll be driving a security van myself. I thought about it, what would *I* do if *I* was robbed?'

He fingered the uniform jacket slung over the chair next to him.

'There are two options. One – I do as I'm told if I see that the robbers know what the hell they're doing. Two – if they're amateurs . . . I'll overpower them. Leo, I could stop a couple of robbers, be the hero in the papers, and nobody would ever know that it was me behind that mask!'

'There is a third option.'

'OK?'

'What would you do if you realised it was me?'

'You?'

'If I was the one robbing the security van?'

'I would . . . hell, I'd take off my clothes. Lie down. And you could do what you wanted. I'd do exactly what you said.'

A laugh. But it was also grounded in truth.

'But it's too early, I need to gain their confidence, work my way up, get into the system. Then I'll be driving a security van.'

Leo emptied his cup; he'd never done that before at Jasper's.

'Good. The tenth first. Then we'll plan this. You and me.'

Just a few hours ago he'd been sitting alone in his armoury. Now he had a driver, and someone capable of following him into a bank.

'And your brothers? What do they have to say about all this?'

'They don't have anything to say. They're not part of this.'

'So it's . . . just you and me?'

'No. There's a driver too.'

'Who?'

'We'll discuss that later.'

'Just three?'

'There's one more.'

80

THEY PARTED AS friends with a common goal. First a small robbery over the holiday season to fund the coming year's activities, then the planning of a much larger robbery next Christmas. *Target* – the main branch of the Central Bank. *Loot* – the forty to fifty million brought in each day from Christmas shopping and then sent back out again to fill the ATMs. The beating heart of commerce would be hit by a cardiac arrest. With Jasper on the inside, the impossible had suddenly become possible. And if they were talking about those kinds of sums, and about finishing it, maybe he'd be able to convince his brothers to join in one last time.

The biggest Swedish robbery ever. And then disband for ever.

Leo stopped the car in front of the gate. There had been piles of leaves in the garden last time, now there were no leaves left. The frozen grass crunched under his shoes and ice crystals stuck to his cheeks, swirled around him, flashing in the morning sun. He nodded to a man holding a newspaper under his arm while kneeling in the snow by the fence, apparently examining it.

'Is my father inside?'

'Leo?'

The man, Steve, stood up and took off his glasses.

'Leo – it's been a while. You don't visit your dad very often.'

Steve was the owner of the house and lived in the slightly larger apartment upstairs. They greeted each other, and now he could see what Steve had been looking at. Several of the green pickets were broken in half.

'Is he in?'

'I think so. His car's parked over there.'

Same yellow Saab estate, now in even worse shape. It stood in the same place it had been in last time, but was parked at more of an angle. Steve shook his head, scratched his neck.

'He drove straight into it.'

Steve glanced meaningfully at Ivan's car, sighed, then looked at the fence, sighed again, and pointed to the tyre tracks in the grass right next to the broken planks.

'Straight into the fence.'

'But he's in now?'

'He's there, but he won't open the door when I knock.'

'Then I'll make sure he knows it's *me* knocking instead.'

Steve wasn't listening, he was busy jiggling one of the boards as if it were a loose tooth.

'Your father can be rather . . . difficult at times. But never this bad. Just sitting there and shutting himself in. And he's always paid the rent on time. Now he doesn't even do that.'

He pulled up the board a little more, then with a jerk it came off.

'And besides, he borrowed money from me.'

Leo peered towards the ground floor of the house, all the windows covered from the inside, quilts and blankets over curtain poles. Like a wartime blackout.

'When did you last see him?'

'Yesterday, when he came home from the off-licence. I tried to talk to him, but he just slammed the door shut in my face. He's been drink-driving . . . I did try to talk to him.'

'He hasn't, well, said anything that seems . . . odd?'

'Odd?'

'Something important, that might be weighing on him. You usually chat, don't you?'

Steve shrugged.

'No. Nothing. He hasn't said a thing. At least, the only thing he said to me was he thought I should . . . and this is a direct quote . . . "go fuck a cactus". And if I didn't, and I'm quoting again, he would "push a handsaw up my arse". I have a spare key, but I don't dare enter. Don't misunderstand me, I like Ivan, he can be difficult and he has a hell of a temper but he's also smart and funny and . . . Leo, right now, I don't recognise him. Honestly, I'm really worried and a little scared. He's intimidating, he hasn't been like that before, not to me anyway. I don't understand what's happened.'

Leo nodded. His father had solved his problems in the same way he always did. He'd been drinking and fighting, but not talking. And the anxiety that had crept up on him now sneaked away again.

'I'll take care of it. How much does he owe you?'

Steve's whole posture finally relaxed just a little.

'Rent. Plus his debt. Eight thousand altogether.'

Leo took his wallet out of his back pocket, and counted out six thousand kronor in 500-kronor bills.

'You'll get the other two later this week. And I'll fix the fence. OK?'

Steve was just about to take the money when Leo pulled it away.

'But I want the spare key, too.'

Leo put the key in the lock and turned it. Darkness. And then the stench of prolonged confinement, in the midst of which was the smell of his father. He turned on the lights. On the floor were heaps of cut-up newspapers. The table was covered with wrinkled Keno tickets, crumpled wrappers and raw onions, which always took over a room when they were peeled, plus a pair of scissors, articles cut out of newspapers, a glue stick and a lot of wine bottles, all empty. And there, on the sofa, was something black in the blackness – a thick black binder sunk into the worn leather. He sat down and leafed through it. Page after page, clip after clip – articles about the Military League. Pictures of broken glass and his own masked face and eight bullet holes in a cashier's window.

A fucking cuttings file.

His father had done his research. He wasn't guessing, he'd known. A father collecting everything that was written about his sons, so he could read it again. As if he were . . . proud.

He wasn't sure if his father had ever felt that way before. And Leo felt the discomfort all the way down into his stomach. He slammed the folder shut and proceeded to one of the two closed doors.

Ivan Dûvnjac lay perfectly still in the darkness. Leo hurried over to the edge of the bed, put a finger to his mouth until he felt something faintly like breath, then moved his whole hand over both nose and mouth. The cautious creak in his father's throat turned into an angry snoring, he grunted and threw his arm like a stray sledgehammer.

'Pappa.'

Leo grabbed his shoulder, shook it slightly.

'Pappa!'

The big body turned over slowly, never opening his eyes.

'Look at me! Dad!'

Ivan opened his eyes, at least halfway.

'Leo . . .?'

He grabbed hold of Leo's outstretched arm and heaved himself up with difficulty, until his bare feet were on the floor.

'How the hell did you get in here?'

'What are you up to, Dad? Fighting with your landlord, driving drunk into his fence, telling him to go to hell, threatening him. What if he'd called the police? What if the fucking cops came in? You're lying in here like a knocked-out walrus, while Steve gives out the spare key, and they come in here, look around this pigsty and find . . . this.'

He threw the black folder into Ivan's lap.

'The path from you to me isn't very far, is it? If they found this, don't you . . . here, in the home of a father with three sons! "Let's check them out."'

Ivan looked at the folder of cuttings, but he didn't throw it, he carefully put it on the bed.

'You'd be handing over your own sons! Your fucking boozing would ruin everything again!'

He pulled down the blankets and forced apart the curtains. More light. Ivan ducked, as if trying to get away from it.

'Look at me, Dad, and listen. Because I'm here to offer you a job.'

'I have a job.'

'Bullshit. I've just given six thousand kronor to Steve out there. And he said you owe him even more.'

He waited while the tired eyes stopped blinking and the daylight sank in.

'A job offer. Because I'm a man short.'

Ivan was still squinting as he got up and silently left the room, with some difficulty.

'So you're a coward. You're not man enough for it.'

Leo followed him.

'You have to fill up on wine just to dare to go to Grandma's house and throw a Molotov cocktail.'

'Yes. That may be me. But I don't snitch.'

'I didn't snitch on you!'

'You—'

'I was ten years old. And this . . . this doesn't work any more. So knock it off.'

Piles of newspapers on the floor. Heaps of food scraps on the table.

The image of a father. Ivan pulled his hand through his disorderly hair and looked at his son.

'If you keep on with this, Leo, they'll hunt you down like an animal. They won't let you go on like this for ever! There are pigs who sit around in cars, but there are others who have the same weapons that you do. They're waiting for you to make a mistake, and then . . . then they'll put a bullet in you. You can't beat them – you can't.'

'I'm doing this with or without you.'

His father had sat down on the worn-out sofa. He looked almost small.

'Do you need me?'

'Are you in?'

'Do you need me or not?'

'We need you.'

We need you. Leo had said it. His three sons needed him.

'I'm in.'

Leo nodded, then pulled down the thick blanket that hung in front of the kitchen window, dust dancing in the bright light.

'Not another drop from now on.'

81

HE COULDN'T REMEMBER the last time he'd wrapped a present, if he'd ever done so before. She'd always been the one who wrapped their Christmas gifts, late at night, while their three expectant sons slept.

Ivan lifted the bulky parcel, weighed it in his hand. Red glossy paper, then gold ribbon. The scissors lay on the table, and he pulled the sharp edge along the flat, hard plastic surface of the ribbon, as Britt-Marie used to, so it would twist into small curls which she arranged around the perfectly tight crisscrossed ribbons until the whole thing looked like a rhododendron in bloom. It didn't work now. No matter which way he pulled the scissors or tried to bunch it up, it turned into spiky, thorny bushes.

The label should sit on top, in the middle, near the golden bushes. He attached it firmly, then used a blue ballpoint pen whose ink wouldn't take, so he switched to black, which worked better.

Merry Christmas from Ivan.

He carried the parcel from the kitchen table into the narrow entrance hall and put it down next to the others, near the front door.

An empty Christmas present next to other empty Christmas presents.

He was about to go back and wrap a new parcel, but stopped. He was shaking again. It found its way through his dry skin. And he had to stand still until it subsided a bit, he didn't want them to see it.

It would get worse by tonight. Even worse tomorrow. Getting the alcohol out of his body was like forcing out another person who'd moved inside him, who'd made himself at home, and who under no conditions wanted to move out again.

He had shaken less this morning. He'd stood in his own bathroom and pulled his hand over the tight, freshly shaven skin. His eyes looked so watery and small, as if hiding, not wanting to see the curly, grey hair on the sides of his head, the nose that was bigger now than when he'd come to Sweden.

He could feel stabbing pains lower down in his body. All the time. Cruel stabs in his stomach and side where he imagined his liver sat, behind where his kidney should be. He'd drunk wine every day and night, for how long he had no idea, but he knew it would take at least three days before his nerves returned to anything resembling normal. The fucking stabbing he could live with. But to rob a bank while this poison was leaving his body, while his nerves slipped out through his dry skin – that he feared.

There was a way. To drink. Not very much, just enough that the devil inside would leave a little more slowly, without making so much damned noise. To level out the anxiety. A glass of wine every other hour. No one would notice.

But he'd promised his eldest son not to touch a drop. And so he'd left the razor and the bathroom without stopping by the half-full bottle on the cutting board. He had gone straight into the bedroom with that stabbing in his side, to a worn brown leather suitcase with equally worn-out handles, and packed two pairs of jeans, two pairs of new underpants, two pairs of socks, two shirts and a light grey suit. He hadn't known then if he would be allowed to stay here at Leo's house. Maybe they'd celebrate Christmas here. Ivan, Leo, Felix, Vincent. First rob a bank together. And then celebrate Christmas.

He held out his hands to make sure they'd stopped shaking. He adjusted the empty parcel, which lay on top of the others, and went back into the kitchen again, to the table with the wrapping paper and ribbons and tape and gift tags.

'And this time, Dad, do you know who this is for?' asked Leo, who sat opposite Anneli. Each had their own wrapped-up present in front of them.

'M-E-R-R-Y C-H-R-I-S-T-M-A-S D-A-D . . .'

He spelled what he was writing aloud.

'. . . F-R-O-M Y-O-U-R S-O-N L-E-O.'

This empty parcel was significantly smaller than the one Ivan had taken out into the hall, and Leo dropped it into the brown hessian sack along with the others.

'A happy family, Dad,' said Leo. 'Doing the things happy families do, wrapping presents and celebrating Christmas with the relatives. You didn't expect that, did you?'

His hands shook on the table, but no one noticed. He grabbed the glass of cold water next to him and drank, without spilling any of it. There were two empty chairs at the table – but they weren't here yet.

He'd left his basement in Ösmo for this house in Tumba, knocked on the front door. There were bells hanging on it, which sounded brittle and beautiful as they vibrated. Leo had opened the door, and Ivan had put his leather bag on the hall floor and hung up his black coat. He'd felt Leo's hand on his shoulder, some kind of welcome, and for a moment he considered hugging him, but changed his mind. A woman had approached him, humming the Christmas carol that flowed out of the speakers on the wall. He hadn't even known that his eldest son lived with anyone. He had held out his hand and said hello to this Anneli, who told him he was very welcome, and then took him on a tour of their Christmas-decorated house. It was only when they got to the guest room that he realised she was involved. Leo had stood by the sofa bed waiting for them, and together they had revealed the room under the floor. He'd climbed down to the missing weapons he'd only seen on TV, but it wasn't really the weapons he was struck by – it was the ingenious design, and he stayed down there asking questions as one builder to another. For a moment he felt at ease. Together again. Father and son. And he had wanted to ask then: *When are Felix and Vincent getting here?*

It had been dark outside the kitchen window when they started wrapping, but there had been glimmers of light from the last of the rush-hour traffic; now only the occasional car temporarily interrupted the silence.

They took away the cardboard and paper as Leo pulled down the blinds and unfurled a map so big that it hung over the edges of the table like a tablecloth. Ivan tried to interpret it, read where they were going to strike tomorrow: one place in the middle called Heby and another to the left called Sala. Small towns he'd heard of but never visited. He guessed they lay a hundred kilometres or so northwest of Stockholm.

There was a knock on the door.

Ivan suddenly became aware how tense he was, how he held the air in his chest and his heart started to pound, as if after all these years he'd changed his mind and didn't want to meet them.

He sat there and wriggled in his chair, while Leo went into the hall. It was possible to hear the door handle turning and the brittle jingle of bells, just like when he'd arrived a few hours earlier. Then someone laughed, and hands pounded on backs.

They're hugging each other. My sons.

And God in hell how I need a drink.

A voice that might belong to someone in their twenties, though it was a little higher than he had expected – neither he nor Leo talked like that. Ivan strained to listen. Could it be Felix? Or Vincent? He'd be quite big by now too.

He walked towards the hall. That couldn't be Felix, could it? He had been darker and more like his father – this guy didn't have anything of Ivan in him. Nor was it Vincent – Ivan thought he might recognise him, if only vaguely.

'Hello . . . I'm Jasper.'

Not even the hands seemed right. His boys' hands were thicker; these were fine-boned and were enveloped by his own hands.

'Ivan.'

'I know. I grew up in Skogås. Used to spend a lot of time at your house, remember?'

Ivan shook his head.

'Well, I remember you. Damn, you cut off some guy's hair in the pizzeria, and then you gave them a beating one after the other.'

The man whose hands didn't belong to either of his sons went into the kitchen. It was clear he'd been here before, and his voice seemed elated as he said, *Hello Anneli, look who's here.* And she laughed, but it wasn't genuine, he could hear it, she was laughing because she thought she had to.

Ivan stayed in the hall. He didn't want to leave it, not yet. Maybe more people would come? He took a last glance at the door as Leo pulled it shut, and then gazed out through the narrow window instead.

No. No one else was coming.

'So he's part of this too?'

'He has been from the beginning.'

The map still lay on the kitchen table. Leo took up two 10-kronor coins from his pocket and placed them on the spot marking the town called Heby.

'The bank's here. And here, about two kilometres away, is the police station, manned by no more than one or two cops half the week. The day before Christmas Eve, they'll be off home around this time.'

Leo tapped one of the coins on the map and the table.

'Pappa? Are you following me? You stand here, outside the bank, easily visible. Anyone approaching needs to know that we're armed.'

He pushed the golden coin that indicated the police station towards the bank.

'The cops shouldn't be there. But if they do get the idea to intervene, it's your job, Pappa, to change their minds. A shot in the air. If it's not enough – a shot over their heads. If that's not enough, put as many shots as you need in the bonnet of their car. And if that still doesn't deter them, you'll have to protect yourself and Anneli, who will be in the car. Pappa, look at me! *If* you have to shoot – aim for the body.'

The two coins were now joined by a slightly larger silver 5-kronor coin, which Leo placed on the map about two kilometres north, next to a road that cut through one of the green forested areas.

'We'll leave the bank and drive the first getaway car here.'

Ivan looked at the map and at Leo's hands, pointing and moving the coins. But he wasn't paying attention. Two vacant seats. They hadn't come.

'Are you listening, Pappa? We cover the car and move through the forest . . . here. Two hundred metres . . . to here, to a car park, and to the second car, which is loaded with Christmas presents and Christmas food. From the stolen car to the rented car. And when we're inside, we change into our Christmas clothes – the happy family heading home to celebrate Christmas.'

'Is it just us? Us . . . four?'

'It's just *one* bank. We don't need anyone else.'

'Felix? And Vincent? Where are they?'

He looked back and forth several times between the empty chairs and Leo, who just sat there in silence. Then after a while he appealed to that Jasper fellow and the woman Anneli. None of them responded.

'Look here, Dad.'

The gun had been sitting in a bag on the floor, wrapped in a bath towel. Not the kind he'd used during his own military service over thirty years ago, but the same principle, and Leo started to disassemble it into four parts.

'A butt. A stock. And here . . . Dad, the mechanism, and inside the mechanism . . . here, the bolt. You move it a quarter turn and pull it out. Now you. Assemble it. And then we'll go through how you use it.'

Four parts in front of him on the table. He didn't want to touch them, or put them together, if he did it would become a deadly weapon. He'd known what his sons were doing, but hadn't quite understood the implications. *He* was the one who was to hurt people.

'Pappa? You have to know this, inside out. Just like when you taught me how to punch with my whole body, remember?'

His hands held on tight to his jeans. If he let go, it would be clear he couldn't keep them steady. He studied the parts; after a while he picked up the bolt and put it into the mechanism, turned it, but couldn't get it to click like it should. He could feel them standing around the table, watching him. He put it back in again, turned it, looked for parts to fasten to it and was suddenly overcome by doubt – not their doubt, but the kind that came from within and demanded that he drop the weapon and tell them that this was madness.

'Pappa, one part at a time,' said Leo, putting his hand on his. They hadn't touched each other in that way since . . . he'd forgotten when.

Ivan turned it. Once. Twice. Three times . . . it clicked into place! His hands were definitely shaking but he hid it well.

'Good. And now the rest.'

The mechanism. Stock. The bolt. One piece at a time until the weapon was complete.

'Are you with us now, Pappa? It's important, you have to be able to do this tomorrow. I don't want to see you let off a stray bullet or hit someone by mistake.'

Leo took the gun out of Ivan's hands.

'This is the safety – and the latch should *always* be on S. Until the cops are coming – then you switch it to P. Not A – that's automatic, twenty shots in two seconds, and you have no idea what they'll hit.'

Jasper had been standing some distance away, waiting. Now he stepped forward, took the gun out of Leo's hands, sank into the firing position between the kitchen table and stove and aimed at the lowered blinds.

'Listen, Ivan? Look at me. You aim and exhale as you take the shot – and remember to press your *whole* body against the butt to counteract the recoil. We don't want you to hurt your shoulder, right?'

Jasper put the safety on and inclined his head slightly to one side.

'Can you do like I did? Show me.'

An automatic weapon lay across Ivan's thighs like an oar, because some brat who was here instead of his sons had put it there. And now that brat was giving him orders, asking him to stand up like some jerk and aim.

'What did you say your name was?'

'Jasper. And I—'

'Were you at the pizzeria when I gave *another* loser who talked too much a beating?'

'Yes, I saw it all through the window when you—'

'Somebody else who thought he'd tell me how I should behave?'

Leo already knew what would happen when Jasper started his lesson. But he wasn't sure if Ivan had fully understood the magnitude of what they were going to do tomorrow.

'Pappa?'

'Yes.'

'Get your coat on. I want you to come with me.'

'What are we going to do?'

'Steal a car.'

Ivan stood in the hall again, near the presents. And couldn't decide what irritated him more. The nerves that shook him from inside or the ceaseless Christmas music.

He'd been waiting for a minute, wearing a coat that had no lining and his slightly too thin shoes, when she waved at him.

'Could you come up here?' called Anneli.

She stood on top of a stepladder in the living room by the tree, a string of lights in her hands, the green wire wrapped carefully around the branches as she fastened it light by light.

'I have my shoes on.'

'It doesn't matter.'

Ivan did as she said and they looked at the tree, assessing it. They clearly didn't see the same thing. She seemed satisfied, hummed again, started moving silver bulbs around. All he saw was some poor tree that had been taken from its natural place in the woods.

'These ones are real,' she said, picking up a couple of the gifts that were crowded around the bottom. 'Most of them are for Sebastian. That's my son. He'll be here on Christmas Eve. To celebrate with us.'

The Christmas star lay on the windowsill. She handed it to him.

'I can't reach, can you?'

The Christmas carols were suffocating him. He took the star and wrapped its wire tail around the top of the tree.

'Perfect. Wonderful!'

She looked so happy that the tree was finished; to him it simply looked even more overloaded.

'Thank you, Ivan. Will you help me with those parcels down there, too?' she asked, gesturing to the sacks of empty packages.

Carrying the light hessian sacks, one in each hand, they went to the rental car. Anneli opened the boot.

'Half of them should be here, the first thing someone would see if it were opened tomorrow. It'll be around three o'clock, so it'll still be just about light at that time, and if they're here and in the back seat and the rear window, you'll see them from above. It was my idea.'

She looked just as proud now as she'd been of the tree. It was cold, and he was shivering, while she couldn't decide if the blue or the green package should be next to the gold one. She moved them from the seat to the rear window and from the rear window into the boot.

'What are you up to?' asked Ivan.

'It should look nice.'

'It does look nice.'

Leo passed behind them, a bag over his shoulder.

'We'll take your car, Pappa, and dump it when we've got another one.'

Ivan followed Leo towards the gate and the car parked outside, which was half-filled with tools and paintbrushes.

'That Jasper . . .' began Ivan.

'Yes?'

'Who the hell is he?'

'One of my oldest friends. Don't you recognise him?'

Ivan found the car keys in the inner pocket of his black coat.

'Do you trust him?'

'Excuse me?'

'Do you trust that pretend soldier?'

He opened the car door, and they sat in their seats, the keys in the ignition.

'Listen . . . Jasper is the kind of guy who never hesitates,' said Leo. 'He does what I tell him to do. If something unexpected happens tomorrow, if they stop us, if they get close to us . . . he'll stand his ground.'

————

Anneli watched Leo's and Ivan's backs from the kitchen window, waiting for Leo to turn round, for their eyes to meet in that way that had become part of her, but he didn't – he would always retreat into himself in those last days before a robbery, into a world he didn't share with anyone. She'd also become aware of something else: a father and his son. She had never seen them beside each other before, and now as they walked there shoulder to shoulder, their closeness became obvious, something they themselves were unaware of.

The living room was too dark. Anneli pushed a plug into the wall socket and a wreath lit up. She knelt by the tree and readjusted two parcels lying under the widest branch. She wondered if Sebastian would be happy – his face was always so focused when he opened presents, so full of anticipation. It had been a long time since they'd celebrated Christmas Eve together, but this year she'd have time to pick him up after they hid the getaway car and money and destroyed the weapons. She might even have time to cook a ham and put the herring in lime juice and fresh coriander and sugar and parsley and vinegar and leave it overnight in the refrigerator. They were going to have a real Christmas, as a family, just Leo and Sebastian and her.

She'd bought a horn for his bike, and an ice hockey helmet with flames on, exactly as he'd asked for. She started wrapping them up on the low coffee table.

'And what do you want for Christmas?'

Jasper. She hadn't heard him. He liked to sneak around.

'What do you mean?'

'I was thinking . . . I have time to get to Åhlens department store. This time of year they stay open until nine? I can't spend Christmas here without giving you anything.'

'What did you say?'

'If I'm going to be here, then I have—'

'You're not going to be here. We're going to rob a bank together. Then we'll celebrate our Christmases separately.'

'Leo asked me, and I said yes. So it'll be us. The family's getting bigger.'

He sat in Felix's armchair and rocked gently, as Felix always did.

'No. No. You are not going to be here.'

'I thought, this is like a fresh start. Right?'

'Did you hear what I said? *You are not going to be here.*'

'And I think, if I'm guessing right, we can probably get over a million. And then . . . we'll just keep going.'

She didn't answer.

'Anneli, what do you say to that?'

She didn't look at him, carried on taping the parcel up instead, but it didn't turn out exactly straight.

'What do I say? That you haven't understood a thing. That you will not be celebrating Christmas with us because you don't belong to our family. That you . . . that you don't understand that you're just a little fucking soldier! A dog that runs after sticks whenever his master calls him.'

She tore the paper off, started again.

'Don't you realise that you're not his brother? You're sitting there in Felix's seat but you *are* not a real brother!'

She stared defiantly at him, knowing he was prepared to hurt people to get what he wanted. But he just started rocking again.

'Anneli, I've known Leo a hell of a lot longer than you have. He has never and will never let anyone like you get in his way. Leo has his brothers. You know that damn well.'

He put his hand on his breast, clenched it, pounded it a few times.

'Leo has his brothers.'

Then he got up, walked towards the stairs, but stopped halfway.

'I *am* a soldier. A damn good soldier. And a good soldier knows exactly what to do – so I know exactly what the hell I'm going to do tomorrow. Do you know?'

And then he saluted.

'I'm not the weak link. You're the one driving the getaway car – and how many banks have you robbed? What if the cops stop us and you're the one who has to roll down the window? And you're the one who has to say, "Oh, officer, are you doing a breath test?" If that's you . . . for fuck's sake.'

And he carried on towards the stairs and then down to the armoury, which was his responsibility.

———

Jasper wiped a cartridge clean, pushed it into a magazine, then the next and the next, until the magazine was full and he could wipe it and then put it among the others. A pile of sixteen magazines free of fingerprints; he always wore eight, Leo wanted six, and Ivan would get two.

Sitting down here thinking about the next robbery – the big one, fifty million – he felt a little calmer, but the irritation that ran in front of him and roared at him didn't stop altogether. *A little fucking soldier.* Anneli didn't know shit about what they were planning to do in a year's time! Not a damn thing! *Not a real brother.* She was a ticking time bomb, he could feel it, and wanted to scream it at Leo. He wanted to warn him, but he couldn't do it, it would sound wrong. Ideally, he would have liked to push a gun barrel into her forehead and explain that she would disappear completely if she so much as considered talking. But he wasn't going to make the same mistake again, not like with Vincent. You can't teach somebody who doesn't want to learn. He had been right though. That's why he was the one sitting in the armoury polishing away fingerprints, not Vincent. He would be proven right by Anneli, too, dammit.

He looked at his watch. They should be in touch soon.

Row after row of automatic weapons. And something else, in a grey-green wooden box on the top shelf, still unused. He lifted up the lid. Hand grenades. They'd got hold of them at their final exercise, too. And he would take three of them with him tomorrow. Just as a precaution. Without saying anything to Leo.

———

Leo and Ivan drove in silence through the winter darkness in a newly acquired Ford Scorpio, stolen from a deserted car park in Södertälje. They passed Strängnäs and turned onto the exit for Highway 55.

'Can you handle this?' asked Leo, glancing at his father.

'What do you mean "handle"?'

'Not drinking.'

He wanted to see the strength, the limitless power he'd grown up with. He didn't understand this man so well. His father was no longer so easy to read. He had to know if the man who'd taught him to punch with his whole body was still in there.

'If the cops come, you'll encounter them first. Can you handle it?'

'I'll shoot if I have to.'

'Aim and shoot?'

'I think I know how a damn rifle works!'

They were silent as they drove through the countryside of ancient Sweden, rune stones and Bronze Age tombs at every other intersection. Past the road to Arnö, the island they'd rented a cottage on for a few summers when they were still a family, over Hjulsta Bridge and the roundabout that separated Enköping from the E18, and then the last couple of kilometres on Highway 70. His father had raised his voice and that was good – but it wasn't enough, he had to be pushed further.

'So I don't need to hide the booze tonight?'

Ivan clenched his hands, Leo saw it. Clenched them and let them lie in his lap.

'Leo, damn it . . . are you trying to give me orders? Is that what you think you're doing? Like a *real* leader?'

'You didn't answer. The bottle, Dad. The bottle! I have to know. Are you going to drink this away?'

'If you're such a *real* leader, where the hell are your brothers?'

It was that kind of aggression he wanted to see, that it was still there and came instinctively. And that his father could control it, that he'd learned how to focus it.

'Is that why you're here? You thought we'd do this together, like a big fucking family . . . damn, don't you get it? If I still had Felix and Vincent with me, I'd sure as hell never need someone like you, Dad.'

The eyes that had just been hidden behind sombre thoughts were now clear and black – a look that could turn into a beating at any time. And Ivan's hands weren't shaking at all.

'Then why aren't they here? With their leader?'

'They don't want to be. Simple as that, Pappa.'

'Are you enemies? My sons? I taught you to stick together.'

It was still in him. And he'd been able to control it. And if he could control himself, then Leo could also control him.

'No. They just don't want to. And when someone doesn't want to do something, you don't force them to. I learned that long ago. And I'm not forcing you either. If you're not up to it, Dad, say so now.'

The last exit. The road narrowed, its bends limiting visibility. Farmland turned into shapeless darkness outside their window.

'Leo, are you really going to do this?'

Up ahead, the first lights of the low-rise buildings and the few family rentals that formed the small town of Heby.

'I mean . . . with them? The pretend soldier? A buffoon who thinks we should attack Russia? And that woman who rearranges fake presents trying to make them look nice? Can she even drive a car? Listen, Leo. Have you really thought this through?'

'I've thought of everything. There's just one problem: you. You are the only risk.'

'This is insane, Leo!'

'Nine bank robberies. I know what the hell I'm doing.'

Ivan saw it all so clearly now. It had always been him in charge. But in this fucking car that wasn't even theirs, in the icy wind that danced through the rolled-down window, it was his eldest son.

Heby was even smaller than the town he lived in. And at this time of night it was completely dark except for a kiosk at the small bus station, the pizza and kebab restaurant opposite it and the video shop. And there it was, in a rendered low-rise building with its lights on, squeezed between a tobacconist and a dentist. The bank.

'That's where you'll stand tomorrow, next to those brown wood slats that mark the entrance,' said Leo, pointing.

They rolled slowly past.

'Or do you think it's *insane*?'

Then the town ended. It was really just a single street, then a beautiful white church on the hill, and then the main road again.

A few kilometres north, they drove through dense forest, around a sharp bend, then two kilometres west. On the right-hand side stood a fence with a double row of mailboxes that belonged to a scattering of summer houses. Leo slowed down and turned off the paved road onto gravel, passing two large barns and a tractor. It was there they'd stop tomorrow, a natural parking spot between densely growing tree trunks. He got out, went into the woods and came back with a bundle of fir twigs already bound together in his arms, and they quickly covered the car, before starting the walk back through the black forest.

'We'll go the same way tomorrow. In about two hundred metres, we'll reach the next car.'

The only light far up above the branches came from the white dots of stars, surrounding a burning half-moon. Leo tried to look at his father, but only heard his heavy breathing as his out-of-shape body ducked under the stubborn branches.

'Dad? Say it right now.'

'Say what?'

They stopped, engulfed by blackness, standing just an arm's length apart.

'So I can reconsider. Say it now. Here. Between us. Say you can't do it. I can take it, but I want to know now – not tomorrow at breakfast.'

Before Ivan could answer they heard tyres approaching on the gravel. Headlights shone through the tree trunks. It was the same rental car that had been parked outside the house in Tumba, packed with colourful and empty parcels, with Jasper behind the wheel. Leo started towards it.

'Leo?'

He was pushing aside branches when Ivan grabbed him.

'Leo, look at me.'

A heavy, needle-laden branch between their faces.

'You, *look* at me.'

Ivan pressed the branch down, broke it off.

'I'm your father. I can do this.'

82

A LIGHT KNOCK on the front door. It is almost inaudible, but somehow it migrates through the house.

Anneli was standing at the worktop, cutting thick slices of bread for sandwiches, and Ivan stood next to her dicing cucumbers and tomato for a salad, a midnight snack, fuel for bank robbers. Jasper sat in the armoury with the hatch open, oiling tomorrow's tools, and Leo sat in an armchair in the living room with a map spread out on the table, studying alternative escape routes.

They jerked to a halt, prepared themselves. Nobody had any business being here, less than a day before the operation.

Leo crept to the bedroom window and angled up the blind, but couldn't see under the porch roof from there, so he went down the stairs towards the front door. A hand had been pressed over the peephole.

Another knock.

Jasper emerged from the armoury with two automatic rifles, handed one to Leo, who placed it on the shelf in the hall and covered it with a jacket, and then crept into the kitchen with the other.

'Go upstairs. And take Anneli with you,' Leo whispered to his father. He waited until they disappeared up the stairs before opening the door.

'So have you been bad or good?'

The two of them. Here. Leo relaxed and smiled.

'Come in.'

He hugged Felix and Vincent. His brothers were back.

'Come in, damn it!'

Jasper approached from the kitchen, gun in hand.

'I guess the whole family's together!'

'You're not part of this family,' said Vincent, unable to look at Jasper for more than a moment.

Anneli came down from upstairs. And behind her, Ivan, who stopped halfway down. Felix crumpled up into immediate anger.

'What the hell is *he* doing here?'

'It's obvious what he's doing here,' replied Leo.

'No, it's fucking not!'

'You left. Someone had to take your place.'

Ivan continued down the stairs.

'My boys,' he said, smiling a little more broadly with each step. 'Vincent, you're so big now. And Felix . . . see, Leo, they're here now!'

It was so crowded in the little hallway. Leo felt squeezed from two directions. Behind him, his impatient father wanted to go forward and say hello, in front of him his two younger brothers had no intention of doing so.

'We want to talk to you. Me and Vincent. Alone,' Felix said to him.

Leo nodded towards the room with the safe in the floor, and the three brothers went in and closed the door.

'I know what you're thinking,' said Felix, once they were alone. 'But we haven't changed our minds. We're not here to rob banks.'

Felix took an envelope from his jacket's inner pocket.

'Here. Seventy thousand. That's all we have left. If you need money, if that's why, then take it, Leo. And forget about robbing that damn bank!'

At first Leo had just stared at the envelope. Now he realised.

'You come here, *here*, Felix, like fucking Santa Claus handing out Christmas presents. And then what? Seventy thousand will only last a few months.'

'Then we'll move back here, if you want us to. We still have a company, don't we? A real construction company? We can do what we did before. We can build houses together.'

The envelope hung in the air between them.

'Vincent, do you still agree with him?'

'I don't know.'

'Don't know?'

'I don't know!'

Leo inclined his head a little to one side, and smiled.

'But what you do *know*, Vincent, is that you can't stand sitting at home and worrying about it either. So it's decision time. We're going tomorrow.'

Felix dropped the envelope that nobody wanted.

'So you're going to rob a bank together? Seriously? You . . . four?'

'Yes.'

'Leo, that envelope is yours. I'm leaving now. I didn't come here to rob a bank – I came here to stop you from doing it. And you will never ask us that question again. Not me, not Vincent.'

He went to the door, opened it, turned round.

'Vincent? I'm going back home tomorrow morning. Our tickets are already booked. You have my number if you want to go with me.'

Ivan got up from the kitchen chair, as if he had been waiting.

'Wait!'

Felix didn't.

'Wait, I want to talk to you!'

He just barely got hold of Felix's arm.

'Let me go, damn it!'

'Listen to me, we haven't seen each other—'

'Listen? To you? You're gonna rob a bank with your own son?'

Ivan let go.

'Felix. My boy. I'm here to see you. You. Leo. Vincent. I thought we could . . . work together. All of us.'

'What?'

A few metres between them, but close enough to tell that his breath was different, didn't smell of alcohol.

'Do you think I would want to rob a bank . . . with you? Do you think I even want to be in the same room as you? After what you made me do to my mother? Do you really believe that? You can go to hell!'

'You have to let go of that someday, Felix, it's not me you're angry at . . . you're angry with him, the man you knew when you were little, who wasn't much older than Leo is now. Let go of it. And look at me now, I'm not the same. You have to let go.'

'I have to . . . let go? Can you answer me one thing – who opened the fucking door when you came and smashed in our mother's face? Was it me? Was it Vincent? Was it Leo? Do you remember? Or should I let go of that, too?'

He took a step closer to his father. He cleared his throat, collecting saliva. And then he spat.

It landed a little higher this time, not on the cheek and neck as with his mother, but it ran down the old man's face in exactly the same way.

'What the hell are you two doing?'

Leo ran out of the side room and pressed one hand against his father's chest and the other on his brother's chest, forcing them in opposite directions.

'Now leave, Felix.'

Vincent stood there. Alone. And he watched his father wipe away the saliva with his shirt sleeve and Felix open the front door.

'Wait!'

He rushed out into the hall, past his father, past Leo.

'I'm going with you.'

83

IVAN HAD BEEN lying there for an hour, maybe two, when he suddenly realised what it was. The smell was bothering him. He sat up and held the pillow to his nose. Yep. That was it. The intrusive smell that was so familiar; the pillowcase smelled of Britt-Marie.

Had she slept here?

It pulled him back. He was there. *Snitch*. She buzzed around him, and he was sitting again on the edge of a completely different bed – in a jail cell just days after a Molotov cocktail had been thrown – and he had been betrayed. *Snitch*. And a policeman had opened the cell door with a bandage around his right hand and stepped in uninvited, wanting to talk.

Ivan hadn't wanted to talk.

Still that damned pig had stood there demanding answers.

```
- How . . . could you bring your own son with you?
- What are you talking about?
- I'm talking about your ten-year-old son, and
how you took him along to incinerate your wife.
His mother.
- I've got nothing to say to you.
- Listen, your son Leo seems like a good boy, he—
- I don't want to talk to you. I don't have to.
I'm sitting in a jail cell, but I decide when I
want to talk. So leave. Get out of here!
- You don't have to talk to me. Because your son
already has. Leo's already told us everything. How
you made the bomb. How you took him in the car,
parked it on the road, how you went through the
raspberry bushes, how you waited there gaping
before you threw it through the basement window.
- I didn't throw any bomb. And my son would never
talk.
- But he did. And everything went so smoothly, he
did so of his own free will and his mother was
there. I sat down at your kitchen table with your
son for over an hour.
- So some fucking cop got my son to sit for an
hour informing on me?
- Yes.
- Then what the hell happened to your hand? My son
would never talk. In my family, we don't snitch.
```

- He talked because he needed to talk, don't you
understand that? You're his father, Ivan. For his
sake, tell me what happened. So he doesn't have
to bear this alone.
- Get the fuck out of here! Now!

That fucking smell, he couldn't get rid of it, even though he tore the pillowcase into pieces and threw them out of the window. He went into the hallway, cold and dark. He was sneaking around like a child in his son's house, and she buzzed around him until he was dizzy and slipped and hit his hip on the sink and his foot on the kitchen table. He didn't want to be back there, back then. *You're the only risk.* He'd walked beside Leo, and they had broken into a car and driven it to the getaway site, and his son had looked at him and accused him before they even started. A risk? Buzzing around someone's head is a fucking risk. Snitching on someone is a fucking risk. Not a drop in forty-eight hours, and his hands shook, and several times he'd almost thrown up, but hadn't, and he knew there was a whisky bottle in the corner cupboard, and then the fever made him shake even though the house was no longer cold, so he sat down at the kitchen table and now froze from the inside as well, and maybe there was a bottle of wine next to the whisky, and he lay down and punched at the air because it buzzed and buzzed and buzzed.

84

JASPER WAS SITTING up. Irritated. It wasn't just the uncomfortable sofa cushions. Or the sheets that were too thick. Or the light that seeped in through the leaky blinds. She was the one who kept him awake. Anneli. The weak link. And he was the only one who could see it. A weakness only becomes apparent when it is subjected to pressure, and under pressure she'd fall apart like a porcelain egg. Crushed. Ten minutes in an interrogation room, and she would squeal like a baby. He felt sorry for Leo. He was stuck with her, could never get rid of her. She would always have a hold on him. Go to the police. Or just talk too much, to a friend or somebody else, someone at a bar, and then the uniforms would kick in the door. And if they did, he knew what to expect. A life sentence. For the bomb. A prosecutor would insist on sentencing them for endangering the public and the offence would be aggravated.

If she talked it would mean a life sentence.

Anneli would point him out first because she'd never liked him, he'd felt that from the beginning. At that illegal club in Handen. She'd been there by herself, drinking rosé cava, hot as hell, that's what he thought, beautiful and natural. They'd talked at the bar, he and Anneli and Leo. He had seen how she laughed and her lips whispered a little closer to Leo's ear with each fresh glass. He hadn't even existed.

85

LEO HAD FELT her waking silence for a few hours now, her bare skin so close to his own as she had turned and twisted, the sheets in her flapping arms. He knew why, she was trying to imagine a sequence of events she'd never experienced before. She wasn't Felix, didn't have his steadiness, the qualification for waiting behind a steering wheel for three minutes while a vault was being emptied, leaving the crime scene so quickly that no one saw anything, no one followed them, and at the same time slowly enough that no one responded or even noticed. Without Felix, they'd need two people outside the bank this time. His girlfriend would drive and his father would face any potential attacker. Inside, he and Jasper were exchanging roles. Leo would go in behind the security glass and clear out the tills and the vault, while Jasper controlled the customers and cashiers lying on the floor.

He felt a sharp elbow between his ribs, against his back, as her arm flailed in that land between sleep and wakefulness. He grabbed it gently, stroking her, soft skin against his fingertips.

'Anneli? Listen? Don't think about it any more.'

She turned over, and her eyes shone clear in the darkness. He kissed her forehead and her cheek.

'I'm not nervous, if that's what you think.'

'I think you are. Try to sleep.'

'"Leo has never and will never let anyone like you get in his way. He has his brothers." Jasper said that. And he thinks he'll be here afterwards. I can't stand him.'

'It's not about him, Anneli. Right? That's not why you're lying here twisting and turning. It's about tomorrow. And I understand why you're afraid.'

She heaved herself up on her elbows.

'Don't you understand, Leo? Listen – *I'm not afraid*. I'm actually glad I'll be going along, that I won't have to sit here listening to that radio to find out if you're alive or not. And then . . . it'll be nice to not have your brothers, and him, here afterwards!'

She poked him again, in the same place between his ribs, not very hard, but deliberately this time.

'The only thing I *don't* think is nice is that you trust that psycho out there on the sofa.'

'Anneli? This is how it is. We're going to do this together tomorrow. Therefore I *choose* to trust Jasper. Just like I *choose* to trust you and my father. Because I have to. OK? Go to sleep.'

He rolled towards the edge of the bed, over it, feet on the cold floor. He needed some peace. He waited until she was asleep before closing the bedroom door gently and walking towards the stairs.

Jasper was on the sofa. Awake. With four automatic weapons in front of him on the coffee table.

'Jasper? What the hell are you up to?'

'Cleaning the weapons.'

'You've already cleaned the guns. They're ready. And you need sleep.'

'It's going to snow tomorrow. A lot.'

'I saw that. But not till the afternoon – and then we'll be on our way home. Go to sleep.'

Jasper put down the gun he'd just oiled again.

'What if we're stopped. Leo? What if the cops are suddenly standing there. Have you thought about that? If she can do it?'

'Do it?'

'I don't trust her. If—'

'Jasper? We're going to do this together tomorrow. Therefore, I *choose* to trust her. Just like I *choose* to trust you and my father. Because I have to. OK? Get some sleep.'

He was the one holding it all together. That had been the case when Felix and Vincent were involved too, but it was more obvious now. Leo went down the stairs, avoiding the step that always creaked. It was quiet inside the guest room, but he closed the door, just in case. Into the kitchen. Half a glass of water from the tap that always coughed before giving in and releasing the liquid.

Anneli, Jasper and himself. All awake. Only his father, who he'd been most worried about, was asleep.

He drank another half glass of water, went out into the hall again, and was taking the first step back up the stairs when he heard his father's voice behind him.

'Leo? Leo, can you come here?'

Pappa's voice sounded different, and not because he was whispering, or because it was hoarse and low, but because he was . . . pleading. His father – who never asked anyone for anything, who outlined how he wanted things to be and then expected them to be just so – had pleaded with Felix at the front door and ended up with spit in his face, and now he was pleading again. It felt uncomfortable.

'Dad, what are you doing here? You have to sleep.'

He hadn't seen him in the darkness. He lay on the kitchen sofa in his underpants. Leo stayed in the doorway and could see the shaking from there.

'Sit down here, beside me, just for a minute. I want to tell you something.'

He went in and sat on the edge of the sofa, while Ivan sat up. Side by side. Two pale torsos. Leo, in his twenties, who had just started his journey, and Ivan, who was more than twice his age and was no longer going anywhere.

'I . . . maybe I didn't always do right by you when you and your brothers were little.'

'You did what you did, Dad. No more, no less.'

'But Leo . . . it wasn't right.'

'Stop it.'

'I could have—'

'I don't give a shit about that stuff now. I don't want to hear any more.'

'Leo, it's important for me to say this. You were just a child.'

'Just a child?'

'Just a child, Leo. And I know you didn't mean to.'

'Mean to?'

439

'To snitch.'

'Snitch? Are we going there again?'

'No, but—'

'Listen to me now! Once and for all! I didn't snitch on you! That's not who we are. We do the opposite! Even when you tried to kill Mamma, we *all* took the blame. And that's why I think I opened the door, and why Felix claims he did, and Vincent says it was him. That's how fucking far we are from being snitches!'

'Leo . . . I . . . I don't hold it against you, not any more, you saw that, didn't you? Felix . . . and I did nothing. Felix spat in my face and I didn't raise a hand. Spitting in someone's face is the greatest insult of all! If someone else had done the same thing, I would . . . have hammered the bastard! But not my son. I didn't do it.'

He wasn't aware of it, but as he spoke, he rubbed the flattened knuckles of his right hand.

Something that happens to them after inflicting repeated blows.

'Stop it! Don't ever talk to me about my childhood again.'

'But Leo, why don't you want . . . I want . . .'

Leo made to walk away, he had no more energy for this.

'It was open!'

The house had gone completely silent. A kind of peace. As he went towards the stairs, Leo realised what his father had just said.

'When I . . . and your mother . . . there in Falun. It wasn't locked. I was able to push down the handle and walk right in. Past Felix and Vincent and you.'

Leo sat down on the first step. It squeaked. It always had.

'You hear, Leo? None of you opened the door.'

86

HE WAS GUARDING a door with a large pane of glass in the middle and brown wooden slats on either side. The door of a bank that was being robbed at this very moment. And he was one of the bank robbers.

Ivan wasn't afraid. He didn't feel that way because he wouldn't allow himself to, he couldn't afford to – that was his son running around in there wearing a black mask and carrying an automatic weapon. But it felt like *something*. Shame. Terrible shame, clinging to him like the small child who had once clung to his back, little fingers digging in between his shoulder blades, preventing him from striking her face again. The terrible shame when that other, smaller face had stood in his way, forcing him to let go and allow her to flee across the bloody, slippery floor. All day those fingers had ripped at his back, while time stood still, and soon the world would realise they were robbing a bank and that his son was in there behind him.

Ten minutes to three. The ground was covered with powdery snow that muffled the sounds outside his mask. Just half an hour ago the asphalt had been dry and the landscape grey. Now he could see their footsteps in the snow, two each from the car to the bank, Leo's, his own and Jasper's. They were supposed to be in there for three minutes. Two and a half left. And if it kept snowing like this, their footprints would almost be gone by the time they got back to the car.

He held his gun in front of him, facing the street and the few shops, glanced over his shoulder and saw Jasper's back in the middle of the room, while his eldest son continued past a large green plant and behind the counters. And up ahead, still in the car behind the wheel, also wearing a ski mask, sat Anneli.

He looked at his watch again. Forty-five seconds. Suddenly time had frozen, and the shame was moving forward at the speed of light – and the desire to get away from this place, to swallow a big gulp of red wine, to never look his sons in the eye again, was unbearable.

Leo glanced quickly over his shoulder. Pappa was still out there, in front of the door, his gun ready. He was holding firm. It had been the right thing to *choose* to trust him.

Sixty seconds.

Leo waited outside the vault while the trembling hands of the branch manager tried to insert the key in the lock. The man was around his father's age but lankier, with fingers like pointers. He was just about to tell him to calm down when he heard the hush of the security lock, a heavy sigh as the pistons left their stronghold in the reinforced frame and the door slid open.

He'd almost forgotten how it felt.

To walk into the room. To force the customers and staff onto the floor. To be the master of a room for one hundred and eighty seconds. Planning and calculating, and then standing in front of an open vault and seeing that everything had been done right.

The only time it had felt like this before with Pappa was another time when they had practised and planned together to carry out a plan and it had worked – it had been just as easy to punch Hasse with Pappa standing on the balcony as it was to rob a bank with him standing outside right now.

There were bundles of cash on the shelves of the vault, even more than there should be: 100s in bundles of ten thousand kronor, 500s in bundles of fifty thousand, and 1000s in bundles of a hundred thousand.

Everything was there. Nothing had been stored in the night vault.

When Leo ordered the banker to get inside, sit down and keep his back against the wall, he heard the excitement in his own voice. He couldn't believe that there could be so much money on the shelves of such a small bank.

He adjusted his shoulder bag and held it open like a gaping mouth as it swallowed every banknote he pushed in – and no dye packs. He counted quickly. At least three and a half million kronor! More than the double robbery, more than the triple robbery. In a little shitty bank, in a little shitty town with Pappa on guard and Anneli driving.

A woman was talking on the police radio about a bank robbery in Heby, and another woman replied to say a patrol car was on its way from the police station in Sala. None of it mattered to Anneli: she'd drive back just as she had memorised and practised over the past week with Leo in the passenger seat. Not even the snow covering the road, melting on the windscreen and being scoured away by the wipers mattered. Those outside the car, hiding and watching, who would later give their statements without ever knowing that it was a woman who sat behind the wheel, didn't exist to her. The only thing that existed was encapsulated in a predetermined pattern that she and Leo had created together. Just the two of them, no one else.

Maybe that's why she saw Leo first, even though all three of them were walking away from the bank, Leo carrying a bag over his shoulder that seemed stuffed full.

And when the car doors slammed, she did what she was supposed to: started in second gear, rolled down the wide pavement and onto the street, speeded up at the church with its black tower. Then right and, almost immediately, right again, around the town and out onto the main road. The gentle snowfall had, within just a few minutes, turned into a blizzard, soft snowflakes with white hard tips. But she was unmoved – she knew every bend and what speed to keep at all times.

'Three million!'

He'd shouted that several times now.

'*Over* three million!'

Anneli had never heard Leo's voice sound like that; it was exploding, becoming almost hoarse he was so happy. Even Jasper's laughter in the back seat felt good. She didn't care at all that the visibility was getting even worse, she still knew how she should drive. Soon left, there, at the mailboxes. She even put on the indicators and giggled to herself – a stolen car that had just been used in a bank robbery and she . . . was putting on the indicators. She giggled more loudly as she turned left onto the snow-covered gravel road. And then, just because it felt so good, and Leo sounded so happy, she put on the indicators again as they turned onto the tiny forest road crossed only by the occasional deer or hare, and again as she turned into the natural parking space between otherwise dense spruce trunks.

They climbed out of the stolen car and into the raging storm. They were changing their clothes again, from robbery gear to Christmas outfits. They'd done it. *She'd* done it. She would soon be exchanging a screwdriver in a stolen car for the keys of a rented car filled with elegantly wrapped Christmas presents. She searched for Leo's hand, holding it tightly as they ran.

87

THE DETECTIVE DEPARTMENT of the City Police was filled with the smells of mulled wine, coffee and Christmas cake, and someone had even positioned an ugly little plastic Christmas tree between the coffee machine and the vending machine.

John Broncks stayed in his office. He didn't participate. In fact, he had never participated, didn't celebrate the approaching Christmas Eve, the things that families did. They had barely celebrated it even back then. He had done so on a couple of occasions – long ago – sitting at a pre-arranged time in a visiting room with a warm cake on a rickety table. Sam had baked and brewed coffee like all lifers did before a visit, and without saying a word about it, they'd both chewed the soft cake as if it was any old Monday.

He looked at the computer screen. An alarm. Just a few minutes ago, in a small town over a hundred kilometres away. The Sala police were on their way. The Uppsala police were on their way. *They* had a real reason to avoid drinking mulled wine.

Broncks sighed.

Piles of ongoing investigations lay on his desk.

Fickle snowflakes chased each other across the Kronoberg courtyard.

There was always someone willing to use violence to get what they wanted, and on a day like this, it justified his work; it was important to stick around at least a little longer.

He called Karlström, whose answer was accompanied by the sound of studded tyres driving over grinding asphalt.

'Did you see it?'

His boss was already halfway home. But at least he'd answered.

'John?'

'Yeah?'

'It's Christmas Eve tomorrow.'

Someone honked a little too long, annoyed. John guessed it was the driver behind Karlström.

'And . . . Heby? John, I don't even know where that is. Somewhere in the Uppsala district. But I know what you're up to. Don't use this as an excuse to refuse to go home. It's not ours.'

Now there were several honking horns; everyone, like Karlström, was heading home to their evening gin and tonics.

'And John? Listen. Seriously? Who robs a bank the day before Christmas Eve? Someone with no traditions.'

There was crackling. The phone changed hands or places.

'Wait. I'm just putting on my glasses.'

It crackled again. John Broncks wondered if his boss had stopped or if he was driving slowly without holding the steering wheel, while he read the car's computer screen.

The honking got even louder, indicating the latter.

'Two. Two patrols already in place. And another one on its way. You can see that on your screen, too. A hundred and ten kilometres, John. Let them solve their own problems.'

88

THE DECEMBER DARKNESS was transformed into something furious, aggressive, a massive white wall of snow that encircled them and became a different kind of darkness. The wipers' rubber strips beat despairingly against the glass, and Anneli slowed even further – they'd planned to go at ninety but that had turned to seventy and now barely fifty.

They should, according to Leo's calculations, have gone more than ten kilometres. Now, he guessed they'd gone no more than a couple or so on a road that in place of hard shoulders and lanes had high walls of snow.

Anneli slowed further – in front of them other cars crept forward.

Two, maybe more. To overtake them was impossible. Both the first and the second time she tried, she was forced to stop, return to her own lane. Since visibility was only a few metres, the oncoming traffic was impossible to see until it passed their side window.

But she seemed to be in control, so far. Anneli balanced it with soft wheel movements, maintaining the interplay of brake, accelerator, gearstick, as the tyres failed to grip. Leo put his hand against her cheek, stroked it, and she smiled.

He adjusted his rear-view mirror. Jasper, behind him, leaned over the weapons case counting magazines and cartridges. Ivan, behind Anneli, clasped his left hand tightly in his right, knuckles a bloodless white, a stream of sweat running from his hairline down over his pale skin. He wiped it with the dirty handkerchief he always kept in his pocket.

Withdrawal.

His father had handled it before – every time he decided to quit for some reason. But never like this. Never while on the run from a bank robbery.

'If you sleep, Dad, it'll be easier. Lean back. This is taking longer than it should – but in about an hour and a half we'll be home.'

That's when they met the car.

He'd actually seen it in the distance, two headlights bright as they broke through the blizzard. But it wasn't until it was almost alongside them that he realised what it was.

A single driver, in uniform and with eyes straight ahead.

And there, on the side of the car, six capital letters almost obscured by snow.

POLICE.

They were already here.

'Jasper?'

'I saw.'

'Get your weapon ready. And make sure you and Dad disappear under those presents.'

The car passed. It seemed not to have seen them. Leo was very aware that the bag between his shins was full of cash.

'Smile,' he said to Anneli. 'Drive and smile. We're a happy family.'

It had been a single cop. Beard, short hair. In his fifties. And he'd looked straight ahead, continuing in the direction of Heby, and was then swallowed by the snow.

Jasper and Ivan sat up again, the Christmas presents on their laps on the floor and on the shelf in the rear window. Ivan closed his eyes. Next to him on the narrow seat, Jasper opened the trunk and let the gun slide down again. And then stopped.

'Ivan? Are you awake?' Jasper asked.

'Yes.'

'Where the hell are your magazines?'

'We don't need them now.'

'The magazines? I just want to know that everything's where it should be! That's my job.'

Ivan didn't like the man he was sharing a seat with. But he was sweating outwardly and trembling inwardly. So he did as he was asked, began searching for the little bag that should be sitting on his stomach.

It wasn't there.

'They're . . . gone.'

'What do you mean "gone"?'

'They're in . . . the other car. They must still be there.'

'The getaway car?'

'Yes.'

Leo had only been half listening. Now he turned round.

'Dad? Fucking hell, Dad!'

'Yeah?'

'Did you touch them?'

'Yes.'

'Without gloves?'

'I . . . think so. When I packed up. When we changed clothes.'

'Turn round, Anneli!'

Jasper leaned forward, lowered his voice, as if Ivan and Anneli shouldn't be able to hear.

'Leo? We can't turn round now. You surely understand that? We can't go back. The cops are already there!'

'Should I turn round or not?' Anneli asked Leo again, desperately. She was still in control, but her movements were increasingly jerky.

'Leo, listen to me,' Jasper whispered. 'I realise you don't want to leave any tracks. But it's not worth it. We're not in any police files.'

'Yes, Anneli,' Leo replied to her.

'None of us. That's why—'

'My dad,' said Leo, cutting Jasper off. 'Those are *his* fingerprints. *He's* got a police record.'

89

LEO RAN STRAIGHT into the white wall, rushed through the woods, through the deep snow towards the car they'd just left covered with pine boughs. He tore away the branches and opened the back door where his father had been sitting, jumped in and searched the seat, the door pockets, the shelf in the rear window. It wasn't there. He crept in, hands across the driver's seat, passenger seat, on the dashboard. Then the floor. Fingers in thin leather gloves groping in the dark across the rubber mats, to no avail.

Only one place left. Under the seats. He pressed down his body, stretched out.

And there. Under the front seat, in the middle. There it lay. The bag. He pulled it out, opened it. Two magazines. Bearing his father's documented and registered fingerprints.

And he ran again, deep breaths and a breast that throbbed and ached as blood was pumped in, pumped out.

Back in the car, they sat in silence. They knew, of course, that there were already police cars in the area. Down the forest road again. Past the barns and out onto the country road.

They'd just started driving back in the right direction. Maybe the wind had eased slightly. Maybe that's why he could see it when he checked the rear-view mirror.

The same police car. The same cop, who would soon realise that he'd passed that car just a few minutes earlier, and that it had taken a very strange path in the middle of furiously drifting snow, right after a bank robbery just a few kilometres away.

Leo put his hand on Anneli's arm.

'It's there, behind us. Just keep on driving normally.'

He checked the rear-view mirror again – it wasn't far between them, twenty-five metres, tops.

'Same speed, same distance. It shouldn't get any closer.'

He saw how she was looking in the rear-view mirror, too.

'Just focus on the road, Anneli. And Jasper – give me the gun.'

Jasper pulled the weapon from the trunk and passed it between the two front seats. Ivan had been sitting quietly ever since Jasper discovered the two magazines were missing. Now he took hold of the headrest and pulled his whole body forward until his mouth was near Leo's ear.

'Leo? Son, what are you going to do?'

'Finish the shit you started.'

The gun rested in Leo's lap while he cocked it.

'Anneli, in about two hundred metres there's a road that turns off to the right. Fairly wide, paved. Turn in there. If that cunt follows us then stop when I tell you to.'

'What the hell . . . you . . .' began Ivan.

'Nothing will happen if he keeps going.'

She put on her indicator, slowed down and veered to the right.

Leo was breathing slowly and deeply to prepare himself. The exit was five metres away, ten, fifteen. Then the police car turned off, almost invisible in the dense snowfall, a predator following them.

'Stop.'

Anneli hit the brakes and the car's tyres slipped on the icy ground; she pushed down the clutch, adjusted the steering wheel with tiny movements. Until they stopped.

Until Leo opened the door and left the car with the gun in his hands.

John Broncks was still sitting in his office with a computer monitor and a radio, following a bank robbery that was 110 kilometres away. The last of his colleagues had passed his open door, giggly from the mulled wine, wishing him a merry Christmas, and he'd smiled at them and pretended to look busy even though he wasn't.

Three patrols were now in place. A fourth was on its way from Uppsala. According to witness statements, three or four robbers had fled in a passenger car, which had just been seen travelling in a northwesterly direction from the crime scene, on a minor road through an area of summer houses which lay somewhere between Heby and Sala.

He massaged his sore lower back, walked in a tight circle between the window and the desk, yawned.

A cup of silver tea always brought him to life. With the kitchenette finally free of Christmas celebrations, he walked towards the hallway to brew a new cup – but was stopped at the door. First, by the sharp beep from the communication radio. Then a colleague, eager.

'I see them. A car with several passengers.'

A patrol car from Uppsala. A lone policeman.

'I'm following them.'

John Broncks went closer to the desk and the radio. The car was a few metres away from the policeman, but a hundred kilometres from him.

'It's turning off. It's stopped. It . . . I'm stopping.'

The sound of his car slowing down.

'Someone . . . from the passenger seat . . . someone's climbing out. He's holding something. A gun! And he's aiming at . . . me!'

Whirling snow. But Leo could clearly see the uniform. He raised the gun and waited. The door on the driver's side opened.

His finger on the trigger.

He waited, but no one got out. The uniform just sat there.

So he fired.

A first shot at the engine. And a second. And a third.

449

Until the lone policeman ran out of the car, threw himself on the ground and rolled down into the snow-filled ditch.

Four more shots – all into the engine. That car wouldn't be following them any more. He kept his eyes on the ditch as he went back and sat next to Anneli.

'Drive.'

The situation had changed. To reverse past the police car and continue along the original escape route was no longer possible.

'Where?'

'Straight ahead.'

Leo knew where they were – in the middle of an area of uninhabited houses – though he didn't know how to get out of there. But there was always a way.

The lone policeman's voice had fallen silent. But it had been easy to understand, even via the radio, what had happened.

A car door had opened: he'd got out. Steps on the snow: he'd tried to escape. A dull thud: he'd thrown himself into shelter.

And then – four more shots. One by one. Burst mode.

Then only the wind.

'They've driven on.'

He was alive. He wasn't even hurt, from the sound of his voice. But he was still down, probably on the roadside, and it was clear that as he spoke, he was starting to realise what had really happened.

'He . . . just stepped out. Methodical. Determined. I was sure I was going to die.'

And – could have happened.

'He fired at the car and the engine block. An AK4. I saw it.'

When Broncks heard the gunfire, there was no anxiety left. He rushed out into the corridor again, towards the stairs and the garage and the car. More than six months and not a single sign of life. A night spent making one last phone call that should have forced them out. It hadn't. A few more letters and a few newspaper ads before all contact suddenly ended, and Broncks had begun to doubt himself. Maybe he'd made the wrong decision, misjudged Big Brother. Despite the tips that continued to pour in from the public and an investigative team filling up with profilers and detectives, no breakthrough had come. And as spring became summer and then autumn, he increasingly thought he felt Karlström's glance – ten years of trust had begun to crumble.

The day before Christmas Eve, and it was as if all of Stockholm had gone home. Christmas trees were lit up in each apartment. After a couple of minutes of driving he passed the tolls at Alvik Bridge at high speed, going towards the E18 west.

'This is Broncks.'

I wasn't wrong. I didn't misjudge Big Brother.

'I told you to go home,' answered Karlström, his voice accompanied by Christmas carols and children's voices. John Broncks remembered last Christmas, his visit to that beautiful house in that beautiful neighbourhood. A year ago. And he was investigating them, still.

'I'm in the car, heading for Heby, just passing Rinkeby.'

'John, damn it . . .'

'It's them.'

He reached the Rotebro junction and the traffic light shone red as he drove right through it. Karlström waited, silent. Then he turned the phone towards the room, and the sound of Christmas carols got louder.

'Do you hear that, John?'

An old-fashioned gramophone. A needle scratching against vinyl. 'I'm Dreaming of a White Christmas'.

'Christmas songs, John. Ham. Mulled wine.'

'I want the national SWAT team.'

'John?'

'I know it's them.'

'According to a witness outside the bank, the one who stood guard was significantly older than the others, slower and stiffer than the ones inside the bank.'

'It's them.'

'And there's never been an old man involved before. Right?'

'Lennart?'

In ten years he had never used Karlström's first name.

'Yes?'

'We've never been this close. But my colleagues in Heby need reinforcements. They've already shot at one of the cars.'

'White Christmas' was finally over. Now it was 'Frosty the Snowman' – a cheerful children's choir singing a happy Christmas song.

'John, I can't contact the police chief tonight and ask her for the national SWAT team, not the day before Christmas Eve. Or any day at all if it's not our district and if there's nothing to indicate that it *is* them.'

'Faster, Anneli!'

'I haven't driven this way before. We didn't practise—'

'Faster! We have to get out of here before they close off the roads!'

The snow danced in their headlights in the middle of a dark forest.

Leo had unfurled the map over his knees and the gun that lay there – moving his finger along the road they were on right now, while the car lurched violently and he bumped his shoulder and head on the side window.

'I don't know where we are, Leo, I—'

'Just keep driving!'

She drove, but she wasn't present any more, she was back there with the seven shots he'd put into a police car. They had opened fire. Those that shoot can be shot at.

'When we pass those summer houses, there's an exit to the road. Four kilometres. Just drive the way I tell you!'

She'd known that those guns could really be used, but she had never allowed herself to think about it.

'Anneli?'

Now she had to think about it. They had already been used.

'Anneli, stop!'

Weapons that could kill.

'Stop! I'll drive!'

She heard his screaming now. Stop here? In the woods? Why would she do that? And as she looked in the rear view mirror, searching for the police car they'd shot to pieces, the bend came closer and the wheel slid between her hands.

'Turn!'

All three men yelled at the same time.

Too late. Her whole body braced against the brake pedal as the car slid, all four wheels gliding helplessly into the ditch, then tipped over the edge, going down as the snow was hurled at the window with a defiant sigh. There it stopped. The impact inside the car was hardly noticeable. The silence was more tangible. It confirmed that the unthinkable had happened. That there was no longer a getaway car to escape in.

Leo pushed open the door, which was forced back by a snowdrift. He turned his body, his back to the dashboard as he braced himself and kicked, again and again, opening it a little more with each kick. He crawled out and stood in snow that reached above his knees.

'Jasper, you take the weapons. Pappa, you take the money. Everybody out now!'

One by one, they stepped out into the snowstorm. Jasper with the handles of the weapons case over his shoulders like a backpack, Ivan with three and a half million in a sports bag in his arms, Anneli with blood gushing from her nose.

'Here. Take this,' said Ivan, offering his handkerchief. She wiped her face and cleaned herself off with snow.

'Sebastian? Leo . . .'

'Come on.'

'What will he say? What will . . . he's supposed to be coming tomorrow. To our home.'

'Anneli? Look at me. We are going home, now.'

'He's coming tomorrow. We're celebrating Christmas. And we've . . . fired a gun at someone.'

She pulled her thin coat more tightly around her body, climbed out of the ditch and onto the road. Leo opened the boot and threw all the carefully wrapped gifts into the snow, heaving out the bag that held the jackets and trousers used in the robbery.

'It'll be cold.'

A jacket for Anneli, who didn't even try to catch it, one for Jasper who snapped it over the jacket he already had, and one for Ivan who accepted it, but then dropped it in the snow. He wasn't cold.

'Four kilometres to the main road on the other side. If we can get through the forest, no local cop can challenge our weapons, and it'll take ninety minutes to get reinforcements here. We have to keep the distance.'

It was snowing, but the white wall was no longer there, it was more like a soft curtain, fabric billowing in slow motion. Easier to see. Easier to be seen. They started walking across the field, towards the edge of the forest, when Anneli stopped abruptly and sank into the deep snow on her knees.

'I don't want to go on,' she said.

'Damn it, Anneli!'

'I don't want to. I've never wanted to. I want to . . . go home.'

'Get up right now!'

She sat there in the snow. And wept.

453

'I said yes. To a question you never even asked! And now I'm . . . here.'

He took her hand, trying to pull her up, but she resisted and he let go.

'Anneli!'

'I don't want to.'

'We can't stay here any longer!'

She'd made up her mind. She was going to stay – a decision as firm as her will to give up. Jasper turned back.

'I told you, Leo!' he hissed. 'I told you she was the weak link! She'll talk! We can't leave her here, Leo, not alive!'

Leo grabbed him, pulling him close.

'So what the fuck do you want to do?'

'They pick her up, and she'll point us out, one by one! All of us! Your brothers too!'

Jasper was right. The snowstorm had drawn all the strength out of Anneli in just a few minutes, and the only remaining life was in her confused eyes, which refused to face Leo or the reality that would catch up with her as soon as she was sitting in a warm police car.

'Do you . . . want me to shoot her? Well? Is that what you're saying?'

'Yes.'

Jasper grabbed the gun hanging on his shoulder and cocked it. But the only thing Leo could think about was how long Anneli would last in an interrogation – one hour, three hours, five hours – and how far he'd be able to get if he let her live, compared with if Jasper shot her.

And just as suddenly his head cleared and he rushed in between Jasper's raised weapon and the woman who he'd chosen to share everything with him.

'Anneli!'

He crouched down next to her, making sure the whole time to keep his back between her and the barrel of the gun.

'Listen to me!' he screamed.

She barely looked at him.

'Don't you remember, Anneli? When you rob a bank together, you can never leave each other!'

He pulled off his leather gloves and wiped the cold tears from her cheeks, holding her thin face between his hands, trying to find her gaze.

'Get up now, for Christ's sake – you have the energy! Come on!'

But she remained, sinking deeper into the snowdrift. And the woman

454

in front of him was someone else, not his Anneli, the one he'd always been able to rely on.

'She'll turn us in!'

Now it was Jasper who was screaming, while at the same time threading his left arm through the leather strap to stabilise the weapon's muzzle.

'Leo, I'm waiting! Give me the order, and I'll shoot!'

Leo saw Jasper moving slowly in a semicircle around him to get a good shot, and then around his father who was standing stock still as he had the whole time, doing nothing that would give Leo some direction. Not a word. Ivan was a dark, motionless shape around which thousands of snowflakes danced.

'No!'

He was the one who'd planned the robbery. *He* was the leader, and *he* had to make the decision.

'Secure your fucking weapon, Jasper!'

He grabbed hold of the muzzle and twisted it away.

'Don't you understand, Leo? She'll turn you in!'

'She is not going to die.'

That was just how it was. They were here because he'd relied as much on his father as he had on Anneli.

'If anyone is going to die here, it's me and Ivan – because we're not finished with each other.'

Because once again, someone had left their mark on the crime scene.

'We're leaving now, do you hear me? She's staying here, and we're going on.'

He kissed her, but she didn't meet his lips. He could feel her warm breath so clearly in the cold wind.

And it was strange, but sometimes you just know when it's the last time.

90

FELIX MOVED A dessert plate, a half-drunk glass of beer, and one of those dull maths books Vincent had spread out all over the place, and put down a tiny plastic Christmas tree, the smallest kind, which could stand on a kitchen table like a houseplant. The artificial Christmas spirit, the illusion that everything here was just like everywhere else, that's how it had always been as long as he could remember – always too much, false, strained, ruined each time by his father's yelling, demands, folly. A plastic tree on a kitchen table corresponded exactly to what Christmases had always been – small.

He should have felt calm: this was an evening in a new life with no past. His little brother close by in the armchair in front of the TV, a remote control in each hand, clicking between TV channels.

Yet calm was the one thing he didn't feel.

'Turn it off. Everything.'

'I have to.'

'And I don't want to know. Turn it off, damn it!'

Vincent had been sitting there for six hours, watching news bulletins as the anxiety seeped out of him.

The men, who robbed the Savings Bank in Heby at gunpoint, are still at large.

'Turn it off!'

'I will not.'

'I don't want to know. I'm fucking well here. In Gothenburg! I'm not there!'

Police reportedly tracked the men and have now surrounded the wooded area where they are believed to be.

Felix sat down in front of the plastic Christmas tree and drank the other half of the beer in the glass. It was lukewarm. He could feel the anxiety creeping through Vincent's pores, mouth, nose, and he remembered the only time he had smelled death – one of the neighbours, who'd lain alone for a long time behind closed doors had had just such a smell.

The police are advising anyone in the area to stay indoors.

He couldn't take it any more, almost throwing himself into the living room and snatching the remote controls from Vincent's hands, turning off the TV. Vincent looked at him in surprise, grabbed the phone lying on the coffee table, and hit one of the few saved numbers.

'Don't call them!'

Too late. The call had already gone through. And Felix could see it in Vincent's face. Hope. There might be others. Others who had also scouted out Heby and chosen this particular day. They didn't know, couldn't be completely sure, and it could— *Hello, you've reached Leo and Anneli, we can't come to the phone right now, but . . .* and then the long beep, and Vincent hung up.

Now they knew.

Felix grabbed the phone and threw it at the wall. It fell apart.

'He couldn't leave it alone! He had to keep going, even though we moved here and . . . fucking hell, Vincent!'

He kicked the plastic fragments of the mobile phone and slapped his hands against the walls and doorframes, and Vincent's smell was even worse now. He rushed into the kitchen, to the four Christmas presents that lay under a stool in one corner, two each, and picked up one of them – oblong and rectangular, with wrapping paper that was not completely smooth because he'd wrapped it himself.

'This one was for you.'

He handed it to Vincent who opened it, paper and ribbons falling in a pile on the floor. A box. And inside – a bottle of whisky. Single malt. Felix got out two clean glasses and filled them all the way up to the brim. They drank until the glasses were empty.

'He'll never give up,' said Vincent, filling the glasses again. They drank again.

'Do you understand, Felix? I should have been there!'

He wept, first quietly, then violently.

'I was supposed to be there, Felix . . . damn, damn!'

And he didn't smell any more, the tears that never seemed to end rinsed him clean.

'You understand that, right? He'll never give up – not alive.'

The snow came up to Leo's knees. The winter cold cut through shoes, jackets, skin. And the wind had become a storm again, whipping, hunting, defying.

I'm going straight through.

Those bastards will never get close, never demand answers.

Straight through.

Leo first, Jasper last and Ivan between them, moving forward in Leo's tracks, his breathing strained, hands clenched tightly in his pockets, ski mask pulled down over grey hair. Twenty minutes. Halfway there. The forest opened up into a large glade, an easier passage, and they zigzagged across, making time, leaving their pursuers further away.

Until Leo, who was in front, started to sink. Quickly. Up to his waist, his chest. This was no open glade. It was thin ice over a bog. Icy water rushed into his trousers, his jacket, and his shoes stuck fast in the mud.

'Leo!'

Ivan, with short steps, came as close as possible, and then stretched out his hand to Leo. His son was stuck. He crouched down, the soles of his boots hard against the slippery surface, and pulled. Then the ice broke. One leg went down into the black water, one leg still on the edge of the ice, while he hauled Leo with all his remaining strength. Then the bog, as suddenly as it had grabbed hold, decided to loosen its grip.

They heaved themselves up and rolled onto solid ground, lying next to each other until the coughing that had started somewhere deep in Ivan's lungs slowly subsided.

'Leo, you can't go on. Not like this. You'll freeze to death.'

It was below zero and the wind howled. The mud and water that covered his son up to his chest would soon turn to ice.

'They're on their way! We have to keep ahead of them!'

He didn't look at his father or at Jasper as he set off, teeth chattering. Ivan caught up with him and grabbed his jacket.

'Did you hear what I said, Leo? Don't you understand! You have to dry off! Otherwise it doesn't matter how fucking far you get!'

Leo broke free and started walking again.

Straight through.

Ivan caught up with him once more.

'There are some summer houses! Over there . . . on the other side of the clearing, see?'

The house wasn't very big. Red panelling, white trim. Nestled among protective trees. Just like any other Swedish summer house.

'Go, damn it!' said Leo, pushing him away.

'We're going inside to get you dry.'

Ivan pointed into the woods.

'*Then* we keep going. If you don't dry off in this weather, Leo, look at me . . . you could die.'

———

John Broncks parked next to the little square where the bank stood just a mini-market away. A small town that could have been Ösmo or Ullared or Rimbo or Kungsör, a few thousand inhabitants and a town centre with shops, a bank, a library, all concentrated in a small area – they'd also been methodical in their choice of crime scene, had always chosen places with limited police resources, easy to get into and out of.

The rest was similar, too.

The billowing tape around the roped-off area, forming a square around the bank's two windows, in order to keep the curious away. The closer he got, the more confused, frightened, weeping people. Inside the bank there were shot-up cameras and a security door open to an empty vault. A uniformed police officer, who had just finished interviewing someone, met him and pointed towards the exit.

'I'm gonna have to ask you to—'

'John Broncks, City Police, Stockholm.'

He examined a badge that looked the same as his own.

'Broncks?'

'Yes.'

'My name's Rydén, Heby police. You're pretty far from home.'

'I know.'

'We already have patrols from Heby and Sala and Uppsala here.'

'I know that too. And I think I know who you're chasing.'

Broncks spent fifteen minutes talking with customers and cashiers who'd been inside the bank when two masked men ordered them to lie down on the floor. He picked up cartridges manufactured for Swedish military automatic weapons, and on an eight-second video clip saw both the leader and the shooter, the ones he called Big Brother and the Soldier.

It was them. No black jumpsuits, and just two of them inside the bank. But it was them.

More than a year of hunting, and he'd never been this close.

The local police station was near the entrance to the town, and Broncks had gone past on his way to the bank without seeing it. He now found a modest building that resembled a brick house, decorated with gnomes and wreaths just like the much larger headquarters in Stockholm, with even the same half a cake and half-finished cups of coffee inside. A Christmas party interrupted by a bank robbery.

Rydén showed him in, and they passed the interview room where a woman sat staring blankly – thirties, blonde, a blanket over her shoulders and a hot cup of something in her hands – as she listened to questions from a female police officer. She listened but didn't answer at first, and when she did reply her responses were vague, as if she was in shock.

'What did they look like?'

'Don't know.'

'You don't know?'

'They had . . . masks on.'

'Who is she?' Broncks asked Rydén.

'We picked her up on an unmade road near the summer houses on the way to Sala,' he answered, careful to turn his back to the interview room and lower his voice. 'The robbers hijacked her rental car. She was running around confused in the middle of a snowstorm, we almost ran over her.'

Hijacked her car? This group didn't use escape cars they hadn't procured themselves. They chose them carefully and hid them where a pursuer wouldn't think to look. Broncks wanted to go back into the interview room to talk to her himself. He'd do that soon.

A map hung across most of the wall, with Heby at the centre. Rydén ran his gloved hand northward along a road that led from the grey squares representing the town centre and the bank, turned several kilometres later at a junction, then walked his fingertips along a small road westward.

'Here, on the edge of the forest, she was wandering. They'd forced her to stop the car, let them in and then drive. She was scared, and it was slippery. We found her car in the ditch, full of abandoned Christmas gifts. And from the car, we observed clear tracks in the snow. Three pairs. Straight into the forest. Easy to follow.'

'And the first getaway car?'

'We're still searching.'

Broncks still wanted to go in and interrupt the questioning.

'They forced her to drive?'

'Yes.'

'A rental car? Full of Christmas presents?'

'She was on her way to see her family.'

'Whose name was it rented in? And what was inside those Christmas presents?'

Rydén opened the door to the next room. A colleague was interviewing an elderly couple who had been pushing a shopping trolley across the square when the robbers' vehicle reversed outside the bank. He went in, interrupted the conversation, and returned to Broncks.

'We'll know in ten minutes.'

John Broncks turned to the interview room where the woman sat.

'Is it OK if I listen in?'

The butt of the gun smashed right through the brittle window of the door. A hand and an arm reached between the sharp fragments of glass to the lock inside the door. The door banged against the gable as Leo opened it and the wind snatched it from his grip.

A cold hallway. Windless. And no snow.

The power switch stood on the wall under the hat rack. But the ceiling light remained off.

'Dad? The main fuse.'

A simple kitchen. A sofa, a dining table, two chairs. Crowded, but with room for four. A wood-burning cast iron stove and next to it a birch basket filled with old newspapers, pieces of wood and boxes of matches.

'Jasper, there was a phone line out there. Find the socket and the phone.'

Two small rooms next to the kitchen, a living room, a bedroom. Jasper searched through cupboards, drawers and small baskets on the floor, while Leo opened the wood-burner's black iron door, placing strips of newsprint and thin needles at the bottom and filling it with two logs.

A thumping sound came from the hall. His father had found the fuse box and the main fuse. Electricity rushed through the old wires, and the ceiling light came on.

Newsprint flared up, wood chips crackled.

His father handed him a pair of work trousers and a tracksuit he'd found in the hall and sat down at the old pine table, moved the dish of mummified autumn pears and replaced it with a packet of thin cigarette papers and the last of his tobacco. Two rolls left, no more. And he usually smoked twenty a day. He needed it now more than ever, if he wasn't going to open the things that stood on the tile shelf between the stove and sink. Four bottles. Swedish vodka and Canadian whisky, a bottle of wine from South Africa and another one from Greece, something sweet and brown that he'd drunk before.

461

'Leo, you need to take your boots off. Dry them before we go any further.'

'We had ninety minutes. Total. We can only spend half that here.'

'You have time to dry them. You'll freeze otherwise! Gangrene. Then they have to amputate, I saw it when I lived . . . there. It starts with your toes, then your fucking foot turns black and begins to rot and then . . . death spreads upwards if you don't cut it off, Leo.'

He did as his father said, untied both boots and placed them in the middle of the black cast iron stove top that was getting hot, then changed into the two pairs of trousers from the hallway, both too short and too tight.

Ivan put his shoes on each side of Leo's, lit a newly rolled cigarette, inhaled deeply and let out a swirling, meandering cloud of smoke while he grabbed one of the still unopened bottles . . .

'Dad, fucking hell! Do you think that's a good idea?'

. . . and handed it to Leo.

'Vodka. Take a sip, it's good for you, it gets the blood flowing.'

Leo drank straight from the bottle and knew his dad was watching him the whole time. He'd done that the whole evening, and it had felt strange, as if he were being judged, as if he were a kid and an adult was assessing him, approving.

'What the hell are you up to?' asked Leo.

'Nothing.'

'Bullshit, you're looking at me like that!'

'How?'

'Like that.'

Ivan looked away, past his son, so as not to disturb him.

'Leo, we . . . you . . . might need to reconsider.'

'Reconsider?'

'Sometimes you just have to accept things.'

He'd just finished drinking and screwed on the cap. Now he twisted it off again and put the bottle down on the table between the tobacco and his father's trembling hands.

'What the hell are you talking about? I never give up! That's you, Dad! What exactly do you want to do? Is that why you wanted to come to this fucking cabin! Drink then, damn it! Drink!'

Jasper was in the doorway with a telephone under his arm.

'I found it,' he said, interrupting. 'It was on a shelf in the bathroom. And the socket's in the corner by the radio.'

The boots on the stove were not completely dry, but they were drier. The bottle stood in front of his dad, open until coarse and shaking hands chose to screw the cap shut.

While Leo went into the living room, to the telephone socket.

Broncks was in the interview room listening to the woman with a blanket over her shoulders struggle to answer each new question. After just a few minutes it was clear that she wasn't confused, she was pretending to be. And she wasn't doing it particularly well.

'I have a couple of questions,' he said. 'What do you say, can I jump in?'

His younger colleague shrugged and Broncks assumed that meant *do what you want, I want to go home and eat some Christmas ham.* He sat down on the only empty chair and introduced himself.

'Broncks, City Police, Stockholm.'

Her hand was cold, thin.

'Anneli.'

'I've been listening for a while. You say you were on your way to your relatives', and that you always drive there along this road. Then suddenly they were standing there. Masked robbers in the middle of the road. They wanted your car. Is that correct?'

'Yes.'

'And they threatened you?'

They never use unknown getaway cars.

'Yes.'

'With weapons?'

They choose them carefully and leave them in position themselves.

'Yes.'

'And they wanted you to give them a ride?'

And they would never let a driver this fragile, scared and stressed, be the key to an escape plan. Unless I've succeeded. Unless I've finally forced Big Brother to the point of desperation, taking risks, making mistakes.

'Yes.'

John Broncks held her cold and lifeless hand a second time. Then he went out and started searching for a free room. But the police station, which looked small from the outside, seemed even smaller inside. With both temporary interview rooms occupied by witnesses, and the few offices equally busy with conscripted personnel, only the kitchenette was left. Broncks closed the door in order to speak confidentially; while the call was going through, he picked up some leftover crackers from a dish on the Christmas snack table.

He heard those happy songs before his boss put the phone to his mouth.

'John?'

'Yes.'

'It's still Christmas Eve tomorrow.'

'I'm in Heby.'

'Do you know how to make a real Christmas *mumma*, John? A classic Christmas *mumma*. Do you know?'

'Three minutes. Closing time. Military weapons. Shots fired.'

'You take some cold ginger beer and—'

'That's what I knew when I headed here.'

'—two bottles of beer and—'

'Now I've picked up the shot-up cameras, looked at the cartridge cases from military weapons, talked to witnesses.'

'—a bottle of porter. Then you mix them together.'

'And – *I've seen them*. On the surveillance tape. The two inside the bank. Big Brother. And the Soldier.'

'I think you should go home and try it, John. If you don't know where to go and need a reason to feel part of something, there's nothing I can do about it. But I can command you to *not* use your badge.'

Broncks couldn't remember ever raising his voice to his boss, it wasn't his way of arguing, just as it wasn't Karlström's way. So when he did it, screaming inside this enclosed pantry, they were both taken by surprise.

'You and I have sat next to each other, watching them on the surveillance tapes from nine other robberies! I've lived with them for over a year! I know it's them! And now, Karlström, they've shot at us, the police, for the first time. They're under pressure, we're close . . . and these people, I've said it before – *they use guns like they're the tools of their fucking trade* – if we get any closer without backup . . . there'll be hell to pay!'

He screamed until his throat hurt. His last words were hoarse and strained his vocal cords, he'd forgotten that he could feel like this.

'Wait a second.'

Broncks heard Karlström put down the phone and cross the carpet to the music, which got louder then died completely. Then he heard him continue up the stairs and into his office, with its view over the bay of Stockholm.

'You're sure?'

'I'm sure. It's them. Armed with automatic weapons that they will use – have used. I don't want the Heby police and the Sala police running in there. I don't want to see dead colleagues. I want the national SWAT team.'

It was quiet. That fucking music was gone. Just Karlström breathing.

'I'll contact the police chief with your request.'

'I've already done that.'

'You've . . . already done it?'

'When I was driving here. Because every minute that passes is the difference between life and death. So they're on their way. I just wanted you to come to the same conclusion. It doesn't look good for a detective to take that kind of initiative without his superior's permission. And I said I had it.'

They'd drunk almost all of Vincent's Christmas present. A few hellish minutes had stretched into a hellish half-hour.

> The robbers, who earlier today opened fire inside a bank in Heby in Western Upland, are still at large.

Vincent was subdued, collapsed on the sofa with two remotes, alternating between television and radio news broadcasts. And Felix paced back and forth between pulled-down blinds in an apartment that seemed to have shrunk, a cell of seven square metres.

> During the chase automatic weapons were fired at the police. The SWAT team was called in and has arrived at the scene.

Shots fired at the police. The national SWAT team.

Felix poured, drank the last of the bottle. A cell with no windows. That was how it felt.

There was another bottle. Vincent's other Christmas present. This time Felix didn't even pour any for Vincent.

Then the landline rang.

'Hello.'

His voice. You're alive. Is everyone alive?

'Felix, how are you?'

They're hunting you.

'I just wanted to talk to you.'

'Is he with you?'

'Who?'

'Ivan.'

'Yes.'

Someone was moving something in the background. Maybe Ivan. Or Jasper.

'If it goes to hell, Felix . . .'

'They're already in place.'

'If it does, I want you and Vincent to disappear.'

'The SWAT team. They're in place. They said it on the news.'

'They're not.'

'That's what they're saying! The national SWAT team.'

'It's not possible. It would take them too long to get here.'

'Don't do anything stupid!'

'I'll say it again. If it goes to hell, Felix, you leave that apartment. Disappear. Any-fucking-where at all.'

'Why should we?'

'You shouldn't take the heat for something I've done.'

'No.'

'What do you mean, no?'

'I'm not running away.'

Vincent lowered the volume on the radio and the television.

'Why do you have to be so damned stubborn, Felix! Just for once – do what I fucking tell you to do without arguing!'

'I don't rob banks any more. And I'm not running away after some bank robbery either. I'm staying here. *We're staying here.*'

Vincent was now standing next to him, leaning towards the narrow gap that separated the telephone from his ear.

'Do you want to talk to Vincent?'

He hadn't even finished the question, hadn't received any response, before Vincent snatched the phone from his hand.

'Leo?'

'Yes?'

Their youngest brother stopped short, held the phone tightly to his mouth, trying to say something that had been said to him so many times.

'Leo . . . you . . . we're going straight through them.'

Five hundred kilometres away.

'Right, Leo?'

And in the same room.

'Yes. Straight through, Vincent.'

Behind the door they'd chosen to shut.

'And Vincent . . . Felix isn't listening. So you have to listen. If this ends badly, *if* it does . . . then you have to take care of yourselves. Do you understand? *You* have to finish this in *your* way. In your own way. Whatever you do, Vincent, you're doing the right thing. You hear me? Whatever happens . . . what you do is right, no matter what.'

There was a small plastic Christmas tree on the table.

He hadn't seen it before. Felix must have bought it.

His brother didn't even like Christmas.

'Leo?'

'Yeah?'

'I should have been there.'

'No, little brother . . . you shouldn't.'

———

Broncks stood in front of the wall with the giant map on it. A large cross in black ink marked the place where a car – which he now knew had been rented in the name of Anneli Eriksson and had been transporting fake Christmas presents – lay in the ditch. The fleeing robbers had made their way from there on foot through a vast wooded area covered by half a metre of snow – he guessed at a speed of three, possibly four kilometres per hour, no faster. He looked at the clock, counted, and drew a circle with the cross at its centre, six-kilometre radius. A search area that hadn't become too big. And, with reinforcements in place, it would soon be narrowed.

'I'm going in again,' he said to Rydén. 'And when I'm done, contact the prosecutor. She should be arrested and taken into custody. I don't know how she's involved – but she *is* involved.'

He went into the interview room, to the woman who was still pretending to be confused.

'Anneli?'

She was looking down at the table, the floor.

'Anneli, look at me when I'm talking to you. I want you to tell me everything you know. If you don't, this could end very badly.'

467

'What do you mean, "everything"?'

'Everything you know. About the people in that car. The ones who robbed a bank. I want to know what their names are. If you can communicate with them. How they're armed. I think that's important. If you ever want to see them again.'

She looked at him for the first time for real, without that dissembling gaze.

'Anneli . . . how are they armed?'

Not long, but long enough. She knew what he was talking about. She knew what the men running around in that forest were capable of.

'In order to protect them, we have to know what we're up against.'

And she was scared.

'Do you understand, Anneli? We have to know. If we're going to take them alive.'

'Put on your shoes.'

'Leo, damn it . . .'

'Shut up, Pappa! We have a head start, and we're going to keep it! Jasper – water, food, take whatever the hell you can find!'

'But the SWAT team . . . Leo, son, listen to me, you have to—'

'No, you listen to me! *No bastard will ever get close to me again! Nobody!*'

The storm and wind had died down. Weak light from the stars above the trees. It would be a quiet night. And their trail would be easier to follow. But it would also make it easier to move forward – out of the reach of those hunting them.

Leo was pulling on his boots, jacket, bulletproof vest and grabbing his gun when he noticed something. Not clearly, more like a glimpse of something that you become aware of without understanding it.

Except back then, when all this started, he'd been the one using darkness as cover. Now others lay in the dark watching him.

First, to the left of the kitchen window, it seemed as if a shadow had come alive and was moving beside a tree. Then, to the right, as it moved to the next tree, a shadow with a half-blackened face. And finally, when he lay down on the floor and crawled to the window to get a better look, there were multiple shadows carrying weapons similar to his own, moving in a wide arc around the house. And if he really was seeing all this –

468

events that seemed so strangely familiar – it felt in some way as if it was all taking place at the same time.

'They're here!'

He turned to Ivan who was sitting in an armchair in the living room, and Jasper who was searching the kitchen cupboards for anything edible he could pack into the weapons case.

'They're already here!'

Ivan sat there as if he were paralysed, leaning back in the chair, while Jasper ran first to the window to see what Leo had already seen, then to the jacket hanging over the armrest of the sofa. He carried it to the kitchen and took a hand grenade from one of its pockets, placing it on the table. Then another. And another.

'This group, what we've done – it's not going to end like this,' urged Jasper. '*We* aren't going to end it like this.'

Three grenades. Beside them he laid out the bag that held the magazines, evenly spacing them out in a new line.

'Jasper, you're fucking crazy – grenades?'

'Grenades, Leo! Tomorrow, when we're on the front page, it will be with our hoods pulled down! They won't fucking be able to point to us and say, "So that's what they look like." Tell me what to do, Leo. I'll do anything you want. You know that – anything! We can't die like failed robbers or end up in a fucking cell in some fucking prison! Then there'll be no group left!'

He cocked his weapon, aiming into the night, ready to shoot the shadows.

'For fuck's sake, calm down,' said Ivan, standing and walking over to the lined-up arsenal. 'If you want to die, you'll manage it tonight, I can guarantee it. But you're not the only one in here, you fucking idiot! So stop waving your gun around!'

'Jasper. That's my name! Go ahead and shoot your mouth off, you're damn good at it, you always have been. You can even hit people in the face. But you can't fucking keep track of your equipment! It's your fault we're here!'

He sat down by the hand grenades, just as lonely as he'd felt when he decided to take them from the armoury. He'd known the two civilians wouldn't measure up.

'They're deploying now! Don't you get it, they're doing exactly what we've been doing for a year without you, you old bastard! Deploying! In order to strike! So I'll wave my gun around as much as I want to – somebody out there already has me in their sights! I can feel it. *I can feel it!*'

Leo crawled along the floor and sat down between them.

'Leo? Are you about to let this fucking fake ranger . . . what should we do?'

That pleading tone was back in Pappa's voice. Leo didn't answer. He turned to the wood stove and warmed his face. The bag still lay on the kitchen floor. He opened it, put his hand in, and took hold of two bundles.

'These are . . . almost thirty per cent cotton. Fabric. Did you know that, Dad?'

A stack of 100s and one of 500s.

'It makes the paper a little stiffer. More difficult to tear. Know how I learned that? I washed them. Acetone and water. Quite a few of them, actually. They'd been stained by a dye pack that exploded. And then I had to dry them.'

He pulled open the small square door on the front of the wood stove.

'The fucking fabric shrank in the drier; they got too small and couldn't even be used in petrol pumps. I didn't know that before, that there was fabric in paper money. I got through thousands of kronor before I realised they had to be dried on the line.'

Leo pushed in the first stack of notes, the 100s.

'What the hell are you doing!' Jasper screamed, but not from rage, from surprise.

'Should we give up? Leo, we can't fucking let them take us!'

'Then get down on the floor. You said it yourself, they've got you in their sights.'

He pushed in the second stack, 500s, and they flared up too.

'It's good you're burning every fucking krona,' said Ivan, sitting on the floor beside his son, the fire at face level. 'Because sometimes, Leo, you just have to accept it.'

Leo felt a violent and intense heat like a thin shell across his face.

'Accept it? They'll never get this fucking money.'

Leo put his hand in the bag again, both hands, deep. Six bundles left. Only 500s now.

'Not the money. And not me.'

The fire continued to devour the banknotes, and he shoved and pushed more bundles through the open door and then locked it with the simple bolt.

'They won't take me. Do you understand that, Dad? *Not me.* So either get your gun or crawl out the door. They'll take care of you out there, you know that, don't you? Like they usually do. From now on, Dad . . . do what you want.'

The heat from hundreds of thousands of kronor felt the same as the heat of a log, but the flames ebbed more quickly.

There was complete silence. Ivan had sat down at the corner table in the living room, protected by two walls, his hands trembling as he rolled his very last cigarette with the very last of the tobacco. Leo pushed and prodded in more money as the bundles turned into hot coals. Jasper crawled around trying to peer through all the windows, following the movements of the shadows while he cocked and switched the weapon to automatic fire.

From now on, everyone could do what they wanted.

John Broncks had seen eyes like those before.

You. Or me.

But these eyes, which Broncks now met, belonged to his own side, embedded in a black face mask.

The national SWAT team. Sixteen elite police officers deployed in the snow and taking cover behind thick fir trunks, with automatic rifles and sniper rifles.

The search area had finally shrunk to nothing.

Four heavy vehicles, at Broncks's request, had left headquarters and fifty-seven minutes later rolled down the country road just a few kilometres northwest of town, cars rebuilt and reinforced until they were almost like small tanks. Meanwhile, a K9 unit had followed the trail from a getaway car to the house they'd just surrounded. Tracks all the way up to the front door. Six feet, three pairs, and he now knew that they belonged to a father and a son and his son's childhood friend, armed with Swedish AK4s and with plenty of ammunition. She'd finally told them, the woman who had pretended to be confused, right down to the exact number of magazines each of them wore in their homemade vests.

'How much longer – if you were to guess?' Broncks asked the squad leader.

'We're in no hurry,' he replied.

'The dog handler estimates they've been there about thirty minutes.'

'We're waiting for the right moment.'

It had stopped snowing. The chill had subsided. John Broncks was looking at a scene from a beautiful Christmas card. That's how it looked. Peaceful. A brightly lit cottage, snow soft as cotton along the gutters and on the fruit trees, smoke coming from the brick chimney.

It was no Christmas card.

The light in what was probably the kitchen had been lit by armed robbers, who on their way there hadn't hesitated to shoot at the pursuing officers. And who in the course of ten aggravated robberies had fired more shots among living people than any previous Swedish criminal gang.

The SWAT team had already tried to call them once.

Now he dialled the number of the house's landline. They could hear it ringing inside through crevices and windows. It was an attempt to urge the people inside to come out voluntarily, with their hands up. A repeated ringing that eventually ended without anyone picking up the phone.

Either way, they got their answer. All the lights were extinguished simultaneously.

They wouldn't be giving up.

91

THREE AND A half million kronor is less than you'd think. It doesn't even fill up a duffel bag. And when you push bundle after bundle of it into crackling orange flames, they turn to ashes that hardly take up any space at all.

Ivan lay down on the living room floor.

'Leo?'

His son passed close to his head as he crawled towards the window, so close that he could have grabbed on to his boots. His whole body hunched over, tense, as he gently unlatched the windowpane and pressed it outwards, until the snow on the ledge was pushed away.

A small gap. Their way out.

'I know what you're up to.'

Ivan got up on his knees beside his son.

'Leo, don't do it.'

Weak light outside in the clear cold. Scattered stars, the waning half-moon. And in the window, he could see the reflection of their four eyes, just as they'd once looked at each other in the narrow space at the top of a graffiti-covered mirror, riding up in the lift. He'd run downstairs in his bare feet, down seven storeys, convinced he had lost him.

'*Don't do it.*'

The reflection of four eyes in the glass. They were just as clear to Leo. And he knew what he saw in two of them.

Doubt.

'They'll use tear gas, Dad. That's always how they start. They *think* they can surprise us. That's when we get out. Here. Through the window.'

This man, older and weaker than the one he'd once hung on to while he threw punch after punch, the only time he'd embraced him and understood how powerful that body was.

'That's when we get our opening, like right after the first few shots in a bank robbery, when only we know and can act. Maybe the fuckers think they've figured out what guns we have – but they don't know shit about the hand grenades. That's how we strike. How *we* attack *them*.'

He'd hung around that neck once, hugging him away. *Don't do it.* This wasn't the same body; now it was exhausted, its power drained.

'If we don't act when we get our opening – then it's too late. We'll never get out of here.'

Doubt. That's what he saw. As only someone who is powerless has doubt.

'When the tear gas gets here we'll throw two grenades out, right away. They're not counting on that. You and I get out first while Jasper holds them back with as many magazines as he needs. We take cover and do the same thing until Jasper's made it out. We have plenty of ammunition. You can do it, Dad, dance and hit, dance around the bear. It's bigger, but we can win, we can take it, if we dance and hit well. Right?'

Ivan stood up. He wanted to take hold of his son's shoulders, hold them tightly, shake him and scream until he listened.

'If we dance around them, we can win. If we strike when they think they have the upper hand. Pull your mask on, Dad, and get ready!'

'Win?'

Ivan didn't hold him, that would end in disaster. And he didn't scream. But he was finally able to speak.

'Why did you burn the money if you thought you could get away? If we meet them out there with guns, it'll go to hell. It'll go black. It'll rot. Death spreads upwards.'

As Leo was listening to him, he wasn't getting ready. And if he wasn't getting ready, he couldn't rush out there, to the people surrounding them preparing to shoot.

'That guy there, who thinks he's a ranger, running around talking about "no masks" and "front pages"! Leo? How the hell can you listen to that shit? Felix and Vincent, do they have to see you dead on the fucking front page, is that what you want?'

'And since when did you give a shit about them? Put on your fucking mask now!'

Leo pulled the black fabric over his face, obliterating his facial features.

'I told you. I'm never sitting there again! Opposite some fucking cop! *Never!* Put your mask on now, Dad! Otherwise I'll leave you here!'

His son was on his way. Out. Away. He wasn't listening any more.

And that power, whatever remained, an echo of someone else in another time, of another man, that power disappeared completely now, and he did the one thing he still could.

'Leo, I know you didn't snitch on me.'

Snitch.

'I've always known.'

Snitch.

'I mean what I say, Leo. You didn't snitch on me. I know the police lied to me. That you didn't talk. I saw the bandage on his hand.'

A black mask on his face. A cocked gun in his hand.

It didn't matter.

Leo wasn't preparing for war any more – it had worked. As long as Ivan got him to listen, he could also keep him alive.

'Then why the hell did you say it?'

'I thought it was better that way.'

'You thought it was . . . better?'

'Yes.'

'How the hell . . . first you smash everything, then you just give up and wait for the police to arrive. And then you blame me!'

His father was now looking up at him from the floor.

'You've kept on with that,' Leo continued. 'Kept on and on! *Snitch*. It never fucking stopped! And you thought it was . . . better that way?'

The others, out in the dark, were in position for an attack.

And Jasper, who was crawling across the floor behind him with a hand grenade, put his finger through the pin as he approached the other living room window.

'Leo – if we don't leave now we're going to die!' said Jasper.

'Wait,' hissed Leo.

He saw Jasper push the curtains aside and stick up his head, peering out.

'I see them! We have to get out! They'll shoot the shit out of us!'

'Shut up!'

'Now, Leo! Before it's too late!'

'Jasper? Shut up! I'm talking to my father, can't you see that!'

He'd already cocked his gun.

'Better . . . that way? Dad? *Better?*'

Now he raised it.

'It's you I should fucking shoot! Not them! You!'

Leo breathed in, held the barrel of the gun steady, and he felt utterly calm. There was no shaking. Not in him or his father.

92

THAT WAS WHEN the first window shattered.

They'd chosen the kitchen.

A spinning tear-gas grenade spread its white vapour cloud from the warm kitchen into the living room. Then they were running, all three, into the bedroom as the next tube smashed the window and started to spin. And when the two gas clouds met, they turned into a gas avalanche.

'Lie down!'

Leo threw himself on the floor. Ivan threw himself down beside him, while Jasper stood in his black mask.

'Damn it, lie down! Jasper, you have to . . .'

But he couldn't have heard the end, as it was drowned out by three shots fired from somewhere inside the white cloud. He had time to think that, in all that light, Jasper's blood looked redder than he expected as it fell on him.

That was when his eyelids started to twitch, convulsively, and the tears gushed out of him as ducts and mucous membranes ceased to function.

'Drop your weapon!'

Muffled voices coming from gas masks above him, in the midst of the gas avalanche, and they were screaming.

'Lie the fuck down and don't touch your weapon!'

Leo was blind. His tongue burned and his chest was like a balloon that needed to burst and he threw up, from deep, deep within. Someone pushed him to the floor, screaming and constraining. Someone else bound his legs, kicked him several times in the side. And someone else held his hands. He couldn't breathe, couldn't think, but the hand that held him felt familiar, big, the callouses where they'd always been.

His father had talked and talked, deliberately delaying, throwing him off balance, and he hadn't had time to run outside.

And suddenly it was real, what could never happen. Being arrested had never been an option.

But now it was the only one left.

93

CHRISTMAS EVE MORNING. Or dawn. Or late night. John Broncks had no idea.

He knew it was dark outside and that the city was still asleep. And here he sat, a detective alone in his office, staring at a taped-up cardboard box with his door open to the silent corridor. And it didn't feel like it should. Even though a fourteen-month investigation – theories, frustrations, hunting, hopelessness, anger, and sometimes even hatred – was over. Even though Big Brother now sat just a few hundred metres away in a cell somewhere else in the police station, and the Soldier had been transported to the Karolinska hospital's intensive care unit. Even though Little Brother and the Driver had been found in a rented apartment in the centre of Gothenburg, with detectives in place outside and a SWAT team ready to go in. And even though two of them had never before featured in the investigation – the older man now in a local Uppsala prison and the woman in the female section of Kronoberg jail, one floor below Big Brother.

Even though he now knew this had all been about a family.

Three brothers. A childhood friend. A girlfriend. And a father.

An entire family.

He should be celebrating, laughing, cheering. But he wasn't. Fourteen months – and nothing.

Maybe he should never have called her. Maybe that was why.

It had felt so right.

He had gone out to the car that was outside Heby's small police station and found it completely covered in snow. He'd retrieved the shovel from behind the front door of the police station and thrown half a metre of snow from the road onto the pavement, then pushed even more from the roof and windows and bonnet with his arms, and finally scraped down the membrane of ice that clung to the windscreen and refused to let go. A slow trip back through the chaos caused by the snow. He'd just made it to Enköping when he first called. They hadn't spoken to each other for a long time. In the last few months they'd only seen each other in the company of their colleagues on opposite sides of square tables in conference rooms, or quickly said hello on their way in opposite directions down the corridor. He'd called, but hung up after only one ring. After another ten or twenty minutes, he'd called again. And hung up when she answered. Twenty or thirty kilometres later, near Jakobsberg, it rang four times before she answered, and her voice had been sharp, and he'd sat silently with the phone in his hand.

'John? I can see it's you.'

He held the phone to his left cheek and ear.

'John, what are you doing?'

Pushed it hard.

'John, you, it—'

'It's over.'

'Over?' Sanna's voice changed, no longer so sharp. 'I've been trying to explain that to you for so long! I'm so happy to hear that, relieved, that you understand, John, I—'

'No, I mean, *they're* over now.'

'Pardon?'

'We got them. Tonight. Heby. *It's them*. Three brothers and their childhood friend. The youngest had just turned eighteen. None with a record. We were chasing a bunch of brats, who've turned Sweden upside down. Fourteen months – and it's over, Sanna.'

It had been quiet for a while after that, because neither of them really knew how to carry on. And it had been possible to hear two lives. She had recognised the sound of someone sitting in a car, going somewhere. He had recognised the buzz of voices in a home, someone surrounded by people.

Children's voices. One crying a little, one asking for Mummy.

'John?'

'Do you have . . . are those children?'

'You woke us up.'

'You've got kids?'

'Two. A girl, she's four. A boy, almost two.'

'You never said anything.'

'Why would I?'

The hum was clearer now, as if she'd turned the phone to more directly capture the sound of the two children who'd just woken up.

'John?'

She'd said she was looking for closure – because she needed it. He hadn't realised that there was that kind of closure.

'It's Christmas Eve. Night. In a few hours . . . I have to—'

'Merry Christmas.'

'You know, John—'

'That was all. Merry Christmas.'

Then he'd driven into the city. And taken a detour through the still heavily falling snow. Past the Northern Cemetery and past a grave covered by snow.

Past someone he thought about more dead than he'd done when he was alive.

On through a city that would soon awake and stay indoors in the warmth of family and Christmas presents. To a police station as empty now as when he'd arrived there an hour ago.

An entire family. And her closure.

He'd gone to his office room and moved piles of folders aside. The investigation would soon leave his desk and become evidence for the prosecution in an upcoming trial – four thousand pages of preliminary investigations on nine bank robberies, one security van robbery, 221 stolen automatic weapons, attempted aggravated blackmail of the police, and a bomb that had exploded at Stockholm Central Station. And instead he started to approach another preliminary investigation. One that lay in a taped-up box that had been packed up so long it had served as a visitor's chair.

He cut away the tape that had been wrapped several times around the box, folded open the flaps, and left the room. Out into the deserted corridor and into the kitchenette to the last drop of mulled wine and some leftover gingerbread cookies in a basket.

Returned to the room.

Walked restlessly around the now open box.

A family. Closure.

He pictured Sam standing between two guards as he left the visiting cell of the prison 225 kilometres away, turning to him and whispering, *I never want to see you again.*

John Broncks decided right then. He approached the box. The thick stack of papers was hiding under empty folders and outdated calendars. Another investigation. One that eighteen years earlier had formed the basis for another trial and a life sentence.

He'd already called Sanna, and she had two kids. He didn't even know where his mother lived any more. And calling Sam wouldn't work either, since this was about him.

He grabbed the crisp cover page.

DISTRICT: Stockholm UNIT: Homicide CRIME: Murder

All these years, from a teenager to a man in early middle age, and he'd never even touched it.

The first pages resembled the beginning of every preliminary investigation he'd ever worked on. The primary report. Then the list of defence lawyers. Then another report. Then a quick overview of the persons involved. The printout of an emergency call from a heartbroken and shocked woman at 02.32 a.m.

It was there, twenty-three pages into the initial interrogation, that the similarities ended. With the sixteen-year-old John Broncks.

He hadn't even remembered that someone had talked to him.

> Lead Interrogator (LI): Did you know about it? What your
> brother was planning to do?
> JB: Know about it?
> LI: Had he told you he was going to kill your father?

It was strange. He didn't remember it at all. Until he read his own answers. He could have been the cop doing the interview. Maybe he had been, in each and every investigation. And maybe he would be again, tomorrow, when the interrogation of a father, an older brother, a middle brother and a little brother began.

LI: The knife, John?

He knew exactly what the next question would be. Before he even read it. That was a police officer's task, to seek the truth, to bring order to a random series of events.

LI: You know we found it under *your* bed?

He knew the question, but never the answer. *Sometimes . . . she usually pretends to faint.* Everyone has their answer. *But you must understand he deserved it?* Their own explanation for their violence. *If I'd wanted to kill her . . . I would have.* He knew the question, but never the answer – not then, not now.

LI: And I wonder, John, did you maybe hold the knife as well?

He'd read more when he got back. The interview with his mother. The interrogation of Sam. The forensic report with pictures of a bed and bloody sheets and a knife with small sharp teeth for scaling fish. And the autopsy of a man with three holes in his chest near the heart. But first he needed to visit someone he knew and yet didn't know at all.

94

IT WASN'T FAR, he didn't even have to go outside. Via three locked doors within the detective department of the Stockholm City Police, through Interpol, Witness Protection and the forensics department, to the taller building facing west – the Swedish Security Service, the National Police Board, the monitoring department, Kronoberg jail. He hadn't been here since last spring when he'd got some help analysing two late-night conversations; the more the authorities emphasised the need for cooperation between divisions, the less it seemed to happen.

This time Broncks took the lift to the seventh floor. He got out and knocked on the prison guard's door. It was the middle of the night and he'd come unannounced. But the young and friendly fellow on the other side of the glass rolled up the hatch and explained that if Detective Broncks sat down and waited for a few minutes, then he would soon be able to visit the suspect, who had arrived a few hours earlier and was now being kept in the western detention hall.

He did so, sat down and waited.

On his way to a locked cell, away from an eighteen-year-old investigation.

From a family, to a family.

What was family? He had no idea any more.

Perhaps a family was something strong, with built-in solidarity, and was therefore a place where violence became purer, more brutal – it turned inwards, against its own, against those its cohesion should have protected.

'Broncks?'

No one to talk to. No one to share with before it's too late. Sometimes it ends in a cemetery. Sometimes it ends here.

'Broncks? Hello?'

'Yes?'

'You can go in now.'

He heard a scream from the first cell, a dream or terror, it sounded the same. Then three silent cells. And then sound coming from two cells, but no screams, more like someone doing push-ups in one and someone talking to himself in the other – when days became weeks became months, it was easy to turn your days upside down.

He stopped about halfway down the hall. Detention Cell 7.

'And you're sure you'd prefer to be by yourself?'

'Yes.'

'You can have an alarm if you want. It's small, fits in your pocket. For safety's sake.'

'Thank you. It's not necessary. Just a short visit.'

The prison guard's keys scraped against the door as they were turned twice.

John Broncks let the heavy metal door slide open. A tall, athletic, blond man, much younger than he had imagined, was sitting on the bed and staring straight at the wall.

'I'm John Broncks. And I'm the one who has been investigating you.'

The blond continued to stare at the grey concrete.

'Investigating what?'

'A lot of bank robberies. A rather large weapons theft. And a bomb that will be considered terrorism.'

'I don't know what you're talking about.'

'I think you do . . . Anna-Karin. And we'll start discussing it tomorrow.'

'Nobody will *discuss* anything tomorrow.'

'You've spoken to me before. People like you do that sometimes. Talk. So that things don't go so badly for their younger brothers.'

The prisoner wore clothes with the prison symbol on his jersey, white chest and brown trousers. Clothes that the person who'd sat there before him had also worn.

Now he turned round. Blue eyes. Thin lips.

There he was.

'I don't snitch. We don't snitch. That's not how we operate.'

And then he turned away again, towards the concrete wall.

'You can go. Since I neither want nor need to speak to you now.'

John Broncks lingered in the stuffy air. Breathing in institutional dust.

'I don't want to talk to you either. That wasn't why I came.'

He went out again, holding the door, waited in the corridor until a prison guard with a big bunch of keys arrived.

'I just wanted to see what you looked like under the mask, Big Brother.'

95

TIME.

He always knew precisely how much he had.

He no longer had a wristwatch with red hands and light-brown leather strap. Pappa had been wearing that. But he didn't need it, never really had, the clock was always ticking *inside* him as he counted the time that remained.

Tick. Less life left. Tick. Less life left. Tick. Less life left.

The heavy iron bars in a grid formation on the cell windows. From now on, he couldn't, he mustn't, do what he always did – think in terms of time. He was locked up. And someone in here who knew exactly how many seconds, how many breaths had passed, wouldn't be able to breathe at all.

Without the days and seasons no bastard could reach him.

He'd tried once before. And it had worked. If he didn't participate, if he refused to exist alongside others, the closed door would just be a door he went straight through.

Uniformed men had stood outside then, too. At home. In the apartment. Pappa had thrown a bomb and a house had burned and Mamma and the police had been waiting on the other side of the door he'd locked.

Felix beside him on the bed, Vincent in his arms.

We'll go straight through them. Straight through.

He'd go straight through this too. The door. The police. The interrogations. He didn't have to say anything unless he wanted to. He was locked up, but he would decide for himself whether or not to open his mouth.

They each sat behind their own locked door. They weren't together. But they would be reunited later. That's how it always was.

If they didn't think and didn't count time.

If now was then and then was now.

About the Author

'**Anton Svensson**' is a pseudonym for Stefan Thunberg and Anders Roslund.

Stefan Thunberg is one of Scandinavia's most celebrated screenwriters. His body of work spans popular TV series such as Henning Mankell's *Wallander* and Håkan Nesser's *Van Veeteren* as well as two of Sweden's biggest box office successes in recent years: *Hamilton* and *Jägarna 2*. While Thunberg achieved fame as a screenwriter, the rest of his family became infamous in an entirely different way: his father and brothers were Sweden's most notorious bank robbers, dubbed Militärligan (The Military League) by the media. *The Father* is Stefan Thunberg's debut novel.

Anders Roslund is an award-winning investigative journalist and one of the most successful and critically acclaimed Scandinavian crime writers of our time. Roslund is part of the *New York Times* bestselling author duo Roslund & Hellström, who are recipients of many prestigious awards, including the CWA International Dagger, the Glass Key and the Swedish Academy of Crime Writers' Award, and who boast sales exceeding five million copies. Films and TV series based on Roslund & Hellström's novels are in the works, both in Hollywood and Europe. *The Father* is Anders Roslund's seventh novel and the first he has co-authored with Stefan Thunberg.

The truth behind the fiction

Anders Roslund: To write a novel based on true events is to shatter reality and then put it back together again, and the only way to do this is to begin by finding the novel's Heartbeat: the central conflict that drives it towards its inevitable end. So, Stefan, what is the heartbeat of this story?

Stefan Thunberg: An event that has haunted me for more than twenty years. It was 23 December, the day before the Christmas holiday, and three bank robbers were pursued by police through a raging blizzard after they had driven their getaway car into a ditch. When I saw it on the news, I knew immediately that two of them were my eldest brother and my childhood friend – but slowly I realised that the third had to be my father. I couldn't understand how my brother and father had, after years of conflict, decided to commit a bank robbery together – the last heist ever carried out by the 'Military League'. That night in the snowstorm they fled into a forest and, as the noose tightened, they hid, exhausted, in an abandoned summer cottage. Surrounded by elite police, with no way out, father and son had to resolve the conflict that had followed them throughout their entire lives – throughout *my* entire life. What did they tell each other during those hours, before the police shot tear gas into the cottage and stormed it?

AR: When did you first find out what your brothers were doing?

ST: I was there when they began planning to break into the weapons bunker. I came home to my brother's apartment and found the others eating pizza and discussing how best to pierce a concrete floor. After that, the first few times I was around they would pause when I arrived, but soon they just continued as if I was part of it. After all, I was one of the family: between us brothers there were never any secrets. And then, after they had committed their first armed robbery, I was sitting there on the sofa as they congratulated themselves, high on adrenalin, and we followed the police hunt on the TV while working our way through a case of Kronenbourg beer. It may sound strange, but that's how my brothers and I had been raised by our tough dad – to never, ever, betray anyone in our family.

AR: Which of the main characters are invented and which are more closely inspired by reality?
ST: The three brothers, father and mother in the novel are all closely inspired by reality. Jasper is a fictional character, though elements of him are inspired by a combination of two friends who each took part in some (though not all) of the robberies. They weren't present in my childhood as early as the book describes. Also, in the 'present' section of the book, Jasper has a dramatic function that does not correspond with either of those friends in reality. The character represents alienation, someone who will never be respected on the same terms, never accepted into the brother-hood, and is therefore used by Leo to carry out tasks he does not want to give to his younger brothers. His presence in the story clarifies that the bonds between the brothers are stronger than everything else – for better or worse – and this reinforces the disruption when those bonds crack. Anneli is fictionalised, especially her family situation before she met Leo. Her son Sebastian is inspired by several different kids. John and Sam Broncks are purely fictional characters, constructed to portray the real police work and as a reflection of Leo's situation.

AR: What about time and place?
ST: We haven't changed any locations, neither in the childhood nor present parts, but we have excluded some locations and compressed the flow of time – the robberies in the book take place over 14 months, but in reality it was 26 months.

AR: Did you find it hard writing about your childhood?
ST: On the contrary, the childhood aspect gave me the opportunity to participate in the story without being portrayed as one of the characters. My experiences, my presence, have been placed in my brothers' bodies in the book, especially Felix, because in reality *I* am the one closest in

488

age to 'Leo' and hence I was often the one experiencing the things that Felix experiences in the book: it was *me* lying there on the floor watching my father and brother making Molotov cocktails to throw into the house in which my mother was hiding. So the situations in the childhood sections of the book are not less true; on the contrary, that conflict between father and son that I observed so clearly in reality is the truth inherent in the story's resolution years later in that snowstorm.

AR: Which, for you, were the most important events we changed from what really happened?
ST: We never went in a completely different direction, but of course there are anomalies: how and why the smiley face was shot into the bank's safety glass; Anneli's involvement, because in reality, the person she is inspired by actually drove the getaway car on more occasions than the character in the novel; and most of all the bomb, both in terms of which bank robbery the bomb was a part of, and of Jasper setting it to deliberately explode, which was an accusation made in court but of which the robber in question was found not guilty.

AR: As you know, we did a lot of research, but how much also comes from your memory?
ST: At first, I tried to avoid written documentation as far as possible, and instead tried to recreate the situations, with you, based on my own emotional memories. But, of course, it's impossible to solely do that if you want to achieve the best results, especially when working with another writer. We were eventually forced to dive into one of Sweden's most extensive police investigations ever, including the preliminary investigations and the hearings with my family that I, up to the start of this writing process, had never read – and *that* had consequences. For quite some time afterwards I suffered from severe anxiety. I ran from the writing both literally and psychologically, but came back to it when we decided to shatter reality and rebuild it as fiction.

AR: What really happened to the robbers?
ST: They were all arrested and convicted with the harshest possible sentences

because of the nature of the crimes, a sentence that was unique at the time, bearing in mind they never killed anyone. In the hearings, it was made very clear I hadn't been involved and in Swedish law one does not have to testify against one's family. And my mother and I got a unique insight into the Swedish prison system after many, many visits to several different prisons over many years.

AR: How did your brothers react when they read the book?
ST: They've all reacted in their own ways. One of them (who inspired 'Felix') called me right after he finished reading the book and said, 'Stefan, I hate you, but I love this fucking book you guys have written', then he hung up the phone and ended our relationship – we haven't spoken since. Another (who inspired 'Vincent') didn't say a word after several readings of the book, but after the fifth he said in a low voice, 'Now I understand what you've done; this is me back then, it's me as a seventeen-year-old that you've portrayed, not the man I am today.' Finally, my third brother (who inspired 'Leo') was deeply moved, and wrote a fantastic letter to me in which he explained how he now understands the madness to which he had exposed himself and those around him.